Ascension

LAUREN DANE

Ellora's Cave
Romantica®
www.EllorasCave.com

An Ellora's Cave Publication

www.ellorascave.com

Ascension

ISBN 9781419964237

Edited by Ann Leveille.
Cover art by Syneca.

Electronic book publication June 2007
Trade paperback publication 2011

ASCENSION

Dedication

So many people to thank on this one!

First of all and always most of all—I want to thank my husband, who is unfailingly supportive of my writing. Without his help, his love and support, without him to bounce ideas off and um, well, without his research assistance, I couldn't do this. Me + You = Camaro's hood and full moon.

And Laura Bradford—The best agent any girl could ask for. This book is much bigger and better than I'd ever imagined it could be because of her help.

Ann Leveille—Editing me can't be that fun ;) and yet you do it over and over and you never fail to make me a better writer. Thank you for correcting my grammar crimes and explaining parallel construction to me over and over.

Tracy and Renee—What would I do without you two? All I have to do is ask and you not only read but you give helpful suggestions and advice. I am fortunate indeed in knowing you both.

And of course Anya and Megan—I'd say for being my crit partners but you're both so much more than that to me. Thanks for all the laughter and great advice.

Author's Note

Ascension is not set in the same universe as my Cascadia Wolves. The stories and Pack hierarchy and history are very different and the Cherchez Pack will go on a journey that is quite unlike that which my Warden family will endure. I hope you all enjoy these wolves with their stories as much as you do my Cascadia wolves.

Trademarks Acknowledgement

The author acknowledges the trademarked status and trademark owners of the following wordmarks mentioned in this work of fiction:

Babeland: Toys In Babeland, LLP

Band-Aid: Johnson & Johnson Corporation

Chevrolet Suburban: General Motors Corporation

Esquire: The Hearst Corporation

Jell-O: Kraft Foods Holdings, Inc

Kool-Aid: Kraft Foods Holdings, Inc

Subaru Outback: Fuji Heavy Industries Ltd.

Tiffany: Tiffany (NJ) Inc.

The Twilight Zone: CBS Broadcasting Inc

Thermos: Thermos L.L.C.

Prologue

Kari Warner walked down the alley, well aware that *something* was following her. No, not following—*stalking*. The alley was wide and the sounds of her heels as she moved along quickly echoed through it, bouncing from the dingy walls back at her. Heart in her throat, her quick walk became a slow run. Fear choked her as she heard the corresponding quickening of the footsteps of her pursuer. Cursing her stupidity, she sent out a brief prayer, exchanging chocolate for safety.

Leaving the nightclub a few minutes before, she'd known she should've taken the long way. But she'd been so tired and had opted for the shortcut through the alley. She'd gone that way a dozen times before.

She felt the weight of eyes on her, watching, measuring, waiting. The corner and the streetlight were only half a block away. Hope bloomed in her chest as she began to believe she was going to make it. The light cried safe haven. She held onto the light like a lifeline.

Suddenly a low growl split the air and the hair on her arms stood on end. A queer electric hum began at the base of her spine, riding up into her hairline.

What was that? her panicked mind screamed.

Eyes wild, she looked up to see a massive dog jump at her, knocking her over, ripping into her flesh with its teeth. She drew in breath for a scream but in those short milliseconds her throat was crushed as its jaws closed in over her neck and bit down. Razor-sharp teeth tore at her. Its unbelievably strong jaw gripped tight as its head jerked from side to side, shredding her neck. Her hands pushed against the massive head as the long muzzle pressed against her open wound. Her mind, unable to accept the entirety of the experience, slipped into a state of unreality for a long moment and she felt herself drifting away. *No!*

Fighting, body screaming for air, she pushed up frantically, trying not to panic. Her strength ebbing, she had a hard time gaining purchase as she kept slipping in the blood she was losing. Her hands grappled with the dog, the hard muscles rippling beneath the fur. She wanted to just crawl away, to get far from the thing now tearing into her stomach with its teeth. But it was so strong, so big, that she couldn't knock him away, or even off balance enough to get away. *God, he's so soft,* she thought until everything went black.

Chapter One

Beep, beep, beep, beep, beep.

Everything hurt. Kari tried to swallow around the fire in her throat. Her eyes fluttered open.

"Kari? Get the doctor, she's waking up! Kari, honey?"

Kari tried to focus on the man next to her bed. It was Jack, her brother. He gripped her hand until she winced.

"Sorry." The grip lessened but he didn't release. "How do you feel, sweetie?"

She tried to speak but all she could manage was a croak. So she just smiled at him, hoping to reassure him. Cool hands offered her a straw and urged her to take a drink.

"Small sips, don't drink too much or you'll be sick," a woman's soft voice cautioned.

Kari had to fight against her instincts because the cool water felt so good on her abraded throat and she wanted to gulp it down.

"That's it. Good, Kari. I'm going to set the water down for a moment, okay? I'm just going to check you out. See how you're doing." The owner of the voice moved into Kari's line of sight. She was a nurse—no, a doctor. Large brown eyes looked her over. Close-cropped chic gray hair and a long tall frame completed the package. The embroidered name on the blue coat said "Dr. Elaine Kennedy".

"Kari, can you try to talk?" Dr. Kennedy's cool hands smoothed over Kari's throat where the dog had bit her. Panic rose momentarily as she recalled the size of that dog, the intelligence she remembered in its eyes. As if sensing her panic, Dr. Kennedy made a soothing sound and touched Kari's arm softly before undoing the front of her gown to look at her stomach. Kari relaxed. Something about the other woman made her feel more secure, safe.

Kari swallowed a few times. "Wha…what happened?" Her voice was hoarse, raw.

"We don't know exactly. You showed up in the driveway of the emergency room. You were pretty beaten up. We got an anonymous call that you were out there. Do you remember anything?"

"Dog. A big dog jumped me." Kari moved her free hand to her stomach where the dog had ripped into her flesh and was surprised that there were no stitches there. "It bit me, tore into me, here." Craning her head to look took too much effort and she slumped back, exhausted, against the pillows.

The doctor looked at her kindly, smiling as if she were not quite right in the head. "It will all come back to you with time. But you can see for yourself that you have no wounds there, just some extensive bruising. Your throat took a beating though. Looks like your larynx was pretty severely damaged. You had a concussion and some swelling on the brain, which has lessened considerably."

"How long have I been here?" Damn, it hurt to talk. She tried to swallow but it was so painful. "Water, please," she asked and Jack brought the straw back to her lips.

"Three days. You came in at two thirty on Saturday morning. It's Tuesday."

"Jesus. Three days?" Groggy, her head hurt. No—her entire body hurt. And where on earth did the dog go? Had she imagined it? No, there was no way she could have imagined such a thing. That dog had been massive. She could still feel the razor-sharp teeth rending her flesh. The silky texture of the fur under her hands. She tried to work it through but she kept losing track. The medication made her drowsy, messing up her thought processes.

"Will she be okay?" Jack watched her, concern written all over his face.

"Well, her pupils look good, reactive like they're supposed to be. Her pulse has remained strong. The swelling has gone down to nearly normal. It looks good for her. We will of course keep her in for at least another day or two for observation, just to be sure."

Dr. Kennedy smiled at Kari, patting her hand before walking to the door. "Just take it slow, Kari, and everything will be all right. Get your rest now. Have your brother help you bring the level of the bed up a bit. Watch some TV or listen to a book on tape. I'll be back in a few hours."

* * * * *

"You are so lucky that Elaine was on shift." Andreas angrily paced the elegant, wood-paneled library. "She just called. Kari has regained consciousness and will recover." He slammed his hand down onto the side table so hard it split into pieces. "Idiot! I told you it wasn't the plan to change her for another month or two. Until after I'd met her and she'd gotten to know me."

Michael, the man in the chair receiving the angry lecture, winced. His blond hair fell over his eyes, hiding his expression.

"You've got to stop breaking the furniture, Andreas. Does she remember anything?" A third man walked over to the table and picked up the wood, tossing it into the trash. His long black hair shimmered against the golden tone of his skin, brown-black eyes glittered behind thick lashes. The face had a savage beauty to it—the nose not quite straight, a small scar bisecting his left eyebrow, the lips lush but holding a not-so-subtle hint of danger.

"Elaine says Kari reported that a big dog attacked her," Andreas gritted out, glaring down at Michael. Fists clenched, rage vibrated through him. His Mate had been put in danger and his plans to meet and woo her without frightening her had been upset. His primal need to protect her, to bring her to him in a way that made her most comfortable, had been challenged. "Lucky for you the wounds have healed already so Elaine was able to blow them off and focus on the concussion. She wouldn't allow too close an examination by Kari's brother so no one saw the bites but Elaine and Henry."

Laurent Cole dusted the wood off his hands and grabbed an apple before tossing himself into a chair nearby. He watched Andreas pensively. "What are we going to do?"

"It's too late to delay. The change has already started. Elaine told the brother she's going to keep Kari in the hospital for another two days but we have to get her out before that. She'll be totally healed by then and it will look suspicious. Problem is, I don't know how we'll deal with the brother." Sighing, he sat down and ran large hands through wheat-blond hair that touched the top of his shoulders. His amber eyes were intelligent but could be merciless in defense of those he loved and protected. His body was tight with stress and barely repressed fury.

"We don't have a contingency. This wasn't meant to happen for another two months. Full moon is in three days. It's clear to Elaine that Kari is changing already. The wounds have healed so fast. We have to have her with us at full moon. She can't transform the first time alone, she wouldn't survive. We don't have the luxury of slowly bringing her into the Pack." Andreas' voice was weary, face resigned.

"We'll have to go to her and explain. Or rather, we'll have to bring her here and explain. Make amends. She won't believe us, of course, so that'll make the transformation even more difficult. I hate to start off with her with distrust and fear. I wanted it to be different." Andreas looked out the window at the pine trees surrounding the large house, toward the lake and sighed. He felt so out of control of the situation and it ate at him.

"She'll have to deal with it, Andreas. She has no other choice. *We* have no other choice. We need her," Laurent said with an elegant shrug. "The Pack needs her."

Phillip, the final man in the room, growled. "If Michael had just kept his shit together we wouldn't be dealing with this." One leg crossed over the other, swinging back and forth. The movement seemed casual but there was menace there just beneath the surface.

"But he did. And so it has to be done. She may well hate us all for a long time but it's too late anyway. She's going to transform in three days and she'll be far worse off without us than with us. Michael will have to explain himself to her later. The Pack needs an Alpha-bitch. We need to continue and we can't do that without females." Laurent's tone was matter-of-fact.

Andreas got up and paced the room, thinking over all possibilities. After a few minutes he stopped and turned to them. "We'll bring her here tomorrow. Elaine'll help us get her out of the hospital. She and Henry will have to drug Kari and drive out. It will probably be necessary to keep her locked up for a bit. We can't have her trying to escape out here. She could get lost easily."

"What about the brother?" Phillip asked.

"Maybe we can bring him over later. For now, well, we can't say she's dead or he'll want to see the body. We can't just take her or he'll wonder where she's gone." Laurent fell silent for a moment before speaking again. "He lives in Boston, he's a cop there. I think I need to call the Lieutenant for the Quincy Clan. If I remember correctly, at least one of their Pack is on the police force there. Maybe we can arrange to have him go back suddenly." Making his mind up and getting a nod from Andreas, Laurent left the room to make the call.

* * * * *

Kari had the dream again. The moon hung heavy and fecund overhead and it pulled at her blood. The scent of forest, fur, filled her senses. She ran. The pads of her paws sank in the loam of the forest floor. Her breath came in pants, steaming in the crisp air in ribbons of frosty white.

A dog—no, a wolf—came to her and rubbed the side of his muzzle along her own, his amber eyes alight with the joy of freedom, the joy of the run. Another wolf, this one black as night with splashes of gray on his haunches, approached and it appeared that he was *grinning* at her. He bumped her, pressing his body to hers playfully. There was an overwhelming sense of rightness about the moment and a terrible sadness washed through her when she awoke. Alone.

* * * * *

Andreas Phinney sat in the window seat and watched the sun rise over the lake. He, Phillip and Laurent had all run the night before. He was tired but in a good way. His muscles held residual warmth, the aches were ones that would make his sleep deep and restful. He'd need to take a good solid nap before Elaine arrived in the late afternoon with Kari. He had a feeling he'd need all of his energy to deal with her and the resulting situation.

He was a werewolf. One of the very few who were born that way. And not just any werewolf—Andreas was the Alpha wolf of one of the most important packs in North America, the Cherchez Clan. Important due to size, strategic placement of Pack lands and the influence his Pack and family held nationwide and had for generations.

There weren't a whole lot of female werewolves. And of those, not all of them had the necessary biology to be able to crossbreed. Kari didn't know it but three generations ago her family had two werewolves born to it. These cousins many times removed were born to the Appalachian Clan. Andreas knew this because the genealogical records of werewolfkind were kept meticulously. Chances were excellent that Kari would be able to bear his children. Thankfully, that biology was also what enabled her to survive the transformation.

Andreas hated having to force transformation on her. Her old way of life had ended and she didn't even know it yet. She'd have to be guarded at all times, especially in her first year. Protected from other werewolves who smelled the chance to challenge her. Protected from herself until she could control the change better. And once she did get pregnant, the next generation of the Cherchez Clan would be guarded at all times.

Laurent walked into the great room, bringing him out of his reverie. "It's done. The Quincy Clan does have two members on the police force, one of whom happens to be the third in command. Apparently a case the brother worked on is coming up for trial. He probably won't have to testify but they'll make him believe he's needed. I've spoken to Elaine, she knows what to expect. She and Henry will take Kari out once the brother leaves."

"All right. Thank you, Laurent. I want Phillip with her at all times. Sean is coming later today. I wish we could have a few women with her."

"You can't cling to what-ifs anymore, Andreas. She'll be here. She's our new Alpha. She might not like it but she'll have to deal with it." Laurent was a man of exceptional bluntness. It made him an extraordinary bodyguard and Lieutenant and an equally exceptional best friend

"I've sent out the Call. There will be a Gathering Saturday. The entire Clan should be here. We'll have a full house. Make sure Anna and Gregory check the cabins to be sure there are enough linens and firewood."

"Of course." Laurent nodded to placate Andreas. In reality, he'd do no such thing. Anna and Gregory had run the house for decades and knew their jobs better than any of them did. Laurent had no intention of risking life and limb by telling Anna how to take care of guests.

"Oh and Laurent? Be sure that Kari's room is comfortable, please. I want flowers and those personal effects from her apartment that Michael brought put out. She'll be a prisoner for a while, yes, but she's my Mate and I want her to feel as comfortable as she can under the circumstances. She's an Alpha, I want her to be treated like one."

"It's done, Andreas," Laurent said and left the room.

*****

"Dr. Kennedy! Can I have a moment please?"

Elaine Kennedy turned to wait for Jack Warner, who was jogging down the hall toward her.

"I just got called back home. A case I'm working on just got to trial. I may have to testify so I need to be there. I hate to leave Kari. What can I do for her? Will she need some help once she gets home? Should I hire a nurse for her or something?"

Elaine put her hand on Jack's arm. "Don't worry, Jack. Kari will be here for another day or so and then she'll be ready to go home. She's recovering very well. If she does need help, her insurance covers home health care and I'm sure she's got friends who can pitch in."

"Well, she doesn't really. That's the problem. She just moved to Seattle from Atlanta about six months ago. She has co-workers who can probably help but she doesn't know many people."

Which made taking Kari Warner even easier. But without a doubt, her new Alpha would be cared for completely. "Well, it doesn't sound like you have much choice. Kari is a sensible young woman, she'll understand. She really will be fine, you know."

He nodded. His conflicting responsibilities showed clearly on his face. "Thank you so much for all of your help, Dr. Kennedy. If you'll excuse me, I need to go tell her. Oh, and you'll keep in contact with me about her recovery?"

"Of course! I know it must be hard for you to be all the way across the country when you're worried about your sister. But she'll be ready to go back to work by the middle part of next week." By then she'd have quit her job and would be leading the Pack but there was no need for Jack to know that yet.

Smiling warmly, Jack shook her hand and thanked her one last time before entering Kari's room.

She turned to catch his grin, blushing that he'd caught her annoyed muttering over the television remote.

"Hey what's up?" Winking, he sat on the edge of her bed.

"Not much, I'm bored. I have a headache but I feel pretty good otherwise. How about you?"

Taking her hand, he smoothed a thumb over the spot where her IV had been. "I just got called back to Boston. One of my cases finally went to trial and I might have to testify. I have to leave in an hour and a half. I'm sorry. I feel like shit for abandoning you."

"Jeez, Jack. You've been here since Sunday, right? Rushed off and came out here and sat around while I was unconscious for a few days? I'm all right now. Honest. Go home. Do your job. Send the bad guys to jail. Don't feel bad. It was good to see you. Next time come out when I'm able to show you around Seattle, okay?"

He hugged her tightly. Since their parents died in a car accident when he was fifteen and she twelve, he'd been taking care of her. She knew he felt awful for having to leave but she trusted he knew her well enough to know she was okay with it.

"Be good, okay? Doc Kennedy told me you'd be going home tomorrow or the next day. She says that you shouldn't need it but your insurance covers home health care."

"There are a few people at work that would help if I asked. Truly. Don't worry about me! I'm a big girl and I feel just fine. I can't wait to get out of here! I love you. I'll call you when they release me and I get home."

He kissed the top of her head as he stood. "Rest. Oh, and no more alleys, Kari. Talk to you soon." He blew her a kiss and was gone.

A while later the male nurse came in and took blood and gave her some pain pills for her headache. They made her sleepy so she lay down and took a nap.

* * * * *

An hour later, the man came back in to check on her and then went out to the doctors' lounge. Elaine saw him and walked into the hallway to meet him.

"She's out. Let's get this show on the road. I just called the airlines and the brother is on the plane and in the air," Henry said quietly into Elaine's ear.

"Okay, I've filled out her release papers and they're filed. Why don't we wheel her down to x-ray and I'll pull the van to the loading dock? I'll meet you there in ten minutes."

"Right." Henry left then, going into Kari's room, putting the pink "discharged" placard in the slot above her bed. He rolled her out of the room, looking for all intents and purposes like he was wheeling her to get an x-ray. Instead, he took a right rather than a left and pushed her out to the deserted loading dock, where he easily picked her up, gently of course, and placed her into the waiting van.

He returned the bed to the area outside of x-ray, where other empty beds were sitting, and jogged back to the loading dock and jumped into the van.

"Call the lodge, Henry. Tell them we're on the way," Elaine said as they pulled onto I-90 going east. "We'll be there—barring any trouble—in about three hours."

The drive was fairly routine. They had to give Kari a shot about an hour away from Star Lake Lodge, the seat of the Cherchez Clan. She started to wake up but Elaine wanted to be sure she was still under until they got her settled in at the house. It would be better to avoid panic as long as possible.

Pulling off the main road down the long, wooded drive toward the lodge, Elaine finally began to relax. The main house loomed ahead of them, three stories tall, faced with windows and large timber beams. Decks ran the entire length of the ground floor. Pretty flower gardens surrounded the lodge and led down the path to the lake and the many cabins there. The lake cast silvery light up onto the windows. It was home even though she didn't live there. It always gave her a feeling of belonging.

When they pulled the van to a stop, Andreas and Laurent came out to help. Andreas opened the door and stared down at Kari. Wonder lit his eyes as he took in the beautiful golden hair, curls softly framing her face, the gentle mouth, the bluish smudges under her eyes. He'd never seen her this close in person before but her genetic code sang out to his. She was his Mate, no doubt about it, he could smell it. Leaning down, he put his face to the crook of her neck and inhaled her. She smelled of the hospital, of antiseptic and cleansers. Beneath that she smelled like the forest, the deep woods where the loam on the ground cries out with fertile beauty. His body tightened, attraction and desire, electric, shot straight to his cock and wrapped around his heart. She was his. He was hers.

He picked her up, marveling at how very small she was in his arms, and a protective glow burst through his senses. Gently, as if she were the most precious thing in the world, he carried her up the great winding staircase and into her room adjoining his own.

"When will she wake up?" he asked Elaine, placing Kari on the bed with care.

Elaine dropped to her knees, brushing the side of her face against his calves. She kept her head bowed in a submissive pose at his feet. He touched the top of her head, caressing the side of her face and she stood, not meeting his eyes.

"In about an hour. She'll be hungry then too. She's healed remarkably well. Michael really hurt her, Andreas." Elaine frowned at that. "It was so much more violence than was necessary."

"He said she fought him hard and hit her head as she tried to get away." Admittedly he felt pride in the fact that even as a human Kari fought her hardest to survive. She was most definitely his queen. He also felt a rumbling of rage, again, thinking of the many ways the situation could have gone wrong—could still be complicated because of his weakling of a cousin.

"Yes, that's certainly what it looked like and how she described it. If she hadn't been an Alpha, she probably wouldn't have survived. She lost an incredible amount of blood and the perforated bowel would have killed her if the blood loss hadn't."

Anger radiating from him, he clenched his fists at his sides until he saw Elaine's nervousness. Willing himself to relax, he touched her face to calm her. "She remembers?"

"Most of it, yes. I think I managed to convince her that her concussion messed her memory up. That she'd been mugged or assaulted." Elaine shrugged.

"Ah, well. One way or the other she'll know the truth soon enough. Did the brother get off okay?"

"Yes, we made sure he was on that plane before we left the hospital. She'll have to talk with him in a day or so. He'll be suspicious if she doesn't. I'll call him later tonight to fill him in on her progress, stave him off a bit."

"Thank you, Elaine. You've done well by me and my Mate."

Chapter Two

Kari awoke, feeling like she was wrapped in cotton. Her eyes opened to find she wasn't in the hospital. Confused, she looked around and saw that she was in a large room with wood-paneled walls. Light shafted over the blankets on the bed. A real bed, not a hospital bed. Flowers burst from vases on every conceivable surface, filling her view with a riot of color. Beneath the sweet scent of the wildflowers there was the clean smell of beeswax on the furniture. More distant, fresh air and the crisp scent of pine trees and verdant moss. Faintly, she heard water lapping against a shoreline of some sort.

She continued to study the room until her eyes focused on Dr. Kennedy, who sat on a nearby chair reading a mystery novel.

"Dr. Kennedy? What's going on? Where am I?"

Looking up, Dr. Kennedy placed her book aside and stood with a smile. "Kari, you're awake. Good." Getting up, she quickly checked Kari over and stepped back, apparently satisfied with the results.

"Where am I?" Kari repeated.

Dr. Kennedy smiled and took a deep breath. "Well, Alice, you just fell down the proverbial rabbit hole. I'll start simple. You're at Star Lake Lodge. It's up in the Northern Cascades about an hour north of Leavenworth. You'll be here for a while."

"What? Why?" Alarm began to creep through her system.

"Well, the why is pretty complicated and I'm not the one to tell you everything. Your life changed that night in the alley, Kari. It wasn't a dog that attacked you. It was a wolf. A werewolf."

"A what?" Kari laughed. "Am I on drugs? My head injury is worse than I thought because I swear I heard you say I was attacked by a werewolf."

"No, you aren't on drugs and your head is fine. And yes, you heard correctly. You were attacked by a werewolf."

She sat up and winced, a bit dizzy. "So *you're* the one on drugs then? There are no such things as werewolves."

"Ah, but there are, beautiful."

Kari turned in the direction of that deep voice and found herself looking up into the face of the most breathtakingly handsome and masculine man she'd ever laid eyes on. He was easily six-and-a-half feet tall, broad-shouldered. Thick, muscular arms and thighs and a long lean stomach were obvious markers of his strength. He had large hands with beautifully long fingers. Wheat-blond hair brushed his shoulders, loose, holding a slight wave through the thick silk that made her fingers clench with the desire to touch it. Eyes the gold-brown of whiskey took her in. Lips, full and ripe for kissing, held a natural smile. His voice flowed over her like water over a river stone, smooth and deep. The man was a complete package of devastating attractiveness. Despite the seriousness of the situation, Kari felt her body respond to him.

"Kari, I'm Andreas Phinney. Welcome to my home." Reaching out, he took her hand in his and electricity flowed back and forth between them, bringing a gasp from her lips. Smiling in a cocky, self-assured way, he planted a kiss on her palm.

"Why am I here and when can I go home?" A bit breathless, Kari pulled her hand out of his grasp.

Andreas sat down on the bed next to her. The heat rising from his skin in waves enveloped her, dizzying her. "Kari, the next few days are going to be hard for you but please believe that I will do everything I can to make them easier. Not just me but everyone here. Before we get to any long explanations, let's get some food into you. Are you hungry?"

Annoyed, she waved her hand at him. "What? No, I'm not hungry. I want to know what the hell is going on here!" Well, she was hungry actually, but fear was overtaking hunger pretty well right then.

Andreas sighed and looked at Dr. Kennedy. "Elaine, can you please go and ask Anna to prepare a tray for Kari and bring it up? She and I are going to talk a bit."

As Dr. Kennedy left, Kari backed up against the headboard, scanning the room, looking for something to use as a weapon.

"You don't have to fear me, Kari. Not ever. I would never hurt you." Andreas' voice was soothing.

"Yeah, well, forgive me for not believing that. I don't know you. I'm in your house. And no one seems to want to tell me anything other than some farcical nonsense about werewolves."

"All right. From the beginning, the unabridged version. I'm a werewolf. The leader of the Cherchez Clan. My father and grandfather before him held the position I hold now. You were marked by a werewolf in that alley on Saturday. Michael—the wolf who changed you—got a bit excited and lost control. He's very sorry and will continue to be until you are well enough to decide on his punishment. You weren't supposed to be marked for another few months so that we could ease your transition."

Mouth open in shock, Kari sat there speechless. He seemed so normal. Hell, Dr. Kennedy seemed normal too. Just went to show how people could be totally lucid and yet completely batshit crazy at the same time.

Ignoring her look, he continued. "Anyway, when you were bitten—marked—the saliva that carries the virus got into your blood and is already working. The marks are gone, aren't they?" He went on without the answer. "We need more female wolves. There aren't a lot of natural werewolves that are female. So we must, from time to time, find human women who have shown a biological ability in their family tree to not only survive the change but to be able to mate and breed with us once changed.

"Werewolves can be created when a human is bitten by a werewolf. But it's more complicated than contaminated saliva being introduced into their system. Not all werewolves can do it and not all humans survive. In fact, many don't because the bite has to be deep and severe enough to cause a certain level of trauma in the body, and many humans die from the wounds before they can transform. Moreover, only werewolves who are born so can create new werewolves.

"You're one of those very special human women, Kari. Four generations ago your sixth cousins were changed and gave birth to werewolves, and a generation after that one of your ancestors was an Alpha, a leader. You're meant to be my Alpha-bitch. My Mate."

Fury pushed down the rising panic. "Your what? Oh no you didn't! You did not just call me your bitch. On top of being dangerously stupid, are you some kind of cult? Get the hell away from me! Jesus! Bitch? You want to see bitch? I'll show you bitch! I want to go home. I don't want to play this game anymore. You need help."

Elaine showed up with the tray, looking concerned. Andreas shook his head once and motioned for her to set it down on the dresser near the door.

"*This* is your home, Kari. You *are* home. I mean no offense by my use of the word bitch. This isn't a cult. This isn't a game. I know you can be happy here once you figure out we're telling you the truth. I'm sorry for the way my cousin brought you over. It's against all of our rules, you know. But we can get through this. You were meant to be here. Can't you feel that?"

Kari stood then, nearly tripping over the bed coverings. She realized with a start that they were the ones from her apartment. A sinking feeling dropped like lead in her stomach. Suddenly her life was a bad episode of *The Twilight Zone*.

"This isn't happening," she murmured, willing it to be true. It wasn't. "Look, whoever you two are, my brother is a cop. He'll know I'm missing. Please, please don't do this. I want to go home now." She blinked back tears.

"I'm sorry, Kari. I don't want you to be scared or unhappy. Two nights from now is the full moon, we're having a Clan Gathering and you *will* transform and take your wolf form. It'll be painful the first time but it's also exhilarating and beautiful. You can't do it alone. Especially not the first time." Smiling at her sexily, he said softly, "I can't wait to run with you."

Kari stood there openmouthed. Okay, she'd take pissed off over terrified any day. She could work with anger. Dropping the comforter, she stalked toward the door. "No way, people. No way, no how. I'm a fucking software engineer for god's sake. I don't even read horror novels. I don't watch scary movies. This has gone on long enough."

Another man stepped into the doorway, nearly as tall as Andreas and just as wide. He had strawberry-blond hair that twisted in a long braid down his back. His eyes were the color of the summer sky, vivid blue. He had a sprinkling of freckles on his cheeks and nose and was smiling at her like he told people they were werewolves every day of the week. He was also blocking her exit.

"You can't keep me here against my will. This is kidnapping!" *Damn it!* What was this place? "What's next, are you planning to rape me?" She was quickly losing the battle to hold back hysteria. Her heart was beating so fast she could see her pulse in her wrist. She tried to remember if the self-defense class she'd taken before she left Atlanta had covered this type of situation. Was she supposed to stay calm and get trust or was she supposed to be angry? Damn, she knew she should have paid attention instead of watching the sunny day outside of the big windows.

"Kari, please!" Dr. Kennedy urged. "You're getting worked up. No one is going to hurt you. Get back into bed and eat. You don't look very well."

"*Worked up!* Well excuse me." She snorted. "Who is Mount Dude here and why is he blocking my way?" She jerked her head toward the man in the doorway.

"I'm Phillip, your bodyguard. My life is yours."

Her eyes widened for a moment and she bit back the sarcastic response that burned her tongue. "Uh, yeah. Well how about a ride into town then?"

"I can't do that, Alpha."

"Alpha? Special. You think I'm a werewolf too?"

"A werewolf queen," Phillip said. Amusement lit his eyes.

Oh of course, a queen too. If you were going to be in some delusional werewolf cult, you may as well dream big. This kept getting better and better.

Andreas still sat on the bed looking delicious but slightly confused. Why was it always the cute ones who were crazy? Scanning the room, she noted the locks on the windows.

"I have to go to the bathroom. Is that allowed?" Maybe she could find a way to escape in there.

"Of course, Kari." Andreas pointed to a door. "Right through here."

Holding the gap in her hospital gown closed, she stomped past. After slamming the door in his face with vicious satisfaction, she frowned, noting the lack of a lock. She also noted that while there was a window, it was at least seven feet off the ground, long and narrow. Even after dieting a month she'd never get through it. There was a skylight but it was even higher up than the window and it had no opening she could see. She quickly did her business while looking for possible weapons but came up empty. Not even a razor, *damn.*

"Are you all right, Kari?" Andreas asked through the door.

Opening it with a jerk, she glared at him. "What, a girl can't even pee in privacy now?"

Andreas took a step back, hands open. "I apologize. I just wanted to be sure you were all right. Won't you eat? Now that you know there is no avenue of escape? I'm sorry we have to keep you here. I truly am. But after you've transformed you'll be free and you won't have the desire to leave."

"Like I'd eat anything you people gave me. How do I know it hasn't been drugged or poisoned?"

"Kari, the last thing any of us would do is harm you." Andreas had the gall to look hurt that she'd even suggest such a thing.

"Did ya ask me if I wanted to come here? Did you get my permission to take me from the hospital? You kidnapped me! Don't want to hurt me indeed!"

Phillip stepped into the room. "Would it help if I took a bite of everything first? To show you it's all harmless?"

"I want you all to leave, please." She had to think.

They all stood there.

"I said *please*. I asked nicely. I've shown you more manners than you've shown me."

"Kari, love, let's sit and eat together. You need to keep your strength up, you're healing still." Andreas motioned to the tray of food.

"Get the fuck out of here now!" she screamed shortly before bursting into tears.

"If that's what you want. I'm sorry you're so upset. Please calm down." Andreas' voice was soothing, pleading. He looked confused and unhappy and she almost felt guilty for making him upset. Almost.

"Then let me go home." Unable to bite back a sob, she slid down to the floor next to the bed, tears scalding her cheeks.

"Please, Kari. Please let me comfort you. Don't be frightened of me." Andreas crouched next to her, reaching toward her slowly.

Scooting away from him, she slapped at his hands. "Oh my god, you are the limit! You kidnap me, hold me against my will, and you want to comfort me? I shouldn't be afraid? Get out, get out, get out!" She pulled herself into a tight ball, yanking her comforter over her head, shutting down.

Dimly, she heard them all walk to the door and close it. Waiting until the storm of tears had passed, she poked her head out of the covers. She was alone. She walked into the bathroom and noticed that her clothes were hanging in the closet. Opening the dresser drawers, she saw her underwear, socks and sweats folded and put away neatly inside.

With nothing better to do and trying not to let herself freak again, she wandered the room. Walking over to the large set of windows, she looked out. It was a truly magnificent view. For a prison anyway. She could see the large lake and the forest abutting the land. Trees were only cut back enough for the small cabins dotting the shore. A large deck with an outdoor barbecue area and tables looked well used. It looked homey, comfortable, the kind of place you dream of making your own home into. "So what, is this a werewolf summer camp or something?" she muttered.

Thinking it might clear her head, she decided to take a chance and shower. Stepping in, she let the hot spray envelop her as she tried to think her way out of the mess she'd fallen into. There was no way she was just going to give up. She'd been through a lot in her life and she would get out of there or die trying.

* * * * *

"Well, she's something else," Phillip said, eyes lit with amusement.

"She's so unhappy and frightened." Misery and agitation warred on Andreas' face.

"What do you expect? Less than a week ago she was a highly paid software engineer on her way home from a nightclub when a wolf jumped her. She regains consciousness in a hospital three days later. Suddenly, her brother is gone and she wakes up to find her doctor and a bunch of strangers have drugged her, removed her from the hospital, are insisting she's a werewolf and won't let her leave. Of course she's afraid," Phillip said reasonably.

"I would never hurt her! I just want to comfort her, calm her fears." Andreas stood up and began to pace.

Andreas didn't just feel bad that Kari was upset, it was hardwired into him to feel responsible for her wellbeing. Not only because he was an Alpha, but because she was his Mate. He had to choke back panic at not being able to help her, and that was an entirely new experience for him. All of his life he'd been able to comfort the wolves of his Pack. He was exceptionally attuned to them and he knew—without undue vanity—it was one of his greatest gifts.

"You have to show her that, Andreas. She can't be expected to know. Especially under the circumstances. She doesn't know any of us. She's alone and frightened. Give it time, she'll come around. Michael really fucked it up," Phillip growled. The light of amusement in those eyes faded to extreme annoyance.

"Yes, well, he does that," said a cultured voice.

"Sean!" Andreas turned and enclosed his brother in a hug.

Sean, a near carbon copy of his brother but for the difference in hair color, looked closely at Andreas. "How are you? I take it Kari arrived safely?"

"She's here but she's pissed off and scared." The worry and agitation were back in his voice.

"Her world is not the world where men kidnap women for Mates and breeding other species." Sean raised a brow. "You'll win her over. You're sure she's your Mate then?"

Andreas' anguished look faded, replaced by a smile. "Yes. I've never scented another female like that. She smelled like the deep forest—earthy, fertile, rich. I wanted to roll around in her." He laughed at the memory. "She feels...smells...*is* perfect."

Sean nodded. "Good. Then we'll all convince her. She'll get over this and you'll have a story to tell your grandchildren."

* * * * *

Back upstairs, Kari rubbed her hair dry with a towel and hung it up, putting on jeans and a T-shirt with her red cardigan over it. Admittedly, having her stuff there made her feel a bit better. Then again, they'd probably planned it that way.

Her stomach clenched and she felt lightheaded. She needed to eat. Thinking back, all she'd had was some broth and tea the night before and some toast and half an egg earlier that morning. She wasn't good at skipping meals. It touched too many bad memories.

Wrinkling her nose, she looked at the food on the tray. It'd gone cold and looked completely unappetizing. Beside that, she was concerned they might have drugged it.

Twisting the doorknob, she discovered it was locked. *Great*. She pounded on it. "Hey! Werewolf jailers!"

Moments later the door opened and Andreas came through. "I see you've freshened up. You look better. Do you feel better?"

He smelled delicious. It drove her insane and that made her mad. She didn't want to look at him and want to take a big bite. Or lick up the wall of what she knew would be an impressive chest. Or feel the heat of his flesh beneath her hands as she rode… She gave herself a mental smack in the forehead. *Focus!*

Truth was, she didn't get a feeling that this guy posed her any harm. He felt safe. Then again, she wasn't sure how much she could take that feeling for, considering he'd kidnapped her and was holding her against her will. Hardening her resolve, she refused to let herself be taken in by him. Even if she felt like jumping on him. If she got out of this alive, she was going to enroll in a computer dating service or something. Clearly she needed to get out more.

"I'm hungry. But I'd like to take Phillip there up on his offer to be my taster."

"If it would make you feel better, of course. Would you like to come downstairs and eat with all of us? We can make you something suitable. I believe I heard Anna say we're having roasted chicken and mashed potatoes with vegetables and salad. I think there's ice cream too," he tempted.

"I'll definitely be your taster for all of that. Anna's a great cook." Phillip grinned.

"Shall we?" Andreas held out his arm and after looking at him suspiciously she took it. She pretty much had to, she was weak just from showering and getting dressed and hadn't eaten a full meal in days. She'd have loved to storm past him but wasn't sure her legs could support a weak mince much less a full-blown dramatic sweep. And a sweep had to be dramatic or what purpose was it? She sniffed her annoyance.

As they walked down the large staircase, she could see down into a great room that rose up, open to the second floor. Giant banks of windows faced views of the lake, forest and a large garden and deck area. Through the great room they came into a large dining room. The long wooden table that dominated the space must have easily accommodated forty people.

Popping her head out of the kitchen, Elaine smiled as she sighted Kari. "I'm going to get you something you can eat. Go and sit down and I'll bring it to you. Is iced tea all right or do you want hot tea?"

"What, no Kool-Aid?" Kari mumbled. "Iced please, no sugar."

When they walked into the dining room proper there were already ten other people there. All of them smiled expectantly at her as they stood. *Eeek!*

Andreas escorted her to the head of the table, pulling out the chair to his right. "This is your place, Kari. You'll be at my right hand. Please sit. I'll introduce everyone once you're sitting and eating."

With a raise of her eyebrow she sat and Phillip sat next to her. Elaine came out bearing a plate for her and a tall glass of tea.

"May I?" Phillip gestured at the food, and at her nod took a bite of everything and a swig of her tea. She watched him and after three particularly loud growls of her stomach and a few minutes she decided to dig in.

At that, the tension broke and people started talking and passing platters of food around.

Once everyone's plates were filled, Andreas tapped on his glass with a knife to get everyone's attention. "This is a truly special night. Kari Warner—your Alpha, my Mate—is finally here. She's a bit frightened and nervous and thinks that werewolves are bullshit, but she's here. Let's welcome her into our Pack. Our family."

There were cheers of approval and Kari watched it all in a daze. Andreas gestured toward a tall man who mirrored him except for coloring. "This is my brother Sean. My Second." The man stood up and smiled at her. Approaching her chair, he sank to his knees and touched his forehead to her calves.

"I'm pleased to meet you, Kari. Welcome to the Cherchez Clan. My life for yours." He moved back and stood up and walked back to his seat on Andreas' left.

"This is Laurent. Laurent is my bodyguard, my Lieutenant and my Third. More importantly, he's been my best friend since we were twelve years old."

Laurent was another giant, though not as broad-shouldered as Phillip, Andreas and Sean. He approached in the same way that Sean had. Although he moved with rippling menace, she had to admit that she didn't feel personally threatened. Clearly this was a man who could use his body as a weapon, and quite skillfully. He dropped to his knees and said the same words Sean had.

Her sense of unreality deepened as the introductions continued. A near-hysterical laugh threatened to bubble up from her diaphragm.

"You know Phillip and Elaine already and also Henry." Kari turned to see Henry was the male nurse who had been helping her for the last days. Nausea lay heavy in her stomach at the thought that there hadn't been anyone she could trust.

"Skyler Andrews is one of my Inner Circle. He's a trusted advisor but he's also a court jester." There was a deep fondness in Andreas' words.

Skyler approached her and knelt at her feet. "Welcome, Alpha. My life for yours." He looked up into her face and grinned. "God, you're beautiful." Kari wanted to laugh at his irreverence but she remembered that these were not her friends. These people had kidnapped her and thought they were werewolves.

"Watch it," growled Andreas.

Kari's body tightened with fear. The growling thing was really scary. They *sounded* a lot like wolves when they did it. Her imagination was running away from her. Forcing herself to be calm, she reminded herself that she had to control her fear or she'd never get out of there.

Finally the last to be introduced came into the room and wouldn't meet her eyes. Andreas frowned and everyone got very still. "This is my cousin Michael. He's the one who changed you."

Michael approached, and whether or not Kari wanted to believe the werewolf story, she was still freaked by anyone who wished her ill. She drew back.

"Please, please don't be frightened," Michael said softly. "I'm sorry. I was just supposed to be watching you, keeping you safe. But you ran. Your fear came over me and I lost control. I didn't mean to hurt you."

Yep, that was enough for one day. Kari stood up. "I'd like to go back to my *cell* now." Andreas started to rise but she held out a hand to ward him off. "No, Phillip can take me."

Andreas looked hurt but nodded to Phillip, who held out his arm for her. She took it, grateful to get out of the room and away from them all. She didn't respond to any of their good nights.

After watching them take the stairs, Sean turned back to his brother. "Don't be upset, Andreas. You did kidnap the girl. She's freaked." Sean took a sip of wine and continued to eat his dinner.

"She is something else though. You have a good match there," Skye added. "She'll see on Saturday and then she'll know. She'll come around. She'll even forgive fucknuts over there." He nodded toward Michael, who looked forlorn.

"He'd better hope so," Laurent growled.

Andreas had a good heart and had only wanted to give his cousin a chance. But Michael's very minimal control of his wolf was a problem. The attack on Kari hadn't been the first big mistake he'd made. They all knew it.

* * * * *

Phillip led Kari to the door of her room. Holding it open for her, he gave her a reassuring smile. "I'll be out here if you need me. Sometime—probably around two or so—Laurent will take over for me so I can sleep. He's a good guy too. Just knock if you need anything. And I mean anything. Warm milk, a beer, someone to play cards with, an extra blanket. Whatever. I won't tell you not to be scared. I know you are. You don't know us from Adam and here you've been fed a very outlandish line but honestly, look inside of yourself. Trust that. You'll know that none of us means you harm—not even Michael—and what we are saying, outrageous as it seems, is true."

"You're all werewolves then?" Kari asked, eyebrow up.

"Yep. You'll see Saturday. Hell, they'll probably run tonight so you might even hear them. Nothing to fear, though. I'm out here and no one wants to hurt or scare you. Now get some rest."

It looked like he wanted to hug her and give her a kiss but he only patted her arm, and she felt tenderness for him. Until she heard the lock click behind her.

"Stockholm Syndrome," she mumbled.

Chilly, she rubbed her hands up and down her arms. It was cold in the house. Rooting through her dresser drawers, she found some sweats, wool socks and a sweatshirt. She had to figure a way to get out of there and to a town of some sort. But she was damned tired. She decided to nap and then work out what do once she woke up.

She'd set her internal clock for about three a.m. and after a fitful bout of sleep, got up quietly. Silently putting on her sneakers, she eased toward the door. Ever-so-carefully she reached out and tried the knob. *Locked.* She'd expected that but it still came as a disappointment. She went into her bathroom and rustled around a bit through her things until locating a bobby pin and a brooch to use for picking the lock.

She walked back into the bedroom but heard voices outside the door. Quickly she jumped into the bed, pulling the blankets up just as the door opened a crack.

"Kari? Is everything all right?" Laurent whispered. "I can hear that you aren't asleep."

She snorted. "I went to the bathroom. Do I have to clear that with you or am I free to do that small thing?"

He laughed softly. "Sleep well. Let me know if you need anything," he said and closed the door behind him. Hearing the *snick* of the lock, she cursed him. Him and Andreas Phinney and Dr. Kennedy. The whole lot of them.

* * * * *

She woke up as the sun was rising and stretched. The bedside clock read six forty-five. Rustling around, she looked out of the window over the lake before deciding to take a shower. She was hungry but she'd decided to take all her meals in her room. She didn't have any desire to go downstairs and enter into their shared delusion that she was a werewolf queen.

No, if she was going to be a prisoner, there was no need at all to be nice to them or mix with them any more than necessary.

When she walked out of the bathroom Andreas was waiting for her, sitting in a chair near the door, reading the newspaper. With a shaft of sunshine glinting off that gorgeous honeyed hair, he looked more like an ad straight out of *Esquire* than a werewolf. His large, muscled form looked handsome and positively mouthwatering in a soft blue button-down oxford shirt and khakis. Hell, he even wore gorgeous designer loafers. Werewolf indeed. The man looked like casual, rich, elegance personified. That now-familiar tightness hit her body as her nipples hardened. The betrayal of her body infuriated her. She tried to breathe through her nose as it was clearly his cologne that affected her so deeply.

"So I take it werewolves don't know how to knock?" She stood in the doorway wearing nothing more than a towel. She was annoyed by his presence and his damnable appeal.

He jerked up at her tone and stared, his lips slightly parted. He dragged his eyes in slow perusal from the tips of her toes to the top of her head. Putting a hand on her hip, she glared at him. "Do I have spinach in my cleavage?"

"I apologize, Kari. I didn't know you would come out here undressed. I'll go and wait in the hall, shall I? When you're dressed we can go downstairs together for breakfast."

"Um, gee..." She paused theatrically, pretending to mull it over. "No. I don't think so. I'm not having any meals with you, Mr. Phinney. If you insist on continuing this ridiculous criminal farce, I'll have my meals here in my room. *Alone*."

"Kari, how can you get to know us if you stay up here?" Agitation rode him. It warred with wanting to coddle her and smooth the way for her. He wanted her to be adjusted to the situation even though he knew it was irrational.

Her eyes widened. "Are you getting testy with me? Get to know you? My god! You are totally delusional! No! I don't want to get to know you. I want you to let me go. I am *not* a werewolf. I am *not* your mate or whatever you want to call it. I don't want to be here. I'm not going to do anything to ease your conscience."

Frustrated, Andreas rubbed his hands over his face. Truth was, he wasn't used to being told no or to having to deal with any real insubordination. He'd been a leader his whole life. People always deferred to him or at least could be made to see the light. And certainly, he'd never experienced a woman turning his attentions away before. This woman was infuriating. She was staring the truth in the face and yet she refused to see it. Surely she could feel how right they were!

With an exasperated sigh, she spun on her heel and went back into the bathroom, slamming the door behind her. He heard the small movements as she got dressed. Despite her frustrating behavior he loved being near her, craved it. She smelled so good. Even through the citrus of the soap and shampoo she used he could smell her elemental earthiness.

She had a fey quality about her. In a world of very large wolves, by comparison Kari was tiny. She couldn't have stood at more than five and a half feet. Her heart-shaped face was framed with all of that beautiful curling blonde hair. Hair that cascaded down her back, stopping just shy of that incredible ass. Her eyes were unusual, a blue-green he'd never seen before. Pert nose and a luscious bottom lip he wanted to nibble on. Her body was curvy and voluptuous. Her breasts made his mouth water and his hands itch to touch her, palm her nipples. He wondered what she'd taste like.

Shifting uncomfortably, as the mere thought of her had made him rock-hard once again, he snorted. It figured that he'd get a Mate like her. The woman had a will of iron. Not one of the sweet easy females that some of the others had, but this tiny persnickety woman with the fiery temper. His lips curved up at the corner as he imagined what it would be like between them when they got naked the first time. She'd be passionate, he could tell that up-front.

The bathroom door yanked open and she stalked out. "You still here? Do werewolves have comprehension problems as well as an inability to knock and an appalling lack of manners?" She stood there, eyes flashing, feet apart, hands on her hips.

She really was magnificent. His hands itched to touch her as he took her in. "Kari, we'd love to get to know you, but if you want to eat here in your room this morning, I'll have Anna prepare a tray and bring it up. You and I can eat together in here. I understand that it's probably a bit overwhelming to see so many people you don't know yet." He sent her a charming smile, cocking his head.

Ooooh! Shivers of delight ran through her as she watched his lips curve, saw the hair slide forward as he moved. Hot damn, the man was a fucking sex bomb. She felt like stomping her foot at the unfairness of having such a hot number be a total nutbag.

Snapping out of it, Kari straightened her back, hoped he didn't see how hard her nipples were and narrowed her eyes at him. "What part of alone didn't you understand? I don't want to do anything with you, Mr. Phinney." She turned to the window, shutting out his appeal. "I'm hungry so unless you wish to starve me, I'd appreciate it if I could eat soon." She flopped onto the bed and picked up the book that Dr. Kennedy had left behind and started to read it, ignoring him. Or appearing to anyway—her body was very much aware of his presence.

He continued to stand there, silently demanding that she look up at him. Instead she continued to act as if he wasn't even there. Sighing with frustration, he turned to leave the room. "If that's what you want, Kari," he said shortly and shut and locked the door as he left.

"That's Ms. Warner to you, dog boy," she muttered, giving the closed door the finger. With forced calm she concentrated on her book. She had to keep her composure and rest. She was going to try to get away again that night.

A few minutes later a knock sounded on the door. At her lack of answer, a head poked in uncertainly. It was Skye bringing her breakfast. He tried to make small talk with her but she kept her resolve and kept her responses minimal. Giving him one last look, she turned away and began to eat while reading her book, effectively dismissing him.

* * * * *

Dr. Kennedy came by mid-morning to check her over. She brought a platter with cheese and crackers and fruit. "Anna wanted to be sure you had snacks on hand in case you got hungry."

With a sigh, she sat on the bed beside Kari. "Listen, I know you're angry, confused and frightened. And you have every right to be. But Andreas Phinney is a good person. He's a leader. He's courageous and strong but also compassionate and he loves you. Yes, I know that to your thinking he can't possibly love you but he's not human. In our world, once you find your Mate—your true Mate—that's it. It's chemical, biological. He loves you because you are his other half.

"No one is going to hurt you. We all care about you because you're his Mate and our female Alpha. Essentially you're our queen. I know you don't believe any of this—I sure didn't until I was changed. But it's true and you'll see that." Standing up, she indicated a bag she'd brought in with her. "There are some magazines and a few paperbacks from the library here I thought you might want to look at. It'll be a long week if you stay in here the whole time."

"Do the people at Harborview know what a whackjob you are? Come on! I've tried to be civil. I've tried nicely asking to be let go. You're a doctor, how can you go along with this? I've been kidnapped. I don't want to be here. Just let me go. Help me get out of here and I won't tell the cops anything."

Elaine looked at her sadly. "I promise that you'll know the truth soon and you'll want to be here. No one will hurt you."

Kari just looked at her and shook her head.

She took her lunch and dinner in her room as well. She was bored out of her mind. She was at the point where she was seriously considering talking to Phillip. Maybe she could befriend him and get him to help her escape.

* * * * *

Andreas was miserable. He snapped at everyone and generally just felt sorry for himself. The separation from his Mate was driving his wolf into extreme agitation.

"Why won't she come down!" he snarled at Sean over dinner. "Does she seriously mean to stay up there until Saturday? I should just go up there and bring her down. Bodily if I have to."

Sean snorted. "Andreas, if you do that, it'll only make things worse. I know that being rejected by a woman is a totally new experience for you and all, but deal with it. You know it's only temporary."

Laurent and Skye laughed until Andreas gave them both a dark look and the guffaws died into the occasional snicker.

"Time, Andreas. Give her time," Sean said dryly, secretly enjoying how this little woman had set Andreas' well-ordered life on its ear.

Chapter Three

When Kari awakened, the light that filtered into her windows was dim. The greenish backlight on her watch illuminated three forty-five. She slowly got out of bed and crept to where her tennis shoes were. She'd worn clothes to bed to be ready when the time came. She shoved her hair into a ponytail and went to the door and tried the knob.

Damn, still locked. Sighing, she pulled out the bobby pin and brooch that had been in her toiletries bag. She and Jack had picked locks when they were younger to get food out of the locked cabinets of their aunt and uncle's home. Shuddering at the memory, she shoved it down before she could think on it too closely.

It only took about three minutes of working before she heard the spring pop open. She grinned to herself—*you'd think werewolves would have more secure locks.* Slowly and carefully she opened the door, heaving a silent sigh of relief when it didn't squeak.

Laurent slept in the chair outside of the door. Creeping past him, she stood at the top of the stairs and peered down. Thankfully, no one appeared to be awake. Sticking to the sides of the stair treads to avoid any creaking, she held her breath until she stole across the great room and over to the front door. Once she'd quietly thrown the locks she walked out into the night.

And suddenly she was free. Elated and apprehensive, she stood on the porch, alone and utterly without a clue as to where the heck she was. Sighting the long drive, she decided to follow it back out to the road. She hoped she'd be able to follow it back to civilization.

The jog back up the gravel drive took about half an hour. She didn't want to overtax herself and had been relieved to find she had a lot of energy. Still, she didn't want to waste time because although she'd put pillows in her bed and pulled up the covers, she knew they'd figure out she was gone sooner rather than later.

At last she reached the road. The question now was right or left? She didn't want to go deeper into nowhere but since she'd been unconscious when she arrived, she didn't know which way they'd come in. Taking a deep breath, she decided that left was always a good choice and started to run down the road.

The post-witching hour darkness was cold. There were no streetlights way out here but the starlight must have been pretty good because she was able to see well enough to run without falling.

After about an hour, she'd begun to wonder if she was ever going to find a town or even another house. Hearing something, she froze for a moment, straining her ears. *Yes*! It was a car coming from the opposite direction of the lodge. God, she might just get out of this yet. That is, if the car would stop for her instead of plowing into her. Who expects to see anyone on the roadside in the middle of nowhere at five in the morning?

She stood in the center of the road and waved her hands, praying that they'd see her. A large blue Suburban came along and—*yes,* it did see her—and pulled over.

Opening the door, the driver poked his head out as he called to her, "Miss? Are you all right?"

"I am now! I've been kidnapped! Could I please get a ride to the nearest town?"

The man got out of the car and came to her then, bringing a blanket that he wrapped around her. "Oh my god! Of course. Get in the car and I'll take you." He led her back to his car and helped her inside.

"Thank you so much." Kari began to tremble with adrenaline. Teeth chattering, she ruthlessly held back tears of relief.

"Are you hurt?"

"No. No, they didn't hurt me. They're all just delusional."

He pulled back onto the roadway and began to drive. "I'm Ryan Salinger."

"Kari, Kari Warner. Thank you for helping me."

"Kari, you said the people who took you were delusional. What did you mean?"

"You aren't going to believe this but they think they're werewolves. That I'm one too and apparently destined to be their queen." She sighed. "My doctor drugged me. Kidnapped me from the hospital and brought me to some lodge. It's all very confusing. God, I sound as delusional as they are."

"It's going to be all right, Kari. I know you're scared but you're okay now. Thank goodness I found you. Something could have happened tonight. You could have been hurt. You're safe now." He gestured at the stainless steel Thermos in the center console. "There's coffee in the Thermos. Want some?"

"Coffee? Oh that would be wonderful."

He smiled at her and motioned to the floorboard. "There're cups in that bag. Grab one for yourself and pour."

Anticipating the warm-up, she quickly poured herself a cup and took a sip, happily discovering cream and sugar were already added. "Oh that hits the spot. I was so cold."

"Good, I'm glad you're feeling better," he said as he turned down a gravel drive.

Shit.

"Where are you going? Oh god, Ryan, this is the lodge." Her stomach sank and she tried the door. It was locked.

"Kari, please. No one is going to hurt you. They've all been worried sick. Luckily I had my cell phone on. I don't usually out here. Andreas called to tell me that you were missing and to be on the lookout for you. I'm so glad I found you and that you were okay."

He stopped the car in front of the lodge and people started streaming out onto the deck and lawn.

Kari stifled tears of frustration. Ryan turned to her. "Kari, please don't."

"Don't what!" Rage exploded through her. "You can't keep me here. It's illegal! Why are you doing this to me?"

Andreas approached the passenger side door and Ryan flipped the lock. "Kari, thank god you're all right. You scared me to death." He reached toward her to pull her out of the car and into his arms but she screamed into his face.

"Do not touch me! Keep your hands off!" She beat at him with her fists, kicking and flailing.

He backed up, waiting for her to get down, but she just sat there. She was done making this easy on them. She was going to be such a pain in the ass they'd willingly drive her to the next town and drop her off just to be rid of her.

Ryan reached out to touch her shoulder and she slapped him off. "You either!"

"Kari, what can I do to make you feel better?" Andreas reached out to her but stopped, hand in midair.

"You can let me go. You can let Ryan here drive me into the nearest town so that I can get home and back to my life. I promise I won't even call the cops or anything. Please, just let me go."

He looked pained. "Anything but that, Kari. You're one of us. I can't let you go. You could end up hurting yourself when you transform tomorrow night. You might even hurt someone else. You don't want that, do you? To hurt someone unintentionally?"

"I. Am. Not. A. Werewolf. You. Are. Not. A Werewolf. There. Are. No. Such. Things. As. Werewolves!" Each word got louder and more insistent.

Skye walked up to the side of the SUV, hands open, palms out so she could see he was unarmed and posed no threat. "Andreas, show the poor girl already. She's scared shitless. Let one of us transform so she can see."

Groaning at his own stupidity, Andreas wanted to smack himself. Why on earth hadn't that occurred to him before? He'd been so dumbstruck by her physical presence and his need to touch her and be with her, his normal logical abilities had been snuffed out. He nodded to Skye and looked back to Kari. "Kari, watch."

Kari looked at Skye as he took off his clothes, handing them to Phillip. Naked? *Well at least the delusion was an attractive one,* she thought to herself as she watched the muscles that lined his body ripple with movement.

Crouching down on all fours, Skye stretched his body and suddenly the electricity that she'd felt at the base of her spine when she'd been attacked by the dog came back. The fine hairs on her arms stood up, the air crackled with power. Before her eyes Skye's smooth skin was lined with jet black fur. His face lengthened and became a long muzzle.

Jesus H., he was a freaking werewolf. The one from her dream, she realized as she saw what was definitely a wolfish grin on his face.

"*Fuck,*" she whispered. "I should have never gone into that alley."

Skye, the wolf—whatever he was, whoever he was—shook himself out and trotted toward her. Scrambling back with a panicked cry, she bumped into Ryan, who, she realized, was also one of them. Another freaked-out cry tore from her throat and she hurled her body into the far back row of seats, as far from them as she could get.

Elaine slowly approached the car and got into the passenger seat. Kneeling, facing Kari, she lowered her voice. "Kari, I know this is a lot to take in. As we've said—normally, we don't do things this way. Andreas would have come to you in human form. Gotten to know you and eased you into our world. Michael made a mistake. He's young. He let emotions get the best of him.

"Your teeth are chattering, Kari. I'm worried about you. Please, come inside. Eat something. Warm up. Let us talk to you about our history, our culture. *Your* history and culture."

Kari blinked her eyes rapidly. This couldn't be happening but it was. If they were werewolves then they were probably telling her the truth about her being one now too. At that admission, her fear melted back into rage.

"How could you do this to me? You didn't even ask me!" She tried to open the back door to get out but it was locked. "Unlock this door!" she bellowed at Ryan, who threw the lock instantly.

Hopping out, she stomped over to Andreas. "Well?" she demanded, hands on her hips.

"Please, come inside. It's cold out here. You're shivering."

She ground her teeth and stalked toward the front door, everyone giving her a wide berth. Thankfully, she sighted a roaring fire in the great room and headed over to it to warm up. The shock and the adrenaline were wearing off. She knew a system crash was imminent.

"Henry, can you please bring some coffee and pastries?" Andreas asked as he walked toward her. Grabbing a throw from the back of a couch, he reached out to hand it to her, staying back. "Put that around yourself."

Wrapping the blanket around herself, she nodded her thanks and sat on the raised hearth.

Laurent gave her an admiring look. "Nice job with the lock."

"My brother and I used to have to steal food from locked cabinets when we lived with my aunt and uncle after my parents died. We learned to pick locks then," she said, chin up.

Laurent nodded. "Perhaps you'll teach me sometime. It's not a skill I've learned."

She just looked at him, exasperated. "Look, I'm not trying to be hateful or anything but I'm *so* not down with this. While I'm willing to admit I believe you're all werewolves and maybe even that I am now too, it doesn't mean I'm moving in like happy freaking families or anything."

Andreas sat down on the couch, very near her. So near his scent—that damnable cologne of his—enveloped her senses and she had to resist the urge to lean back and sigh happily.

Turning her body toward him, she took the mug of coffee that Anna held out to her and wrapped her fingers around it. "I've come inside. Tell me."

"Kari, *belle loup*, I can't apologize for making you into one of us. I *can* apologize for how it was done. It's not our way. At least not in this country, in this century. We didn't mean to have to kidnap you and hold you against your will. We didn't want to scare you."

"*Belle loup*?"

"Beautiful wolf. You will be, you know. Your fur will be golden. I can tell that now."

"Yeah, yeah, okay, smooth talker. You're still in deep shit. Keep talking."

Skye laughed as he approached the fireplace, clothed and human again. Grabbing a cup of coffee from the tray, he sat on the floor as near to her as he could without scaring her.

"We need females—*loup de mère*."

"What is it with all of the French? English please."

"He means we need females who can carry on the lines. Mother wolves," Phillip explained from the chair across from her.

"I speak French because I am French. My family is. This Clan is. Werewolves originated in France and China at around the same time." Andreas' deeply sensuous baritone stroked over her like a caress.

She exhaled sharply. The panic was back but what the hell? In for a penny, in for a pound. "Okaay. So why me?"

"Your ancestors have bred before. Have been changed and borne offspring. You have an Alpha in your family tree."

"What?"

"Not every female can bear children successfully. We don't know why that is. Our Clan is led by natural werewolves—those of us who were born as werewolves. This Clan could be thrown into upheaval if I don't have sons. I've been looking for a Mate for twenty years, failing to find her. That is, until I was in Seattle at a conference and I saw you. Or rather, smelled you. We investigated you, and after looking into your background, I'm convinced you're made to be my Mate. *La reine de loup*, the wolf queen to my wolf king."

She stood up. "Wait a minute there, buster! Of all the arrogant... You stalked me and had me investigated? You made me into a werewolf so I could breed for you? Are you kidding me? All of this without even *asking* me! You have some nerve, king or not." Now fully enraged, she folded her arms just under her breasts.

Andreas put his head in his hands, but not before getting a look at the breasts straining against her sweatshirt. "Why can't you just accept this?"

"Andreas, if I may?" Elaine asked, seeing her Alpha's frustration.

He groaned and nodded.

"Put at its most basic? Yes. Part of what you'll do as a Mate—as our queen—will be to have children. But Kari, we didn't make you just to breed for us. You'll be our leader as Andreas is. You'll rule the Pack and work in a national governing body for other Packs. It's difficult to understand because things in the human world are different. The world of wolves isn't so simple."

"I am not a broodmare!"

"No, you aren't." Elaine grabbed her hand. "I was brought over six years ago. Bert, my Mate, and I have two children together. No one forced me. That's not how we are. You are attracted to Andreas, aren't you? Don't lie. Not to me or yourself."

Kari looked at Andreas as he gazed up at her. "Well for goodness' sake, of course! He's a freaking studmuffin. He could be a model. So?"

Skye was laughing again and Andreas sent him an annoyed look, secretly pleased that Kari found him attractive.

Elaine smiled. "Well, it's more than that, isn't it, Kari? Will you try something? It won't hurt you."

Kari sighed resignedly. "Okay."

Elaine held out her hand to Andreas, who stood and approached Kari. "Kari, I want you to lean into Andreas' neck. Put your face against his skin there and take a deep breath. Inhale his scent. Trust me, please."

He was so big there as he stood before her. Imposing and so male. Taking a steadying breath, Kari leaned in. Andreas pulled back the collar of the flannel shirt he was wearing and the heat of his skin blanketed her face. She touched the flesh of his neck with her lips and breathed him in.

The reaction rolled through her with shocking force. A soft cry broke from her lips. Her body tightened, his smell imprinted on her system. It was as if his very cellular makeup was twining around her own. He smelled *right*. Like he was hers. It was like nothing she'd ever smelled before—like the yummiest dessert, the spiciest food. It was sex and comfort rolled into one.

The pull of it made her want to put her teeth in the flesh of his neck and bite down and she knew that he wanted that too. A low growl came from her throat and she felt a tremor run through his body. His hands came up and slid over the skin of her ribs. At that touch, the scalding heat of his hands against the sensitive flesh of her sides, her body tightened.

Nipples hardened, pussy softened, clenched to be filled by him. Her spine arched as she pressed her body into his, wished she could crawl into him forever. If at that moment he'd pushed her back onto the couch and pulled her jeans down to fuck her, she'd have held on and enjoyed the ride. Hell, she'd have begged for more.

Instead Elaine pulled her back. Dazed with desire, Kari looked up and saw that Andreas' eyes were glazed over, breath shallow and lips parted. She had to blink a few times to come back to herself. "Wow," she murmured.

Elaine beamed. "Wow, indeed. Kari. What you just felt was your biology calling out to Andreas', as your Mate. The two of you are *meant* to be together. You could feel that, couldn't you?"

"I don't know what I felt. Lust, sure but other than that I don't know. I know I didn't get all, *hey, turn me into a werewolf so I can have your freaking babies*."

Andreas caught her hand in his, kissing her knuckles. The heat of his mouth sent gooseflesh racing up her arms. "Kari, love, you felt it though. Even if you can't describe or define it just yet, you admit that you felt it? The depth of connection between us?"

Reluctantly she nodded. She had no freaking idea what the hell she was doing and it scared her. Worse, it felt so *right* that she knew she couldn't just walk away from it either. Didn't *want* to walk away.

His eyes glittered with emotion. "Thank you."

She allowed herself a small smile, unable not to be flattered by the intensity of his attention.

"More females will arrive later today. There're eight in our pack, Elaine being one. They generally stay with their Mates. You can count on all of them to help you through this. My mother Jade is the second oldest among us. She can't wait to meet you and I know she'll be thrilled to help you in any way she can."

"What makes you think I'm just going to stay here? And if I do, you think I'm just going to stay at home barefoot and pregnant? That I'm just going to quit my job and drop a litter for you?"

Skye snorted a laugh.

She watched Andreas' jaw clench and then unclench with some effort. "Running a Pack is a big job and I want and need your advice. Generally the Alpha pair run the Pack together. It'd be hard to live in Seattle and keep your old job. Our home is here. But if you wanted to, we could find a way to make it work. And I'd never force you to bear our children. I hope you want to."

"You say you don't force anything but you did. You made me into one of you without my permission, that's force. You drugged me and brought me here, against my will. You kept me a prisoner. That's force. You're asking for my trust but you haven't done much to deserve it."

Andreas hung his head but not before slanting a furious glare at Michael. "You're right and I'm sorry. As I've said, it wasn't supposed to be that way. I wanted to woo you as a human and then bring you over myself after we'd gotten to know each other. As for keeping you here, we had no choice. The first transformation is difficult. You'll need us all to help you. It's not only confusing but dangerous. You'll find the presence of the Pack to be comforting as well as joyous. If we'd left you to change alone, imagine how frightened you'd have been. We're doing the best we can with the choices that have been made and I'm sorry." He looked so sincere that she found her heart softening. He added with a small smile, "I'm not sorry I found you, though."

The force of his energy, his charisma, his being, sucked her under. She fought it. If she was going to change her entire life, she wanted to do it without these damned hormones clouding her mind. Hell, simply the fact that she was standing there considering it was astounding.

"Breakfast, folks!" a voice called out from the dining room.

"How about we have some breakfast now? We can talk more later. I promise to answer whatever questions you have. We can go for a walk, just you and I. Get to know each other?" Andreas' face was hopeful but he kept a respectful distance from her.

Exhaling slowly, she gathered her thoughts. "Here's the deal. I don't know why, but I'm willing to listen. I won't try to escape. For now. But if I want to leave after this transformation, you have to promise to let me go."

"How about we start the negotiations after we've eaten?" he countered.

"Other things are negotiable. My being free to leave is not. I won't be a prisoner."

He inclined his head to her. "As you wish. Now shall we have breakfast so that you can start getting to know me?"

"Fine." She allowed him to guide her into the dining room, where a long buffet table positively groaned under piles of food. The hand he had at the small of her back burned into her. "Why is everyone standing around waiting?" she asked Andreas, only barely suppressing the desire to lean back into him. His touch drove her insane. She wanted more, wanted him to stroke those large hands over her bare skin, wanted the brush of lips, the flick of tongues and the gnash of teeth. The mere thought of it made her feel dizzy.

He paused, pupils widening, nostrils flaring. A faint smile possessed his lips. "They're waiting for us to eat first. Pack order. You and I always get first bite."

"There is no you and I, Andreas."

He chuckled and raised an eyebrow at her. "Ah but there is, *ma belle jeune mariée*. You just won't admit it to yourself." He lowered his voice and put his lips to her ear. As he spoke, the luscious flesh of his lips stroked over her earlobe. "But I can smell how much you want me. Honey, sticky-sweet between your thighs."

Her eyes slid closed for a moment and she gulped like a cartoon character. Shivers of desire broke over her. "You wish," she whispered. Then louder, "Translation please," she said as she picked up a plate and Andreas began to fill it for her, filling one for himself too.

"My beautiful bride." The amusement in his eyes remained and she couldn't help but smile back at him. She'd been busted.

Still, as he filled the plate for her, she rolled her eyes. The whole big guy helping the small woman thing wore on her nerves. She was used to doing things for herself. *Liked* doing things for herself. "I don't even know you. I'm not married to you—nor, I might add, have you even bothered to ask. By the way, I'm perfectly capable of filling my own plate."

"Of course you are. I just want to help you. Is that an evil thing?"

"No, just patronizing."

"Ah, the little wolf is a feminist."

"So what of it? Is that an evil thing?" she asked, turning his words back on him and gaining a smile in return.

"Oh, you're a lot of things I wager. But not evil. So will you? Marry me? Be my Mate? Rule the Cherchez Clan at my side?" As the words came from his mouth he wanted to kick himself for rushing her after she'd agreed to stay and get to know him. He was usually way more suave than this. But she did things to his head. Still, he didn't want to scare her away. He wanted to bend her over and fuck her until neither of them could walk, but he certainly didn't want her any more spooked than she already was.

"You don't know me well enough to know if I'm evil or not. Cherchez? What does that mean?"

"Well, I told you we're French in origin. The Clan left France to come here several generations ago. Cherchez means searcher. We're voyagers, searchers."

"Interesting. That's actually quite lovely. And maybe."

"Maybe? Maybe you'll be my Mate?"

"Yes, maybe. I'll consider it."

He smiled and pulled back her chair for her. "Maybe is a good thing. I could always get my mother from maybe to yes."

She sat down and smiled up at him. "I bet you could. But Andreas, I'm not your mother. Let's get that straight."

He threw his head back and roared with laughter. "I should hope not! You do have a fire similar to hers, though."

Sean sat down across from her. "*Maman* will be very pleased to meet you."

Kari grunted noncommittally and took a bite of the eggs. "Who cooks for this crowd?"

"The oldest of our Clan are a couple who take care of the lodge. Anna cooks and helps with the cleaning and shopping and Gregory, her Mate, is the groundskeeper. We have fifteen cabins as well as the main house. It's a big job and one they've performed well for my entire life. Bigger when the entire Clan gathers. By nightfall tomorrow there'll be twenty-eight of us here. Well, twenty-nine counting you. A full house."

"Twenty-eight is the whole Pack?"

"Yes. That includes my mother and father, who live in Olympia now."

"So what do you do for a living anyway? Living out here in the middle of nowhere still costs money."

"We own a few businesses. We have real estate holdings. I just bought a small software company. For you. It can easily be run from here. Ryan is also an engineer and has experience with software and tech work. Right now he's working as a naturalist for the Parks Department." He nodded toward the man who'd brought her back that morning.

"You bought a company? For me? You didn't even know me until yesterday." Each time she began to get a little comfortable, he'd spring something else like that on her. A girl could only take so much at a time.

"I knew you from the moment I saw you at the Convention Center two months ago. I want you to be happy. Here with me. With us."

"This is all just way too much. What the hell am I going to tell Jack? What about my job?"

Laurent leaned over and squeezed her hand briefly. "I'm sorry. Andreas has been a leader his whole life. He's not used to having his will or his actions questioned. He doesn't mean to be a steamroller, Kari. He just wants to make life easier for you. Hell, for all of us. It's his way."

Looking down the table at the people sitting there, seeing them all laughing and talking like family, gave her a pang of regret. She'd never had any family she felt close to other than Jack. Even before her parents died they had been too busy to be around much for their children. Skye gave her a little wave and she couldn't help but smile at him.

"It's hard not to be charmed by all of this. We're all happy you're here. We can be your family too." Sean looked at her, head cocked to one side.

"How did you know?"

"Well, I wish I could tell you I was a wolfen sort of mystic but I'm not. I'm a psychiatrist by training. I practice in Shaw, a town about half an hour south of here. But I've seen the information about your life. You didn't have a whole lot of closeness and family life as a kid. This has got to be a bit overwhelming. It's not just how we are as humans, although we're all in each other's business. It's how we are as a Clan, a Pack. Touch, laughter, togetherness, it's all part of who we are as a unit. I was born a werewolf. I don't know any other way personally, but I know that humans don't usually grow up with such constant physical closeness to others. That'll take some getting used to. Probably the biggest adjustment. Well, that and the fact that no matter how independent you are and how much Andreas respects that, he's not human and he's simply biologically driven to want to take care of you."

"You were in on the investigation too?"

"Well, not in the sense you think. Andreas wanted to know you, to get a feel for you so he could bring you over in the best way. It really was an accident the way Michael lost control and bit you. Michael is...well, he's our cousin and we love him. But he's low in the Pack because he doesn't have a whole lot of intelligence. Or self-control for that matter. There's been some internal tension in the Clan for a long time between Michael's father, who was my uncle, and my father. Andreas thought that if he let Michael watch you—protect you—that he'd gain some confidence. Feel included. Phillip was there that night too, you know. To be sure something stupid didn't happen. But of course, when Phillip decided to run to the bathroom, you left the club and Michael followed. Not in human form, where he'd be safest, no, in wolf form."

Sean sighed, leaning across the table. Flicking a tendril of hair out of Kari's face, he tucked it behind her ear.

"Michael's a good wolf, he's just dim. He doesn't have anyone to lead him other than Andreas. Andreas wanted to help but only made it worse, I'm afraid. In any case, I hold Phillip and Andreas more at fault than I do Michael."

Kari finished her food and thought over everything that had happened to her in the last several days. As soon as she finished the last of her coffee, Andreas leaned over to fill her juice glass. He also got her another cup of coffee to replace the empty one. It felt odd but not necessarily uncomfortable.

"Anyway, Kari, welcome to our family. If I can help at all please don't hesitate to come to me. I know this will be a rough transition but you can do it. I know you can. What's more, *you* know you can."

"Thanks, Sean. I appreciate it. If I stay, I'll do that."

She knew she would stay. Even at that moment, they were all weaving their spell around her heart. He was right. Her lack of close family made the way they all treated her even more potent. She *belonged* there. She belonged to them.

Surreptitiously, she watched Michael, sitting at the far end of the table. A pang of sympathy cut through her. She should be furious at him. But she looked down the long table, through the ranks of the Pack and saw him—a blood relative of these strong males—and yet he sat all the way down there. It was odd but she felt a sort of kinship with him. In a way, he was an outsider too.

Making her mind up, she stood up and went to sit in the empty chair next to Michael. He looked at her and cast his eyes down quickly, blushing. All around her the room grew silent.

"It's okay, Michael. Not that I'm all that thrilled to have been made into a werewolf without permission or anything, but I understand that you didn't do it to hurt me."

He fell to his knees and put his face into her lap. She stiffened at the intimate intrusion, not knowing what to do.

Elaine whispered into her ear, "It's okay. He's showing his submissiveness to you and his devotion too. You did a good thing."

Reaching down, Kari touched his hair hesitantly, stroking a hand over his hair and neck. She didn't know why, she just knew it was what she should do. When she looked up she saw Andreas looking on with satisfaction and pride.

He stood up and came to her, holding his hand out. "Shall we take a walk now? I can show you around. Unless you are tired from your…adventures?"

Michael immediately backed off and sat back in his chair. "Thank you. My life for yours, *reine*."

She gave Michael a last smile and stood up, taking Andreas' hand. "I'm not that tired. A walk sounds nice. But I'd like to meet Anna first to thank her for breakfast. Can we do that?"

Andreas looked as though she'd just announced he'd won the lotto or something. "Yes, of course. Let's go into the kitchen."

Phillip and Laurent got up and trailed behind them. She turned to look at them and then back to Andreas. "What are they doing?"

"Phillip is your bodyguard, Kari. He'll be with you most of the time. Laurent is my bodyguard and Lieutenant. He's with me most of the time." Andreas opened the swinging doors leading into the kitchen. A tall, beefy, gray-haired woman stood stirring a huge pot of something that smelled heavenly.

"Anna?"

A big grin broke over the woman's face when she turned and saw them. She dropped to her knees and touched her forehead to Kari's calves. "My life for yours."

Kari stiffened. This kneeling thing was just weird. She looked up at Andreas, who nodded as if to tell her she was doing fine. "Uh, I just wanted to meet the woman who made that delicious food," Kari said, reaching down to help Anna up.

"Oh my! Thank you, *reine*. It was nothing. You just let me know what you like so I can be sure to make it for you."

Andreas looked at Anna with mock dismay, "Replaced in your affections so quickly?"

She swatted his behind with a kitchen towel. "You're a scalawag! There's always a treat for you in my kitchen but your Mate, she needs to be spoiled. She needs some meat on those bones." Giving Kari a thorough once-over, she nodded to herself. "I'll take care of you. Don't you worry!"

Kari laughed at that. "Thanks, I think. Can I do anything to help?"

Anna's face dropped in astonishment. "No! Thank you for your offer but you don't lift a finger in the kitchen here. I'm here to take care of you. Not the other way around."

"Well, thanks then. I do like to bake cookies every now and then though. You'll have to abide my presence in the kitchen from time to time."

"Ah well, cookie baking isn't work! It's fun. You're welcome here any time." Anna went back to her giant soup pot and Andreas led Kari out a back door into a large herb garden.

"You may not understand this but in paying her those compliments you honored her greatly. Anna is integral to this Pack in many ways and you've won her over without even trying to. And Michael? Thank you for that."

"For what? Letting him off the hook because he made a mistake? A big one—don't get me wrong—but it seemed cruel to make him feel bad because he wanted to be a bigger fish in the pond than he's capable of and he messed up. I've been there."

They walked a path down to the lake shore. She picked up a few flat stones and skipped them.

"You're pretty good at that." Andreas bent and scooped up a few of his own. Straightening, he winked at her. "I'll make you a deal. A wager if you will. If you can skip it more than me, I'll answer any of your questions. As many as you skip."

"And if you win?"

"You allow me to kiss you."

She laughed, *well, win-win for me then*. "Okay. You're on."

She stood and threw. One, two, three, four, five, six skips. Excellent.

The smirk on her face died as he threw. One, two, three, four, five, six, seven, eight skips.

He smirked at her then. "I'm quite good you know. I've lived on this lake for pretty much my whole life." He stood close to her, looking down into her face.

"Okay, you win. No tongue," she said, trying not to sound as breathy as she felt.

He chuckled then, the sound caressing her skin like hands. When he leaned down she felt like time slowed. The soft brush of his hands over her skin as he moved them to her throat brought a shiver. He held her, fingers cupping her jaw. Her breath caught as he lowered his lips to hers and the kiss was there, a faint brush of contact.

Instantly the electricity she'd felt earlier arced up her spine with enough impact to cause her to arch into him. It crackled in the air around them. She opened up under his kiss and he sucked her lower lip into his mouth and nipped it ever-so gently. True to his word, he kept his tongue in his mouth and admittedly, she was disappointed by that.

He broke off, running the pad of his thumb over her bottom lip. Her body tightened at that small touch and wanted more. Her mouth tingled with the memory of the kiss. Her pulse hammered in her ears and it occurred to her that if he made her feel that way with a simple kiss, the sex was going to be spectacular.

He stepped back and she could think a bit clearer. "Wow," she murmured.

"Yes," Andreas returned softly.

Over her shoulder she saw Phillip and Laurent sitting on a bench, trying to act like they hadn't seen anything. But above them in the house, at least six people stood at the window watching them. Skye gave them a thumbs-up and a dopey grin. She gave him the finger back. Andreas roared with laughter, as did Skye.

"I do so love your sense of humor." He held out his arm and this time she took it without hesitation. "Come, let's keep walking. You can ask questions if you like. You never need permission for that."

"So why the bet?"

"I wanted to kiss you."

"Oh. Well good." It'd been on her lips to reply that he never needed her permission to do that but she held her tongue. She was shocked at herself for taking all of this so calmly. Once she'd seen Skye transform, she'd known that everything they'd all been saying was true and the hysteria that had been building just melted away. She might be sorry later but this all just felt right. In any case, if she was going to turn into a freaking mythological creature tomorrow night, she'd need help.

"So how old are you?"

"I'm forty-two."

Surprised, she stopped and turned to look at him more closely. "No way! You barely look thirty."

"We age differently. We have longer lives than humans do. You will now as well."

"I'm twenty-four, what will I look like in ten years?"

"Much the same most likely. Your hair'll get thicker. You'll be more resistant to disease and cold. Your eyes will take on a more—I don't know how to describe it to you—I suppose a more magical look, the closer to the full moon you get. Your eyes are already so beautiful, such an otherworldly color. In wolf form they'll be incredible."

A blush crept over her cheeks. "Does it hurt?"

"The transformation?"

She nodded.

"Well, it's hard for me to say because I was born a werewolf. Most natural wolves are able to change starting at the onset of puberty. Alphas often earlier. It's natural and painless for us. Apparently the bones hurt a bit as you change, especially the first time. Henry likens it to growing pains. But it happens quickly and there's nothing on earth like being a wolf."

"Can you talk to each other?"

"Yes, but not in words. The Pack shares a common mental link. We send short bursts of sensation, pictures to each other. There's also a lot of touching, growling, howling, whining."

"Are there fights?"

"Yes. Over territory. Over females. Most of the time it's more just show than anything else. Sometimes though, especially if females and territory are involved, it can be bloody." He went on to explain that the Cherchez territory spanned from just east of the Cascades to the Puget Sound and north to Vancouver and south to Eugene, Oregon. There were apparently a whole series of complicated treaties and agreements to keep the Packs from fighting with each other.

"Everyone else is scattered from Olympia to Bellingham. Most of them will be here at least a few times a year and always at Gatherings. We have one at least once a quarter and more often for celebrations like marriages, birthdays, births, that sort of thing."

"That's only seven women, including me. You said there were nine. Who are the two others?"

"Perri lives with her Mate, my youngest brother Devon, in Portland. Unfortunately, she can't have any children, she was in a car accident two years ago and almost died."

"How awful for them, but thank god she's alive."

"Of course! I didn't mean to make it sound as if all I cared about was her ability to have children. But children are important to us, we don't have very many in the Pack right now."

She skirted that one for a moment. "Okay and the ninth?"

"Oh. Well, that's Johanna."

He said it so quickly she stopped in her tracks, turning to him with one eyebrow raised. "Okay, I may be new to the wolf thing but not to the woman thing. Who is she and what is she to you?"

Busted, a wry smile twisted his lips. "As for what she is to me? She's a female member of my Pack. We dated for a while.

She hoped to be more to me than she was, and when I figured that out I stopped it. I knew she wasn't my Mate and I didn't want to lead her on."

"Ah, and she's still hung up on you?"

"For a woman who doesn't know if she's going to be staying here, you sure are curious."

"Yeah, spit it out. We both know that I'm not going anywhere."

He smiled at that, white teeth gleaming. He hugged her tightly and she allowed herself to glory in the full body contact for a few long moments before pushing him off.

"Spill."

He sighed but his smile still lurked. "She's confused. She's been courted by many other Pack members but finds a reason to reject them all."

Kari snorted with amusement. "Of course she has. She's not confused, Andreas. She knows what she wants and that's you."

"Ah but, little wolf, I'm taken."

"Yes, but that doesn't matter to her. I hope there won't be trouble," she said, but all he heard was her agreement that he was taken.

They walked arm in arm awhile longer, until Kari got tired and they went back to the house so that she could take a nap.

"Shall we nap together?" Andreas asked, standing outside her bedroom door.

"Well," she arched against him, unable to resist touching him. "I'm not going to sleep with you but I wouldn't say no to some snuggling." Kari's voice was teasing until Phillip sat down outside of her door.

"What's this?" she asked, face hardening.

"Kari, he'll *always* be your bodyguard."

"You don't trust me. You think I'm going to run. I gave you my word and clearly that's not enough." Her arms crossed over her chest and Andreas felt that wall start to build back up between them.

Praying for patience, he sighed as he ran his hands through his hair. "I *don't* think you'll run. I just want you to get used to Phillip at your door."

Kari raised an eyebrow at him. "Prove it then. If you lock that door all bets are off. You got me? If you treat me like a prisoner, I will *not* feel like a member of this family."

"I wouldn't dream of locking you in, sweetheart. Now will you let me at least lie with you for a while until you fall asleep? I want you to rest. Laurent says that several more Pack members will be arriving by dinner."

She looked up at him through her lashes and stepped aside, motioning him into the room. He nodded once at Phillip and closed the door behind himself.

Kari kicked off her shoes and noticed the room had been tidied for her. Bed made. The flowers made the room smell springlike. She'd worked hard for most of her life. Even when she was a very young child she'd had to take care of herself or Jack did. Just having someone taking care of the basics was luxurious, but slightly uncomfortable all the same.

"Is something wrong?" Andreas moved toward her as she backed onto the bed.

"I...uh, no. I was just surprised to see the room cleaned up and bed made and stuff. You know, I may have lied about not having sex with you." She blurted it out, but looking up at him as he loomed over her, she couldn't help herself.

He stalked to the bed, his body pushing hers. The mattress dipped under his weight as he followed. The way he moved—crawling to her, eyes locked on her—was feral and all barely leashed sexuality. It rendered her speechless, dry-mouthed and wet.

Stopping when he was over her on all fours, he looked at her without speaking for long moments. "I want to kiss and lick and bite and rub all over every inch of your body. I want to possess you and make you weep with desire. I want to make you beg and watch your face when my cock is deep inside you and I make you come so hard you scream." He paused, a smile curving his lips. Her heart stuttered and a hot flush worked through her.

"But for now, you're tired. You ran eight miles just a few days after being bitten." Disappointment tempered lust for a moment until he moved again, leaning down and kissing her. Softly at first, gentle and slow, deepening in intensity and pressure as the time passed.

All she could feel, sense, was him above her, over her. His lips were on hers and then, with consummate skill, opened her mouth under his. His tongue swept inside and he possessed her with nothing more than his mouth. There was no touch of his body to hers other than there. But it was more than enough to make her weak with want.

This kiss was much more than the one outside by the lake. This kiss was the kiss of a man who knew he was going to get naked and hot and sweaty with the person he was kissing. It was a sex kiss plain and simple. His tongue slid along hers, caressed the inside of her mouth, moving in and out in a mimicry of what she prayed he'd be delivering with his cock and like, in thirty seconds. Sharp white teeth nipped at her bottom lip.

He sat back up and she stared at him, dumbfounded and tingly all over. Taking one arm and then the other, he stretched them up above her head. "Keep these here." He grabbed her wrists and held them in one hand, and a dark thrill rushed through her as he clasped her there. "I like the way your breasts are thrust up in this position."

He lay down beside her, his cock hard and pressing into her thigh, the heat of him burning into her through the material of both of their pants. It was a hot reminder of what would be between them.

Still holding her wrists, he kissed down her neck and breathed in deeply at that sensitive spot where neck became shoulder. His tongue, hot and wet, licked over her pulse point and she gasped at the unexpected sensation that rocketed straight to her clit. She felt his mouth curve into a smile at her reaction.

"I like your taste," he murmured.

Damn, the man was a lethal weapon.

His free hand skated over her breasts and down her belly. His fingertips brushed the flesh of her stomach as she felt him unbutton and unzip her jeans. *Oh dear god, yes!* His hand slipped into the open vee of her pants, sliding down to cup her pussy. With a gasping moan she arched, utterly wanton. Desperate for more contact. At that moment, Kari was fairly sure she'd never wanted to come more in her entire life.

Clever fingers delved between slick labia and through the folds of her cunt and she cried out at the intensity of contact.

"Damn it, you're so fucking wet and hot," he hissed, mashing the heel of his palm down over her mound and clit as two fingers slid up into her pussy.

Kari writhed, wanting more, but his hand held her wrists and her jeans held her legs. A low moan broke from her as he began to finger her, pressing his palm over her clit at the same time.

"So close already, little wolf? You don't know what it does to me to feel your pussy fluttering and clenching around my fingers while you rain honey on my hand. Oh how I want to be fucking you right now." His lips were at her ear as he spoke.

Moving his mouth to her breasts, he sucked and bit her nipples through her sweatshirt as she rode his hand.

Looking down her body, it was like seeing someone else, like a movie. This incredibly gorgeous, totally sexy man with his mouth on her breasts, one large hand inside her jeans as he fingered her pussy. Unreality slammed into her. The werewolf thing was nothing compared to the mystery woman moaning and getting off in the bed of a near stranger.

"Oh Andreas, I..." Her words bled into a long, low, breathy, gasping moan as orgasm shot through her body, wringing out each and every cell in her body.

"Yes, little wolf, come for me now." Andreas continued to work her with his fingers as she arched and pulled against his hold until she finally slumped back against the bed, sated and sleepy.

"Now you," she murmured, and reached for him.

"Let's lie here for a while," he said, turning her and bringing her back into the curve of his body, where he slowly stroked her belly with his fingertips until she fell asleep.

Taking one last look at her and tucking the blanket around her, he kissed her temple and quietly left the room.

Chapter Four

Sitting in his study, Andreas stared out the window at the shimmering gray-blue water of the lake. The yawning emptiness he'd felt for the last two and a half decades had finally eased.

The search for his other half had occupied so much of his existence that at times it'd felt like another person in his life.

He was a commitment kind of man. He'd dated many women but only in the short term, because they weren't his. Aside from a short period in college, he was very discriminating. He tried to always make it clear that he was only interested in a casual relationship. That hadn't worked with Johanna. Kari, clever wolf that she was, figured that one out right away.

That emptiness—that constant search—was finally over and the relief was welcome. The chance to finally let go and love someone in a deep way burned like an ember inside his soul. The arrival of his true partner and equal made him whole at last.

Laurent stood in the doorway and watched his best friend. Andreas carried an awful lot of weight on his shoulders and had from a very early age. He'd always been more serious than his brothers, even as a child.

When Andreas went away to college and grad school, Laurent accompanied him there to serve as his bodyguard while attending classes himself. Laurent had watched the first bloom of a womanizer when Andreas had gotten free of his father's daily influence. A man who looked like Andreas got a lot of attention from women and it went to his head for a few years.

But that had died out soon enough when Andreas had realized what every other wolf male does when he reaches maturity—a warm bed is no substitute for a Mate. Laurent knew Andreas felt that more acutely than most because finding a Mate was necessary not only to the Alpha but to the future of the Clan. Andreas had a lot of responsibility on his shoulders.

After graduation Andreas returned to Star Lake and took over for his father as Alpha. He did it at a relatively young age with confidence and strength. He led with a sure hand. He was responsible for each and every member of the Clan and when they had reason to celebrate he did as well. But he provided a shoulder and an ear when they needed him as well.

Seeing the Andreas who knew his Mate was upstairs readying to join the Clan and his life made his best friend and Alpha different somehow. Laurent had cocked his head, trying to figure it out, when Andreas turned and met his gaze.

"She makes me a whole person," he said, reading Laurent's look. "All of the responsibilities that buried me to the point where all I was doing was going from task to task, day to day—they feel lighter now. She did that. That searching, the emptiness—it's gone, Laurent. I'm warm inside. Complete." Andreas said it in a tone Laurent had never heard from him before, and his chest tightened with longing. He wanted that wholeness too. He was happy for his best friend and Alpha but he wanted that warmth for himself. With his own Mate.

* * * * *

Gregory spent the afternoon cleaning out the planter beds and putting in the flowers that he'd picked up at the nursery earlier in the week. The front of the house was a riot of color even in the cool fall air. White fairy lights lined the gazebo and the trees around the back of the house.

Smiling with satisfaction, he loaded all of his equipment into the wheelbarrow and rolled it back toward the maintenance shed. The place looked magical, fit for a queen. Andreas would be pleased.

Pushing the door open, he put the tools back in their place and the unused potting soil in a corner. He washed his hands off well in the sink and turned to dry them and noticed a gap on one of the shelves. He tried to remember what was there and why it would be gone. It was in an area that had boxes and jars of different chemicals. A few different fertilizer mixes, some sealant that he'd put on the decks and the walkways, some poisons for the rat problem they'd developed last year.

He made a mental note to check with Anna about it later and was doubly careful to lock up behind himself when he left.

* * * * *

Kari stirred when Anna came in to wake her gently. Sitting up slowly, she saw that the light was lower. It was nearing dark. She also realized her pants were still unzipped from her *nap* with Andreas earlier. A twinge of guilt hit her when she realized she'd fallen asleep without making sure he came too.

Her stomach growled loudly and she realized that on top of being a selfish girl in bed, she'd slept right through lunch.

Anna laughed as she heard. "Dinner will be ready in about half an hour. But I brought you some apples and cheese to tide you over. You've probably noticed you're hungrier now. We've got a much faster metabolism. You'll need to eat more food daily just to keep strong and healthy."

"Cool." Kari grinned.

Anna bustled about the room as Kari snacked. "We've got a near-to-bursting house. Everyone is here now except for Jade and Tomas. They'll get here tomorrow morning. They all want to meet you. Why don't I help you get dressed?"

Kari stood up and dusted cracker crumbs from her hands. "That's okay, really. I can get myself dressed."

Anna looked back at the door before moving to close it. "Listen, I don't want to talk out of turn or anything but well… I think you should get very dressed up. Do the makeup thing. I can put your hair in curls. You're already beautiful, this will only accentuate it. It'll help make the right kind of statement."

"What aren't you saying?" Kari eyed the other woman shrewdly.

"There's a female down there who wants you to fail. I think she needs to be put in her place."

"Ah. Johanna?"

"He told you about her? She's trouble she is. Three or four dates and she was already acting like she was queen. When Andreas saw that he backed off in a hurry. Told her up front that she wasn't his Mate. It was just a casual thing, but she's been sniffing around ever since.

"You're a beautiful woman. It's clear as day that Andreas thinks the sun rises and sets with you, but I don't know… Why not just make it really clear to anyone who'd make trouble?"

"You don't like her, do you?" It was nice having an ally like Anna.

"No I don't. She was less than nice to Sean and Ryan and put on airs. Caused bloodshed at a Gathering. A true queen doesn't need to act it, she is it. You are a true queen."

"Flatterer." Kari smirked at the older woman.

Anna laughed at that. "You bet! Now let's see what you've got in that closet."

She allowed Anna to pick out a pair of charcoal gray pinstriped slacks with billowing legs and a pair of cream-colored suede heels to go with. To top it off, she added a blood red silk blouse with a heart-shaped neckline and pearl buttons. Anna put her hair up so that it spilled down her back in riotous curls, pinned with little amber clips that complimented the gold in her hair.

Kari stood back after putting on ruby earrings and blotted her lipstick. Anna smiled approvingly. "Perfect. You're a vision. A queen. Andreas will be by in a moment to escort you down. His jaw is going to hit the ground when he sees you." Anna chuckled at the thought.

"Oh and Kari, remember that a queen never bows or shows fear. Hold your chin up and keep your gaze steady."

Anna left the room, stopping to chat with Phillip for a moment. Kari waited for Andreas, who knocked on the connecting door only moments later.

At her "come in" he stalked into the room and stopped, astonished, when he saw her. "My god, you look beautiful. Red suits you." He dropped to his knees before her. Of course being nearly a foot taller than she was, he was just about eye to eye. "You make it hard to breathe."

He might have been nearly speechless, but she was entirely without words as she took him in. The man was flat-out beautiful. A masculine work of art. His hair was a river of honey rolling over his shoulders. A black turtleneck stretched over the broad expanse of his chest. He was a tall, wide, big man and although cultured, clearly a predator. The barely leashed animal that lurked just below the surface turned her on immensely. Thrilled and excited her and frightened her just a bit. Just looking at him made her lightheaded.

Unable not to, she ran her fingers through his hair. The cool silk of it felt luxurious against her hands. "Oh my, such flattery," she said coyly when she got her voice back. Her nervous laugh died in her throat when she watched his face change at her touch. There was raw greed there and a gasp sounded from her lips.

"Kari, you're... God, I have to touch you." His hands moved up her thighs and over her ass. "I can see the curve of your breasts through the silk of the shirt," he whispered, leaning in and breathing over the thin material. Her eyelids slid closed and she gave herself over to him, to his touch, and held on. "I can't wait to taste your skin again." To underline that, he bit her nipple through the silk of her blouse and camisole and she arched. Her body swayed against him, dancing to a tune he created between them.

She was so wet, so swollen and needy that she squeezed her thighs together to relieve the pressure.

"You smell so right. You want me too," he said in a low rumble that shivered down her spine. Her clit throbbed in time with her nipples.

All she wanted was to lie back and take him into her body. For him to fuck her until she couldn't walk or speak or even think. "Yes. Andreas, I'm sorry about falling asleep this afternoon. I wanted more. I hate taking my own pleasure and not giving any back."

"Little wolf, I wanted to make you come and let you sleep. You needed the rest. And you did give me pleasure. Watching you fly apart in my arms like that, pulling at my hold while you arched into my hand, your pussy grabbing me hot and wet… It's burned into my memory."

She opened her mouth but there weren't words. He stole them from her with his deep, raw sexuality. She'd never met anyone like him before. On one hand he was sweet and solicitous of her, at the same time he had a dark, edgy sensuality that thrilled her right down to her toes. She'd decided to get on her knees to face him when Phillip knocked on the door.

"Dinner is ready, everyone is waiting," he called out, discreetly staying outside.

Andreas stilled a moment, his head over her heart, arms tight about her waist. She bent over him and held him, breathing him in.

With a sigh, some moments later, he stood up, his enjoyment of their moment obvious. He grinned and her pussy contracted greedily. "I'll have to think about Margaret Thatcher for a few seconds to get rid of this."

She burst out laughing. "I'd suggest helping you out with it, but I get the feeling Phillip will start knocking again before we got anywhere good. I'd hate to think of you down there with blue balls."

Looking surprised for a second, Andreas laughed. "I'm afraid where you're concerned, I couldn't stop when we got near anything good." He stole a quick kiss.

Blushing, Kari smoothed down her clothing and went to the door. Taking a deep breath, she joined Phillip for a few moments until Andreas came to stand beside her, holding out his arm for her to take.

With a wink, Phillip moved to stand behind them both, Laurent at his side.

As they descended the stairs, the friendly gazes of the people in the room below amazed Kari. They faced their Alpha couple on the grand staircase. The light from candles and the fire flickered and the room took on a magical glow.

She took a deep breath and her body responded as the scent of Pack rolled through her senses. Her wolf recognized it and stirred. It was unexpected, exhilarating but not frightening.

She looked down, recognized those faces she'd already seen, but saw several she hadn't met yet. Including a female who had to be Johanna. Kari was sure because hers was the only hostile face in the room.

A few stairs from the bottom Andreas stopped and took her hand and brought it to his lips before addressing the Pack. "Thank you for answering the Call to Gathering. As everyone but Jade and Tomas are here, I'd like to formally introduce Kari Warner, *la reine de loup*."

"Not until tomorrow night," a voice called out. *Johanna.* The other woman was tall, very tall. Judging from how she stood out among the rest, Kari guessed right about six feet tall. Her sharp features were accentuated by the way her hair was pulled back at the nape of her neck and deep blue eyes stared with hostility.

Kari heard several people growl at Johanna as she made her way toward them. Phillip jumped *over* Kari and landed on the ground, in front of her, facing Johanna. "You will show the proper respect," he growled out. The energy in the room was so thick and tense it was palpable.

Kari held her chin high and met Johanna's gaze straight on. She knew that if she broke or looked away she'd be letting the other woman win. This standoff was about far more than this one moment. The others in the Clan would look to her to see how she handled herself. Weakness—she had a strong feeling—was not something that werewolves tolerated in a leader.

"Phillip, I'm sure that Johanna means no ill will and was simply pointing out proper Clan etiquette." Sean's cultured voice was calm but sent a warning that no one could fail to hear. He'd stepped forward and, as a result, also stood between Kari and Johanna. Kari realized he was protecting her as well.

"Johanna oversteps herself and that's a dangerous thing." The room suddenly got very still. Kari didn't look at Andreas. She continued to stare, unblinking, at Johanna. But she knew how terrifying he must have looked. His growl was laced with threat. With menace. She suppressed a shiver, glad it wasn't aimed in her direction.

"Andreas, I'm very hungry. I slept through lunch. Let's eat, shall we?" Kari's eyes flicked over Johanna, dismissing her as if she weren't even there.

Andreas relaxed, kissing her temple. "Of course, love. Let's go and get you fed. Everyone else must be hungry as well. Perhaps Skye can escort Johanna outside and talk to her about her behavior." This was said casually, without even a glance at the other woman.

Andreas drew Kari down the remaining stairs and toward the dining room, careful to keep his body as well as Sean and Phillip between her and Johanna at all times.

From the corner of her eye she saw Skye grab Johanna's arm and move her toward the door and out into the night.

"I'm sorry," Andreas whispered into her ear.

"From what I'm told, you did nothing to be sorry about."

"Anna's very quick."

Kari quirked a grin at him. "Just keep that in mind, Andreas."

* * * * *

Dinner was served at the table in multiple mouthwatering courses. Andreas leaned over and spoke quietly in her ear. "The members of the Clan are now going to approach you. They'll repeat a vow. An oath of allegiance and fidelity. It's their way of accepting you as their Alpha."

She nodded. Everyone she hadn't met and who hadn't shown her obeisance the night before approached her, fell to their knees and spoke formal words. Kari felt like a fief lord or something. Their near piety toward her was incredibly touching and meaningful.

When a very pregnant woman approached and began to kneel Kari stood and walked toward her. "No, don't! You'll never get back up," she said laughingly. "May I?" she asked, indicating the woman's bulging stomach.

"I'd be honored."

Kari caressed the bulge and felt a mighty kick from the life within. "Strong. You must be Ellen. Andreas told me about you and your husband. Congratulations by the way, he's going to be a big boy."

Ellen colored and laughed. "Yes, he feels that way. How did you know it was a boy? We only found out yesterday."

"Oh, I don't know. He just felt that way."

Truth was, she'd been doing a lot of stuff that she couldn't explain over the last two days. Sometimes things just popped into her head—she knew the words to say or the thing to do.

"Thank you for your blessings. My life for yours." A man approached and fell to his knees, forehead to calves.

"You must be James." Reaching out, Kari stroked his hair.

James got up and escorted Ellen to a chair at the other end of the table. Andreas came up and led Kari to the seat at his right and sat down after she did. "You're doing well. Already acting like a queen," he said into her ear as he settled in beside her.

Another wolf approached and she felt Andreas tense up slightly. "My life for yours, *reine*," he said and put his face in her lap. He rubbed his cheek along her thigh and it made her uncomfortable.

Andreas growled and Laurent reached over to pull him away. "Alex, knock it off before you get into trouble you can't get out of."

The other man gave a saucy grin and shrugged. "I'm Alex, *reine*. I'm pleased to meet you." He stood up, bowed and walked to the middle of the table and sat down.

The first course was served and she took a bite quickly, feeling bad that they all had to wait for her and Andreas. The silence broke then and a happy rush of conversation and laughter flowed through the room.

Kari watched them all, feeling a sense of place that she hadn't felt before.

Andreas looked at Kari, noting the wondrous smile on her face. "Why the smile?"

"I don't know. They're all just wonderful. This is all just wonderful."

He squeezed her fingers. The relief he felt that she wanted to be there, at his right hand, guiding their Clan, nearly staggered him. What had it been like before? He found the longer she was in his life, the harder it was to remember.

At the second course, Skye came back in with Johanna. Phillip got up and stood next to Kari, Andreas loomed behind her. She turned and looked at both of them. "Sit down please. I don't need protection from a Pack member. Do I, Johanna?" Kari faced forward and spoke as a clear superior to the other woman, who stood before her.

Johanna looked down, careful not to meet Kari's eyes. "Of course not. My apologies for offending you earlier. It was disrespectful." She dropped to her knees and pressed her head to Kari's legs. "My life for yours."

"Remember that," Sean said softly.

"Go and sit down, Johanna. You've missed the first course and you must be hungry." Kari turned back to the table, exposing her blind side to the other woman. It was a risk but she knew that if she didn't act unafraid, Johanna would find a way to attack her later.

Once Johanna sat down, the chatter started again. Kari caught approving glances from several of the other women there. She had to admit a secret pleasure that she was prettier than Johanna. As shallow and petty as it was, she'd worried about that and hey, she was an ex-girlfriend after all. Apparently, Johanna wasn't very well-liked by the rest of the Pack either. Hardly anyone spoke to her in other than the politest of tones. Kari almost felt bad for the woman. *Almost.*

"Don't feel sorry for her," Sean said.

"There you go again with that mind reading thing, superwolf."

He laughed at that. "No, I can see it in your eyes. You see a lot, don't you?"

"Not as much as you do."

"She's where she is because of greed. She's greedy for power. She saw Andreas as a way to garner position in the pack and when it didn't work she shopped her wares elsewhere. Truth is, no one's good enough if he's not king. It's not even about Andreas really. It's about position. He only dated her three or four times, backing way off when he saw she expected something more."

It was Kari's turn to laugh then. "You know, if I had a nickel for every time someone has made that point clear to me today, I'd be a rich woman." She patted his arm. "You care about him, it's obvious."

"Yes, I do. Andreas' entire life has been about taking care of his family. Even when he was a child he thought of the Pack first. It's good to see my overly serious, type A, hyper-successful brother happy. Although I admit to being amused to watching you make him jump through a few hoops."

"You know, Sean, it would be nice if you stopped hogging Kari all to yourself. I'd like to visit with her too." Devon's wife, Kari's soon to be sister-in-law Perri, was one of the most gorgeous women Kari had ever laid eyes on. In a room filled to bursting with big men and tall women, Perri was elfin. Her eyes were so blue they were nearly purple and her hair was fiery red and short. She'd emigrated to the States from Australia after meeting Devon in college four years before. Kari liked her immediately.

Sean shrugged. "I've got to do it now. Once Dad gets here even Andreas won't be able to get to her." He looked back to Kari. "My father loves women. I'm sure he'll be thrilled to have another daughter-in-law to flirt with."

"Well, I don't think I can complain. If he's anywhere as handsome as you three, I'll be in good hands. Plus, I want all the dirt on you." Kari winked.

The way they laughed and teased each other was at once heartwarming and heartbreaking. They had such history and love between them and Kari had never had that before other than with her brother. Suddenly she missed Jack very much.

Leaning over, she whispered to Andreas, "I need to call my brother. He's probably worried about me."

"Of course. How selfish of me to forget about that. Elaine spoke with him last night and told him you were fine so he wouldn't worry. But I'm sure he'll want to hear from you." He stood up and escorted her to the den that was adjacent to the dining room.

He pointed at the phone. "Use this one if you like. Phillip's going to stay with you. I don't trust Johanna. But I do trust you." He looked into her eyes to emphasize the last point before kissing her temple and leaving her to make the call.

She had the freedom, she could tell Jack where she was so he could come and get her. She could escape and yet she didn't want to.

She dialed the number she knew by rote.

"Hello?" The voice that answered was a sleepy mumble, yet belonged to someone who was used to calls that woke him up.

"Oh I woke you! I'm sorry." It was near eleven there. She'd forgotten about the time difference.

"No, don't be sorry. How are you?"

"I'm good. I'm home now. I just wanted to call and check in." Oh how she wanted to share all of this with him! But she had no way to do it and make him understand. Hell, she didn't even understand. It would only make him worry and so she had to wait to tell him later.

"I'm glad you're home. I'm sorry I'm not there."

"Please don't apologize. I'm fine. It was good to see you, even under the circumstances. Next time it can be for a real visit and neither one of us will be in the hospital. I miss you." He laughed drowsily.

"Go back to sleep, Jack. I love you, okay? Be safe and I'll call again soon."

"Love you too, Kari. Talk to you later."

She hung up and stood there for a moment as she pulled herself together. Phillip watched her with a tender look on his face. Unable to resist, she went to him, hugging him briefly.

When she returned to the dining room everyone started to stand. "No, don't. Please. Keep eating."

"Everything okay?" Andreas asked. Her loneliness for her brother rolled off her in waves.

"Yeah. I woke him up. Forgot about the time change."

"I'm sure he didn't mind."

"Nah, he didn't."

"You miss him."

"Yes. He's always been the only person in the world that I could count on. He's more than a brother to me, Andreas. He raised me. He's my best friend. He begged me to move to Boston with him but I chose to come out here instead. I felt like he deserved some time where he wasn't responsible for anyone else. Of course he's a cop, which means he's responsible for everyone."

"He sounds like a good man."

"He is. He's dating for the first time in ages. It sounds serious. She seems very nice. Has a young child. He deserves happiness."

"As do you, little wolf."

"Little wolf?" She arched a brow, not knowing whether to be offended or not.

"I'm nearly a foot taller than you are. I only refer to your physical size. You're a big person in other ways." Reaching out to her, he ran the backs of his knuckles down her cheek. She noticed that he took every opportunity he could to touch her, to caress her.

"Mmm hmm, good save. I could torture you and demand to know if you were saying my butt was big, but I'll save that one for when we know each other better." She fought the grin threatening to curve her lips and lost. "You know, I'm going to need some sort of primer on werewolf behavior. There's so much I don't know and don't understand. I'm afraid I'll mess up."

"Yes, I think that's a good idea. It'll help later when you meet wolves from other Clans. Although now is not a very typical moment for a Pack at a Gathering," Sean said.

"What do you mean?"

"Well, we aren't really big on clothes. I mean, we wear them and all, but to change—to transform—you need to be naked. Most of the time you'll see naked people all over the place."

"Like a werewolf nudist colony?"

He chuckled. "Something like that. It's just easier to change if you don't have to constantly worry about your clothes."

"Oh. So you all change more than just at the full moon?"

"Yes, peaches. We do it all of the time. It feels good to be a wolf. To run and be free? Oh it's joyous."

"But it's thirty-eight degrees outside!"

"We run at a much higher temperature than humans do. Once you transform tomorrow night, your metabolism will begin a final change. Aside from that, when you're a wolf you'll be covered in fur."

Oh, duh. "Well that must come in handy during winter."

Andreas laughed and the sound rolled over her, bringing a hitch in her breathing and shivers of delight.

"So essentially the house will be filled with naked people?"

"Well, naked and in clothing easily removed if we're planning a run. You'll often see naked people coming out of the woods directly behind the lodge. We own all this land—about seven hundred and fifty acres. Those of us who live in the city can't run as often as we'd like so we come up here, knowing we're free and safe to run. It's why I spend three or four nights a week here."

"Okay, I understand that."

"And we touch a lot. I know you got a bit uncomfortable with Michael putting his face in your lap earlier but he needed that. He needed to touch you and be soothed by you. Part of your role as Pack leader is to comfort. To give strength and reassurance. A stroke of the face, a touch on the arm, a caress, a nuzzle, all of these are ways to do that."

"Are there specific ways to do it?"

"You seem to have an inherent idea. What you did with Michael—stroking his hair like that—was perfect. Also, the way you touched Ellen earlier and responded to James, it was just right. Just follow your feelings." Sean looked to her and then to his brother. Both men shared a moment of pride at the way Kari was taking up her new role.

"Well, but aren't there any boundaries? Certain places that touching isn't okay or that are purely sexual or aggressive?"

"Well, when you're in wolf shape, only Andreas should be mounting you."

Kari's face colored. "Mounting?" she said weakly. *Jeez Louise.*

"There'll be no mounting by anyone but me." Andreas cast a dark look around the table.

Sean smirked at his brother's actions. "Yes, Kari. We have sex in wolf form too. Also, it's one thing to smell you briefly. It's a form of greeting. But no one's nose should be close to your genitals for too long. That is aggressive and it's sexual."

Kari wrinkled her nose. Oh lord, this was getting more and more bizarre.

"As for aggressive, it's often more in a look than physical. For instance, earlier, when Johanna stared you in the face and thrust up to the front of the crowd—that was very aggressive. She's submissive and much lower in the pack ranks than any other of the females. That she looked you in the eyes for so long and shoved her way to the front was a major attempt to insult you and your station." Sean sent a dark look over his shoulder toward Johanna at the far end of the table.

"But once you transform and you and Andreas bond, she'll be dangerous to you. She wants what you have and you'll be new to your wolf form. I think you might have to fight her before it's over. I hope blooding is all it'll take."

"Blooding? What? She's four inches taller than I am. She's got at least thirty pounds on me! I can take her? Physically?"

"Kari, in the first place, you're my Mate. That means you're quite literally of better biological stock than she is. You're faster, stronger and more agile. You'll be all of these things and more as a wolf.

"Secondly, she comes from a very easy life. She's never had to struggle for anything and she's power hungry. On the other hand, you've had to work for everything you've ever gotten. You're smart. You look at all the angles. Although walking through alleys at two a.m. is pretty dumb."

"Yes, I'm aware of that fact," she grumbled but he continued after a brief smirk.

"You're resourceful. No one I know could have picked the lock to their room and escaped a house full of werewolves and run the way you did. When Ryan picked you up you were only half a mile from town. Even then, caught and scared, you came back here and screamed in my face—a man a foot taller than you are. You never stopped fighting until you got the evidence you needed.

"If she's stupid enough to challenge you, you'll draw first blood. I have no doubt of it. Your wolf will let you be nothing less than an Alpha. If she pushes it, you'll kill her."

"Oh no fucking way!" Kari stood so abruptly the chair would have fallen had Andreas not caught it. Heads turned and people looked toward her with surprise.

Sean laughed so hard his eyes watered and Laurent merely grinned.

"Sit down, Kari," Andreas said softly, grabbing her hand and trying not to smile.

"I am not killing anyone!" she hissed at him.

"You will if you have to, Kari. You will or you'll be killed and I'll lose leadership of this Pack as well as a Mate. I know it's hard to deal with. I'm sorry. You've dealt with so much in a very short time. But it's the way we live and you're one of us now."

"Oh, lucky me!"

Before she could add anything else, Anna came in with a large covered platter and placed it at the head of the table.

"For you, Kari, in honor of your special night to come." With a dramatic flourish, she removed the lid to expose a gorgeous cake covered in marzipan that was braided and looped in what looked to be vines. Tiny flowers and berries decorated the surface.

Deeply touched, Kari's vision blurred as she blinked back tears. "Anna, it's gorgeous. It must have taken you hours to do this. You're amazing." Without thinking, she reached out and ran her face along Anna's cheek.

"Oh *reine*. I'm honored you like it." Anna's voice was choked with emotion as she fell to her knees.

Kari knelt before the other woman and brought her face up with her hands. "I'm the one who's honored, Anna. You do this Pack proud with your gifts—your kindness and your artistry. Do not kneel to me." She stood and held her hand out to Anna, who took it and let Kari pull her up.

After the cake, Kari went into the great room with her brothers-in-law and Perri while Andreas stayed back to talk golf with some of the others.

Kari excused herself briefly to go upstairs and change into jeans and wool socks while Phillip waited outside.

Once back downstairs she joined Sean, Devon and Perri on the couch. Skye came and sat on the floor, leaning his head back on her legs, and she threaded her fingers through his hair absentmindedly. Perri leaned close on one side and Sean on the other. All around the room she could see small groupings just like theirs where everyone was touching.

From her spot on the couch she could see Andreas talk and laugh with the others in the dining room. They clearly loved him and it made her proud. He looked up then and met her gaze and the heat of it scalded her from across the room.

With a narrowing of her eyes, she also noticed that Johanna had insinuated herself into the group. Snorting derisively, she glanced back at Skye, who'd been speaking to her. His eyes went up to see what she'd been looking at and he gave a snort of his own. "Don't sweat it. She's nothing to him."

Perri agreed. "I don't know why she just didn't leave the Pack last year."

"Last year?"

"Oh she dated Andreas a few times and he put the brakes on that. She actually sniffed around Devon for a bit—the ho—and then she went out with Sean. Once it was clear the Phinney brothers weren't interested, she moved on. Skye wouldn't get near her and Laurent and Phillip hate her so she went for Ryan. Sweet and wonderful Ryan, who really tried. He reached out to her but she broke his heart. Caused a huge fight between Ryan and Neil. Many of us felt she should have been exiled to another Clan but she begged to stay and Andreas relented. He felt sorry for her." Disgust was plain on Perri's face.

"Neil? I don't think I met him."

"He's dead. Ryan killed him. In my opinion—and this is just gossip mind you—but in my opinion, Johanna set Neil up to try to make Andreas jealous. She led Neil on and when he took the bait and mounted her she yelped, making it seem like he'd tried to rape her. Ryan intervened, still thinking Johanna was his girlfriend, and he and Neil got into a fight, a really bad one. Ryan is high in the Pack hierarchy for a reason. Neil was stupid to forget that. He challenged and wouldn't back down. He kept coming back at Ryan and it got him killed. Johanna never showed an ounce of remorse or even kindness toward Ryan, who was obviously upset afterwards."

"Oh," Kari said, distressed suddenly. Turning to face her, Skye put his chin on her knees, rubbing his hands along her calves.

Sean leaned into her side and put his head on her shoulder. "Don't worry, peaches, it's all okay," he murmured. The wolves nearby reached out in some way to touch or caress her. It was almost funny but it did calm her down.

She noticed movement out of the corner of her eye and turned to see Andreas rise and come toward her, sensing her distress. Perri got up and moved to Devon's lap as Andreas sat beside her, pulling Kari into the curve of his body. "Are you well?" he murmured into her ear.

"Fine. I'm okay. Really. Just getting a history lesson." She didn't want to get anyone in trouble with Andreas and didn't know how he'd feel about them telling her about Neil.

"We told her about Neil," Sean said, resettling, moving closer to her again.

"Ah. And you're distressed?"

"I was but superwolf here and his gang of sidekicks seemed to calm me down with a bunch of petting," she said drowsily. Andreas' warmth enveloped her, lulling her into a deeper calm.

"Superwolf? Gang of sidekicks?" Andreas asked, eyebrow rising.

"Well yes. Sean has this way of reading my mind. And everyone with their petting and stroking—it was magic. Like the furry version of the superfriends."

Perri giggled then. "You'll fit into this family just fine."

"Yes," Andreas said, hugging her to his side tightly. He was so big he dwarfed her but she didn't feel threatened in any way, just blanketed. It was a nice girly feeling. She'd never been out with a big man before, it was a bit overwhelming. Well, that was an understatement. Still, not scary.

They all sat there, lounging and talking and laughing. She felt them burrow into her heart as they shared funny stories about each other.

Just after one a.m. Johanna came in. "Shall we run?" She stood in the doorway with eyes only for Andreas. "Andreas? It's a beautiful night for it. Your last one before your queen joins you."

Several people got up and headed out. Their small group all stayed on the couch. Kari looked bored while the other woman actually thrust out her chest in Andreas' direction.

"I'm too tired to run tonight. And I most definitely don't plan to leave my little wolf's side. Don't let that stop any of you though," he added without taking his eyes from Kari.

"Go. Run if you want to. Just because I can't doesn't mean you can't," Kari said quietly once Johanna left the room.

"I *don't* want to. You're so close. Less than twenty-four hours and you'll be running at my side. I can wait. I like being here with you." He looked down at her, so small compared to him. The warmth of protective feelings spread through him when he thought about her and how strong and yet vulnerable she was.

Skye got up and stretched. "I think I'm going to go. I didn't run last night or the night before. Tomorrow is a big day so I need to get back into practice." He grinned at them and headed for the door. Perri and Devon had gone back to their room, lust seeping from their pores.

Kari noticed that she could smell emotions now. She mentioned it and Sean answered, "Part of your new superpowers," as he got up. "I'm off too. A run sounds like just what the doctor ordered. See you two tomorrow." He bent down and rubbed his cheek along Andreas' and kissed the top of Kari's head.

Phillip and Laurent played chess on the other side of the room. The smoky peat of the expensive scotch they drank seduced her senses. The room was empty except for the four of them.

"You did a great job tonight." Kari pulled away to face Andreas when he said it but he brought her to his body again, needing to touch her.

Sighing with satisfaction, she snuggled into him. "Why do you say so?"

"I've spent my life being groomed for leadership but you just do it and make it look effortless."

Turning her head, she stared at his mouth. He noticed, a smile curving his lips. Reaching up, she ran her pinky along the outer edge of his bottom lip. The vibration of his heart, of the rise and fall of his chest drew her in like a spell. She was mesmerized.

"Andreas?"

"Hmmm?"

"So um, several people have mentioned bonding or joining. I'm guessing that me being turned into the werewolf queen isn't some kind of big church, white dress, flowers and a crown sort of deal."

"You'll be declared my Mate tomorrow night. Under the moon at around nine your wolf will surface. We'll run and end up at a lake about three miles from here. There we'll complete the ritual. I'll love you in wolf form."

"Love as in a nice euphemism for hot monkey sex—or should I say hot werewolf sex?"

He laughed, "Yes, it's a euphemism. I'm going to fuck you. Does that frighten you?" He looked concerned but suddenly all she could think about was his cock thrusting into her body.

It took her a few moments to clear her head. "Does it frighten me that you're going to fuck me in general? Oh hell no! I want you to fuck me right now. Does it frighten me that we'll do it in public? It should. All of this should. I mean, a week ago I was writing software. I worked a twelve-hour day.

I ate frozen dinners and watched too much television. I am so *not* the sex in front of a crowd with a guy I met two days before kind of girl."

"Yes, the Pack will be there and we'll be fucking in front of them. And I know you aren't a casual sex kind of woman. Correct me if I'm wrong but you know this—this between you and I, between Alphas of the Cherchez Clan—you know this isn't casual."

She reached out and ran her hands through his long hair, coming back to trace her thumbs over his brow bones, his cheeks, his lips. Her fingertips tingled with the touch of his skin.

"I don't know much. I'm just feeling right now. I seem to have turned off the little voice that's kept me out of trouble for the last twenty-four years. Now I'm going to have sex with you—as a wolf—in front of nearly thirty other people and I can't seem to be bothered by it."

"There's a relaxed sexuality in a Pack. There'll be times when wolves will couple in the presence of other wolves. It's a way of seeking comfort as well as meeting a sexual need. In any case, tomorrow will bind you to our Clan. You'll become Pack."

"Okay." She breathed out slowly. "I know I should be really mad that you made me into a werewolf without permission and kidnapped me and turned my life inside out but I'm not. When I saw Skye turn this morning, when you kissed me at the lake, it all just felt right. This feels like what I'm supposed to be doing. It must be the lust that's made me insane."

He chuckled. "I'm relieved you aren't mad at me and yes, you deserve to be." Pausing a moment, he glanced at his watch. "It's very late."

She looked at the grandfather clock. It was after two, coming up on three. "Yes."

"Laurent and Phillip are probably very tired. I'll put Drew and Carey on to let them sleep."

"Or..."

"Or what?"

"Or we could just have one guard. You know, conserve by only sleeping in one bed." It surprised her when her voice came out in a throaty purr but she liked it. Letting the feeling take over, she rubbed her cheek along his chest and up his neck. Slowly she stroked his body with her own, stopping at his thundering pulse where neck met shoulder and breathing him in. Letting her desire go, she ran her tongue over his skin, gently biting down, taking his flesh and tendons between her teeth. Waves of pleasure rolled through her. Her eyes slid shut and her body ached to be filled by him.

He growled then, deep and sensual. "I'd like that but we can't do anything more than cuddle and kiss. We have to save it for tomorrow night." His voice broke and he cleared his throat.

Kneeling between his thighs, she whispered in his ear, "All of it? Or just *it* it? You took such good care of me earlier today. I'd love to return the favor." Licking along his earlobe, she inhaled. She could smell his lust for her rising from his skin in waves.

He chuckled, low and sexy, and put his hands around her waist. Literally. And it wasn't like her waist was teeny, it was that his hands were that large.

"Well, I'm sure we can work something out." The grin he sent her was wicked and promised naughty naked things. She only barely stopped herself from giggling.

He called over her shoulder, "Phillip, you sleep. Laurent can take first watch. Laurent, do you need Drew to step in for a while?"

Laurent got up and stretched, looking at the two of them with amusement. "Oh, I think I'll be okay for a four-hour shift. Phillip can take over then. He slept while Kari did earlier."

"Fine." Without any further preamble, Andreas picked Kari up and carried her into his bedroom, kicking the door closed behind them.

"We can redecorate it any way you like. It's our room," he said, putting her down gently before pulling off his shirt.

"Yeah, whatever. Get naked and do me."

Standing there watching him, Kari gasped at the sight. His chest was wide and muscled, covered with a smattering of blond hair. His biceps were gargantuan. Not in a bulked-up way, more like the marble muscles of a statue. "Oh grandmother, what big pecs you have."

He laughed, deeper and huskier than he had before. Oh how the sound did things to her! She'd backed up to the bed but she wasn't trying to escape him, she just couldn't hold herself up in the face of his incredible appeal.

He approached with eyes only for her. Being the object of such intense focus made her feel like a goddess. Her heart thundered in her chest.

Reaching out, he pulled her shirt over her head. Some of the pins holding her hair up cascaded to the ground with a pinging sound. She stood there in the silk camisole she'd left on, breath heaving.

Eyes widening, he leaned back so he could get the full view. "Nice. I didn't get the chance to get a good look at these earlier at naptime." A smile rested on those carnal lips as he ran his palms over the soft material, sliding up her ribs, her back and finally around to her breasts. She bit back a moan as his fingertips lightly played over her nipples.

Taking a deep breath, he pulled the camisole off and tossed it to the side. It fluttered to the floor in a pool of pretty red silk. "You aren't wearing a bra, little wolf."

She shook her head. He left her speechless standing there shirtless, the testosterone pouring off him in waves.

"I'm glad I didn't know that. I'm not sure I'd have lasted down there all those hours knowing these beautiful breasts were free under that sweater and a scrap of silk."

A bit of turnabout was necessary or she'd be a damned puddle before anything got started. She tipped her head to look into his face. "So um, about this, *it*. What exactly are our constraints? Because I'd very much like to find out just where that," she pushed him back a bit and then trailed a fingertip down his lower abdomen, hooking her finger in the waistband of his pants, "honey-colored trail of hair leading south ends up." Looking up into his eyes through her lashes, she smiled a moment. "With my tongue." Triumph spread through her as his eyes widened and then slid halfway closed and his chest heaved a few times.

"No climax for me," he whispered, sounding almost in pain.

"What? Why, are your boys sacred or something?" she murmured, brushing her nipples along the hard-muscled planes of his stomach and lower chest. Damn he felt good.

He cleared his throat and brought his hands down the slope of her back to cradle her ass. He squeezed, the tips of his fingers brushing over her pussy through her jeans. "Sort of. It's part of the ceremony. It makes me more potent."

"Are you trying to knock me up already?" Arching her back, she began to lose her concentration. She ground herself into his body and gasped as his fingers pressed upward, finding her clit and pressing over the denim seam lying just over it.

"Yes," he hissed out. "You're killing me, minx. Part of the ceremony is calling fertility down onto the king and queen."

"I wouldn't kill you, Andreas. I need you to have sex with me a few hundred thousand times."

Laughing, he moved lightning quick and she found herself sitting on the bed, her face level with his very impressive cock, straining through his pants. "Oh. My. Well, I suppose I need a look at the goods before I buy them," she mused.

Leaning in, she rubbed her cheek over the hard plane of his belly, catching the flesh around his navel in her teeth. God, the taste of his skin intoxicated her. Salt and pine, tang and musk. She wanted to eat him up in three giant bites and lick the bowl afterward. Instead she ran her tongue around his bellybutton and down the trail of golden hair. The waistband of his pants stopped her. She slid her hands up his thighs and over his cock and even through his pants she felt him jump against her touch.

"Hmmm. That's very nice," he murmured, moaning when she opened the button and zipper to expose emerald green silk boxers.

"Silk." She leaned in and breathed on his cock through the fabric, teasing him as he'd done her earlier. Tightening his hands in her hair, more pins scattered, the pinging sound sharp over the low sound of breathy moans.

Pulling his boxers down, his cock spilled into her hands. She licked her lips. "Wow. Now would be the time in the romance novel where the heroine looks up at the big bad alpha hero and asks him how *that* would fit. I always snicker at that part. But well, I'm beginning to see the point. Don't tell anyone, but I think I just became more than a werewolf queen, I think I just became a size queen."

Andreas laughed. "Well thank you. I think. I'm glad the size of my cock impresses you. And I am now supposed to assure you in my arrogant way that it will indeed fit?"

It was her turn to laugh. "Andreas! You read romance novels?"

"Only the sex scenes."

"The best part." Getting back to work, she explored the velvet stalk of him. He was so hot but soft as the silk of his boxers. She'd never particularly thought of cocks as beautiful but his was. A dusting of golden hair sat at the root. He was fat and the meaty head made her shiver and her mouth water.

Reaching out, she grabbed him in her fist and he gasped, thrusting into her grip. A glistening bead of pre-cum invited her tongue. Leaning in, she licked from his sac to the head. His taste burst through her, overwhelming her senses. She slowly took him into her mouth, tongue swirling around the head. Taking bit by bit until he growled and grabbed her shoulders, holding her away.

Through passion-glazed eyes she looked up at him.

"Oh god, the way you look. Sex drunk. Tousled hair, swollen lips. You want more of my cock, don't you?"

She nodded as his words stunned and seduced all at once.

He groaned. "I'd love to feed you more, Kari, but I can't. Not tonight. Honestly, I'll lose it if you make another pass with your tongue. I've had a permanent hard-on since you came here. I promise you that tomorrow night, after you Ascend, I'll fuck you six ways 'til Sunday."

He laid her back on the bed and leaned over her. "Now the rule says I can't climax but there's nothing in there about you."

"Oh." She faintly felt him remove her jeans and underwear. "I think I like that rule."

His body blocked the light as he straddled hers, raining kisses along her rib cage, his hair sliding over her breasts. "Oh my," she breathed out when he kissed a hot, wet trail between her breasts and down her belly.

"You're beautiful," he said, eyes greedily eating her up. "Damn but I want you. Every last inch of you."

Kari knew the feeling. Knowing she couldn't have him inside her, she had to content herself with running her hands over his chest, his shoulders, his arms, up his thighs and back. The feel of his skin beneath her hands drove her insane. It wasn't just alluring, it was intoxicating and addictive. The more she touched him, smelled him, saw and kissed him, the more she wanted.

He brought his lips to hers. It wasn't a kiss, it was a possession, a devastation of her senses. His mouth ate at hers, devoured her, tasted, teased and tortured. His tongue seduced hers with a wet, sinuous slide. He demanded all of her, took all she had to give and more. His teeth nipped at her bottom lip.

His kisses were heady, thick and sweet. She cried her disappointment when he moved from her still tingling lips to the column of her neck and down to her breasts. Bringing his mouth to first one nipple then the other, he looked up into her face. "You taste sweet. You smell like vanilla," he murmured as she gasped when he bit down.

The same mouth that had drawn her into the maelstrom of his spell with his kisses turned that skill to her breasts. Licking and sucking, gentle scraping of teeth, laving, sweet kisses and sharp ones—the man clearly knew his way around a woman's body. As he was hers now, Kari felt a certain amount of gratitude instead of jealousy to those women he'd learned on. Having a virtuoso in bed was not something she could complain about.

Writhing beneath his sensual assault, she arched into a gasp when one of his hands skimmed over her mound, the tips of his fingers lightly playing over her labia. Spreading her, he dipped into the folds of her pussy and she sighed in satisfaction. She was so wet it wouldn't take him two minutes to make her come.

She felt him smile against the skin of her breast when he found her in that state. He moved back with one last flick of his tongue over her nipple. "You can't know what it does to me to find your pussy drenched and swollen, so ready for me every time I touch you."

He entered her with a calloused finger and slowly teased her. He moved back to continue to pay homage to her breasts while he traced big circles around her clit, never quite touching it. The one finger he'd slid deep into her pussy teased but didn't quite satisfy.

She practically wept with need. "Please, please, please."

He moved down her body and spread her thighs to his gaze, his wide shoulders held her open the way he wanted. "Please? I love a queen with manners." He sent her a cocky grin. "Please what? Tell me what you want."

She blushed. Aside from the occasional "oh god harder", she wasn't much of a dirty talker, although she did usually make a lot of noise. But he made her feel so deliciously sexy and naughty. "Please make me come."

"With my mouth on your cunt? Shall I lick you until you scream so loud the entire house knows what I'm doing?"

A dark thrill slid down her spine. "Yes," she whispered and jerked as his mouth met her pussy and he kissed her, deeply and wantonly, with the same level of devastation he'd shown her lips. "Oh god yes," she gasped.

One hand went up to grasp her breast, fingers rolling the nipple. The other hand continued a leisurely pace inside her, a second finger joined the first. His mouth—*oh his mouth*—found her every sweet spot. He licked through every furl, every fold and dip, he played his tongue over her clit, bringing her up and then backing off until she'd descended a bit only to start again. He'd pushed her so far she didn't care that she arched, pressing her pussy into his face. Didn't care that the noises she made were so loud people in the house couldn't help but hear them.

He left her helpless to do little more than pant and beg. "Don't stop, please." If he did stop, she couldn't be held responsible for her actions.

She felt her climax building from the top of her head to the tips of her toes. The taste, metallic on her tongue, dripped down her throat. Oh god, it was going to be a big one. The kind that made you scream and bite your lip until you tasted blood.

This time he didn't stop until orgasm burst through her cells, endorphins flooding her, wrenching her body, back arching off the bed, wantonly pressing herself into his face as she cried out his name.

On and on it went, wave after wave as he would not back off. Each time she felt her orgasm begin to wane, he pressed forward again, flicking his tongue against the underside of her clit, tickling a slick finger over the sensitive flesh of her rear passage, sucking her clit in between gentle teeth. Three more times she came until she finally had to heave up the mattress to escape his mouth.

"It's too much," she slurred out, drunk with him.

Taking pity on her, he let her evade him and settled in behind her in bed, wrapping his arms around her and holding her against his body.

"So yeah. That was pretty spectacular, your majesty. I may just stick around for the orgasms," she murmured sleepily. "And I don't even need a blanket with you around."

He chuckled into her ear. "Whatever it takes to keep you around, little wolf. I love you too."

Chapter Five

The morning sun on her face, Kari awoke slowly and stretched. Until her movement was impeded. She was enveloped in something. *Oh*! Andreas' arms surrounded her, held her to his very naked, very warm chest. She smiled to herself. The arms of her man. Snuggling back against him, she changed her mind, wanting to see his face. She squirmed, turning over in his arms until she faced him.

He looked peaceful, almost angelic as he slept. His golden hair fell around his face and back. Lips slightly parted, chest slowly rising and falling. He smelled so good. Warm and sleepy and sexy. She kissed around the line of his jaw and laved the dimple of his chin. His arms tightened around her as he started to wake.

"Mmm. This was worth twenty years of looking," he said into her ear, tonguing the edge and dipping inside until she gasped. "But you should be careful, little wolf. I love a good, hard morning fuck. And look, you're right here, naked."

"And oh-so-willing. Stop warning me already and get on with the fucking. But I thought every sperm was sacred?"

A sharp knock and the door starting to open startled them both. Andreas however made no move to cover his nakedness.

"Andreas! Are you still sleeping… Oh!" A tall blonde woman barged into the room. Halting near the bed, her eyes widened at seeing Kari there. She smiled. "You must be Kari! I'm Jade, Andreas' mother. My, you're more beautiful than they said you were."

Oh. My. God. She was lying naked up against this woman's son. Kari felt the heat of a head-to-toe blush.

Jade smiled at her broadly. "Oh honey, don't be embarrassed. It won't be the last time I see you naked. You know wolves and naked, they go hand in hand." She laughed, bracelets jangling on her wrists.

Kari sat up because Andreas had. She pulled the sheet up when he got out of bed to give his mother a kiss after pulling his boxers on. He turned back toward Kari, his arm around his mother. "Mother, this is Kari. Kari, *mon amour*, this is my mother Jade."

Jade bowed her head and got to her knees. Kari got up then, kneeling on the bed, still clutching the sheet to her chest. "No way, no how. You're Andreas' mother! You don't kneel to me."

Jade rubbed her forehead along Kari's thigh. "My life for yours." She stood up and pulled Kari into an embrace. "Of course I kneel to you. Just as Tomas' mother kneeled to me and you'll kneel to your son's *reine* some day. It's the cycle of things. Keep that look on his face and I'll forever be in your debt." She started bustling around the room, picking up clothes and folding them, including Kari's underwear.

"I'm going to shower if that's okay," Kari said to Andreas. He leaned down and kissed her forehead.

"Of course. We'll go downstairs. Come join us when you're ready."

"Will everyone have to wait to eat breakfast? I'd prefer not to hurry if I don't have to."

He laughed, "It's nearly eleven, love. I'm guessing that everyone has eaten breakfast by now so don't rush on their account."

She blushed again and went through the connecting door and toward her bathroom and didn't emerge until she'd taken a very long, very hot shower.

When she opened the door to the hallway, Phillip was waiting, stretched out in the large chair, feet up on the ottoman, reading a novel. He looked her up and down and smiled. "Green is good on you. Although I hear Jade got to see you naked, which, I'm guessing, looks even better than green. Course, I *heard* lots of other things last night too." He grinned wickedly.

A deep blush ran through her as she remembered how loud she had been as Andreas went down on her. "Oh good lord, are you always so full of it?" she teased. And then frowned. "Why are you here? Don't you know I won't escape?"

"No, darlin', it's not about that. As long as there's a Gathering and you haven't sealed the bond and Mated with Andreas, I'll protect you. If I'm not here, Sean or Laurent or Ryan will be. If *anything* happens, you can go to anyone. Anyone except Johanna or Alex."

"I know why to avoid Johanna, but why Alex? I only met him last night, but he seemed sincere enough."

"Alex's family ruled the Flatlands Clan for a hundred years. It was torn apart under his brother's reign three years ago and he came here. I think he meant to challenge Andreas but he wasn't that foolish in the end after all. Still, I don't like the way he lingered around you when he greeted you. Too familiar."

"Face in the crotch too long?" she asked and he laughed, nodding.

"It's good to have you here, Kari."

She took his arm and let him escort her downstairs, where a large gray-haired man shoved him out of the way.

"Get off, Phillip. This sweet little wolf is mine now," he growled playfully.

"You're Tomas, I presume?" Kari asked, laughing at his antics.

"Yes, but don't believe all you hear. I may be seventy years old but I'm still hot stuff. Just ask my wife." He waggled his eyebrows at her, grinning. Tomas was at least six feet tall, his hair was silver. Not gray but the silver of moonlight. He had a beard and the same broad build that his sons had. The combination of Jade's beautiful blonde good looks and this man's powerful masculinity produced some extremely handsome children.

"Seventy! No way. I don't believe it. You don't look a day over forty!"

"Oh you chose well, Andreas. This one is a keeper," he said. Andreas tried to come and take Kari's hand but Tomas slapped it away. "No, you'll get her back later on. Now, my sweet queen, are you hungry? Let's go into the dining room. Anna, who you've charmed already I hear, has saved you a sandwich and some fruit. Then we shall go on a walk." He guided her into the dining room and shoved Sean out of his seat to sit across from Kari.

Anna came out and when she saw Kari she ran back into the kitchen and brought back a tray filled with food. "Here, little queen, a chicken salad sandwich. One of my specialties. I saved you a piece of cake too. Wash it down with a big glass of milk." Flitting around Kari, she blushed as Kari thanked her.

"Hey? What about me?" Andreas said.

"Oh don't pout. There are sandwiches right behind you on the sideboard. I do have some fresh apple cider for you, I'll be right back."

Laurent came in and plopped down, munching on an apple, laughing. "Seems as if someone's been pushed out of the winner's circle, Andreas."

Andreas scowled. Kari tried not to smile as she ate the best-tasting chicken salad sandwich ever made. "You can have half my cake," she said, grinning at him.

"Feh, cake!"

With a grin, she tossed the last bite into her mouth and gulped down half the glass of milk. She sighed. "It's good to be queen." She held out a marzipan apple to Sean, who grabbed it and popped it into his mouth with a grin.

They all burst out laughing, relaxed to see her accept them all so readily.

After wiping her eyes with a napkin Jade winked at Andreas. "Oh my boy. You've found a woman who can keep you in line at last."

This said right as Johanna came in the room. The temperature dropped twenty degrees as Jade turned and gave Johanna her back. Even Kari could tell it was a snub.

Not that it seemed to stop her. "We missed you on the run last night, Andreas. Don't worry, you won't have to babysit your human anymore after tonight." She moved to sit next to Tomas but Sean stood up and growled at her, as did Laurent. Phillip stood behind Kari's chair, touching her back with his legs.

Kari was tired of this woman. She was normally a patient person who let little get to her but she was done with Johanna's sour grapes. "What are you doing?" Johanna turned and looked at Kari, holding her gaze. "You'll lower your gaze now. You show me respect. Your seat is down there." Kari pointed to the other end of the table.

"Who do you think you are?" Johanna asked her and Sean and Laurent moved to grab her but Kari held out her hand to stay them.

Kari gathered herself up to her full height, still at least three or four inches shorter than Johanna. "I'm your queen. That's who I am. Now swallow those sour grapes. He's mine. He was never yours to begin with. If you have a problem with that, don't let the door hit your ass on the way out. No one, *no one*, talks to me the way you just did. If you can understand that, you can stay. If not, get out."

Andreas stood behind her, a low growl trickling from his lips. Kari felt the coiled-up violence emanating from him. In fact, everyone in the room growled. Kari felt her skin ripple and she looked down and saw her fingers lengthening into claws.

Jade saw it too, eyes widening.

Kari's head dropped back as a howl ripped up through her throat and out her mouth in a hot rush. Johanna dropped to her knees and put her forehead on the floor, abasing herself. She backed out of the room, Laurent following, glowering at her.

The tension dropped and just as the claws had come, they left. She sat down, inwardly shaken by what had happened to her body. Phillip dropped to his knees and rubbed his face against her thighs and calves. She took a deep breath and stroked his head and shoulders, drawing comfort even as she gave it.

"Kari," Andreas whispered and she looked to him.

"Are you angry with me? It wasn't my place to tell her to go. I'm sorry but that woman had to be put in her place."

He came forward and Phillip moved out of the way as Andreas dropped to his knees before her and put his head in her lap, cradling her waist in his arms. "*La reine de loup*." His voice the merest hoarse whisper, he rubbed his face along her breasts, over the hollow of her throat, ran the top of his head along her jaw. She reached out and caressed his face, bringing his mouth to her own, kissing him by running her lips along his, rubbing them, sliding them back and forth, the friction delicious.

Looking up at the other faces in the room, Kari was touched and surprised to see their expressions held admiration and affection. Jade stood behind Tomas, her arms around his neck, and they beamed at her. One by one, the wolves, *her wolves,* came to her to bare their necks to her caresses.

* * * * *

Later, they went for a walk. Kari on one side of her father-in-law, Perri on the other. They strolled along the shore of the lake and he told them stories of his sons' youth. He showed them where Devon had ridden his bike off the roof and had crashed into the apple tree, cracking his skull open, where Sean had set up his own mad scientist-like lab and had electrocuted himself.

In his office, he brought out ribbons and letters of achievement for all three boys. He showed off Andreas' trophies for track and field. He'd even kept all of the boys' report cards all the way through college and medical school for Sean. There were scrapbooks and newspaper clippings, the announcement of the births of each son from the local paper. He was a proud father and it seemed utterly foreign but Kari listened happily to the stories he was telling. She didn't have that growing up, but she was glad Andreas did and she knew her children would too.

On the way back up to the lodge, Tomas took Kari aside. "What you did today, my dear… I don't think you understand how extraordinary that was. The first time anyone who is bitten changes, it has to be done at full moon. The power of the moon is the force that brings the wolf and guides the change. You transformed today without that pull. You, by your own power of will, caused your wolf to rise.

"You need to watch yourself tonight. After you fully transform, the change will be like a drug. You'll be distracted, naturally, but you'll need to keep an eye on Johanna. I don't trust her. If she challenges you don't waste your time with blooding. Kill her. Now I know that sounds harsh but you're not human anymore. You're more than that. Our ways have served us for a very long time. She'll kill you if she can and this Pack—my Pack, *your* Pack—won't survive if you die. You're going to bring my grandsons into this world. Males who'll lead this Pack into the next generations. They'll be strong and intelligent, unbeatable. Don't let her steal this because you hang onto human sensibilities in a wolf world." He kissed her forehead and they caught up to Perri.

Chapter Six

Anticipation built throughout the rest of the day. Admittedly, Kari was nervous about what was to come and Andreas picked up on that, trying to soothe her as he could with touches and caresses and the occasional softly spoken word.

After they'd eaten, Andreas led Kari upstairs to their bathroom. A soft gasp of surprise left her lips when she saw that the giant claw-footed tub was filled and steam rose into the air above it. Lit candles perched on every available surface.

"Let me help prepare you for your ascension, my queen." The way he said it, with reverence and love, left her speechless as he undressed her slowly. Each time he removed a piece of her clothing, he caressed and kissed the skin exposed before moving to the next item. That such a strong man served her so gently touched her and bent her heart to his. If there'd been any doubt in her left about how she felt about Andreas Phinney, it was gone in that moment.

When he'd gotten her completely undressed, he quickly got rid of his own clothes and stepped into the tub first. She took the hand he held out and got in, nestling between his thighs. Kari breathed deeply, the scent of the herbs floating in the water soothed her senses.

"The herbs in the water are Anna's special mixture. Rosemary, lemon balm and she said a bit of vanilla just for you because she knew you liked it."

Tears stung Kari's eyes. She held such a feeling of belonging, of being cherished and adored. For a moment panic drowned her as she remembered her life before, without this man and his family.

Sensing it, Andreas leaned in and kissed her temple. "Tonight, in just a few hours, you'll be mine and I'll be yours. This is forever, Kari. And I've never felt so satisfied and sure about anything in my life."

"You'd better be, Andreas. Because I'm trusting you with my whole self. I'm giving myself to you totally. If I lost all of this, if you change your mind, it would break my heart. And then I'd have to rip your balls off."

She felt him wince behind her and then he laughed. "Such a vicious little wolf. I like that." And she felt the truth of it as his cock pressed into her back. "And I'm not going anywhere. If anything, you'll have to beat me off with a stick to keep me away from you. I can't seem to get enough."

Rising up on her knees, she turned to face him. "I'm a buffet, Andreas, come and get me." One of her eyebrows went up and he groaned.

"Don't torture me!" He brought soapy hands to her nipples and rolled and tugged them between his fingertips and a soft moan broke from her lips. "You don't know how much I wanted to rip off your pants and fuck you on the table this afternoon after you told Johanna off. Seeing you that way really turns me on."

He sat her on the edge of the tub. "Spread your thighs." He knelt before her as she did. "Kari, I want you to touch yourself for me. I want to watch you here, flushed with the heat of the bathwater, skin glistening and wet and golden from candlelight. I want to see your fingers on your pussy. Show me what you like."

She was speechless for a moment. But he'd given to her twice when he couldn't come at all. He'd loved her and cherished her and asked for something she did anyway, why not give him a little show?

Her gaze locked with his, she brought two fingers to her mouth and then down her stomach to her pussy.

"Hold me open, Andreas."

Reaching out, he spread her labia with his thumbs.

When her fingertips found her clit she jumped. She'd never masturbated in front of anyone before. It was incredibly erotic and intimate.

"That's the way, little wolf," Andreas growled low, eyes rapt on her fingers.

She tried to give him a show, drawing out her movements as her fingers slid through her wet heat, her clit a swollen bead beneath the pads of her fingers. When she pressed two fingers into her gate they both gasped. The walls of her cunt gripped her, wishing it was him instead.

And as she fucked into herself with her fingers and her thumb went to her clit, he leaned in and licked around her hand.

And that was all it took. A cry came from her as orgasm rippled through her system. A quiet, moving climax that pulled her under for a brief time and then she resurfaced, feeling calm and relaxed.

Andreas kissed the inside of her thighs. "Beautiful." He pulled her fingers from her and sucked them into her mouth and she nearly came again just watching. "Let's go, little wolf. Let's go and do this so I can finally take you in our bed. And out of our bed. Against a wall. On the table. Wherever."

"Oh! Promises, promises."

* * * * *

Just before nine they went downstairs where the Pack waited. The emotions of the wolves, *her* wolves, slammed into her as she began to walk through them out the door.

Most of them wore robes like Andreas', a few were naked already.

Andreas led her into a meadow ringed by trees behind the lodge. The place felt magical, heavy with power. He turned to her. "It's time, little wolf. Are you ready?"

Taking a deep breath, she nodded. He carefully removed her robe, hanging it on a peg in the tree trunk, putting his own next to it. Her heart did a little lurch when she saw him naked again.

Andreas looked at her, so beautiful as the silvery light of the moon shone on her skin, making her glow like a pearl. Her hair hung down over her shoulders and played peek-a-boo with her nipples as she moved. His own personal goddess. The importance of the moment weighed on him, not as a burden, but as a cloak. This was his Pack and here was his Mate. They'd lead together and build a life, like his parents had. The yearning he'd pretended not to have all those years rushed through him and drained away, replaced with satisfaction.

Bowing over her hand, he kissed it and stood again before leading her into the small clearing.

"This meadow is where most of the Clan are buried. You can feel them all here, watching over us. All our major celebrations happen here—dedications of children, Mating ceremonies, first transformations. This piece of ground is the heart of Cherchez." Andreas gestured around the meadow.

Kari nodded, feeling the sense of unity, of kinship with the others there. Her skin had begun to itch. The energy from Andreas hung over her like fog. Her head began to feel muzzy and her hearing was tinny, as if she was listening through bad speakers.

"Let it come, Kari. Don't be afraid." Andreas looked deep in her eyes and she looked back into his, latching onto him like a life preserver.

The Pack formed a circle and Andreas pulled her into the center, under the open sky.

He addressed the Pack but his eyes were for her alone. "Tonight the moon will pull the wolf to the surface and Kari will become my Mate. The Alpha of Cherchez Clan. Your queen stands before you, human for moments more."

"J'honore mon compagnon. I honor my Mate." Andreas held out his hand to her and she took it, kissing his knuckles. *"J'honore mon reine.* I honor my queen." He put a wreath of white star jasmine in her hair. The rest of the Pack repeated the last phrase.

Andreas turned in a circle and spoke. *"Nois faisons bon accueil au loup. Nous celebrons le lien. Nous honorons notre soeur.* We welcome the wolf. We celebrate the bond. We honor our sister."

Kneeling before her, he ran his hands up her legs. "The moon calls the wolf, Kari. Let her come." He drew her to her knees, the need to stretch burned through her. Her bones ached, especially the long bones of her legs. Her fear was muted by the energy of her Pack. Their presence calmed her.

The itching rippling of her skin that she'd felt earlier in the day returned. Her humanity, her woman-skin slid beneath the fur. Her humanness fell away. The wolf within took over, bursting up and through her body, roaring to the surface, and suddenly she blinked. The world was black and white and gray. She looked up at the moon and howled, joined by the voices of twenty-eight others howling triumph and joy.

It was amazing. She shook her head and felt another wolf rub his muzzle along her own. Joy rolled through her—it was Andreas. Even with her black and gray vision she knew he was a golden wolf the size of a small pony. His eyes gleamed with an otherworldly fire. She wished she had her human sight to see him in full color but still, she'd never seen a more beautiful sight.

The jet-black wolf from her dream thudded into her playfully, grinning at her. Skye. As she was nuzzled and bumped by numerous other wolves, she could tell who each one was.

Andreas sent a burst of emotion to her—*run*—and she nodded her head at him, tearing off into the forest, following closely on his heels.

She had never dreamed anything could feel so good. Utterly free. Powerful. She'd have giggled if she were human. Experimenting, she sent a burst of extreme joy to Andreas. He looked back at her for a moment and howled as he ran.

They ran for miles, the forest whipping past. The smells and textures intoxicated her. Finally she scented a lake. It was higher here, the air a bit thinner. She could smell the fish, the birds in the trees, the fur all around her. She slowed, approaching the lakeshore, padding beside Andreas.

Andreas herded her by pushing her with his head in the direction he wanted her to go. She nipped at him playfully and he batted her with a big paw on her hindquarters. He sent a burst of lust so strong that she nearly stumbled. Her legs trembled. This was the moment.

Rearing up behind her, he mounted her. His teeth closed in on her neck, holding her in place. He growled and she whined. She wasn't going anywhere, mesmerized by the spell of this place, of the ritual. Of Andreas inside of her in such a primal way. There was no orgasm for her, just a feeling of possession and pride. The pleasure of being wanted and desired by this wolf at her back. Her Mate, her king.

She felt his climax and he withdrew from her slowly, licking her where he'd bitten, nuzzling her. She got down on her belly and crawled to him, utterly submissive. He stood over her and howled. Finished. She was his. He was hers. Getting on his belly, he rolled over to her and she pounced on him. Playing, they rolled over each other, growling and yipping in joy. Other wolves were coupling as well. Some with their Mates, some were sharing, which she found interesting and wanted to remind herself to ask about later.

A female approached and presented toward Andreas. That bitch Johanna wanted to fuck her wolf? Kari didn't think so.

Even though Andreas turned his back on Johanna, Kari came forward and snarled at her, but the other wolf wouldn't back off. Kari shot over and bit her on her hind leg, drawing blood as a warning. It should have been enough but Johanna came tearing toward her, trying to bite her back. Sean and Phillip started to get in between them but Kari snarled at them both to get back. She had to fight her own battles. If she didn't take care of the Johanna problem now, her status would be in jeopardy. Other females might be having sex with males they weren't mated to. But she was sure that, as king—on the night he bonded with his Mate and queen—fucking other women, wolves, whatever, was not allowed. Even if the rules allowed it, it certainly wasn't okay with Kari and Johanna knew it.

No, Johanna was pushing. She thought she could take Kari and she was dead wrong.

Kari jumped at Johanna, slashing her hindquarters with her teeth, raising more blood. She growled low, *give it up, bitch.* Johanna looked her square in the eyes and lunged but before she'd even realized it, Kari was gone, having jumped out of the way.

Sean stood next to Andreas, two great hulking wolves. Andreas looked supremely assured that his Mate would win. He hadn't even raised his hackles.

Phillip, on the other hand, growled and snarled at Johanna.

Johanna kept trying to catch Andreas' eye. Kari'd had enough. Lunging, she caught Johanna's neck, throwing her on her back, belly exposed. She closed her mouth over Johanna's throat and the song of Johanna's blood slammed into her. Warm and coppery, spicy and intoxicating. She tightened her grip and placed her front paws on the exposed stomach.

Johanna whined and went limp. She'd surrendered. Kari let go and turned her back, snorting. She'd nearly reached Andreas when she saw his head snap up and Johanna's body slammed into her. The bitch had faked it and attacked her when her back was turned!

Kari went limp for a moment to confuse Johanna. When Johanna moved in for the kill, teeth bared, killing light in her eyes, Kari rose up and jumped into her full force. Grabbing Johanna's neck between her jaws, Kari jerked Johanna's head back and forth, avoiding the snapping jaws that tried to bite her. One last savage whip of the neck and Kari heard the crack and dropped Johanna's body from her jaws. She'd broken Johanna's neck. The reality of it hit her human, deep beneath the fur of her wolf. *Oh god, she'd killed someone.*

The other wolves came in and yipped and stroked and touched her. Andreas came and licked a bite on her side. Sean nuzzled into her as if he were looking for wounds. He licked the scratches on her stomach. Her human was in shock but her body, her wolf nature, sang in victory. She'd dealt with a threat effectively. There'd been no choice but to kill Johanna in the end but Kari didn't have to start the fight to begin with.

Andreas shook his head at her, whining and licking her face. Jade came and rubbed against her gently. Andreas put his body against hers and pushed and the two of them ran back through the woods, fur gleaming under the waning light of the moon, until she and Andreas stopped at the tree where their robes hung. He looked at her as if to ask if she was ready to change back. She lay on the ground, belly pressing against the cool dirt and pine needles, her breath visible against the cold. She let her wolf slide beneath her human self and her soft pink skin rose as the furry skin sank.

She said, "Wait," to Andreas, who was still a wolf.

He was beautiful, his coat the color of wheat, his eyes like amber with flame behind it. He was so large that he rose to her chest. She ran her face and hands through the soft fur and his sandpapery tongue came out to lick across her jawline. She held his muzzle in her small hands. "You are so beautiful. Come back to me now, Andreas," she murmured and stepped back. Before her eyes he took back his human self. Coming to her, still naked, he pulled her into his arms.

"Don't feel bad. You did what you had to do. She started it, you had to finish it or you would have never been truly safe," he whispered against her hair.

"I killed someone, Andreas."

"You killed a wolf. Wolves do that. We also kill deer, you'll do that too. You are no longer human, Kari. You're a werewolf, a shapeshifter. You're my queen and my Mate. As of tonight, you rule at my side. You are my wife. You have responsibilities on so many levels. You did what you had to do. She forced it."

Touched, she nonetheless had to deal with what happened. "What's going to happen to Johanna's body?"

"She's Pack. She died as a wolf, she'll keep that shape. Every Pack member has contingencies in place should any of us die. To deal with our human lives. Johanna's human life will be dealt with as she wished it to be in her paperwork. She'll be buried in the meadow. As Second and the healer of the Clan, Sean will conduct the burial ritual before he comes back to the house."

"Good. I like that."

"Part of this world is death, Kari. It's not an everyday occurrence. But it's there. We're predators, not just people with fur. It sounds savage, but it's our reality. Don't let this mar your Ascension. As hard as it is to understand, please know that you did what you had to. She would have killed you, Kari. You defended yourself and you killed her first."

She took a deep breath. True, she'd had no choice. She'd tried to show mercy many times but Johanna wouldn't accept it. It truly had been a kill or be killed situation. Nodding, she gave Andreas a small smile. "I know. It's just hard."

"Good. It should be. You shouldn't take it lightly and you haven't. You did your job with integrity, Kari."

Nodding, she let him hold her, let the steady rhythm of his heart calm and comfort her.

"Come, my queen. I'm now going to make love to you as a human should. And then I'm going to fuck you."

Stifling a smile, she took the hand he held out and they started walking toward the house.

"Let's get upstairs before they all start coming back. If we aren't behind our locked door, everyone will want to talk to you. I'll have to share you and I want you all to myself. And naked."

They ran up the stairs and into the bedroom, where Anna had set up candles, chilled champagne and chocolate-covered strawberries. "Man, you've really charmed that woman," he said, shaking his head in amusement.

"What can I say? I'm very charming," she said in a haughty tone, then laughed.

He poured her a glass of champagne and she took a bite of strawberry, watching him, eyes alight with lust and mischief. So amazing, his woman. He walked toward her, holding out the glass and staring his fill down the lines of her body. Curvaceous thighs and hips, high, full breasts, softly rounded stomach. He'd watched a lot of modern women with dismay. He liked curves on a woman, but so many women today seemed to be so terribly thin. They looked unhealthy when he compared them to the lushness of the woman standing before him, candlelight flickering against her pale skin. His cock bobbed painfully when she licked her bottom lip, clearing a smudge of chocolate.

Taking the glass from him, she held out the other half of the strawberry in her fingers. He took it from her, licking her fingertips, making her gasp. "To forever," he said, holding his own glass up.

She clinked hers against it. "Forever," she agreed and sipped. "Mmmm. Strawberries, chocolate, champagne and naked man. No combination can beat that." She gave him a wicked grin.

He drained his glass in one long swallow and sat it down. Grabbing her hand, he led her to the bed, *their* bed.

"You're so beautiful, Kari. I can't think of a better way to wake each morning than with you at my side. I've waited so long. I was beginning to think I'd never find my true Mate and yet, a few days after meeting you for the first time and I feel like you've been with me forever. You just feel so *right*."

"You sure know your way around the love words, Andreas Phinney. I bet that got you loads of ass over the years."

Grinning a moment, he wisely refrained from commenting. Instead he took her glass and put it down on the table next to the bed and waggled his brows at her with lascivious intent.

Kari smiled at that, shivering as he ran his tongue around the shell of her ear and down the column of her throat, stopping to nibble on her collarbone.

"When I was in high school I read some romance novel about this couple who fell in love the first day they met. I always thought that was a load of hooey. Love was something that only happened for some people. When you brought me here…I was so scared and so pissed off! But at the same time I felt this intense draw to you. When Skye changed it gave me a lifeline, a reason to believe you and to let myself want to be here.

"This is all totally fantastical! Not just the werewolf thing but the love at first scent-sight thing. But I don't know, when I'm with you I believe it. The fairy tale is real. Love, shapeshifters, all of it." She gasped again as his head bent over her breast, tongue flicking out to lave a nipple. "That's very nice."

"In the first place, you think too much. Just accept it. In the second place, I'm here to serve you, my queen."

Grinning, she playfully punched his arm. "Hmmm. Then you should roll over because if you'll remember, I'm the only one who got to come the last three times. I have a bit of catching up to do." She raised an eyebrow and then traced the trail of blond hair from his navel to his groin. "If I recall correctly, I had plans to explore this particular trail in depth with my tongue. You stopped me last night at just a taste but you know, a queen should not be denied her pleasure."

"As you will it, my darling, so it shall be. I'm all yours." Andreas let her push him to his back and she scrambled atop him. "I do like this view."

Looking over his body, spread before her like a banquet, she laughed. "Me too!" Shimmying down, she bent to him, her hair cascading over his bare skin. She traced through the trail of downy hair with the tip of her tongue, tasting his skin underneath. His taste seduced her once more, spicy and salty. She took a deep breath and woodsmoke and pine and an elemental male musk wove into her senses. Everything he was made her eyes roll back into her head.

Kissing downward, she came to his cock and stopped, looking at him with a smile. She drew her cheek over the length of him and sat back up. Running her palms over him and down to cup his balls, she went back to trace a long lick from crown to sac and back up again. She licked over his skin, soft and smooth, feeling the prominent vein on the underside throb. Unable to resist any longer, her mouth closed over his meaty cock head. Her tongue swirled over him, tasting the salt of his pre-cum. Around and down, over the prominent ridge, learning him bit by bit. He tasted so good and right, she hummed her approval. As the vibrations rolled up the flesh of his cock, he groaned.

He ran his fingers through her hair and down her neck. His legs trembled a bit as she took him as deeply as she could. She began to learn the different sides of this man she loved. This encounter was so sweet and gentle, so lovely. Contrasted with the harder edged dirty-talking Andreas of the evening before, it meant all the more. It meant they'd be learning each other for decades to come, never getting bored. Each time they'd been together had been unique and special in its own way. She was a very lucky girl indeed.

"Kari, you feel so good," he murmured, stroking her neck and ears. She felt his climax approach. His muscles tensed and his breathing became erratic, her name a rhythmic whisper from his lips.

She got to her knees to get better leverage and to take more of him into her mouth. His balls drew tight against his body and he hissed when she drew her nails over the taut flesh there.

"Oh little wolf, stop. I've got to be inside you, and right now."

She took her mouth off him and looked up through her lashes. Gently grabbing her shoulders, he pulled her up to lie across his chest. She put her ear over his heart, listening to the thundering rhythm slow down, his warmth soothing.

His fingertips caressed the skin at her hip, swirled patterns on her ass and up her back. She arched into his touch like a cat, or perhaps like a dog. "You take my breath away, Kari."

"That's the point, Andreas." She grinned against his flesh and felt his chuckle vibrate through him.

"You're right." He picked her up and sat her astride his thighs. "Ride me sweetheart," he urged huskily. "I've been dying to be inside you for so long. And remember, first time is making love and then we get to fucking." He winked.

Reaching around behind herself, she grabbed his cock and rose up enough to guide him to her gate. Letting just the head of him sit there, barely inside her, she enjoyed it before slowly sinking down onto his cock. Electric shocks of pleasure played along her spine. Andreas being a big man with big equipment, Kari took it slow, letting the size of him stretch her slowly. She must have looked a bit overwhelmed because he laughed, a low sexy growling sort of laugh. "You did say you were a size queen." And he thrust his hips up to meet her and the last few inches were inside of her.

She arched with a gasp, nails digging into the muscle of his thighs. "A crown I do deserve now that I'm with you. Not that I want to swell your head any more than it already is or anything, and not that I've slept with some huge stable of men, but I've never had anything approaching this big inside of me. It's overwhelming but very, very nice."

He laughed then, belly shaking and sending little shocks of pleasure through her as he jerked inside of her. "Thank you for that. I do aim to please." He put his hands on her hips and raised her up and she took over from there, slowly riding him as his hands caressed her.

Each time she relaxed her thigh muscles and slid down on him, his cock sliced through her, invading her body with his. She felt this acutely, both physically and emotionally. He resided within her in so many ways.

Candlelight flickered off his olive-toned skin, the way he looked there beneath her clutched at her gut—blond hair glinting like spun gold, lips parted, eyes glazed with desire, filled with only her. She took him in there, so large and dangerous but tamed for that one moment in time, and she continued to be amazed that anything could feel so good. Shivers worked through her as his hands palmed her nipples, pulling back, drawing fingertips over her, pulling and rolling and moving forward to palm them again.

Vaguely in the distance she heard the sound of people coming into the house but it was a million miles away from the feeling of this man buried inside of her.

"Andreas?"

"Hmmm?"

"I love you." She bent down, placing a kiss over his heart.

His arms came up and encircled her back. Moments later he flipped her over onto the mattress, leaning over her then, so big he blocked out the light behind them, the effect like sensory deprivation. All she could see, hear, smell and feel was him.

She wrapped her legs around his waist and he slipped in another inch or so. He picked up the pace then, sliding in and out of her faster and harder but still with incredible care. "I love you too, *belle jeune mariée*. I want to feel your pussy come around my cock. Make that happen for me, little wolf."

After that evening in the bathtub, she was past blushing about it or playing shy. And the look in his eyes brooked no room for that even if she'd wanted to. He wanted all of her. And so she slid her hand down her belly, fingertips finding her already slippery clit. Still, reaching down further to the place they were joined, she gathered her honey even as she caressed him each time he pushed his cock deep into her cunt.

"God, Kari," he gasped as he fucked into her body. "You're so sexy."

Smiling, she moved her fingers back to her clit and stroked over it, pressing down hard until her climax approached. Between her fingers on her clit, the new position that brought his pelvic bone against her mound and the size of him, she rocketed toward orgasm with toe-curling intensity.

"Please, I'm almost there. You too." The muscles in her forearm corded as she worked her clit, the other hand clenched his hair.

He growled in approval and began to thrust so hard the headboard began to pound into the wall. "Yes, yes, little wolf," he murmured, body tightening.

"Mmmm. Oh Andreas." Their mingled climax hit with such force that the electricity, the power that was released between them built into a hot wind. Most of the candles blew out and the lights flickered.

Wave after wave of pleasure buffeted her. Back arched, a hoarse cry came from her. Their gazes locked for a moment as she saw the force of his climax come into his face. Andreas threw his head back and roared out her name as he continued to thrust and come deep within her.

Finally after what seemed like an hour he sighed long and hard and collapsed on her, his weight feeling so good as it anchored her to the bed.

Well, good for a moment or two and then it became hard to breathe, and she was already panting from the orgasm. She squirmed underneath him, "Andreas," she pleaded in a gasp and he moved back at once.

"Sorry, love, are you all right?" He tenderly kissed her lips.

"Now that I can breathe I am." Laughing, she took a few deep breaths.

He lay on his side, facing her, head resting on his hand. The other hand was tracing along her body. Her fingertips drew through his hair and down along the line of his jaw. Those moments were theirs alone.

The noise from downstairs was growing. "That's some party." She glanced toward the door.

"Yes. We should go down soon."

"Really?" she asked, disappointed.

He chuckled. "They got a queen tonight, a new member of the Pack. You bested one of them on your first transformation. They want to be with you."

At the memory of Johanna, she tensed up.

"Little wolf, don't despair. It is the way of things. You did what you had to do to protect yourself and your Pack. It's your job."

She sat up. "I killed someone, Andreas. That is not my job. I started that fight. I should have just walked away."

He sat up, grabbing her chin and turning her to face him. "No. Damn it, Kari. Think like a wolf! She presented herself to me—to your Mate. On the night you Ascended and transformed. Not only was it bad form, it was out of line. You protected what was yours. You blooded her, as was your right and duty. She should have stopped then. She chose to attack you. Even when you had her by the throat and she surrendered you walked away. You let her live and showed mercy. When she faked surrender and then chose to attack when your back was turned, she meant to kill you, Kari. She broke the rules of combat and you defended yourself. You did what you had to do.

"You didn't kill a person. You aren't human and neither was she. She lived according to Pack law. Law she broke several times today alone. You enforced it. That's what a true leader does, Kari. It's easy to lead when things are good but if the Pack doesn't obey the rules, things happen and can get out of control very easily. It's the job of an effective leader to keep the Pack safe. Sometimes that means discipline. You showed them tonight that you're willing to fight for them. For what's theirs, and that you're willing to kill for them too." He kissed her forehead.

"They'll hate me."

He laughed, squeezing her to him. "Listen. Do you hear them?"

She listened and heard laughter and loud talking. All joyous. "Yes."

"And does it sound like they're celebrating you or hating you?"

"Celebrating. Andreas?"

"Yes, little wolf?"

"Don't you think you'll get tired of being so much wiser than me?"

He laughed again and stood up, bringing her out of the bed with him. "Kari, you're wise beyond your years. You didn't grow up in this world, I did. It's only natural that I'd know more than you. But I give you six months until you're smarter than I am about all of this."

She went into their bathroom to clean up a bit and came back out just as he walked into the large closet and brought back a red bundle. "This is for you. To wear when we go downstairs." He handed it to her and it unfurled in her arms.

She held it before her in wonder. It was red silk. A robe with slits on each side to her upper thighs. Black fabric-covered buttons lined the front and embroidered wolves circled the mandarin-style collar. It was breathtaking.

Gasping, she held it to herself and squealed, jumping up and down with girly delight. Much to his amusement.

"I like that. Do it again. Your breasts are even more attractive when you jump around," he said, grinning.

"You sure it's not too much for your heart, old guy?" She smirked at him and slipped the robe on over her head, fastening the buttons that ran from her waist to the throat. The sleeves were long and bore the same embroidered wolves along the edging, flaring at the wrist.

He stood back and smiled. "Beautiful for such a smartass. Drew created it. He's a clothing designer. I have one as well. It's blue. Or, Drew said, it's royal blue. Fitting, no?" Turning, he pulled his robe out. It didn't have the thigh slits and the sleeves were shorter but the blue was perfect for him.

"You look like a pasha. Very handsome."

Smiling, he brought her to him, kissing her passionately.

"If you keep this up, I'm not going anywhere other than back to bed. And I want to. I want to keep you in here all night long, making you come over and over. Damn this whole being king business." Smiling ruefully, he straightened up, letting her go.

"You can make me come over and over after the party. Nice erection," she teased and walked toward the door.

"All for you, my queen," he said huskily as he joined her.

Out in the hall, Laurent enjoyed a glass of wine as he stared down at the crowd below. He turned to her and bowed. "My queen. You look beautiful."

She rolled her eyes at him. All of the "my queen" stuff was getting old. "Thanks, Laurent. You don't look so bad yourself. Naked becomes you." Winking, she swept past him.

"As it does you," he returned and then grunted when Andreas slugged him on the arm.

Kari went downstairs to greet everyone. Approaching Drew, she kissed his cheek. Gesturing to the robe, she grinned. "This is the most beautiful thing I've ever owned. Thank you so much for creating it."

"When Andreas told me about you and then showed me a picture, I just saw you as an empress. The silk had been sitting in my workshop for two years, just waiting for the right person. One of the women who does embroidery work for me took one look and suggested the embroidered wolves to line the collar and the wrists, the major blood points."

"Wow. I'm even more touched that so much thought and care went into this. Does she know? Is she a wolf too?"

"No. Just a very wise woman."

"Where on earth did you get my picture anyway?"

"Uh." Worry crossed his face, making Kari suspicious. "I don't know. You were sitting near a fountain in an outdoor café of sorts. Your hair was free, you had on lavender. A pretty skirt and blouse."

She patted Drew's arm reassuringly. *Andreas.* Turning and scanning the area, she found him lounging on the couch, like the pasha he so resembled. Of course, she wasn't surprised to see him surrounded by other males from the Inner Circle. "Please excuse me, Drew. And thank you so much again."

He smiled, touching his hand over his heart. "'I'm honored that you find it to your liking. Come by my shop anytime. I'd love to make you other items."

"I'd like that too." Her sincere smile for Drew turned into a glare as she turned to face Andreas and make her way over to him. Oh he was in big trouble.

"Uh oh," Sean said as he caught sight of Kari making her way over to them. Of course, she had to stop every few steps to greet someone else.

Andreas looked up and saw her face as she glared at him but the glare transformed into a beautiful smile as she turned to face one of the Pack, who rubbed his cheek along her thighs while his partner kissed her hands.

"You're obviously in trouble." Laurent grinned.

"I haven't done anything," he said defensively and then glared at Sean. "You take an awful lot of joy from this, Sean. You're next you know." Andreas was glad he had so many people around him, his little Mate looked spitting mad. Whatever it was, he was sure he'd hear an earful.

"She's quite delicious, Andreas. Does she have a sister?" Carey asked, watching Kari weave her way toward them, her legs showing with each stride. Despite the fact that many of them were naked or nearly so, the effect of the brief flashes of Kari's bare skin was quite sexy.

"She has a brother. He's human. Stop ogling my wife." Andreas growled. A look around the room showed that many males watched his Mate. Even the mated ones watched. Hell, even the women watched her. She exuded a thick kind of sensuality. She also had an inherent maternalism. Add that to the musk of the sex they'd had earlier and the fact that she was their queen and she made the perfect wolf girl. Aside from annoyance and a mild jealousy, that she was so desired turned him on. She was his and others wanted her.

There were times when a female who was mated might have a sexual interaction with a male not her Mate. At the Gathering tonight he'd seen Perri with Sean and Luna with Laurent. He'd slept with Perri himself a few times in wolf form and once in human form before she'd married Devon. He had the feeling that Kari didn't know that though, and there wasn't any way he'd be telling her any time soon.

He knew for sure that he was glad that for the most part, the wolf king and queen, once mated, didn't step outside their relationship. He wasn't sure he could imagine seeing her with another male and he felt so deeply about her he felt no desire for anyone else.

Finally Kari made it across the room to where Andreas held court. What should have taken thirty seconds had taken half an hour after she'd had to greet everyone and accept congratulations, including a special thank you from Jade for the way she'd dealt with Johanna.

She kept walking and the huge men lolling around at Andreas' feet simply rolled out of her way. Coming to a stop when she reached him, she put her hands on her hips.

"Skye, stop looking up my robe," she snapped and he laughed, reaching out to caress her leg. Rolling her eyes at him, she turned to look down at Andreas.

"Is something wrong, little wolf?"

"You want to tell me how a picture of me taken without my knowledge ended up in Drew's possession?"

Oh, that. Oops. "Oh, that. Well, you remember that I told you that I saw you at the convention center and then I tried to find out all that I could about you. Phillip and Michael watched you to keep you safe. Sometimes they took photos of you. You knew I found out about your childhood."

"Pictures of me? Through some sort of telephoto lens? Like a stalker? How many pictures do you have and what sort pictures are they?"

Busted. He didn't dare look at Phillip, who'd taken several pictures of her in her apartment, two of them with her in states of undress. It had been more to see what sort of body she had, to assess her breeding ability, and she *so* wouldn't understand that. It *was* sort of bad when he thought about it.

"Why do you look like you swallowed a bug?" she accused.

Skye wheezed with laugher. Sean joined him. Oh the two of them had trouble coming to them when they found the right woman. He couldn't wait.

"*Cherie…*"

"Don't you start with all your French love words. Tell me now. Are there naked pictures? Do you have any of me changing at the gym or out on dates?"

"Dates? You went out on dates and did things you didn't want photographed?" he asked, sputtering.

"Don't you change the subject! Answer my questions." She looked at him imperiously. It would have been more effective had he not met her eye to eye, even though she was standing and he was sitting.

"You do, don't you? You pervert! I want them, every last one, to be destroyed. Oh!" She looked down at all the men around Andreas. "Have you all seen them too?"

That sobered Sean and Skye quickly and Phillip just looked at the ground, trying very hard to be still and hope she didn't notice him.

"WELL?" she demanded.

Andreas started to say something but she held up her hand to tell him to be quiet. "These members of my Pack were going to answer a question their queen just asked them," she said very softly.

Now Andreas knew enough about women to understand that they were far more dangerous when they got quiet than when they were loud. In fact, *damn,* his mother snapped to attention at Kari's tone and hurried over, concern on her face. Well, maybe she'd step in and save him from his tiny Mate.

"Andreas! What have you done to upset Kari?" she demanded. So much for thinking his mother was going to save him.

"He's got naked pictures he took when he was spying on me. And it appears that all of this lot has seen them." She gestured to everyone seated around Andreas.

Jade looked at Andreas. "Is this true? Son, you invaded Kari's privacy when she was naked and showed the pictures to your buddies? It's like tenth grade all over again."

Everyone nearby groaned at that, along with Andreas, and Kari started to grin. "So wait, this pervert thing has a long history?"

"Oh let me tell you. Come on, let's get the girls and go grab a bottle or two of wine and meet over in my cabin. I'll tell you all about it," Jade said, laughing.

Kari started to follow her out and turned back to Andreas. "I'm waiting. Go get those pictures and give them to me so I can destroy them."

He stood up and approached her, eyes down. He tried to hug her but she stepped away from him. He whispered to her, "I just used them because I couldn't have you."

She leaned in and whispered back, "And you won't be having any more of me if you don't give me those pictures."

Andreas sighed. "Phillip, please bring me the folder so we can put my beautiful queen's mind at ease."

She spun to face Phillip. "You too?"

"I'm sorry," he said and sprinted into Andreas' office. Moments later, he came back out and handed Kari a folder.

Her face colored when she opened it and saw the pictures. There were a few of her walking around in underwear and no bra as she was getting dressed in the morning, and one of her in a towel. "You perverts! What, were you in a tree across from my apartment complex or something? Did you all have a good time? Did I pass muster?" She wasn't really mad anymore but she planned to make Andreas pay just the same.

"You're a beautiful woman, Kari. We'd all be very lucky indeed were we to find mates as luscious as you." Sean tried not to smile.

"Hmmph. That Eddie Haskel routine won't work on me, Sean." She tossed the pictures into the fire and handed the folder back to Andreas. "This is going to cost you, you know. I love clothes but I didn't really make enough to buy what I liked until just recently. Now that I have to leave my job, I think a new wardrobe might make me more inclined to forgive you and let you back into my bed." Grinning wickedly, she spun, walking out of the room, making sure to put extra sway in her hips. She wanted Andreas to get a view of her ass and her loose breasts jiggling. She got to the door and looked back over her shoulder. *Yeah, he'd seen.*

Andreas threw back his head and laughed. "I'll toss a nice two- or three-carat wedding ring in there too, little wolf."

"Okay," she said, flouncing off, Phillip in her wake.

Andreas turned around and growled at the laughing men he faced.

* * * * *

It was after three a.m. when Andreas and Kari were finally able to climb the stairs to their room. Even at that late hour there were still people talking and snuggling all over the place, drinking and playing cards. Sean and Ryan smoked nasty-smelling cigars out on the deck.

"I'm going to have to go to Seattle and clean out my apartment and give notice at my job. We need to work out how this company you've acquired for me will be run and where. I also have to deal with Jack. I certainly can't tell him I'm a werewolf." She snorted. "But I do need to tell him I've moved and quit my job. I have no idea what to tell him about you. He's going to think I'm crazy for moving in with some guy I met a few days ago."

"I'm not some guy, I'm your Mate."

"According to Pack law, yes. But according to human law—the law I've lived under my whole life, the law that Jack lives under—you're some guy I've shacked up with."

"It's more than that. You insult the bonding," he said, angry.

She sighed. "I'm sorry, I didn't mean to. It came out wrong. I respect that and I do consider you to be my husband according to Pack law. But part of my life is in the human world, with Jack. I don't know, I guess I'd feel better if there could be some human marriage ceremony too."

He sat on the bed. "Okay, I understand. I'd hoped that you would consider Pack law to be enough. You're the Alpha. You're their queen. But I want to make you happy. We can have a human ceremony if you wish."

Oh god, she'd hurt his feelings. His pride. She sank to her knees and crawled toward him, touching her face to his feet, rubbing her cheek along the lines of his calves, being a submissive wolf. Letting him know how much she accepted him and the laws he upheld as Alpha. They could deal with the realities of legal situations in the human world tomorrow. For now she just wanted to love him, show him she respected his world.

Reaching down, he stroked her hair, growling softly. She felt the vibrations through his bones, through his skin. His utter maleness, the musk of man and wolf, swirled around her.

She looked up at him. "My life for yours," she said softly and saw the shimmer of emotion in his eyes, joy had replaced the pain.

He pulled her up to him, rubbing his cheek along her face, over her neck. His hands stroked over her skin softly. He murmured, "I love you, little wolf. Thank you for your apology and your fealty."

Stretching up, she wrapped her arms around him tightly until a hand in her hair pulled her back enough so he could bring his lips to hers. There was nothing gentle or hesitant in his kiss. But his arms, his arms so strong and large, cradled her as if she were the most precious thing he'd ever seen.

He moaned as she pulled his bottom lip into her mouth and laved it with her tongue. His tongue, hot and wet, swept in between her lips, tickling the roof of her mouth, caressing the flesh between her cheek and gums. Pulling her tongue into his mouth with gentle suction, he stroked over it with his own. He mocked the in-and-out motions of sex and she whimpered with need, rocking her hips against him. Her hands, which had been on his chest, began to push his robe back until she was able to stroke the hard, bare skin beneath it.

He broke the kiss and stood, tugging the robe up and over his head quickly. Tossing it aside, he pulled her up to stand while he took hers off. Leaning in, she flicked the tip of her tongue across first one nipple then the other. He shuddered and gooseflesh broke out.

"You make me want to dominate you. Tell you what to do. Make you do it." His voice was low and taut with need.

"Sounds gooood…oh yes…to me," she gasped as he lowered his mouth to her breast and softly bit the nipple. Andreas understood the fine line between pleasure and pain. He bit just to the point of pain and shivers ran down her body, straight to her weeping pussy.

Kari's hands went to his cock but Andreas shook his head and dragged her over to the small loveseat in the alcove near the windows. Sitting her down, he moved her hands back above her head, moving her fingers to grasp the back of the couch. "Leave them there, Kari. I love the way you look when you're posed like this. Your tits offered up. Your back arched.

"I want you to stay still. Can you do that? If you can be good and listen to me, I'll reward you." His voice was serious and laced with authority that did wicked things to her body. She nodded mutely.

"Good," he said, drawing her thighs apart, leaning in to rub his cheek over her mound. "Your panties are soaking, Kari. Why is that, do you think? Hmm? Is it that you want me?"

She was dying to arch into his face to show him just how much. "Yes," she gasped as he stroked a finger over her desire-slicked labia.

He stood up and she whimpered. Staring up at his naked body, so fucking beautiful there in the low light, Kari licked her lips, aching to have him in her—mouth or pussy, she wasn't choosy.

"Suck me off, Kari. Lean forward, but leave your hands where they are." He knelt on the couch, thighs astride hers, and placed his hands on her head. As she leaned forward he cradled her head, helping her to keep her position. He groaned as she took him into her mouth. "Make me nice and wet, Kari." Honey flowed, coating her pussy, hot and sticky. While he'd been dominant a bit before, this was a new level. It appealed to a dark part of her soul. Thrilled and excited her, and she wanted more.

She obliged, coating him while sucking him lightly. Her saliva made him nice and slick and he slid between her lips easily. His hands fisted in her hair. "Oh yeah, Kari, that's it. Harder now."

His pace sped up. Kari wasn't so much moving her mouth on him as he was moving himself in her mouth, controlling the pace with his hips. Fucking her mouth, she realized, and the sheer carnality of it thrilled through her system.

She swirled her tongue over the head each time he dragged out of her mouth and flicked her tongue on his sweet spot underneath the head each time he pushed in. "Kari, yes. Oh man. Your mouth is so hot, so slick. I'm going to come. Yeah, oh god, yessss." He hissed as his cock began to pulse as he came, filling her with his seed, nearly overwhelming her.

He continued to stroke into her mouth until he'd gone soft. Caressing her face, he kissed her forehead. "That was very good, Kari. Did you like that?" he asked huskily, moving off her and coming to kneel between her thighs.

She looked up at him, using all of her self-control not to whimper and beg him to fuck her. *Was that a rhetorical question?* "Yes."

Slowly running his cheek up the inside of her legs to her thighs, he stopped and parted her, looking intently. "I can't get enough of how fucking pretty your pussy is. Like a flower. I love your pussy. I love the way it feels around my cock. I love the way it tastes. I love to watch it clutching me when I'm inside you."

"Ooh." Kari's response was involuntary. His words were driving her over the edge.

He leaned back and looked up at her. "What is it, Kari?"

"Please, taste me."

"Here?" He licked the inside of her thigh.

She shook her head.

"Here?" He laved her navel.

Kari whimpered then in frustration and anticipation but all she got in return was one of his wicked smiles.

"Where, Kari?"

"Lick me, oh god please. My clit!"

He hummed as he lowered his lips to her pussy and she nearly broke into tears of relief. He licked in one long line from her core to her swollen, needy clit. "It's hard for me." He drew it into his mouth, grating his teeth over it lightly, making her gasp and thrust her pussy into his face.

He leaned back. "I love it when your pussy is wet and swollen for me, Kari. So wanton. All for me."

"Yes!" she snapped, frustrated that he'd stopped. She arched up and he moved his head back.

"Ah, ah, ah! Should I make you come?"

"Yes. Oh god yes, please, please, please."

He gave her that damned patented sex god smile and lowered his face her. She was so close already that once he eased two fingers inside of her and flicked the tip of his tongue over her, once, twice, three times, she went off like a bomb.

Fingers clawing at the back of the couch, she screamed and clamped Andreas' face into her pussy with her thighs. Her back bowed at the intensity of her orgasm but he didn't stop, he gripped her hips with his hands and kept her pussy in his face. Kept at the hard pace, flicking his tongue over her clit with a featherlight touch. It was too intense. She'd moved her hands and had him by the hair, trying to pull him away when another climax hit. Sweat poured off her body, she shook violently, screaming and moaning, trying to pull back, to escape the intensity of his mouth.

"Please god, stop. It's too much," she gasped out. With a chuckle he stopped, pressed a kiss to her belly and stood up, looking down at her with greedy, glittering eyes.

Quickly, he flipped her over and faced her toward the back of the couch, arranging her so her ass was up in the air. Rapidly, his palm met that tender flesh and the shock of it morphed into a slow building fire on her ass and thighs as he gave her several more slaps.

"You moved." The velvet dangerousness of his tone strummed along her spine. She trembled with anticipation over what he'd do next.

Luckily, she didn't have long to wait before he nudged her thighs wider and knelt between them. The wide head of his cock pressed against her gate. Taking a deep breath, she began to roll her back into him. He put his hands on her hips, stilling her. "No moving, Kari. I'll tell you if I want you to move," he ordered and she stilled. "Good." He petted the skin on her back softly. "I'm going to fuck you now. Is that what you want?"

"Yes," she whispered, her body thrilling at the whip crack of his words.

He nudged his cock back, just barely against the cheeks of her ass. Kari stilled mentally. She'd never had anal sex before. She wasn't sure she wanted to either. Once, in college, a boyfriend had put a finger inside of her while he was going down on her. The idea was interesting but there was a lot of cultural baggage that came along with one's ass and Kari didn't know if she wanted to jettison it or not.

"Kari." Andreas spoke and she heard the tremor in his voice. "Have you ever had a cock in that tight little ass?"

She gulped. "No."

He moved his cock down, back to her pussy. "We'll have to change that. Not right now though, it's something we'll have to work up to." Without missing a beat, he plunged inside of her so hard and deep he nudged against her cervix. She shuddered.

He rammed into her hard and fast, his balls slapping against her mons on each thrust. Kari gripped him with her vaginal muscles and felt him start to tremble. "Your pussy is so fucking tight. Squeeze me."

He moved a hand that had been pinching a nipple down to her clit but she choked out, "No. Too much. Just fuck me."

"Come for me now, Kari. I want to feel your pussy grasp and pulse around my cock," he gritted out.

She didn't know if her body could take it but she wanted to try. Wanted to please him even as she pleased herself. "Can I move?"

"Yes. Do it, Kari."

She dropped a hand to her pussy and softly stroked herself, circling around her clit instead of touching it directly, stretching the hood, stroking skin on skin.

"Pet yourself. That's the way." Reaching around her body, his fingers met hers. She though he was going to help but after he drew his fingers through her very wet folds a few times he moved his hand away. Suddenly he was back, slowly stroking down the crack of her ass and then over the bud of her anus. She gasped, freezing up.

"Trust me," he murmured, lips against her spine for a brief moment before he moved his body back, continuing his relentless pistoning in and out of her pussy. She realized then he had more access to her ass.

Kari willed herself to relax, to concentrate on her hand as it circled her clit, dragging herself higher and higher. Andreas' middle finger stroked her, wet with her juices, and slowly he worked it in.

"Easy, little wolf. Relax."

At that point, hearing the desire-taut character of his voice, Kari realized that he was more turned on than she was at the intrusion. Continuing to slide his finger in, past the first knuckle, he pressed into her inexorably until he'd penetrated her to the webbing of his hand. He slowly started to stroke in and out of her and she realized that he was also touching himself through the thin wall that separated pussy from anus.

Oh god, knowing that, coupled with all the sensations that bombarded her—new and unused nerve endings being stroked but his fingers, her hand on her clit, his cock moving deep into her cunt—brought her orgasm rocketing through her with electric intensity.

Her pussy gripped the girth of his cock, showering him with cream. He moaned and with a last deep thrust he came. Kari felt his cock pulse over and over until he exhaled with a long shuddering breath and pulled out.

Picking her sweaty, boneless body up quickly and easily, he walked them over to the bed and put her under the sheets and joined her, as always, bringing her into the shelter of his body.

"That was the single most incredible sexual interlude I've ever had," he said into her ear.

"Yeah," she manged to stutter before falling into a deep, sated sleep, her head against his rising and falling chest.

Chapter Seven

Kari woke to an empty bed and enjoyed the moment of solitude. Wincing, she stretched her sore muscles before rolling herself in the sheet on Andreas' side of the bed, wrapping herself in his scent. The night before had been pretty spectacular as nights went. As sex went it was spec-fucking-tacular.

With a smile, she poured herself a glass of water from the bedside pitcher and drank it down in two gulps. Teach her to drink so much in one night. She was lucky she didn't have a headache. She did have a nasty taste in her mouth, though.

She heard noise downstairs. Laughing and talking and the smell of coffee rose, strong enough to motivate her to get out of bed. She padded into the bathroom and took a long hot shower.

She towel dried her hair and got dressed, leaving her hair free behind a headband. She had a moment of dizziness as she pulled a sweater on over her head and realized she was starving.

Outside the door Phillip and Ryan sat at the table in the loft area playing cards and drinking coffee. Phillip smiled sheepishly when he saw her. Still feeling bad about the pictures, she guessed.

"Morning, boys," she said, reaching out to touch them both as she walked past. Andreas saw her and yelled up to Phillip to keep playing his game, that he'd take it from there.

As she descended the stairs, Kari took a long greedy look at her man. Wearing a pair of low-slung jeans and a T-shirt, he looked quite edible. He smiled, drawing her to him when she reached the bottom of the stairs.

"Good morning, little wolf." He kissed her lightly.

"Mmm. You taste like coffee with cream and cinnamon. I want more. Lots more."

"Oh you'll get more, Kari. After breakfast we're going right back to bed. Let's get you fed. You'll need your strength." His voice was low, eyes glimmering with sensual promise. "Anna made *you* cinnamon buns but let me have one. Let's go into the dining room, see if she'll let me have another."

Seated at the table and watching the byplay between Andreas and Sean over the cinnamon rolls, Kari rolled her eyes but shortly afterward broke out in a cold sweat.

"Are you all right?" Laurent asked her, coming over to crouch next to her chair.

"Elaine! Come in here, please," Andreas bellowed.

"I'm all right. I just felt a bit nauseated for a moment. I've been through a bit in the last week you know. It's probably just the flu."

Andreas shooed everyone away from her when Elaine came into the room.

"Kari isn't feeling well. She went all pale," Laurent told Elaine.

"Just a dizzy spell. A bit of nausea. I'm all right," Kari insisted.

"Just the same, let me look at you." Elaine put her medical bag on the table and popped a thermometer in Kari's mouth, causing her to gag. "Okay. Well, let me check your pulse and look into your throat and ears."

After she'd given Kari a cursory look-over she put her things back into her bag. "You look okay. You're a bit warm but we run warm anyway. Why don't you go and lie down for a bit?"

Before Kari could protest, Andreas swooped in, picked her up and carried her toward their room.

"Bring her some tea and toast please, Anna," he said as he started up the stairs, leaving Anna scurrying into the kitchen to make her a tray.

"I'm fine! Put me down!" Kari protested as Andreas walked into their room. Phillip followed behind them, looking worried. "Are you going to be like this every time I sneeze, Andreas Phinney?"

He laid her gently on the bed, propping pillows up behind her. "I'll be however I need to be to protect you," he said shortly.

Anna came in with the tray and sat it down on the bed. "Here, eat it slow. You'll be right as rain in no time."

"Thank you, Anna," Kari said, patting her hand.

Andreas started to pick up the toast and feed it to her. She grabbed his wrist. "That is not necessary. I can feed myself you know." And then had to bolt into the bathroom to throw up.

She could hear Andreas yelling for Elaine again and then he pounded on the door to be let in.

She sat on the bathroom floor, trying to catch her breath. "Leave me alone for a moment!" she yelled back, thanking her ability to shut and lock the door as she'd entered the room. A girl needed a bit of privacy now and then. Jeez.

"Kari, you will open this door right now or I'll break it down. You know I can."

She crawled over to the door and unlocked it and he nearly fell in over her body as he rushed inside. He fell to his knees beside her. "Baby, are you all right?"

"*YES*. I told you, it's probably just the flu."

"We don't get the flu, Kari. You're beginning to spike a fever," Elaine said, checking Kari's lymph nodes again. "Open."

Kari opened her mouth and Elaine made a distressed sound. "This is more irritation in the mucus membranes than I like to see after vomiting. Damn it. Your eyes are clear. You haven't eaten anything that others haven't, have you?" Elaine asked, looking worried.

"I had chicken salad yesterday that Anna made just for me but I don't think that's it."

Cramps wracked her body and she doubled over in pain. "Kari?" Elaine said, but it sounded to Kari like she was underwater. A thick sweat broke out all over her body and she started shivering. Elaine spoke but Kari couldn't understand her.

"I… Oh shit," she mumbled and everything went black.

Andreas looked down at the shivering, doubled-over body of his Mate, trying not to panic. She smelled wrong. "Elaine, what's that smell?"

"Poison. Jesus, she's been poisoned." She started pressing Kari's stomach to see what her kidneys felt like, if her internal organs were swollen or hard.

Kari looked up at them, mumbled and passed out.

Elaine stood up and took charge. "Andreas, get her to one of the cars. We've got to get her to a hospital right now."

Andreas picked her up and they all ran down the stairs. Phillip had started the SUV and waited for them. Sean didn't know what was going on but jumped into the backseat, helping Andreas hold Kari. Phillip got behind the wheel and Elaine got in next to him, Ryan shoved into the front seat with them.

"We're taking her to the hospital in Wenatchee. I'll call later," she called out to the puzzled group as they tore out of the drive and onto the two lane highway.

"She's going to be all right," Sean said to Andreas, who looked more scared than Sean cared to admit. Elaine was on the phone, speaking to the hospital to get them ready for Kari.

Ryan called the lodge and explained to Anna what had happened. Anna was to set aside any of the leftover chicken salad, just in case. He admonished her not to say anything about poison to anyone other than Tomas, Skye, Laurent or Devon.

"Laurent and Devon are on their way. Your dad had to take your mom back to their cabin, she's very upset," Ryan said over his shoulder to Andreas, who nodded blankly before going back to rocking Kari's unconscious form, stroking her hair and speaking softly to her.

Sean stroked gentle hands over Kari's legs, up under her pants. She was soaking wet and clammy. Her eyes fluttered beneath closed lids.

"What's taking so long?" Andreas' voice was laced with fear.

"I'm driving as fast as I can, Andreas. This road is narrow. If we got into an accident it would kill her," Phillip answered calmly.

Ryan turned in his seat and put his hands over Andreas' as he stroked Kari's hair and face, lending his strength to his Alphas.

Twenty minutes later—a land speed record—they pulled into the emergency lane of the hospital. Andreas jumped out, directed by Elaine, who had him place Kari on a waiting gurney. Ryan went to move the car and Sean, who practiced out of that hospital, helped Elaine get Kari through the ER quickly.

"We need to pump her stomach right now," Elaine said to the attending physician as he approached them. "We think she's been poisoned. She's vomited. She's got a high temperature. She passed out less than half an hour ago and has been in and out of consciousness."

She continued to fill the other doctor in as they ran down toward a set of double doors at the end of the hallway. There a nurse approached Andreas. "You'll have to wait here."

"Like hell I will. That's my wife!" His hands shook as his voice cracked with anguish and rage. The nurse took a step back, pale at the sight of such a large man so close to losing control. The emotion radiated from his body in waves.

Elaine had never heard him in such a state before. She turned to him. "Get yourself together, Andreas. You can't come in. We need you to stay out there. Someone will be out to you when we know anything."

Grabbing his arm, Sean pulled him back. "If you don't calm down, they're going to kick you out of here. You terrified that nurse. Andreas!" He put his face close to his brother's. "Focus, damn you! Get it together. Come back to the waiting room."

Andreas blinked, seeing his brother, anguish twisting his features. "I can't leave her."

"You aren't leaving her. You're right here. Elaine will stay with her the whole time. Now please."

Numb, Andreas allowed Sean to lead him into the waiting room to sit down. A moment later Ryan, Laurent and Devon came in and sat down around Andreas. Phillip stood there, looking down the hallway, before striding over to Andreas. Dropping to his knees, he exposed his throat. "I failed her. Kill me, Andreas."

Snapping out of his numbness, Andreas looked at Phillip. Then at Ryan and Devon, at Sean and Laurent. Men whom he'd grown up with. Men he loved. His stomach clenched and he reached out to draw Phillip close.

"No, Phillip, *I* failed her. Someone poisoned her. A member of our Pack. If you can't trust your Pack, who can you trust? You did your best by her. You'll continue to do so when she recovers. For now, get up. This is a public place."

"I don't deserve your trust." Phillip's eyes remained downcast.

"Did you poison her?"

"No! Of course not! I'd die for her. I love Kari like a sister."

"So why don't you deserve my trust? Enough, Phillip. Enough guilt. I don't blame you and you know she won't either."

"I need someone to call Skye. Have him ask Anna who was in the kitchen yesterday when she was making those sandwiches for Kari. I know it wasn't the bread, I ate some of that. Everything else she ate, at least that I know of, others ate too."

Glad to have a task, Phillip got up, taking his phone outside to make the call.

"Oh, and Phillip?" Andreas called to him.

"Yes?"

"No one leaves yet," Andreas said and put his head back in his hands.

* * * * *

Back at the lodge, Skye listened intently as Phillip relayed Andreas' orders. "Okay, I'll do it. I'll call you back."

He hung the phone up and went to go speak to Anna, who was beside herself thinking that it was her fault that Kari was ill.

He did his best to reassure her and get her to focus on who may have been in the kitchen around the time she'd made the chicken salad for Kari. Right then it was the only thing they had to go on.

"Well, you know how it is at a Gathering. Everyone under my feet. You were in here, grabbing milk and stealing apples. Drew brought me a flat of peaches. Alex came in and got something out of the pantry. Johanna was here to grab a cup of coffee. Andreas came in with Tomas and tried to get me to make him a sandwich with the chicken salad. I relented later and made him a turkey sandwich with the bread I made that morning. Thank god he didn't eat the chicken salad too. Ryan came in and got a beer and Ellen came by for a bowl of ice cream. I think that's it. At least within an hour or so before, during and after."

Alex and Johanna. The two pack members he trusted the least. Johanna certainly hated Kari. But Kari, the sweet but surprisingly vicious little wolf she was, had taken care of that threat. Alex had sniffed around Kari a bit long for Skye's tastes but had been properly submissive at all times. He trusted Drew with his life. There was no way Tomas would hurt his daughter-in-law and he didn't believe Ryan or Ellen capable of hurting a woman they had both seemed to really take to. He knew that *he* hadn't done it. Hell, if Andreas hadn't been around, he'd have jumped on a woman like Kari.

Kari would unite the Pack as never before in his opinion. He knew Andreas adored his Mate. He knew Anna's loyalty to Cherchez ran so deep she'd die herself before allowing any of them to be hurt. So back to Johanna, who was dead. And Alex.

After a quiet word to Gregory about the issue of the missing poison from a few days prior and an order to check on what they had on hand and it anything else had gone missing on the property, Skye went out to speak to the rest of the Pack who'd gathered in the great room. They'd kept the number of people who knew Kari'd been poisoned as small as possible. Laurent wanted to see what people's reactions were as they all found out.

"I don't know anything new. Kari's being examined now," he said. "I'd like to talk to you all to see if you saw or heard anything that might help us figure out what's wrong with her. She's still unconscious and hasn't been able to say anything."

* * * * *

Back at the hospital, Elaine held Kari's hand while they pumped her stomach. Her blood—which was handled personally by Sean, as werewolf blood was so different from human—showed positive for a common poison often used illegally on animals. Whoever had poisoned Kari did it knowing that she wasn't human.

The doctor administered a medication meant to counteract the poison. All they could do now was wait. Kari's newly transformed system could fight off illness and damage ten times better than any human could and that gave them hope. If she'd been human and given the poison it would have killed her within hours.

But the more Elaine and Sean talked about it, the more they doubted it was the chicken salad. With their metabolisms, it seemed unlikely that the poison would have taken so long to affect Kari, and then so severely. Kari transformed the night before and had been in a fight with Johanna. If she'd been poisoned before that, why hadn't it affected her then?

They moved Kari to intensive care and Sean went out to talk to Andreas and the others to fill them in.

Andreas looked up at his brother expectantly.

"She's stable now. Her temperature is still high but it's not necessarily a bad thing. It's the body's way of fighting off illness. She tested positive for poison, Andreas. They had to pump her stomach and give her a medication that will help counteract the effects of the poison to her system."

"Will she be okay?" Andreas' jaw hardened.

"It's hard to say. We don't know when or where the poison came from. But Elaine is with her and she thinks that the chances are good. Kari is strong, Andreas. Very strong."

Andreas looked over at Devon. "Call the house. Get them to bring that chicken salad here so it can be tested. Also, have Gregory check the shed for the poison used on Kari."

"Wait a sec, Devon," Sean interrupted. "We're not so convinced it's the chicken salad. The time between Kari eating the sandwiches and her getting sick is really long. She transformed and fought off a challenger without a whole lot of effort last night. When you two came back to the lodge, did you eat or drink anything?"

"We had champagne. Both of us did. Two bottles. They should still be either in our room or the recycle bin in the pantry. There were chocolate-covered strawberries. I only ate half of one but Kari, the little piglet, ate a whole tray." He paused. "Do you think it could have been the strawberries?"

"I don't know. Anything else?"

"No, I don't think so. We drank the champagne and ate the berries at around midnight. We came downstairs and didn't eat or drink anything that others weren't drinking or eating. I know before she came to bed, the women all went out to *Maman's* cabin to drink wine and gossip but I think they all drank the same stuff." Andreas turned to Phillip. "You were there. Did they eat anything? Did Kari eat or drink anything that anyone else didn't have?"

"They drank a few bottles of wine. Jade had a bowl of peaches and everyone ate a few, me included. I think they might have eaten popcorn or chips, but they all did. I didn't see Kari take anything that others weren't also eating or drinking."

"Devon, have Anna send the chicken salad anyway. Have Skye ask her about the berries."

Devon went out to make the call.

"Can I see her?"

"Yes, for just a few minutes. She's still in intensive care." Sean led him down the hallway to the double doors of the unit so they could get to the elevators to ICU. They rode the elevator in silence.

As they entered the ICU, Elaine stepped out. "Stay with her. I'm going to call a friend and see what he can tell me about this poison. I want some idea of time so we can narrow it down. We have a murderer in our Pack," Elaine said in his ear.

The truth of it sliced through him as he walked into the room and looked down at Kari's small, frail form. She was so pale, eyes sunken, lips nearly blue. He sat and took her hands in his own, stroking her soft skin.

"Little wolf, I'm here. You need to wake up now. The time to be sick has passed. We have so much to do—a new wardrobe and a ring to buy. A wedding to plan. I need you. I love you," he said, trying to stay strong for her sake.

Running his hands along her legs and arms, he smoothed his face over hers, through her hair, kissed her lips a thousand times. Listening to the steady beeping of the heart monitor, he sat and spoke to her of their future.

* * * * *

For the second time in a week Kari awoke to the sound of a hospital heart monitor. It was bright, but even as her eyes adjusted she could smell that Andreas was nearby. Immediately she calmed, his very presence a balm to her.

She took a deep breath and swallowed hard, trying to speak.

"Kari?" Andreas moved toward her, hope lighting his eyes.

"Water," she whispered.

"Nurse? Elaine?" Andreas walked to the door and called out. A woman entered the room. "My wife's awake and asking for water." Andreas' voice was gravelly from emotion and strain.

The nurse leaned over Kari, checking her eyes with that damned penlight she'd come to hate. "How're you feeling, Kari? I bet your throat is pretty raw about now."

Kari nodded.

"It's from the tube they had to insert when they pumped your stomach. It'll feel better soon. Instead of water you can have chipped ice to keep the dryness down and soothe your throat. The doctor's on his way. I'll go and get that ice for you." The nurse patted Andreas' hand gently and smiled at Kari before leaving.

"God, you're awake. I've been so worried about you."

"Stomach pumped? Why?" she gasped out.

"You were poisoned, Kari. We don't know how or who yet."

Tears sprang to her eyes at the thought that one of the Pack would want to hurt her.

Shaking his head, he kissed her tears away. "We'll find them. Meanwhile, we have to deal with the police. Thank goodness Carey is a local cop. They've put him in charge of the investigation," he said quietly. The Pack would mete out justice on their own. Bringing humans into the mix meant that they took a chance on discovery.

"Good, you're awake!" Elaine walked into the room with another doctor, who introduced himself and checked on Kari before handing Kari's care over to Elaine and getting back to the ER.

Two orderlies came and moved Kari's bed into a private room on another floor. Andreas refused to leave Kari's side so Elaine went down to let everyone else know what was going on.

Within minutes Andreas was pacing the room and growling at all of the people who kept coming by to check her vitals or drop things off. When Sean came in, Andreas nearly lunged at him. Sean met that aggression with a raise of one brown-black eyebrow and walked over to Kari's bed.

"Hey, peaches. How are you? No, don't talk. Elaine told me your throat was sore because of the tube. We've got your back, okay? No one—nothing is going to hurt you," he said solemnly and pressed a kiss to her forehead, rubbing his face along her cheek. "I love you, little sister."

Kari smiled weakly, reaching up to touch his hair.

"Don't tire her out," Andreas growled but Sean just smiled at him and plopped down in a chair.

Next came Phillip. "Kari, please forgive me. I failed you. I'm so sorry."

She reached up and caressed his face. "No apologies," she whispered hoarsely. Kissing the tip of her finger, she put it to his nose. He fell to his knees then, jostling her bed, and she tried not to grimace in pain. Her stomach felt like she'd been run over by a herd of elephants. Elaine had said that the vomiting and the stomach pump caused the muscle soreness.

Andreas came over and lifted Phillip away, moving him to the door. "Neither of us believes you failed. No apologies are necessary. Don't make Kari say it again, oaf," he grunted with affection in his eyes.

Laurent, Ryan and Devon tried to come in but Andreas chased them off. "She's still weak. Everyone has to go now. Phillip will be outside the door. I'll stay here. Go back to the lodge and find who did this."

Sean just looked up at him, crossing his leg over the other. "I'm not leaving."

"You're my Second, Sean. You need to go back to the lodge. The Pack needs direction right now."

The bickering and negotiating went back and forth for so long that Kari swallowed hard and croaked out, "Shut the fuck up already. Sean, go back to the lodge and take Andreas with you. He looks like hell. Make him rest."

They both turned and looked at her, surprised. "Our little wolf is coming back, I see," Andreas said, looking relieved.

She rolled her eyes. "Go."

"No, that won't be happening. Sean will be going because he won't want to upset you and because the Pack needs him. But I'll be staying here. No arguments. I won't leave you."

She would have pointed out that the hospital was full of people and Phillip was still there but she knew he wasn't going to budge.

"Okay, but at least rest. I'll agree to you staying here but you need to sleep."

Sean shrugged. "She's right. When everyone leaves, take a nap. You're no good to anyone if you're too strung out. I'll go back home, for now at least."

"Oh all right. On your way out, make sure that Phillip and Laurent make arrangements with each other so they can get some rest as well," Andreas said, stretching out in the chair Sean had vacated. A large enough chair for a big human but Andreas still spilled over the sides. He looked over to Kari. "You too," he ordered. She was so exhausted that she obeyed, promptly falling asleep.

* * * * *

The moment Sean, Ryan and Devon walked back into the lodge they were surrounded by people asking after Kari.

Privately, Skye told Sean that Carey had taken the chicken salad and the platter that had held the strawberries to the hospital so the toxicologist could test them for poison. Gregory had found that some of the slug and rat poison he'd had in the shed was missing a few days before and that the door was always unlocked unless children were visiting. He hadn't found anything else missing.

Jade looked awful and clung to Sean and Devon tightly. "Is she going to be okay?" she whispered.

"She was awake when we left. They've moved her out of the ICU and into a regular room. She felt well enough to try to argue with Andreas. So well she actually told us to 'shut the fuck up' when he and I were bickering." He grinned at that.

Jade relaxed a little. "She's such a little thing and Andreas loves her so much. I can't imagine how he'd react if something happened to her."

Sean kissed his mother's cheek. "*Maman,* she's a fighter. She might be little but she's strong. She's already recovering. Because of that Andreas is looking better too. They'll both be home soon."

He turned to Anna. "Has Carey been up and gone through their room yet? Let's not touch it just yet. The police will want to see it," Sean said urgently.

"Police? Why are police involved?" Ellen asked as she waddled over.

The Pack had gathered in the great room and stared intently at Sean. Most of them thought Kari had food poisoning. It was time to come clean and tell everyone the truth. Skye and Carey had already interviewed everyone and Alex and Johanna were at the top of the suspect list.

"Kari was poisoned."

Outraged gasps and conversation rolled through the room.

"Who would do that to her? Why would anyone want to hurt Kari?" Drew asked.

"Kill Kari," Skye amended.

"We don't know," Sean said quietly.

"It had to have been one of us," Michael said.

"Johanna hated her, that much was clear," Alex said.

Sean wondered if Alex was trying to divert attention from himself, and then he hated that he had cause to distrust his own Pack.

"Yes she did and she's dead," Jade said, not sounding sorry in the least.

"When did it happen? How did it happen?" Perri asked, coming to hug Devon tightly.

"We don't know really. Elaine's going to call a toxicologist friend of hers, a shifter, to see if we can't narrow down a timeline. Kari only ate a few things that others didn't and they've been taken to be tested. If anyone can wrack their brains to think about whether they saw anyone near the shed where the poison was kept or if they saw Kari eating or drinking anything anyone else didn't, that'd be really helpful."

"Could it have been accidental? Like maybe she got a hold of something when we were running last night?" Alex asked.

"Good question. We'll know more when we figure out how fast this particular poison acts on us. Human biology doesn't count. But for now, Andreas wants everyone to get back to their homes, jobs and children. Those who want to stay are welcome, of course."

Sean looked at his Pack, understanding now why Andreas made him come back to the lodge. They wouldn't have gone so easily if Skye or Ryan had given the orders. They needed to care for Kari but not to lose sight of the rest of the Pack too. Sean realized for the thousandth time what an exceptional leader his brother was.

His parents decided to stay on for several more days, as did Devon and Perri. Others would return if needed.

Life crawled its way back to normal as Anna made lunch boxes for everyone who was leaving and laid out a lunch buffet for those staying.

Chapter Eight

Kari woke up and couldn't move. When she looked down to see why, she saw Andreas' huge body sprawled protectively over her own and hanging off the sides of the rather small bed.

"Andreas," she said softly, stroking his hair.

He jerked awake and jumped down in front of her bed, crouching.

"Andreas, it's okay." She reached out to touch him and he relaxed, turning to her.

"You look much better," he said, running his hands all over her, checking to make sure she was all in once piece.

"My throat doesn't hurt anymore and my stomach doesn't feel like it was trampled on by elephants. I feel much better. The headache is even gone." Her eyes widened as she looked around the room.

"Oh my god, what is all of this?"

The room was filled with flowers. There were at least twenty baskets, bouquets and nosegays in the room, on every available surface and even on the floor.

"Oh, they started coming two hours ago. News travels fast." Andreas couldn't help but be touched by the fact that his Mate was already held in such high esteem. The Supreme Alpha of the United States' Territory had even sent a huge plant and fruit basket.

"Oh. Wow. That's nice. I don't know what to say, I've never had this many people concerned about me before. It's nice but a bit nerve-wracking. I hope I can live up to all of these expectations."

"I have no doubt you will."

A knock sounded on the door and Elaine, Carey, Sean and Laurent came in.

"Did Phillip eat?" Kari asked. "He's feeling so bad. I don't want him to neglect taking care of himself."

Laurent looked at her, a huge smile on his face.

"What?" she asked. "What is up with you guys and that damned smile?"

"It's just nice to have an Alpha-bitch—a queen to take care of such things."

She cringed. "About the use of the word bitch—it's weird to me. When you call me a bitch, I can't help but feel insulted."

"No offense is meant, Kari. For us, a bitch is a female. You're a female Alpha werewolf in our Pack," Sean explained.

"I know, it's one of the million and a half things I'll have to work on and get used to, I'm sure. Anyway, no one's answered my question."

Laurent stuck his head out into the hallway and called Phillip into the room. "Ask him yourself, Kari." He moved a basket of Gerber daisies out of the way and tossed himself into the chair.

"Phillip, you look terrible. Have you eaten?"

"A bit a few hours ago. I haven't wanted to wake you or Andreas. I'm fine."

She sat up. "You are not fine. I'm ordering you to go and get something to eat right now. A big giant heaping plate of something. Juice and milk too. Go on. You can't be an effective bodyguard if you're rundown and sick, can you?" She reached out and grabbed his hand and ran her face along it.

Phillip blushed, his pale skin red all the way into the collar of his shirt. "As you wish." He nodded at Andreas and turned to Laurent and Sean, who assured him they'd stay until he got back.

"Oh, and Phillip?" Kari called after him. "Andreas'll be coming with you. He hasn't eaten either." Andreas started to protest but she held up her hand. "Don't even think about it. What kind of leader wants his men to do things he won't do? You haven't eaten in hours, Andreas. Go. I'm quite sure that everyone can wait until you return." She glanced at the others in the room. "Can't you? It doesn't look like you've got the culprit under your shirt or anything." When Carey grinned, nodding at her, she turned back to Andreas. "See? Bring me back a donut." She grinned and Andreas sheepishly moved to follow Phillip out of the room.

"I'll be back in less than half an hour. In fact, I'll bring it back here. I want to hear that report. Elaine, can Kari eat?"

"Jell-O and broth. No donuts."

"We'll be right back," he said and left.

"So who wants to kill me?" Kari turned to Carey.

"We don't know. Let's wait for the rest until Andreas comes back. He'll be annoyed if he misses anything." Sean grinned. "What's with the garden?" He motioned to the flowers.

"Dunno. Andreas said they started arriving a few hours ago. I haven't seen the cards yet."

"Well, let's look, shall we?" Elaine approached a giant basket with fruit and a beautiful plant in the center.

The others all got into the spirit and opened and read cards out loud to her to pass the time. There were flowers from Pack leaders from across the country and even a basket of cookies from the Clearwater Clan's Alpha, which were promptly gobbled down by Sean and Laurent.

She smiled at them all, watching them bicker and laugh as they made cracks about the appropriateness of the notes or the baskets.

Andreas came in, his tray loaded with three plates of food—sandwiches, cartons of milk and juice. Phillip followed in his wake, his own tray equally laden.

"See, you were hungry," she said to them.

"Yes, well. I'm a growing boy." Andreas sat the tray down on Kari's bed and tossed sandwiches to everyone. He put a plastic mug with chicken broth and a bowl of Jell-O on Kari's food tray and moved it within her easy reach.

She slowly drank the broth and saw that Andreas had also brought a mug each of beef and veggie broth. She was bummed by the lack of donuts though.

"Okay, so he's back, what's the scoop?"

Carey explained that they'd interviewed everyone but no one seemed to have caught anything suspicious. People had been near the shed where the poison was kept but they all admitted it up front. But the big bomb was that there'd been no poison in the chicken salad, the bowls, the strawberries or the chocolate. And the lab tech said that he didn't think that it would have taken so long for a reaction anyway.

Elaine agreed. "I spoke to my friend, who says it's very difficult to poison a werewolf because our systems process things so quickly and efficiently. This particular poison, to have made her sick when it did, would have had to be ingested within an hour or less of the first symptoms. Whatever it was in, Kari ingested it this morning, not last night or yesterday."

Kari looked at them, puzzled.

"When did you first start feeling sick?" Carey asked.

Kari thought back over the hours. "Let's see. I felt slightly dizzy just before I got in the shower but it passed quickly. I came downstairs and sat down to eat, felt dizzy again. That's when Andreas brought me upstairs and laid me down. Right after that, I had to get up and run into the bathroom to throw up. I had sweats and cramps then, and then I guess I must have passed out."

"It's a good thing you did throw up then. Got rid of the bulk of the poison. The stomach pump took care of the rest,"

Elaine said and Kari grimaced, thinking of how much her throat had hurt from the tube.

"Okay, so it had to have been something you ate or drank before you came downstairs. Around the time of your shower. Can you think of what that might have been?"

"I woke up. Andreas was gone from bed and I rolled over onto his spot and stretched." She smiled at him. "It was still warm so he couldn't have been gone that long. I grabbed a glass of water from the pitcher on the nightstand and went into the bathroom. Nothing to eat or drink other than that. I brushed my teeth, but it was in the shower, after that first burst of dizziness."

"What pitcher on the nightstand?" Andreas asked.

"There was a pitcher of water with a glass on the bedside table on your side of the bed. You don't think..."

"Kari, there wasn't any pitcher in the room when I went through it. Sean, do you remember one?" Carey asked.

"No. The champagne bucket was there. The empty bottles and the champagne flutes, the tray that held the strawberries. No pitcher of water. In fact, there wasn't anything on Andreas' bedside table at all other than the phone and the lamp."

"Did the water taste funny at all?" Andreas asked.

Carey picked up the phone and called the house and had Anna run up to the bedroom to check for the pitcher just in case they'd missed it somehow.

"Well, I drank the glass in two gulps. I was slightly hungover. There was a nasty taste but I thought it was my mouth."

Carey looked up from the phone in his hand. "Anna and Skye searched the room— nothing. What did the pitcher look like?"

"It was clear glass, wide rounded bottom and fluted top. A lemonade pitcher. The cup was one of the regular glasses from the kitchen. The kind we use every day."

Carey relayed that to Anna and then paused as she spoke back to him. "No kidding? Okay, have Drew put it aside then. Try not to touch it with your hands. I'll be by to look at it in a bit." Sighing, he hung up the phone and turned to them.

"She says that the pitcher showed up this morning in the dishwasher. She was mad because she normally handwashes them. She figured someone had used it the night before and taken it back to their room or cabin. It's been washed. She also said she's got forty of those milk glasses and at least ten were in the dishwasher this morning."

"Why would she wash anything with Kari being poisoned!" Andreas exclaimed.

"She ran the cycle after you'd left for the hospital. No one knew she'd been poisoned yet."

Andreas sighed. "So can you get anything from the pitcher now?"

"I doubt it. The water in the dishwasher is pretty hot. I'll go and see if we can get prints from it anyway. Don't count on it though."

"So you're telling me we're no closer to knowing who tried to kill Kari now than seven hours ago?" Andreas asked, voice dangerously low.

"We know a lot more, Andreas. We know that the poison had to have been in that water pitcher and that someone went into your room and brought it down to cover their tracks. That's a hell of a lot more than we knew before. We know it wasn't Johanna or anyone that was here at the hospital, unless they were working with someone else at the house. It's not everything but we have a lot of things ruled out, which is just as important as what we don't know."

After several long moments of silence Kari broke in with orders. "Okay, if there is nothing more, I'm going to send everyone home. And I mean everyone. Take the flowers to the nurses' station and have them donated to people who need them. Take the plants and the food home, we still have guests,

I imagine. Please write on the cards what they sent so I can send thank-yous."

Andreas turned around and stared at her, openmouthed. "Kari, how can you think about that right now?"

She sat up straighter and pulled the sheet around herself. "Listen here, buster. It's been a tough week all around, filled with outrageous and outlandish things. This is just another of them. It's not in my nature to fall apart." She glared at Andreas.

"What should I do, Andreas? Should I wail and scream and cry about the unfairness of the world? The way I see it, I've got you and the Pack, minus one person who hates me. It's more than I've ever had so I'm really doing pretty damned well in the long run."

His gut clenched but he knew she didn't want his pity. "Of course not. I'm sorry for assuming you couldn't handle this. You're entirely capable of dealing with this. But I'm not going anywhere and neither is Phillip. You'll have a guard on you twenty-four hours a day, no matter where you are. And you don't eat or drink anything that someone else hasn't tasted first."

Elaine nodded her agreement. "Good idea. I'll be getting you released tomorrow, Kari. You're almost completely healed and that'll be hard to explain. I've had to take care of your blood tests myself. Your liver and kidneys are just fine. A transformation will help when you get home. A run will speed the regenerative effects of your system."

"You need to go back to Seattle, Elaine. You've been here since Thursday and I know you need to get back to work," Andreas said. "Let's get her released and home so you can get home too."

"You want her released today? Tonight?"

"Yes, if possible. You say she's well enough and despite what happened earlier today, we can protect her better at home than here. Frankly, I believe Alex is responsible for this. I can't believe it of anyone else."

"I don't know, Andreas. I tend to agree on motive but he wasn't one of the people seen near the shed," Laurent explained.

"Really?"

"Really. It was Ryan, Skye, Pierre, Luna, Michael, Tomas, Gregory, Devon, Peter and Sean. Of those, Sean was with you on the way here. Everyone else is a possibility."

"There is no way my father or brother would hurt Kari. Nor would Skye. Ryan could have killed Kari quite easily when he found her after she'd run away."

"Michael? He's been awfully upset since he made Kari," Sean said.

"Upset because he failed. He could have killed her that first night. And he's an awfully submissive wolf."

"Except that he went against orders and made Kari without permission. That's pretty aggressive," Elaine said.

"I don't know. He seemed sincere when he asked for my forgiveness. He's been very kind to me," Kari said. "I hate this. I don't want to accuse anyone."

"I know, peaches. It's very difficult but it's necessary. We have to find out who did this. It's not only for you but for the Pack as a whole. You can't have people around who would betray us like this. None of us are safe this way."

"But has anything like this happened before?"

"Not in the eight years that Andreas has been Alpha. But this kind of political machination is sadly typical in many Packs. Our structure of governance is not democratic. Leadership usually goes from Alpha male to oldest son. There can be challenges, but you've got to beat biology, which usually works to make the Alpha the strongest wolf. Usually killings are done in outright challenges amongst the Pack."

"What happens when we find out who did it?"

"We take care of it. Everyone out. Kari needs her rest," Andreas ordered, ushering people out of the room.

"I'm going to go and talk with the lead physician on duty tonight to see if we can't get you released. Why don't you all wait here until I get back?"

"Good idea," Andreas said as Elaine swept out of the room. "Hey, what happened to that platter of cookies?" Andreas looked around the room.

"Uh, Kari ate them," Sean said innocently.

"Hey!" Kari said, throwing a pillow at him. "Just for that, take these flowers out to the nurses' station."

"They looked good too," Andreas growled and sat next to her on the bed. "I'm so glad you're okay. I was so scared I was going to lose you."

"I'm not that easy to kill. Plus, you owe me a ring and some clothes."

He laughed softly.

"Laugh while you can, wolf boy, I've got expensive taste."

* * * * *

The lights were still burning when they pulled onto the drive leading to the lodge.

Andreas insisted on carrying Kari inside and made everyone stand back while he carried her upstairs to their bedroom. He laid her on the bed gently and she held onto his neck. "I need a shower. I feel grungy. Wanna keep me company?"

He laughed suggestively. "No, little wolf. Let me send Anna up. If I come in there with you I'll do things I'm not supposed to. You need to rest."

She pouted. "I don't want Anna. I want you. My back needs washing. Surely you'd rather do it?"

He sighed dramatically. "Okay, if you insist." He followed her into the bathroom, turning on the water for her, getting it hot while she got out of her clothes and laid out some towels.

"You too." She motioned at him. "Can't take a shower with clothes on." Without waiting for an answer, she stepped into the tub and backed into the spray, moaning.

Andreas stood there for a moment as he fought with himself. She'd just been through a terrible trauma and he should leave her alone. On the other hand, she seemed well enough and was inviting him in with her in a clearly suggestive manner.

He wanted to be with her. No, he *needed* to make love with her to reassure himself that she was alive. She connected him to the world in a way that made it impossible to resist her, even if his cock hadn't been so hard it felt like it weighed three hundred pounds.

Making his mind up, he quickly stripped and stepped in after her. She smirked a moment and he bent to kiss her quickly as he grabbed the soap and her sponge. Bubbles, fragrant with vanilla, lathered on the sponge and his hands when he began to scrub her back while she washed her hair. He shouldn't have been so damned turned on by the simple act of taking a shower with his Mate but he was. The intimacy of bending down and bringing the sponge over her skin, of ministering to her and taking care of her shot straight from his heart to his cock.

She turned to rinse off and he soaped up her arms and torso, trying to stay detached as he came to her breasts but failing miserably as he watched the soapy bubbles slowly running down and over her puckered nipples.

Seeing his intense interest, she smiled archly and walked the last step to him, bringing their bodies together. Like a cat, she rubbed her soap-slicked body against his.

"Kari," he warned. "You just got home from the hospital." No one on the planet would have been convinced by his words. Or his hands, which were running down the curve of her back toward her ass.

"I'm a werewolf. I heal quickly. I'll let you do all the work. Come on, I can see you want to," she said, eyeing his considerable erection.

Chuckling in defeat, he cupped her ass, squeezing. He kissed her hungrily. A kiss filled with love and passion but with an edge of desperation and fear. She answered his need for her, opening her lips to let his tongue inside, moaning. Her taste shot through him with intense sweetness. His arms tightened around her as the water cascaded over them both.

She grabbed his cock between soapy palms and he groaned, arching into her. He thrust into her grasp, building himself up as he continued to feast on her lips.

"Wait, let's get out," he gasped.

She shook her head. "No. Let me finish this." She continued to slide her soapy fist over his cock. "Lean back."

He started to argue but couldn't resist the feeling of her hands on him. Leaning back, he put his back against the tile and looked down at her.

Hand over hand, she took him through her fists over and over. "Andreas, I love the way your cock feels. So big and hard, like you. When I see how much I affect you, it makes me feel faint."

A hand job never felt so good. Andreas moaned as climax approached. "Kari, god damn, how do you do this? Make even the simplest touch so incredibly erotic? I want your hands on me, your mouth. I want to be inside you. I want to touch every part of you." He reached out, drawing a fingertip down the valley between her breasts. "I want to put my cock here and fuck you slow while you hold your breasts together for me."

She increased the speed and he put his hands over hers, grasping tighter. "That's it, little wolf, oh fuck yes."

He came as his eyes locked with hers, hands over hers, the heat of his semen on his belly. Her lip caught between her teeth as her breathing sped up, water cleaning them both.

Finally he reached behind her and turned off the taps and brought her to him, kissing her soundly.

Lips still on hers, one arm banded about her waist, holding her against him, he carefully got out of the tub. Quickly he grabbed a towel, throwing it over her back. He pulled away from her to begin to dry her off. Her disappointed cry at his absence tightened low in his stomach and he quickened his pace. She grabbed the other towel then and dried him off at the same time, tossed it into the hamper when he picked her up. He carried her to their bed, laying her down on fresh sheets.

He looked down at her naked body, flushed with the heat of the water and wanting him, her eyes gazing back, bright and wide, a sensual smile curving her lips. She was his and there and alive and vibrant. Joy surged through him, twinned with desire and love.

Leaning down, he started at her toes, slowly licking and kissing a path up her body. Swirling his tongue around her ankle bone, over the luscious muscles of her calves. Over the sensitive and delicious skin at the back of her knees. Her scent, the scent of her want of him drew him upward over the velvety flesh of her inner thighs. Carefully he skirted her pussy and kissed up her belly, up the underside of the curve of each breast and the valley in between, along her ribs and arms, over her collarbone, licking through the hollow of her throat, around her neck and the shell of her ear. With soft sighs and moans, she writhed beneath him.

"God, the noises you make are going to make me lose it again before I can even get inside of you." He took a nipple into his mouth. It was hard against his tongue as he sucked and she arched into him with a cry of his name.

"I do love a man with such a short recovery time."

Her hands roamed across his shoulders and down his spine. She squeezed his ass and then moved around his body to grasp his cock in one hand and his balls in the other. He groaned and shifted higher so she could reach him more easily. Her hands on him like that, giving him pleasure with such abandon, made him crazy.

He moved back, disentangling himself from her grasp, and locked gazes with her as he settled between her thighs. "I love the way you taste, Kari." Looking down then, he spread her open with his thumbs and looked his fill at her.

"Damn, so beautiful. Pink and glistening. Your clit is swollen up for me." He leaned down and flicked it several quick times with the tip of his tongue. "Looking so damned sweet I can't help but want to lick it."

"Oh..." Kari breathed faintly.

He chuckled. "I think I've made you speechless. Hmm, do you like dirty talk, little wolf? Shall I tell you how I'm going to eat your sweet pussy until you rain your honey all over my face? And then I'm going to fuck you long and hard and watch your breasts as they bounce while I do it."

A flush moved up her body and he moved back to her pussy to get to work. Dipping two fingers into her and hooking them, he knew he'd found her sweet spot when she gasped and arched off the bed. "Yes. That's the ticket. I know you like being heard too. Night before last you were so loud, I felt you get even wetter when I made that comment about everyone hearing you. Would you like that? Knowing that you made some of them touch their cocks after hearing you? Imagining me fucking you? Part of me likes that. The idea that I have something they all want."

He tasted every fold of her pussy then. Every dip and bump. He teased the underside of the hood of her clit and sucked it into his mouth, just slightly abrading it with his teeth.

He knew she was just on the edge, her thighs trembled and her moaning and begging had increased in intensity. She was slick and swollen and he'd never been more turned on in his life. Her taste, the sounds she made and the thought of how his sweet wolf was not so sweet in the bedroom ramped him up even as he drew her ever closer to orgasm.

Drawing the flat of his tongue up and over her clit again and again, he stroked her G-spot with his fingertips until she came, her entire body seizing up, thighs clamped around his head.

Backing off, her pussy still spasming around his fingers, he laid his head on her thigh and watched her, licking his lips, enjoying the way her eyes widened and then went half-lidded.

Kari watched him as he lay there wearing that arrogant smile. Of course, he deserved to wear it. The man's mouth was a miracle. Aside from the way he'd gone down on her like she was the best thing he'd ever tasted and couldn't get enough, the dirty talk really rang her bell. Did she like the idea that Laurent or Phillip heard her coming and it made them hard? Deep inside she guessed she did.

"Inside. Andreas, I want you inside of me," Kari breathed out as he dipped two fingers inside of her, drawing his thumb up to her clitoris, drawing slow circles with it. "Oh my. Stop. Please. I need you." Reaching down, she tugged gently on his cock to underline her point.

He moved over her on all fours and sat up, back against the headboard, legs straight, spread out on the bed and pulled her to him. "I'll do the work, just sit on me," he growled and it sent shivers cascading down her spine.

Straddling his body, she reached back and grabbed his cock, guiding him true. She loved that moment where she felt both how ready and hard he was but also the wet heat of her own body crying out for his. The anticipation of those seconds before she began to slowly sink onto his cock, taking him deep into her body. And so she did. Her pussy's muscles stretched to accommodate him as she moved, delicious pleasure shooting up her body. She bit her bottom lip at the pleasure of the sensation. At how full he made her feel.

Bracing herself, she placed her hands on the wall of his chest before leaning in to run her tongue along his nipples, garnering a hiss of pleasure in return. She hadn't really given much thought to male nipples before but Andreas' cinnamon-colored ones beckoned her mouth and fingers. She loved the way he reacted as she ran the edge of her teeth over them. Loved being able to make him react as wildly as he made her.

Keeping her from exerting herself in any way, he used the muscles in his arms to slowly raise and lower her over his cock. Giving him such control over her movements was incredibly erotic.

She moaned and he smiled at her. "Even in pleasure you like to chatter," he teased.

"Are you saying I'm a moaner?" she gasped as he sped up her movements over him. His cock sliced through her over and over, dizzying her.

"No, little wolf, you're a screamer, a gasper, a talker, a moaner. I enjoy it greatly." He grasped her bottom lip between his teeth gently and ran his tongue over it.

She added a grinding swivel as he lowered her each thrust and he made his own gasp.

"You like that?"

He responded by intensifying his thrusts and speed, bringing her down hard but not too hard onto him, until she thought she was going to explode with pleasure.

"Omigod. You feel so good," she whispered in awe.

She felt the muscles of his stomach tighten, watched the sweat run down his face. Her own climax was approaching. "Come with me, Kari," he groaned and moved his hand so his thumb came down and flicked over her sensitized clit, sending her over the edge with a crash.

He followed, the spasming of her internal muscles around him coupled with her breathy moans and squeals finally proving too much to endure. He arched his back, holding her tight against his body as he thrust up into her deeply, biting his lip until he tasted the metallic spice of his blood to keep from screaming her name. Instead a hoarse cry issued from his lips.

She fell forward over his chest, boneless, chest heaving.

"Andreas? Kari? Is everything all right?" Jade asked, knocking on the locked door. She sounded puzzled. Probably the very idea of a locked door in the house was unusual to her.

"Fine, *Maman,*" Andreas answered hoarsely and Kari tried to stifle a giggle.

"Andreas, are you having sex with that poor girl? She just got home from the hospital. Leave her alone!"

Kari couldn't help it then, her giggles erupted and caught Andreas as well.

"It was her idea," he protested through laughter and Kari hit him with a pillow.

"Some protector of my reputation you are!" Laughing, she got off his lap and grabbed her robe, putting it on quickly. Tossing Andreas' at him, she went to the door and opened it.

Jade rushed in, pulling her into a hug. "Are you okay, dove?" she asked, feeling Kari's forehead.

"I'm fine, really. I feel much better. In fact, I'm starved. I wonder if Elaine would let me eat?"

"You don't hate us?" Jade asked.

Kari turned to her, dumbfounded. "Hate you? Why on earth would I hate you?"

"My son had you kidnapped, he turned you into a werewolf, and not even a week later you're challenged by a low-level Pack member that you have to kill and then someone tries to poison you. How can you not hate us?" Jade wrung her hands, eyes not meeting Kari's.

"Thanks, *Maman*. It's always good to remind her of the bad things," Andreas said sarcastically.

Kari took Jade's chin in her hands and turned her face toward her own, to meet her eyes. "I don't hate you. I was angry and scared when I was brought here. And yes, I would have preferred it if someone had asked me before simply choosing to turn my entire life upside down. But truthfully, I wouldn't have believed it if Andreas had told me he wanted me to be a werewolf with him. I wouldn't have gone on seeing him. I would have missed out on the way I feel about him now. The way I feel about all of you.

"There are definitely things that I need to work out with Andreas but I'm here to stay. Bizarre as it sounds to even say it, I love your son, Jade. Even after just a few days and a shaky start, I love him and I know he loves me. I trust that.

"Some really bad stuff has happened to me this last week but the best stuff of my life happened too. In the whole benefit-cost analysis, I come out ahead."

Jade dropped to her knees and hugged her around the waist, her face pressed into Kari's stomach. "I'm so glad. We love you too." She looked back at Andreas, who was still lounging on the bed, naked, and smiled at him. "You did have your way with her. I can smell it."

Kari stepped back, blushing. She had a lot to get used to. She wasn't a prude by any means but this was just too weird. "Okay, enough of that. Way was had. It was my idea. He actually tried to put me off but I pressured him. Moving right along, is Elaine here?"

Andreas chuckled and got up and kissed her on the top of the head affectionately. He pulled on a pair of sweats and left off the shirt. Not like she'd be complaining about that.

Jade stuck her head out into the hall where Laurent and Phillip were sitting, drinking scotch. "Can one of you go and get Elaine?"

While Laurent jogged downstairs in search of Elaine, Jade popped back into the room and started brushing Kari's hair, braiding it for her.

"My mother never did that. I've never had anyone braid my hair before. Thank you," Kari murmured as she leaned back into Jade.

Jade kissed her temple gently. "I'm sorry, little one. Every little girl should have her hair brushed and braided by her mamma. I always wanted a girl to do that for. Luckily my boys all kept long hair and let me brush it. Even Laurent let me brush his. Of course, only Phillip let me braid it. As you can see, he still wears it that way today."

"It looks lovely too. All of that gorgeous strawberry blond hair falling down his back in that braid. Very sexy," Kari said loud enough so that Phillip could hear.

"Hello, husband here," Andreas grunted.

Elaine came in the room. Kari saw Phillip standing outside of the door, smiling but looking toward the stairs so she couldn't see him blush.

"You look so much better already," Elaine said, checking her over. "Must be the sex." She winked.

Kari moaned and put her hands over her face. "Oy. You wolves and the sex comments! It must have been murder as a teenager to have everyone be able to smell if you had sex."

Jade laughed. "Those girls that my boys used to hang around with couldn't hide it from me."

"Girls huh?"

"Yes, the boys went to school right here in Star Lake. Laurent came to live with us when he was eleven. His mother died and his father was human and thought he'd do better in a Pack. Phillip came a bit later. He was ten, just a year younger than Sean. His mother was my best friend. She mated with a man from a Clan in France. They died in a terrible fire, on a cruise ship of all places." She looked sad at the memory.

"Anyway, they all dated the little human girls from town. Some of them still live there. In fact, one of Andreas' old girlfriends owns the grocery store here. We'll have to take you over there soon. She dumped my boy for some other human. The gall of that girl."

"*Maman*, that was twenty-five years ago. I think we can let it go now," Andreas said, laughing.

"Oh really? Then why does she always give you the eye when you go into the store? I've seen it, Andreas. She always tries to rub those gargantuan breasts on you."

Kari snorted at that.

Andreas just rolled his eyes.

"Kari, your vital signs are great. You're healthier now than you were when we brought you here on Thursday."

"Cool. Can I eat solid food now?"

"I don't see why not. Just keep it simple for tonight. No steak or anything like that. Tomorrow you can have a normal breakfast. I'm going home tonight but if you don't feel well, don't hesitate to call. In an emergency, Sean has a medical degree too, and there's a shifter who's a doctor in Moses Lake."

"Is he one of ours? A Cherchez?"

"No, he's a bear."

"Huh?" Kari asked.

"There are more than just werewolves, Kari. There are werebears and werecats—which are generally cougars here in the US, but there are werejaguars in South America and weretigers in Africa and Asia."

"Get out!" Kari said, wide-eyed.

"I'm serious."

"Do you all hang out together?"

Andreas laughed. "No, not really. In human form we might be in the same restaurant in a city. But just as bears and wolves and cats wouldn't get along in nature, different species of shape-shifters generally avoid each other."

"This is so bizarre. I had no idea. How come no one knows?"

"It keeps us alive, Kari. If humans knew they'd want to kill us and or experiment on us. Cage us and exploit us. Keeping our existence silent is the safest way to stay alive."

"Next thing you'll be telling me that there are vampires and mummies too."

"Not that I know of." Andreas shrugged. "But who knows. There could be but they've kept quiet like we have. We've stayed safe all these generations because we've kept to ourselves. If there are vampires, my guess is that they keep quiet out of self-preservation."

"Okay, okay, enough for one night. I'm starving and Elaine needs to go. Let's rock." She went to the open door, winking an eye at Phillip as she walked past.

Anna was pleased to see her up and around and made a big deal of getting her settled at the table. She brought out a big bowl of soup and motioned for Kari to wait. "Let me take a bite of everything first."

"No. I'm sorry but this isn't going to play out this way," Kari said.

Andreas looked tired. "Kari, you have to let someone taste your food and drink first. You could be poisoned again."

"I will not live that way, Andreas. I will not suspect my Pack like that. It's disrespectful. And I won't live in fear. It's ridiculous and *you* wouldn't do it."

"What I would or wouldn't do is not at issue," Andreas said.

"Oh please, can the cavewolf routine. Of course it's at issue. You wouldn't do it for exactly the same reasons I won't. Isn't that right? And don't lie."

He rolled his eyes at her. "Kari, it's my job to protect you and every other member of this Pack. You especially."

"You are *so* avoiding the question. G'hed, answer it. Or don't, I know the answer already anyway." She pulled the soup bowl to her and put a heaping spoonful in her mouth, narrowing an eye at Andreas.

He sighed. "Do you make everything so difficult, Kari? I don't know if my heart can stand it," he said.

She snorted. "Yeah, whatever. You want me to go back to Seattle then? I'll probably be safe outside of the Pack and you can have a nice quiet life with old big boobs at the A&P."

Jade burst out laughing and Skye and Sean looked at them, puzzled. "Clearly we missed something good," Sean murmured.

Andreas narrowed his eyes back at Kari. A battle of the wills had erupted and he didn't like it one bit that this tiny scrap of a woman held him by the short hairs. She was right in a sense. One couldn't live forever in fear. And having a taster would eventually make people feel alienated from their Alpha pair. On the other hand, she was his Mate and he wanted her safe.

"Oh my god, Anna! This cornbread is so good I could eat the whole pan!"

Andreas stifled a groan of annoyance. Hell, Anna ran off to get Kari more food without even looking in Andreas' direction. His little wolf had won them all over in just a few short days. Well, all but one anyway.

"Kari, you're ignoring your safety," Andreas urged.

She waved her hand at him dismissively as she cleaned the bowl out. "Look, are we back to that again?"

"We never left—" He was interrupted when Kari turned to Sean and Skye.

"What do you two think?" she asked, gulping half her glass of milk.

"Oh no, thank you. We'll just watch," Skye said and Sean nodded.

"Smart boys," Jade murmured as she watched the interplay between Andreas and Kari.

"Cowards," Kari muttered and then turned back to Andreas. "I'm not ignoring my safety, Andreas. I'm very aware of all of the bad things that can happen to me. I'm a woman, I was born aware of all the bad things that could happen to me. But I won't, *will not,* give in to this bullshit, petty, cowardly terrorist who tried to poison me. It's divisive to the Pack. I won't have it and I'm not going to argue about it any further."

Sean applauded, smiling at her, and Phillip and Laurent joined him. "She's right, Andreas. I hate to take sides, I know how worried you must be and so am I. But she's doing what an Alpha does—putting the Pack first. Let's make her as safe as we can without giving in. Our Pack is our family. We cannot let this betrayer undermine that."

"But..."

"No buts, Andreas. She's right. She's an Alpha. It's her job to lead this Pack, be strong for this Pack, every bit as much as it is yours. If she shows distrust to all for the act of one, they'll feel slighted," Jade said.

Devon and Perri walked into the room and sat down at the table. "What did we miss?" he asked.

Sean just laughed.

* * * * *

The next morning Kari decided to call Jack and check in. She rarely went more than a day without talking to him and she missed him. Not wanting to wake Andreas, she eased out of bed and headed to the office. She smiled when she saw the roaring fire already built up in the great room. Gregory and Anna were wonderful that way. She wasn't sure if the lodge could survive without their care.

Still, she was disappointed when she got Jack's voicemail. She wanted to share all the excitement of meeting Andreas, even though she'd have to be very circumspect in giving the details. She left a brief message with the phone number for the lodge.

"Hey, little wolf. Where'd you go?" Andreas asked as she tried to sneak back into the room.

"I'm sorry I woke you. I wanted to call my brother."

He held the blankets back and motioned his head that she get into bed and she obliged, snuggling against the hard heat of his body.

"You didn't. I woke up while you were gone. Funny how fast I've gotten used to you in my bed next to me. How did Jack take the news about us?" He kissed the top of her head.

"I didn't get a chance to talk to him. He's out. I left a message." It still made her sad. Jack was all she had in the world aside from the Pack. She had this great news but couldn't share it. As it was, she'd have to edit out ninety percent of the story. Loneliness welled up inside her, despite her joy at finding Andreas.

"I'm sorry. I'm sure you'll talk with him soon. So what's on the menu today other than lots of sex?"

"I need to go into Seattle. I haven't been to work in a week. My apartment has been empty all this time. I need to tie up loose ends."

"Let's negotiate. I'll come with you to your apartment. We'll give your notice and I'll help you move anything you wish and bring it back here. In fact, call your boss from here and quit."

She sat up and leaned against the headboard. "Um, no. How is that negotiation? If I recall correctly, negotiation means each side puts forth a plan and both people give a little to get a little. You just told me what to do. Here's what *I'm* going to do. I'll go back to my apartment and figure out some way of getting out of my last three months of the lease. Then I'll figure out what to move here and what to get rid of. I'll probably need to spend the night down there. I'll meet with my boss face-to-face and work out something that doesn't leave him in the lurch. I can't just quit over the phone, Andreas. Jonas gave me a chance when a lot of others wouldn't even read my resume. I won't just abandon him. You can come with me but not into the office when I'm talking to him. I'm an adult woman. I don't need you there."

"I thought you'd want me there." His eyes flashed with hurt and it sliced through her, even though he was being bossy.

She reached out to caress his cheek, smiling softly. "Don't pout, Andreas. I do want you there for most of it. You can't get your feelings hurt every time I express my need to be independent. I like working. I like my boss and my job. But I'm quitting and moving up here to be with you. You have to let me deal with my responsibilities in my own way. I'm willing to give, and give a lot. But you can't have everything your way. Big bad Alpha wolf or not."

She didn't miss the twitch of a smile even as he tried to hide it. "All right, I'll try. What'll you do with your new company? Right now it's running itself. Not much is happening but you'll want to develop your own stuff, won't you?"

"I had forgotten that you bought me my own company. I'll have to look it over. I'd really like to write games. It's been something that I've dabbled in but haven't been able to do as much as I've wanted to."

"So do it. Kari. I'm a very rich man. Well, *we're* very rich. You have the time and money to do it, so follow your dreams."

"I still have to leave my job gracefully, Andreas. It's about loyalty. You of all people should be able to understand that." She moved to stand but he grabbed her wrist, pulling her back to him.

"You're right. I do. Let's get ready and get on the road. And by getting ready, I mean let's have sex," he said with a grin.

Managing this big man was going to be a full-time job. She laughed as he made quick work of divesting her of her robe. The best job in the world

* * * * *

Her apartment seemed so cold and small after being at the lodge. She spoke to her landlord, who was unhappy about releasing her from the lease early, so they decided they'd hold the place for a few months, leaving some of the furniture there so that Pack members could use it if they needed to stay in Seattle.

There were thirty-eight messages on her machine and her mail was being held in the apartment manager's office. Work had called a few times. Jack had called the day before. And Frank, the man she'd sort of been seeing but had pretty much broken it off with, had called.

Before Andreas could say anything about that, she grabbed the phone and called work and arranged to meet with her boss in an hour. When she turned to go into the bedroom to pack up her clothes Andreas stood in her way, glowering. "Who is Frank?"

"He's a man I used to date. I hadn't gone out with him for a few weeks. Nice enough guy, but not for me."

"I should say not! I'm for you," he said arrogantly.

She laughed, patting his arm. "Of course you are, love."

She went into the bedroom and started packing clothes into the boxes they'd brought with them. Michael had brought a few bits and pieces to the lodge but the bulk of her stuff was still there. Andreas smiled appreciatively as he watched her put her lingerie into a box.

"You have very good taste in underwear. Now what exactly happened with this Frank?"

"Thanks, I love fancy panties. Do you want a detailed sexual history and if so, will you be giving me yours?" she said flippantly, folding things and putting them into boxes.

"Okay, fine."

"You really want that?"

"Yes."

She sighed. "Okay, suit yourself. In detail then. We had sex once, it was okay. His dick was thin. The experience was not very satisfying. I like some girth on a man. He had an okay technique in bed. Seemed to like doing it and put some effort into making me feel good—which is more than you can say for many men. He was totally silent when we fucked, which I found to be unnerving. We broke up because among other things, he had an odd obsession with porn. Loved it. Had stacks and stacks of it. Just creeped me out that the guy probably had thousands of dollars worth of porno.

"Before Frank, back in Atlanta, I went out with Geoff Pierce for two years. The sex was pretty good. We were young but eager to learn and try new things. I broke it off when I moved out here. I have no doubt that he's married now. He's that kind of guy, which is lovely but not what I wanted from him.

"Um, before that there were a few guys here and there. I was a virgin until I was nineteen. Matt Smith was my first. A totally mediocre experience. He didn't seem to know that most women can't climax during intercourse without some sort of direct clitoral stimulation. In fact, he didn't make much of an attempt to find out where my clit was, the selfish pig. He was not an oral sex guy. Well, giving anyway, he liked getting. And frankly, I may just be twenty-four and all, but if a man wants you to go downtown, the bus had better travel both ways if you know what I mean.

"All in all, I've had intercourse with four men, including you. Not very exciting or wild. Is that what you wanted?" She turned to him, stifling a smile at his pale face.

"More than I wanted. Thanks for the visuals."

"You did ask. I tried to stop you. For what it's worth, I don't really want your sexual history, unless you've had sex with people I know. And then again, maybe not even then," she said.

The thought of her having a sexual life before him unnerved him to a certain extent. He also knew it would be a good time to tell her about his sexual experience with the other females in the Pack, but the need to have her right that moment pushed all of that out of his head.

Instead he took her to the plush carpet and captured her lips with desperate passion. "I want you," he breathed into her mouth as he nibbled on that luscious lower lip. "I want you every way I can have you, every moment I can have you."

The need to have her, to touch her and possess her, burned through him. He wanted his touch to erase the thought of her past with anyone else from her head. He wanted to give her a thousand orgasms, bring her so much pleasure that all her waking hours were filled with desire for him. For his touch.

Her eyes widened in surprise at the intensity of his response but she gave in, lids sliding halfway shut as his hands caressed her.

Bending down, he captured a nipple between sharp white teeth, through her blouse and her bra. It wasn't enough. Hissing in pleasure, she arched into his mouth, wanting more. Hands yanked his shirt up, her nails raking over his skin, digging into the meat of his muscle. The sharp sensation of it drove him, tested his control. Breaking contact momentarily, he tore his shirt up and over his head, summarily removing hers as well. She lay beneath him, desire-tousled, pleasure drunk. Her breath came in short pants and he reached down, unsnapping the front closure on her bra. Her breasts came free and he stilled for a moment, taking their beauty in. High, perky and mouthwatering, her nipples large and hard at his perusal.

"So pretty. Your nipples are so damned pretty, Kari. They make my mouth water. I want to bite them and lick them and tug on them all day." To underline that, both hands reached out to her nipples, fingers rolling and tugging until she began to whimper and writhe beneath his touch.

His need caught hers, engulfing her. Drowned her and set her on fire all at once. She wanted him so much it robbed her of breath. Her skin burned where he touched her, tingled in the wake of his glance. Never, not with any other man, had she felt such a level of desperate need to be with someone. To feel desired and possessed and the center of his attentions.

Desperate for more contact, she arched her hips, rolling them to grind her denim-clad pussy against his cock. The seam there pressed against her swollen clit and she moaned softly.

"Jesus, Kari. The way you are, damn it, you're so fucking sexy."

Despite the intensity of the encounter, joy bubbled up and out her mouth as a laugh. Her hands frantically struggled to get his pants unfastened and he pushed her away with a groan and pulled them off himself. The moment he moved back into her reach she grabbed him with both hands as he spilled out of his underwear, and he yelped. She let go, afraid she'd hurt him.

"No, god, no. Don't stop," he panted, putting her hands back around his cock.

He practically ripped her jeans from her, the panties followed. Pausing, he looked down at her. Desire deepened the color of his eyes and she was caught up in them. His lips were wet from licking her nipples, swollen from kissing her. His gaze went back to her breasts and he leaned over, touching them, kneading them. "I want to fuck these," he said in a deep rumble.

She opened and closed her mouth a few times but there weren't words. The power of his want of her rendered her speechless. Nonetheless, her body responded. Her pussy gushed cream and her nipples hardened to the point of pain. It was all she could do to nod slowly.

Without taking his eyes from hers, he took her hands and put them where his were. She found herself holding her breasts together, creating a tight channel of flesh for him. For his cock.

A cock she was unable to resist as he slid in between her breasts with a hiss of pleasure. Leaning down, she swirled her tongue around his glistening cock head each time it came toward her. That sweet, tangy taste of him tortured her senses over and over.

"Sweet heaven," he stuttered, stroking himself through the tight passage. What a sight she made there! Spread out beneath him, wanton and sexy. Her gaze met his as she licked over the head of his cock, looking into him with such depth of feeling that he felt he was falling into her. The sight of her pink tongue lapping at him each time he thrust, lips swollen, small hands holding those luscious breasts together as he fucked them brought a shiver through his system as he felt his climax approach, quicksilver up his spine.

Growling, he pulled back and turned her over. "That's it, little wolf. Ass up, head down."

He knew she was soaking wet, he could smell her pussy, hot and ready to be fucked. Without preamble, he spread her thighs and plunged deep and hard into her cunt. Crying out, she arched back to meet his thrusts.

He kneaded the globes of her pretty little ass, keeping her wide open to his strokes. Looking down, he watched his cock disappear into her sweet pussy and come back out, slick with her juices. He loved the way it looked as her body clutched his each time he pulled nearly all the way out. Loved the depth of color of her labia as her pretty cunt flushed for him.

And her ass. Her ass was so pretty. The little bit of anal play he'd given her the few nights before had only sparked his desire for more. He stroked a finger over her rosette, she stiffened and then relaxed with a shaky sigh.

"You're so pretty. You have no idea how much it turns me on that you trust me," he crooned and she relaxed a bit, waiting.

Sliding his fingers through her pussy to gather her lube, he stroked a thumb over her ass and then pushed into her slowly. She tensed up and he pet her with his free hand, making soothing sounds. Reaching around, he flicked a fingertip over her clit and she groaned, relaxing enough for his thumb to slip into her more easily. The muscles in her pussy clenched and his balls drew closer to his body.

"Hmm, you like that, don't you? One of these days, very soon you know, I'm going to put my cock here. Fuck this pretty little ass while you beg me for more."

She moaned softly in response.

Sweat rolled off his body as he slammed into her, fingering her ass as he went. The fingers of his other hand stroked in time over her clit. She wriggled back against him with soft mewls of pleasure and entreaties for more.

When he pinched her perineum between the thumb inside of her and his index finger he knew it would push her over. And he was right. Her spine curved and a long, soft moan broke from her as she came.

Her pussy clenched and fluttered, gripping his cock in a tight wall of hot, wet flesh. How in the hell could any mortal man withstand the sight of her there, arched, flushed and writhing with pleasure with his cock buried deep inside her? It was certainly a task beyond his control. A bone-deep shudder broke up his spine as he orgasmed, feeling as if his entire body was shooting through the end of his cock.

"Oh for… Your cunt is so fucking hot."

The totality of being taken in such a feral way settled into her skin. By this man who had such a raw, deep abiding need for her—it would have terrified her from anyone else. But from Andreas, it made her feel more alive. Made the scent of the pine trees outside more crisp, brought more resonance to the sound of the rain against the windowpanes. The weight of him, his hips curved around hers, brought a deep satisfaction to her soul.

It was so much and yet just enough. Right up to the brim of sensory overload. Edgy, dark, thrilling. Sex with Andreas could be soft and sweet but more often sharp and exciting. His need for her was sharp and sliced through her. The tang of it rode the edge of pleasure-pain that awakened something deep within her. A need to be desired with that nearly uncontrollable force. The yearning for fingers digging into the flesh of her hips, of teeth grasping the tendons in her neck to hold her still. She didn't have words or explanation for this dark lure of his immense sexuality but she loved it nonetheless.

With a long groan, her legs gave out and she collapsed to the carpet. He slipped out and followed, pulling her into his body, his face in her hair.

They both lay curled into each other as they caught their breath. Kari turned to face him, kissing his forehead. "Wow. That was…wow. Andreas, what brought that on?"

"You did. You always do. Just being with you, hearing you talk about sex with anyone else. I had to have you. Each time is better than the last, little wolf. Even now I want you again."

No one had ever known her body so well. Had played her senses, emotions and responses with such expertise and passion. The raw need in him when he touched her was addictive and overwhelming but those moments on the floor, the carpet biting into first her back and then her knees had been the most powerful sexual experience she'd ever had. She craved him like nothing she'd experienced before.

"Well, even now I want you to have me again, but I need to be at Instaware in," she looked at her watch, "fifteen minutes. We need to get going."

He stood and helped her up. They both groaned at sore muscles and then laughed. She freshened up quickly and they left. Andreas waited in her office, needing to make some business calls anyway.

* * * * *

The meeting with her boss was easier than she'd thought it would be. He was sad to see her go but there was an easy enough replacement in the temp that had been handling her work when she was out. Kari had been cheered by his request to call him when she got her own business up and running.

Free of any other responsibilities, they headed to Seattle to go shopping. When they walked into Tiffany he stole a look down at her and smiled at the stunned look on her face as she took in all the rings.

He sat in front of the case she peered into. "Go for it. Whatever you want, it's yours."

She would have jumped up and down squealing were she not inside of the mecca for women everywhere. Home of the blue box. Instead she gave him a quick grin, replaced by a more mature smile, and perused the array of rings beneath the glass. A salesperson came over to help.

Kari knew what she wanted—a pear-shaped diamond with twin sapphires to either side. She'd seen it in the window as she'd shopped at Pacific Place a few months back. The band was platinum, nice and sturdy. Simple, not a whole lot of flash, but the diamond was a carat and the sapphires were a quarter carat each. Elegant without being gaudy. She pointed to it and the woman pulled it out of the case and set it on a velvet pad. Kari tried it on. It fit perfectly.

Andreas approved, the ring suited her well. "Is there a ring that could serve as a companion to this one?" The salesclerk brought out a men's band with a pave diamond, a sapphire on each side. All of the stones were set within the band and were much smaller than the woman's setting, but he preferred that anyway.

"Do you like it?" he asked Kari.

She looked up at him, eyes shining, cheeks flushed. "Yes. It's perfect." Sliding the ring off when the clerk brought out the box, Kari saw the price tag and blanched. "Oh never mind! Let's look at other rings."

He put his hand on her arm. "Why? Kari, I can see how much you love that ring. You've seen it before, haven't you?"

"Yes, I saw it in the window awhile back. But, Andreas, that ring costs more than an economy car."

"Kari, marriage is a once-in-a-lifetime thing. This ring, these rings," he pointed to the band he'd chosen to complement hers, "are not a hardship. Believe me. I'm going to buy this ring for you. You want it. I want it for you. End of story."

She wore the ring out of the store. His had to be sized and would be ready in a few days. He smiled when he noticed she kept looking at it, watching the light play on the diamond. He'd have to thank his mother for the suggestion to let Kari choose her own ring.

When they were walking back to the garage where the truck was parked, she looked up at him. "So have Laurent and Phillip been with us all along?"

"What? How did you know?"

"I'm a werewolf, duh. I could smell Phillip. And then I saw Laurent when we came out of the restaurant. Why didn't you tell me?"

"I didn't want to upset you."

"I'm not upset that they're here. I understand and I agree that it's necessary. What I'm upset about is you not just telling me up front. Oh my god, look at those boots…" She wandered off in mid-sentence and he stifled a smile. A strong, intelligent woman but still girly underneath. Intoxicating.

"Let them be my penance for not telling you about Laurent and Phillip," he said indulgently. He wanted to shower her with presents to drown out a childhood that had had her picking locks for food.

"Twist my arm," she said dreamily and went into the shop, coming out with not just a pair of boots but a pair of strappy stilettos too that'd been Andreas' idea.

By the time they'd gotten back to the car he'd been weighted down with bags and packages. "It's a good thing we brought the big truck," he joked as they got back onto the freeway going east. Her cell phone rang then. It was Jack.

"Hey there. How are you?"

"I called you at home a few times. What's with the new number you left?"

Taking a deep breath, knowing her brother was going to freak out, she blurted out, "Jack, I've met someone. We're married." Well, not according to human law but Andreas promised to have some sort of ceremony to do that soon.

"You got married? How? Why didn't you tell me? Who is this guy?"

"Oh, it's such a long story. I met him when I got out of the hospital but it's like I've known him forever. The new number is for his house. Or rather, our house. It's at Star Lake, on the water. His name is Andreas Phinney. He's a businessman. Comes from a large family. You'll like him."

"Kari, you married a guy you haven't known for a week yet?" he yelled out and she held the phone away from her ear. "Are you insane?"

She sighed. "I know it sounds completely crazy but all I can tell you is that it isn't. It's right. Come out to visit. Meet him yourself. You know I'm not a flake. I have good judgment."

"Kari, you can't be serious. This guy could be an axe murderer. He could be anyone. I'm gonna check into his background."

"Jack Warner, you will do no such thing! Don't you dare treat him like a criminal and investigate him!"

Andreas put his hand up to interrupt. "Kari, he wants to protect you. I'm sure it sounds very sudden to him. Let him investigate. It'll make him feel better."

"Did you hear that?" she asked Jack. "He says to go ahead."

"Kari, I will. Don't worry. Listen, are you okay? I mean, is there any trouble?"

"I'm better than okay, Jack. I'm in love. He's a good man. Come out. I'll send you a ticket."

Andreas interrupted again. "Kari, we have a jet that can pick him up at Logan and bring him out here if he'd like."

"He has a jet?" Jack asked incredulously.

"Apparently," she replied.

"Okay, I'm gonna check this dude out. When I do, I'm coming out there to meet him. No one's gonna hurt my baby sister."

She laughed. "I love you, Jack. I'll see you soon. You'll meet Andreas and his family and you'll fall in love with them too."

"I'll be calling you tomorrow. I don't like how fast this is moving. You had a head wound! This guy could be preying on you."

She burst out laughing. "You think he's taking advantage of me because of my head wound? Or my huge amounts of money? Oh perhaps my access to the halls of Congress!"

Andreas looked at her askance. "Would you like me to speak with him? Set his mind at ease?"

She shook her head. "He won't feel better until he's done whatever he thinks needs doing to be sure you're on the level."

"Look, smartass, joke all you want but this guy could be the big bad wolf."

Kari laughed so hard she nearly choked. "Oh Jack. Not the big bad wolf. He's not bad at all."

"Okay, baby sister, I'll be calling you. Take care of yourself. Call 9-1-1 if anything goes bad. Should I call the police station in Star Lake to give them a head's-up?"

"No, Jack, don't interfere. Trust me, if he did anything bad, I'd take care of it. I'm not a doormat."

"Of course you aren't. I'm sorry. I hope this is all what you think it is. I want you to be happy. I just don't want some loser taking advantage."

"A loser with a jet."

"Yeah, okay so he's probably—and I say probably because who knows if that's true—not a loser where it comes to money."

"Yeah. So anyway. Check and call me back. I want you to come out soon. Bring Alyssa and her son. There's plenty of room here. A lake to play in, woods to explore."

Andreas nodded at that, he wanted very much for Jack to come and visit to make Kari happy.

"We'll see. I'll talk to you soon. I love you."

"Me too, monkeybutt." She flipped the phone shut.

"So I'm the big bad wolf?" He leered at her.

"I corrected him. I said you weren't bad."

Back home, Gregory and Sean helped unload all of the goodies from the truck and put them away.

She was talking with Drew about having him design some clothing for her when Andreas bellowed at her from inside.

"Jeez! What?" she asked, walking into the house.

He sat in the living room with his mother on one of the couches near the fireplace, wearing a cocky smile.

Jade shook her head at her son and came to Kari. "I told him to use his manners and go and get you. Lazybones. However, he tells me that he bought you a ring, let's see it!" she exclaimed and Kari flashed her hand, being sure to catch the light. "Oh it's gorgeous and very you!" Jade said and Anna rushed over to look as well. Perri, attracted by the excited sounds, came in.

"What?"

"Come and see Kari's ring," Anna said as Perri rushed over and oohed and aahed.

"It's beautiful. I love it!" Perri looked at Andreas. "Nice job. You're aware that you have to do the human ceremony too, right? And not just for Kari's sake, 'cause every girl needs a wedding, but to deal in the human world as her husband too. You can't just tell them you're mated, they won't accept that.

"You have no idea how lucky you were that Elaine and Sean were there at the hospital. Technically, you had no right to see her or make medical decisions for her because you weren't legally her spouse."

He sighed, the panic at nearly losing her and the thought of being powerless to help her passing slowly through him. "I know. I've arranged for a judge to come over next Saturday. If that's okay with you, Kari?"

"Really? I can plan it?"

"Yes, if you'd like. We should invite the Pack of course and the leaders of the neighboring Packs. If you want to invite anyone else, any human friends, do so. We can mix with humans without biting them, you know," he said and she smirked.

"Oh, my goodness! I have a lot to do and not much time!"

"Well, I've taken time off—helpful when one is the boss." Perri laughed. "So I can help with anything you need."

Anna said she'd plan the menu and Jade offered her help with the guest list and any other details.

Sean came and sat on the arm of the couch next to Andreas. "All of this is going to be noisy, I can tell." He chuckled as they both watched the women plan out the details.

"I would be honored if you would help design a dress for me. Do you think there's enough time?" Kari asked Drew shyly.

"I was hoping you'd ask!" Drew said. "Let me think about it for a few hours. I'll run some ideas by you tonight. We can start on it tomorrow. We'll need to so we can finish in time."

"Cool!"

Skye wandered in and sat down across from Andreas. "What's all this?" He gestured toward the women.

"They're planning a wedding," Sean said dryly. He was actually quite happy for Andreas. "Maybe I'll ask the woman I've started seeing to come."

Kari looked around and made her way over to them. "You're seeing someone? What's she like?" she asked, settling herself down in Andreas' lap, snuggling back against his chest.

"I work with her. She's a doctor at the hospital."

"Details."

He laughed. "Her name is Emma, she's a GP. Tall, redheaded, blue eyes. She grew up in Spokane. She's very nice. We've only gone out two or three times. I like her. She's smart and funny." He shrugged.

Kari arched an eyebrow his way. "Invite her. She sounds very nice and you need to settle down."

"Oh no, another woman who wants me to settle down! Heaven help me."

Skye laughed. "Better you than me."

"Think again, buster. I tell you, you have no idea how many women would fall over dead at the sight of the studmuffin factory you've got going here. All of these gorgeous single men. It's a crime that you're all up here away from the city."

Andreas pulled her tight against him. "That's enough noticing how many single men are or aren't handsome. You're married now."

"Married, not dead." She stood up and kissed Sean and Skye. "I'll be thinking about a plan." She winked and went back over to the dining room table to plan the wedding.

* * * * *

Jack Warner sat back in his chair and sighed. He'd called a friend at the FBI and the friend had run a check on Andreas Phinney and the Phinney family. The guy had no criminal record. In fact, he had a history of working with multiple charities and raising millions of dollars for them. He owned a printing company, a construction company, three travel agencies, an import-export business and a golf course. He also just purchased a small software company. One of his brothers was a psychiatrist who ran his own private practice and also took patients at the public hospital. The youngest brother owned an architecture firm with his wife in Portland. The parents were wealthy as well, the mother worked in the state capital and the father was retired from the construction business that the family still owned.

They had a lodge on the lake that had cabins and apparently quite a large extended family. Andreas owned several properties all over the United States. Some that he leased, including two office towers in San Diego and Los Angeles and a condo complex in Seattle, as well as apartments in Portland, Vancouver, New York City and Paris. He did indeed have a jet.

The pictures he'd pulled showed a very handsome, extremely large man. The guy wasn't like the men Jack had seen Kari with before.

He was forty-two years old and didn't look a day over thirty. Why he'd waited all these years to marry a twenty-four-year-old whom he'd known for less than a week was beyond him. Not that Jack didn't love his sister—he did, she was a beautiful, intelligent woman—but these kinds of guys didn't just marry twenty-four-year-old nobodies from Atlanta.

He felt safer now. At least the guy was on the up and up. Still, Jack was suspicious of Phinney's motives. He'd take Kari up on that offer to visit but he'd leave Alyssa in Boston this time. He didn't want to bring her out with Max until he was sure it was safe. And they'd been having some problems of late anyway.

He dialed the number Kari had given him, the one for the lodge.

"Hello?" a deep male voice answered.

"Yes, may I speak with Kari, please?"

"May I tell her who is calling?"

"I'll tell if you will," Jack said.

"This is Phillip. I work for Kari and Andreas."

"Oh, this is Jack. I'm Kari's brother."

"Nice to hear from you. Kari talks about you all of the time. You're a cop, right? In Boston?"

The guy sounded nice. "Yeah. So you work for them, huh?"

"Yes, I'm Kari's bodyguard and I also help with the day-to-day stuff. Andreas has several businesses and that takes a lot of his time."

"My sister needs a bodyguard?"

"Well, she's married to a very rich man, which makes her a very rich woman. Andreas would never take chances with her safety. It's not that necessary out here at the lodge but it's better to be safe than sorry."

"Well, on one hand that makes me feel better and on the other it makes me worry more."

"Let me get her for you. Hold on a second." Phillip set the phone down and Jack could hear talking in the background and moments later the phone was picked up.

"Jack! Hey, monkeybutt, what's happening? I was going to call you tonight."

She sounded really good, he had to admit that. "Really? What about?"

"I'd like you to come out this Saturday. We're having a wedding here at the lodge."

"Wedding?"

"Yes, mine. We had a small private ceremony before but Andreas knew that I wanted something that I could have you at. Something his family could attend too. Say yes, please."

"Of course. I wouldn't miss it. I was just calling to tell you that Andreas checks out. He appears to be a good guy. On paper at least. Although why does a forty-two-year-old guy avoid marriage for that long and then marry so suddenly?"

"He met me," Kari said simply, and it made him smile.

"You have a point there."

"Listen, shall I make the arrangements for you and let you know? You'll stay here, of course. We'll have the jet pick you up at Logan and then have a small connector grab you at SeaTac. There's a small airfield here that will get you about ten miles from the lodge. I'll pick you up there."

"Jeezus, Kari, you have quite the life all of a sudden."

"Yeah, don't I know it. Will Alyssa be coming?"

"Not this time. Maybe soon, though. Right now things are complicated with us."

"Oh. Is everything okay?"

"It's a long story. I'll tell you mine and you can tell me yours when I get there. Are you sure you'll have room?"

Kari laughed. "The lodge has eight bedrooms and fifteen cabins. I was going to put you in the lodge but you can have a cabin if you want."

"You live in a mansion, Kari."

"Sort of. It's pretty overwhelming sometimes. But at the same time, everyone here is so close that it feels intimate. You'll see when you get here. I'll have a car come to get you from the station then and drive you straight to Logan. I want as much time with you as possible. And I want you to walk me down the aisle, is that okay?"

"Okay? Oh honey, that's great. You know I'd be honored."

"I'll call you then with the final details. I'll go ahead and deal with your wedding clothes, so don't worry about that."

"All right. Love you."

"Love you too."

Chapter Nine

By Wednesday morning the lodge was a study in insanity. The phone rang off the hook. Laurent and Phillip handled the business that Andreas had been putting off as he and Kari got to know each other. Sean had to go back to work but Ryan stayed to help with all the preparations.

Drew worked on the dress—a dress so top secret that Kari refused to let Andreas see it. Since it was December, they'd have the ceremony in a large heated tent in the meadow near the lake. Thank god Andreas had connections because an event of that size at such short notice would have been impossible otherwise. Kari was in her element though. She'd smoothly dealt with the details of the seating arrangements of no fewer than five Alpha pairs from neighboring clans.

Andreas stood in his office, looking out into the meadow and over the lake, smiling. He'd come into so much happiness in the two weeks, it was hard to believe that he'd lived otherwise before. Kari was a force of nature, filling the lodge with an irrepressible joy and energy. They ran every night under the starry sky. She was so small and sprightly she was dwarfed by his, Phillip and Laurent's wolves, yet she held her own.

"You know the brother had a friend at the FBI check you out," Laurent said from behind him.

Andreas turned and went back to his computer. "Yes. I knew that. He worries about her. She lives all the way across the country. She's young. He's pretty much been a father and mother to her his whole life. I understand his reticence. And we had her investigated. I'd be a hypocrite to be angry now."

"What are you going to tell him? About us?"

"She doesn't want to say anything yet. I've offered to bring him over but she doesn't know if she wants to ask him at all. I have to respect that. Most of the Pack that have been changed have family members who don't know."

"But they won't be staying here for four days either. We'll have to be careful."

"Of course. That goes without saying."

"He's a cop so he'll be extra observant too. Andreas," Laurent began, moving to close the door. He lowered his voice. "Does Kari know about your past with the females in the Pack?"

Andreas sighed. "No. I've been trying to find a way to tell her. It's not like I'll be sleeping with any of them now. I want no other female. Kari's more than enough. All of that's in the past."

"But it's part of Pack culture. It'll come up sometime. I worry that if you don't tell her it'll get mentioned by someone and catch her by surprise. She's woven a spell around my heart, Andreas. Your little wolf is very dear to me. I'd hate to see her hurt. She didn't grow up this way."

"What do you think I should tell her? Oh, by the way, pass the peas and did you know that over my life I've fucked every single female Pack member except for my mother and Anna?"

Laurent sighed. "Don't be a smartass. She hungers to understand us. To know our ways. Tell her. Tell her that young males often couple with the females of the Pack, even after they're mated. Talk to her about it. Reassure her that you don't want any of them now that you have her. Although frankly, Andreas, I've heard many males say they hoped they'd have the chance to couple with Kari."

"The hell they will!" Andreas roared. "Listen, I know what the situation is but she's mine. I won't be offering her up like that. I'm not closing it off as an option forever, but right now, I won't be sharing."

"Sean and Devon will be expecting it as your brothers. You coupled with Perri on more than one occasion. As the oldest brother it's custom for the Alpha to share his mate with his siblings."

"Don't presume to tell me about Pack custom, Laurent. I *am* Pack law. It's *optional* to share mates and it's not going to happen. Period."

"Okay, Andreas. But tell her. Tell her before she hears it from someone else and it hurts her. Hurts you both."

* * * * *

Late Thursday evening, Andreas and Kari drove out to meet the plane bringing Jack in from Seattle.

Kari rushed into the arms of her brother and he hugged her tight.

Andreas watched the lanky blond gather Kari into his arms. It was clear immediately that he adored his sister and they shared a very strong bond. Andreas knew that it was incredibly important to win the other man over. For Kari's sake if for no other reason.

Kari may not want to admit it to herself but Andreas knew that he'd have to either change Jack or at the very least tell him what they were. The two were simply too close to have such a big secret between them.

And the man was a police officer—he'd begin to realize that she was hiding something from him. That would begin to affect their relationship negatively. And once they had children, it would be even harder to explain a three-month-old crawling and a six-month-old walking.

Jack meant a lot to Kari and in truth, Andreas felt he'd be an asset to the Pack. Someone who knew and loved his Mate in the Pack would provide for more protection and loyalty to her, which would strengthen their leadership as a whole. And he came from good genes, like his sister. The more strong males that sat at the top of the Pack who were loyal, the better it was for Andreas and Kari both.

Jack looked down at Kari. She'd never looked better. Her eyes were bright and the shadow of sadness that had always lurked there was gone. She looked healthy, happy and vitally in love.

"You look awfully good for a woman who was in a coma for three days," he joked.

"Yeah. You look fab too. A bit tired though. I know that plane ride is a killer. Let's get you back to the lodge and into bed. First though," she looked up as they approached the car and locked eyes with Andreas, "Jack, I want you to meet the other incredibly important man in my life. Andreas Phinney, this is my brother and my best friend, Jack."

Jack perused the other man for a moment and then smiled, holding his hand to take Andreas'. Andreas took it and returned his smile.

"Welcome, Jack. It's a pleasure to finally meet you. Kari speaks of you all of the time."

They drove back to the lodge and got Jack settled. As Jack lay in his bed in the cabin on the lake, he thought about the situation. A knock sounded on the door.

It was Andreas.

"Mind if I come in?"

Jack nodded and stood back.

"I'm sorry if I woke you, I just thought that it would be good if you and I could talk a bit. Away from Kari. I know you have concerns and I want to get them in the open so that you and I can clear the air."

Jack motioned to the couch and Andreas sat down.

"Look, here's the thing. Yes, you check out. All the things Kari told me about you are true. On paper, you're a fucking wet dream. But that's the thing that bugs me. I'm not saying my sister isn't wonderful. She is. But why does a forty-two-year-old bachelor marry a twenty-four-year-old he's known for a few days?"

"I met your sister and there was no other option. I had to be with her. The thing between us is," Andreas paused, realizing he really couldn't explain it, even if he could tell the guy he was a werewolf. What he and Kari shared was beyond words.

Andreas shrugged. "I can't put it into words. But I am forty-two so it's not like I can't recognize something miraculous, even if I can't properly explain it. I love your sister. I don't expect you to trust me right off. You don't know me and you want the best for your sister. I respect that. I just ask that you see for yourself. Watch and see how much I love and cherish her."

Jack nodded. He had an instinct about people. This man did indeed love Kari. And he wasn't one to hold a grudge or bias without evidence to the contrary. And what he saw, everything he'd seen up to that moment, pointed to the guy speaking the truth.

"Okay. I appreciate your being so up-front. I like honesty. I'm a blunt man and I love my sister and want her to be happy. Just know that if you prove false and hurt her, I'll be back and it won't be pretty."

Standing, they shook hands and Andreas smiled. "Gotcha. Good night, I'll see you in the morning. Come on up for breakfast any time."

Jack went back to bed. Yes, the guy was on the up and up. He clearly had a major thing for Kari—that was quite clear. He was so large and yet gentle and Kari seemed to have no problems standing up to him. But there was something niggling in the back of his mind. Something wasn't being said, and he would find out what that was before he left or he'd be taking Kari back with him.

Chapter Ten

Kari stood in Laurent's room in front of the full-length mirror as Drew adjusted the dress. Midnight blue silk caressed her skin snugly in a form-fitting spill with beaded spaghetti straps and a floor-length skirt with a slight flare at the hem. Tiny black seed pearls were sewn into a swirling patter along the décolletage—which was pretty daring. The back dipped even lower, to the small of her back.

"Wow," Drew said. "It looks amazing on you. Your body is perfect for this dress."

"Your dress is perfect and makes my body look amazing," Kari corrected. "I can't believe you finished this in a week. You must have not slept at all."

"I had help. But any sleeplessness on my part was worth the result." Drew met her eyes in the mirror and smiled.

Perri whistled. "Kari, you look hot. My god, Andreas is going to pass out."

Earlier, Drew wove a thin metallic ribbon with the same black pearls sewn onto it through her hair, piled in a mass of curls on her head.

Perri, Jade and Anna all had on white silk dresses to the mid-calf with midnight blue bolero jackets to match. The dresses all had capped sleeves and pencil-straight skirts. Good thing that even at seventy years old, Anna was in top form. The bridesmaid dresses were as form-fitting as Kari's and showed quite a bit of skin.

Kari had chosen a bouquet of white roses, a midnight blue ribbon holding them together. She breathed in their heady scent to center herself and her emotions.

Jade stood behind her. "I'm proud to have you as a daughter. I have something for you. A bridal gift." She reached up and Kari felt the weight of each dangling pear-shaped diamond earring as Jade placed them in each ear.

"Oh my goodness. They're beautiful." She leaned back into her mother-in-law.

"Perri has a pair too. Hers have pearls." Jade nodded at Perri, who showed that she was wearing them. "The pearls belonged to my mother and the diamonds to Tomas' mother. I wanted to keep them in the family."

"Okay, all of this has to stop or I'll cry and smudge the makeup job Perri worked on for an hour," Kari said, laughing. "Let's rock. Can someone get Jack for me?"

The ceremony itself was going to be held in the great room. It seemed a shame not to be able to come down that dramatic staircase. Then they'd move to the tent in the yard for the reception.

"Ready? Oh wow, honey, you look breathtaking," Jack said as he walked inside the room.

Jack liked Andreas' family. Despite himself he was charmed by them and their obvious love for his sister. His sister who looked wicked beautiful.

"Thanks. You too. You're made for wearing tuxedos, babe."

Jade, Perri and Anna filed out and Kari could hear the music start as they went downstairs on the arms of Tomas, Sean and Devon.

"Ready?"

"You betcha. Thanks for being here."

"Wouldn't be anywhere else." They walked out onto the landing. Phillip saw them and gave the signal to the string quartet to play the bridal march. Giving her the thumbs-up, he grinned one last time before scrambling downstairs quickly.

When Kari and Jack reached the top of the stairs the assembled guests stood and turned to take her in. She smiled at a few overheard gasps and looked to Andreas, whose mouth hung open in shock. They took the stairs regally and carefully…she was wearing some pretty high heels after all.

Jack announced to the crowd that he was happy to share his sister with a man like Andreas and went to sit down. Kari joined Andreas before the judge, who was officiating. The ceremony was quick, simple and over far too fast.

"I would like to present Kari and Andreas Phinney," the judge said to the crowd, who stood up and whooped, howled—although, thank god, not so wolflike—and cheered.

The reception was a dream. Tiny white lights lit up all the trees that bordered the lake. The tent was nice and warm inside. There was dancing and a band and the food and drink were delicious.

At nearly two, Kari and Andreas finally escaped back into the house. Many of the Pack had gone on a run with the visiting wolves but knew that there were humans about and had gone a few miles into the forest before shifting and had promised not to come back naked.

On the way into the house, Henry and Luna approached and gave hugs and kisses to them both. Kari was a bit taken aback to see Luna's more-than-friendly kiss right on Andreas' lips. She shook it off, thinking it was some Pack thing.

Once inside the house, Andreas practically picked her up and ran up the stairs to their room. When the door closed behind him, Andreas leaned back against it, sighing in exhaustion. He locked it and looked his wife over, giving her a slow, sexy perusal.

Heat flared inside her as it always did when she became the object of his attention in such a way. Her heart began to pound and a flush worked its way up her body.

"I've wanted to jump you all night. That dress is sinfully gorgeous. I don't think I've ever seen a more beautiful and sexy woman," he whispered as reached back to unzip her.

"Drew outdid himself. I heard at least fifteen people ask him for his card. He's an artist." Her voice was breathy as his fingertips brushed her spine.

"You make a fine canvas then." Warm hands skimmed up her shoulders and reversed and the dress slid off and pooled at her feet. She was wearing a silk thong in the same color as the dress. He circled her like the predator he was. "Mmmm."

She quirked up a corner of her mouth and swallowed past the lump of desire. "Who'd have thought they made tuxedos in big bad wolf size. If we're passing out compliments I must tell you that all of your golden hair falling down on those wide shoulders encased in that black tuxedo jacket—very sexy." Bending over to give him the nicest view, she picked up her dress and gently placed it over the back of a chair before turning back to face him. Something about being nearly naked while he was still dressed drove a wave of sharp heat through her. Hunger for him.

The click, click, click of her heels on the hardwood floors echoed in the room against their breathing and the muted sounds of celebration outside and all over the property.

Reaching him, she pushed the jacket from his wide shoulders, tossing it alongside the dress. "I have to tell you I was distracted all night, every time you took the jacket off because I could see that spectacular ass, not to mention the hard-on. Were you hard all night, Andreas?"

"Each time I scented you, touched you, heard you or thought about you." His scent rose from his skin as he heated. Leaning in to take a deep breath, she untucked his shirt and began to unbutton it slowly. Her lips brushed over each new inch of flesh exposed as she unmoored each button.

She took her time. The night was theirs. No one would bother them. It was just about the two of them and no one else.

The shirt followed the jacket and she paused to look at his bare upper body. He stood here, proud and a bit arrogant as she took him in, and she grinned at him. "Cocky."

"You like what you see, little wolf?"

"Oh yes. Yes I do, Andreas. Your body is beautiful and hard and very, very masculine." She dragged her nails lightly down his chest and he hissed as she abraded his nipples and lower abdomen the way she'd come to discover he liked so much.

Reaching down, she skimmed her fingertips just beneath the waistband of his pants. "Now this is the part I like best," she murmured as she unbuckled, unbuttoned and unzipped and gave a hearty "ooh!" when his cock sprang into her hands.

"It would seem I have a bounty of blessings this day," she said as the pants fell down his legs and he stepped out of them, pulling off his socks so that he stood there gloriously naked to her gaze. Nope, no complaints there!

"I don't think I'll ever get over the shock of…well, of you. I mean, my god, Andreas, you're every woman's dream." She quirked up a smile. "It's hard to believe you're mine."

"Well, I am. And the feeling is more than mutual." His words were playful but what passed between them was powerful.

His lips found hers and took them in a way only he knew how to do. His kiss seared her, his lips dominated and possessed her even as they celebrated and cherished. His taste rushed through her as his tongue slid against hers seductively. The way he kissed her left her no place to hide, she was exposed completely to him and he took every bit she had to offer and gave as much.

When he broke away, her hand went to her lips, still tingling from his taste, swollen from their kiss. "You're so good at that."

He chuckled. "Among other things, I hope."

She still had her shoes, a spiky pair of strappy heels that showed off her pretty red painted toenails, and the thong on. "Off or on?" she asked with a saucy smile.

"Shoes on. Thong... Well, I'll get that," he said, going to his knees in front of her. He rubbed his face along her belly. His hands caressed her sides, her thighs, her breasts, coming to rest on her hips. He pressed his face to her pussy and breathed in deeply before hooking his thumbs around the waist of the thong and slowly pulling it down. She put her hand on his shoulder and felt the muscles ripple as he helped her to step out of it.

Looking up at her, he growled, low and sex-laden. "My god, you look like sex in heels."

Backing her up against the door, he used his shoulders to nudge her thighs wider. "Mmm. You're ready for me." His fingers parted her to his gaze. Drawing a fingertip through the folds of her pussy, he pulled her honey up and around her clit, bringing a gasp of pleasure from her lips. Followed by a moan when he brought that finger to his mouth and tasted her, eyes closing as if she were divine.

Those amber eyes opened and looked up into hers. "You. Taste. So. Good. I want more, Kari. I'm going to take it. But you're going to put your arms above your head and hold them there. If you move I'll stop and we don't want that, do we?"

She had no words as he looked back to her pussy again, still open to him. She reached up and grabbed the top of the doorjamb.

He knelt there for several long moments just looking at her. "So beautiful here. Glistening, swollen." Fingertips traced through warm wet flesh, causing her to moan and arch into him.

Bringing one of her thighs up onto his shoulder, he leaned in to taste her. Slowly and single-mindedly he ran his tongue over her sensitive pussy. The wet slide against her slick folds was so good it was almost too much. His mouth loved her gentle and then rough, he was hard and then soft. Bringing her to the very edge, he'd then back off only to start over once she'd stepped back from climax.

Her hands gripped the door. In desperation she whimpered so he looked up at her. "If you don't let me come right now I'm going to explode," she pleaded through gritted teeth.

He chuckled, his warm breath teasing her exposed flesh. "I want you to remember that only I can make you feel this way. Do you know how much I love going down on you? How much I love your taste on my tongue, your honey scalding my lips? Your scent all around me? If I ate you ten times a day it wouldn't be enough. You're mine, Kari."

"Oh Andreas," she sighed, "you do say the best things. Now shut up and get back to work," she said teasingly.

And he did, leaning in and finishing her using fingers, lips, teeth and tongue to push her over not once but twice, until she trembled so badly that only his strength kept her from sliding into a puddle on their floor.

He stood up, her thigh moving to the crook of his arm as he lifted her off her feet, plunging into her in one hard stroke. Arching her back to receive more of him, she knocked the back of her head into the door, hard. She gasped out his name and he moved, one hand holding her ass for leverage as she wrapped her free leg around his waist. He moved the other leg to join it and she locked ankles at his back.

"Oh fuck," he gasped, stilling for a moment. She felt the throb, throb, throb of his cock seated deep inside her. "Just a minute."

Her hands burrowed through his hair and she rained small kisses over his face until he pushed orgasm back enough to begin to fuck her in deep, feral digs.

Each thrust into her body she cried out. He moaned as her nails dug into his shoulders.

"More, oh god, more. Andreas, fuck me deeper. Harder. I need to feel you as deep as possible. I need it."

"Little wolf, I'd climb into your pussy if I could you feel so fucking good around me. I love the way your inner walls clutch at me, hold me like you can't bear to let me go. I love to see you wild for my cock. My sweet woman, all wild and begging for it. God, watching you cock-drunk is the hottest thing I've ever seen."

They made so much noise at the door that Laurent knocked, asking if everyone was okay.

"Go away!" Andreas yelled, continuing to thrust into her.

She heard Laurent's laughter as he went back into his room next door.

"Oh. Yes. Right there. That's it. My god." His onslaught brought a string of sounds deep from her gut. She said things she was pretty sure she'd never even *thought* before much less said aloud to a lover. He brought out her deepest, darkest passion and unleashed her every whim.

He fucked her like a man possessed as she writhed in his arms, begging for more, demanding it. Her back against the door made her feel submissive, caged by him, controlled. It thrilled her.

"Kari, little wolf. You're so hot, so tight. You. Feel. So. Good. I'm so very close. I want you to come with me."

Adjusting herself in his arms, she ground her clit over his cock each time he pressed himself into her body. The friction began to build. Electric shocks of her climax began to spark through her body as they began to race toward orgasm.

His name screamed from her throat as she came, and seconds later he roared. He pinned her then to the door and she felt each jerk of his cock as he came within her. Finally they collapsed onto the floor, laughing, muscles twitching.

* * * * *

Breakfast the next morning was almost as fun as the reception. There were still a lot of people there at the lodge. Anna happily catered to Jack, who quite easily pulled her under his spell. Sean was there with his new girlfriend Emma, who seemed to like him a heck of a lot. The kids ran around, playing with cars and trains and balls until James and Ryan set up an obstacle course on the front lawn and the kids all ran out to try it.

When Kari and Andreas came down, Laurent saw them and his face broke into a gigantic grin. Kari, of course, didn't have the time to do anything herself before Anna had set a cup of coffee and a heaping plate of pancakes before her.

"I didn't get much sleep last night," Laurent said, smiling into his cup and Kari groaned.

"Why's that?" Skye asked, a hint of amusement in his eyes.

"From all the groaning, screaming and thumping next door. I wish I'd had earplugs. I did however learn what Andreas' name sounds like when screamed, moaned and being ordered around."

Kari put her face down on the table and her hands up over her head. She'd never hear the end of it.

"Ordered around? Do tell," Skye said, laughing.

Laurent proceeded, in detail, to describe just what she'd ordered Andreas to do.

Andreas tried not to laugh but Kari really was vocal in bed and Laurent was quite an accurate mimic.

The conversation went on for at least twenty minutes until even Jack was laughing.

"Okay, okay, enough!" she ordered, trying not to laugh herself. "I'd like to eat but before I do I have a few words for you, Laurent Cole. Paybacks are a bitch." She cut into her pancakes as they all made *I'm so scared* noises.

Later, Jack and Kari took a walk around the lake. He wanted to give her his thumbs-up over Andreas and his family but also to get her to tell him whatever it was that was being left unsaid.

"Well, you know I hate to admit I'm wrong. But in this case I'm happy to. Andreas is a great guy and it's pretty clear he worships you."

Relief lit Kari's face. "I'm so glad you like him! He's a good man, Jack."

"Not just him but his whole family. They all seem really nice. A bit touchy-feely but you know, whatever floats your boat."

"Why don't you tell me about what's going on with Alyssa?"

He took a deep breath and exhaled. "It's complicated. I'm ready to either move on to marriage or break it off. I don't see myself dating her for the next however many years. I want to be married, Kari. I'm twenty-seven, almost twenty-eight, and I want a family. On the other hand, she doesn't know what she wants. I understand she's got a kid to worry about, but you know, I've proven to her time and again that I'll put him first. I'm reliable with him. I want to make a life with them both. Love them both. Be their family."

"So what's her problem then?"

"She says she's not ready to be serious right now. She doesn't want to break up but she doesn't want to move to the next level either. We've been dating for a year now. I asked her to marry me and she balked. I asked her to move in and she balked. I don't know—I think at this stage that she likes the way things are and I don't see that changing. I care about her deeply. No. I love her. But I'm not willing to wait around for god knows how long when she doesn't even know if she wants me."

Kari squeezed his hand. "I'm sorry, Jack. She's a fool if she can't see how great you are."

"Kari, how would you feel if I moved out west? To Seattle or even to Star Lake?"

Kari stopped and grabbed both of his hands. "Are you serious? I'd love it. I miss you like crazy."

"When I was here when you were in the hospital I talked with a few folks I know at the Seattle PD. And one of my commanders at the Boston PD knows some people here in Star Lake. Small world, huh? Anyway, I talked to Carey last night and he seems to think that I could come on here or in one of the surrounding towns. The only thing holding me in Boston was Alyssa and since that looks like a bust, I'd like to be near you again."

She hugged him. "That would be so great." Kari wanted to tell him about her new life, about her new family but she had no idea how to broach the subject, so she remained silent. Thing was, she wasn't just a Pack member, she was an Alpha and their house was werewolf central. If Jack did move out there, she'd have to find a way to tell him.

"I'll start the ball rolling once I get back home. I thought I'd give it one last try with Alyssa and if she says no, I'll give notice."

Even as joy at the idea of Jack moving there swamped her, Kari felt a wave of dizziness hit. Overwhelmed, she staggered to the bushes and threw up.

Phillip ran over. "Kari? Are you all right?" Alarm sharpened his voice.

"Must be something she ate," Jack said, sounding puzzled at Phillip's strong reaction.

"I feel nauseated," she mumbled.

Phillip picked her up and carried her quickly toward the house. "Get Elaine. Now," he barked at Skye, who'd come running toward them.

"What the hell is going on? She just threw up. What aren't you telling me, Kari?"

Phillip looked down at him. "She was poisoned last week. It started like this."

"She was what?" Jack yelled and Kari started crying. She felt like crap and he was upset and she hadn't wanted him to know and now he had to know everything and she didn't know how she'd explain it.

"I'll explain later. Please." She pressed her face into Phillip's neck, breathing in his scent.

Phillip laid her down on her bed and went to get a washcloth from the bathroom. Elaine rushed in, followed by Andreas and Laurent.

"What the fuck is going on! Why didn't anyone tell me that Kari had been poisoned?" Jack demanded of them.

"I'll explain it all when we are sure she's okay." Elaine calmly but quickly moved him aside. "Kari, what's wrong?"

"I just felt very dizzy and nauseated. I threw up in the bushes. Phillip ran over and carried me back here. I'm feeling better now that I'm still. I don't have cramps like I did before. I just feel tired and nauseated."

"Have you felt this way at all before?" Elaine asked, using an ear thermometer to gauge her temperature.

"I felt butterflies yesterday but I thought it was because of the wedding. I've been tired but again, I thought it was because of the wedding and recovering from the poisoning."

"Your temperature is normal. You're not showing any of the signs from before."

"All of her food's been tasted," Andreas said and Kari turned a narrowed eye at him. He returned the look without guilt.

"What? I told you I didn't want that."

"I did it anyway. In the kitchens so no one knew but Anna, Gregory, Sean, Phillip and me."

"Bastard," Kari said although she was relieved that she probably hadn't been poisoned. She burst into tears. "How could you lie to me?"

Andreas quickly came to her side and pulled her into his arms, looking confused. Kari was not a woman given to tears like that. Being pissed off, sure. Yelling, hell yes, but not tears for no real reason.

"Kari…well, never mind." Elaine turned to everyone else. "I'd like to talk with Kari alone please. You can all wait outside." She ushered them all out over Andreas' strident protests and Jack's glowering insistence that someone tell him what was going on.

Once they were alone, Elaine turned back to Kari. "How long have you felt moody?"

"My whole life?" She snorted and Elaine laughed. "I don't know, about three or four days."

"Coinciding with the tiredness and the nausea?"

"Yeah. What, do you think I'm pregnant?" Kari snorted with amusement.

"Yes, as a matter of fact I do," Elaine said and pulled out a needle stick and a test paper from her medical bag.

Kari sat up. "What? I've only been having sex with Andreas for a little over a week. Before that I hadn't had intercourse for a month. I had a period in between."

"Kari, werewolves have a different physiology. Our pregnancies mature very quickly. We have four-month gestations. You'd start feeling the symptoms of morning sickness within two days of fertilization of the egg. Tell me, where were you in your cycle before this last week? Count from after the poisoning because I think if you had been pregnant that would have caused a miscarriage."

"Um, I had my period a few days before Michael bit me."

"Twenty-eight-day cycle?"

"Yes. Oh my god, I ovulated this last week."

"Let me take some blood from you. We can't just pee on a stick like human women can. About ten years ago a test strip for human-wolf growth hormones was developed. The werewolf version of the home pregnancy test." Efficiently, she used the needle stick and pressed Kari's finger to the test paper.

Elaine smiled as the paper turned bright blue. "Kari, you're pregnant. You're bearing the next generation of Alphas for Cherchez." She grabbed the bleeding finger, cleaned it again with an alcohol swab and put a Band-Aid on it.

"Oh my god! I'm pregnant?" Kari lay there, stunned.

Elaine looked at her and sat down next to her on the bed. "Yes. Are you okay with that? I mean, I know you started out on shaky ground about the whole idea."

"I am. I really am. I mean, I know what condoms are. I'm a big girl. I knew this might happen, although not this soon. I was human not too long ago, this is all new to me." Kari smiled, tears flowing again. "I'm going to have a baby in four months? It'll be a baby right, not a puppy?"

Elaine laughed. "I asked that same thing! Yes, a baby. Our young can't transform until they hit puberty. They do mature at a much quicker rate, though. Your baby will be walking by six months, for instance."

"Oh my goodness. How about prenatal care? Who do I see for that?"

"I'm it. Don't worry. I've done it several times before. I delivered Josh and Julia as a matter of fact. I can come here for a lot of it but you'll have to come to Seattle to see me at the hospital for other things. The ultrasound, for instance. If you have a good pregnancy there's no reason you can't deliver here at home. Our births are notoriously easy and fast. It's a big plus, quick gestation and quick deliveries. Still hurts like hell, but it's much less than a mother birthing a human baby deals with."

Andreas began pounding on the door, demanding to know what was happening.

Elaine went toward the door. "He's a handsome one but I don't envy you having to deal with him."

Kari laughed. "Yeah. He's worth it but still a pain in the ass."

"I'd wager he'll be hard to manage while you're pregnant."

Kari heaved a sigh. "Yeah. Well."

Laughing, Elaine stopped and made a note to herself. "I'll get you some special prenatal vitamins. You'll have to eat even more than you do now. We can talk more about it later. Shall I tell them?"

"No. I want to tell Andreas first. Privately. Tell everyone else to wait downstairs. I'll have to explain it all to my brother. Oh god, won't that be fun." She rolled her eyes. "JUST A MINUTE!" she yelled to Andreas, who stopped pounding.

Elaine nodded and opened the door. "Just you, Andreas. Everyone else downstairs," Elaine ordered as she closed the door behind Andreas.

"Baby? Are you okay?" He rushed to her, pulling her into his arms.

"Yeah, we're fine," she said, waiting for him to catch it.

"What is it? We?"

"I'm pregnant."

"You're what?" The biggest grin she'd ever seen broke out over his face and he howled so loud she had to cover her ears. He picked her up and danced her around the room until she begged him to put her down.

"I'm nauseated enough as it is, don't spin me." Chastened, he carefully put her down.

"Oh thank you," he said, kissing her cheeks, her lips.

"Thank you? For what?"

"For being okay and not poisoned. For bearing our child, the future king." He beamed. "We have to tell everyone." He rushed toward the door.

"Wait!" she ordered and he stopped. "I have to tell Jack everything now. He knows about the poisoning. He'll know it's impossible for a woman to be showing symptoms just a few days after conception, especially after being poisoned. He's planning on moving out here. He'll have to be told anyway so let's do it now.

"But like me, he'll need proof. So why don't we go down there. Explain it all and then you'll need to shift to show him. Or Skye or Phillip. Sean and Emma left, right? No more humans here now?"

He sighed, clearly impatient and wanting to shout the news to all and sundry. "Okay. You're right." He started to pick her up.

"What are you doing?" She slapped his hands away and stood up on her own.

"You need to rest. I'll take care of you. You don't have to lift a finger until our son arrives."

"Could be a daughter and that would be just as good. I don't want any of this pro-boy nonsense around me. I'm already annoyed with this whole emphasis on having a son, as if daughters don't matter. Our children will be just as loved and important if they're female."

He kneeled down and nuzzled her stomach. "Of course. A daughter bearing your beautiful eyes and curls will be heavenly."

"Fine, you pass. And I'm pregnant, not dying. I can do my own walking, thank you very much. Elaine said that I'd need to eat more and that I could even have the baby here if the pregnancy went okay. I don't need to be treated like an invalid."

They walked downstairs and everyone who was left had gathered in the great room looking nervous. Except for Jack, who looked furious as well.

"I'm fine. Before I say anything else I need to talk to Jack for a second." She went to sit next to her brother, pushing Skye bodily out of the way. He'd started to nuzzle into her side when Andreas came and picked him up and took his place.

Disgruntled, Skye settled in at her feet. Jack raised his eyebrows at that.

She sighed. "This is going to sound completely outrageous, but please hold on until the end. I wasn't attacked by a dog in Seattle, I was attacked by Michael." She motioned toward Michael, who sat across the room. "Elaine checked me out of the hospital, drugged me and brought me here. They told me that I'd been attacked by a werewolf and that I was going to change into one at the full moon on that Saturday. Not only that but I was a Mate to their king, and as such, I'd be queen of their Pack."

Jack's brows rose with alarm but she waved at him to stay quiet.

She quickly sketched out the details of her attempted escape and of Skye changing. His eyes widened when she described the Ascension and the fight with Johanna. And as non-dramatically as she could, she filled him in on the poisoning, explaining the merits of werewolf biology.

She grabbed his hand and took in his pale face. He looked as if he wanted to run out the door.

"Kari, honey, why don't you come with me? We can get you some help," he said softly, eyes darting around the room. She could tell he was calculating his odds of getting her out of there alive if the big guys decided to try and stop him.

"I told Andreas that you wouldn't believe it unless you saw it. You're like me."

"Kari, it's safe for you to change. Perhaps seeing *you* do it would help Jack." Elaine discreetly avoided mentioning the pregnancy.

"Jack, sit there please. I'm going to show you something amazing." Jack just stared at her as she stood up and began to pull off her clothes.

"Kari, you're in a room full of people!"

"Just give me a second," she replied, pulling off her underwear and bra. Skye moved the coffee table back to give her space to change. She got down on all fours and closed her eyes. Letting her human self fall away, she freed her wolf to come to the surface, and when she looked up into Jack's eyes she did it as a wolf.

"Oh holy crap," Jack whispered, staring at her with his mouth open in shock

She approached him and touched his hand with her cool nose and licked it. Hesitantly at first, he touched her head, running a hand through her fur, over her ear.

"It's true. I thought werewolves walked on two legs and attacked people. Hell, I thought they were mythological."

Andreas chuckled. "Only in the movies. We don't attack people. We try to keep our runs in the safety of the wilderness. We don't walk on two legs unless we're in human form. And as you can see by your beautiful sister, we aren't mythological."

"Are you all werewolves then?" Jack looked around the room warily.

"Yes, everyone but you," Andreas answered.

Jack looked around, feeling slightly panicked but knowing that Kari would never allow him to come to harm.

Kari moved away from him, transforming back into her human form, getting dressed. "Bummer," Skye said under his breath and Andreas sent him an annoyed glare.

She came back to sit next to Jack. "So I'm a werewolf. I'm sorry I worried you. It's not like I could have explained it over the phone or anything."

"Well, you've never done anything halfway. And I knew you were hiding something!" he said, satisfied that his intuition was right. Suddenly he stopped and narrowed his eyes at Andreas. "You told me you didn't attack people but Kari said Michael attacked her."

Andreas colored at that. "Yes, you're right. Michael lost control. It wasn't meant to happen that way. It's not our custom to change people like that. I knew Kari was my Mate, that our biologies were meant to be mated, but I wanted to approach her in human form first. Michael knows he was wrong and he was reprimanded. Kari has forgiven him, I hope you can too."

"And the poisoner, what happened to him or her?"

"We haven't caught them. We do know it was one of our Pack. We know it was administered through a pitcher of water left at their bedside but the pitcher got washed before we knew she'd been poisoned. We're on it. I swear to you we won't fail Kari," Phillip said.

"So…what's wrong then? Why are you sick?" Jack asked, turning back to face Kari.

"No, I'm not sick. I'm pregnant," Kari said, smiling, and the entire room erupted into auditory chaos.

"Pregnant? This fast?"

"Apparently werewolf pregnancies only last four months and move quicker all the way around." She smiled at him. "See, you coming out here would be even better now, Uncle Jack."

"This is a lot to take in. You're a millionaire, married and a werewolf who's now bearing my niece or nephew. I can see I need to be around to keep you out of trouble," he said into her ear.

Andreas strutted around like the king he was, the males clapping him on the back. Jade pushed her way past everyone and practically lunged at Kari. "Congratulations! A grandchild. Oh how I've waited for this day."

Kari felt a twinge of sadness for Perri and Devon, whose chances at a biological child had been destroyed by a drunk driver two years before. However, Perri came and hugged her tightly. "I'm so happy for you. I'm gonna be an aunt!" she said happily.

Anna came out, ordering everyone out of her path, and handed Kari a big glass of milk. "Drink it now, there's lots more where that came from." She beamed.

"Damn," the wolf who hated Kari mumbled at the announcement while smiling broadly.

Chapter Eleven

Kari walked out of the bathroom. "My robe is too small now." She tossed aside the red wolf robe that Andreas had given her on her transformation eve.

Approaching her, Andreas ran his hands over her swollen belly and felt the baby kick. At three months along, the skin of her belly was stretched tight around the life inside her.

They'd come to Seattle to get an ultrasound at Elaine's office. They'd spent the night in Seattle, at the Four Seasons, so she wouldn't have to get up early to drive into the city for their appointment.

It paid to have a talented clothing designer in the Pack. Drew kept her supplied with beautiful and colorful maternity clothing. She put on one of the dresses, a wrap that tied just under the bust.

"You're beautiful, little wolf," he growled and circled her.

"We don't have time for that," she warned him with a laugh but loved the way he made her feel so beautiful and desired.

Ever since she'd started showing, Andreas couldn't get enough of her. They were still having sex two and three times a day. Her pregnant body was the sexiest thing he'd ever seen. She was his wife, bearing his child. It made him hard all over just thinking about it.

He laughed and dropped a kiss at the nape of her neck, running his tongue up to her ear. Moaning, she leaned her body back into his. "Stop it now, don't tempt me! We only have twenty minutes to get there and we just had sex forty-five minutes ago. Over there, on the chaise by the window?

Remember? I was on top? You'll have to wait until we get home tonight. Remember that Jack is coming over for dinner."

Jack had just moved to Star Lake the month before. He was in the process of interviewing with the local Star Lake Police Department and also in North Bend. Whichever choice he made, she was just happy to have him around. Being so close again was good for both of them. Alyssa didn't know what she was missing.

Andreas sighed dramatically and stepped back. "Okay, let's get going. Phillip's bringing the car around."

Since she'd announced the pregnancy they'd been even more vigilant with her. Phillip was with her twenty-four hours a day and she knew they still tasted her food and drinks. Phillip actually slept on a futon that they'd moved to the hallway outside of their bedroom door, trading shifts with Skye. Laurent was still next door but was moving out that morning because they were making his room into the nursery.

They arrived at Elaine's office with no time to spare and when her name was called, Phillip started to wait in the hallway. But Kari thought a moment and reached out to touch his arm.

"Phillip, would you like to be in the room when Elaine does the ultrasound? You want to be there when we see the baby for the first time?"

Phillip blushed. "Are you serious? I'd love to. If that's okay with you," he asked Andreas.

"We'd love to share this with you." Andreas never ceased to be amazed at how loving and giving Kari was. Phillip was like a brother to him and it touched him that she seemed to care about him as much as Andreas did.

After Kari changed into a short robe that opened in the front, Andreas helped her up onto the table where she lay on her back. "This is warm," Elaine warned and squirted goo on her belly. "Okay, let's see our new baby. Just watch the screen." She indicated the black-and-white monitor to their right.

"Oh there we go," she said, running the Doppler device over Kari's belly. Kari's eyes filled with tears as she saw the tiny arms and legs of their child. "Do you want to know the gender?"

"Yes," Kari said. She and Andreas had argued about it. He wanted to know and she didn't. So that morning they'd ended up tossing a coin and he'd won.

"Oh!" Elaine said.

"What?" Andreas and Kari both said, alarmed.

"Well look here. *Another* set of arms and legs. You have two babies in there, *reine*. You're having twins," Elaine exclaimed.

"What?" Kari felt faint.

"Right here." Elaine pointed at the screen and yes, there were two sets of arms and legs.

"Oh my goodness. I'm having *two* babies?" Kari said wondrously.

"Yes. A boy, this one." She pointed to the baby on the left. "And a girl, right here." She pointed to the baby on the right.

Andreas stared at the monitor, emotion shining in his eyes. "Two. A boy and a girl. Oh Kari. You're so amazing."

"Hey, big boy, it's not like it was my choice or anything."

"Twins. The first set of twins in at least a hundred years," Elaine said.

"I definitely deserve pie," Kari said. She craned her head back to see Phillip, who was staring at her belly with a goofy smile. "What do you think, Uncle Phillip?"

He leaned toward her and kissed her temple tenderly. "I think you're magnificent. You definitely deserve pie. If Andreas wasn't so much bigger than me, I'd kick his ass and steal you away."

Kari laughed and the babies moved. "They respond to your voice. To the sound of your laughter. They'll know you when they're born," Elaine said and Andreas leaned down and spoke to her belly.

"Daddy loves you two." And they moved toward the sound of his voice.

Elaine stood back and wiped the goop off her belly, allowing Kari to close the robe. "I've printed out some pictures of the ultrasound. Jade and Tomas will want to see and I know Jack will too." She handed them to Andreas while Phillip helped Kari down off the table.

"You're doing well. They're both very good-sized for being twins. I'll be by this weekend to check you. You're only three weeks from your due date so I want you to stay near home from now on."

"You still think it's safe to have them at home?"

"Yes. Twins are harder but as I said, birth is a fairly quick process for us. I'll be there and Ellen is coming too so you'll have two doctors on hand. Plus Anna has been present for the birth of many children in the Pack. It'll be fine."

"Okay. If you say so." She put her dress back on, not bothering to go into the dressing room. They'd all seen her naked before. Phillip lovingly caressed her belly and went out into the hallway first, making sure they were safe.

"Steal her away. I think not." Andreas bumped past Phillip and snorted in amusement. Phillip winked at Kari and she laughed.

"Oh hi, Andreas." Henry and Luna came around the corner. Luna, as always, looked a bit too happy to see Andreas and Kari bristled. *Pregnancy hormones.*

Andreas smiled at them both and pulled Kari in front of him and back into his body. Immediately his hands spanned her belly. "Hello, you two."

"Wow, Kari, you're really looking big," Luna said in that way that sounded like it was an innocent comment but any woman could tell was a dig.

Andreas laughed, "Compared to what? She's still a sprite and more beautiful than ever."

The dig had gone completely over his head and Kari narrowed her eyes at the other woman. "Well, pregnancy has a tendency to do that. Thankfully Andreas seems to find it sexy." *Take that!*

"I'll say. I can't keep my hands off her." Andreas nuzzled into her neck, hands caressing her stomach.

Kari could have sworn that Luna smirked. She'd have to run it by Perri to see what she thought.

"What brings you two all the way out here?" Henry asked. "Everything's okay, right?"

"Oh yes. We had our ultrasound today." Andreas didn't seem to want to tell them about the twins. She thought that it was probably that Jade would kill them if he told anyone but her first.

"Oh great! Do you know the gender?"

"It's a secret until we announce it at dinner this weekend. You two coming out?" Andreas asked teasingly.

"We will now for sure." Henry laughed. "We'll see you Saturday then."

"Bye, you two," Kari said as they swept past them, Phillip leading the way.

Driving back to Star Lake, Kari happily ate her double scoop of chocolate chocolate chip and finally asked Andreas about Luna.

"Andreas, what's Luna's story anyway?"

"What do you mean?"

"She seems…I don't know…less than friendly to me sometimes."

"Really? I hadn't noticed. What do you mean?"

"The comment about me being big just now. It was a total dig."

"I'm sure she didn't mean it that way."

"Ugh. Men are so dumb sometimes. Of course she meant it that way. If I'd have said it, I'd have meant it that way. It goes against the woman's code. You don't tell another woman something like that unless you mean to insult her. It's the way we operate. We take comments that could be perceived as casual, even compliments, and we turn them into subtle insults. It's an art."

Phillip laughed at that.

"I'm serious. And why is she always kissing you on the lips? None of the other females do that."

"Phillip kisses you on the lips," Andreas said.

"Yes, a peck, and I'm with him twenty-four hours a day and he is so totally not on the make. There's a difference."

"Hmph."

"Are you saying it bothers you when Phillip gives me a peck on the lips? Usually as I'm leaving our bedroom? Pregnant with your children?"

"No. It doesn't bother me. It makes me happy that the Pack loves and respects you. I'm just saying that it's not a big deal when Luna kisses me."

"Is she like your sister? 'Cause Perri doesn't kiss you on the lips like that. She gives you a peck."

"Kari, is this one of those conversations that men can't win, no matter what they say? If so, tell me now so I can apologize already and we can avoid the inevitable agony to come."

Her eyebrows shot up and she snorted and turned to look out the window. Butthead.

* * * * *

When they walked into the lodge, Sean was there already, as were Skye, Jack, Ryan and Laurent. All waiting to hear the gender. Andreas held out his hands to silence the tide of questions. "Wait. Let me get *Maman* on the speakerphone. Someone go get Anna."

Kari sat down on the couch only to have four different men get her a pillow for the small of her back, a throw for her legs and a glass of milk. Jack took off her shoes and rubbed her feet. She smiled. *Life was good.*

Anna came into the room with a slice of banana nut bread to go with the milk. *Even better.*

"Okay, I've got *Maman* and Dad on one line and Devon and Perri on the other. Kari, do the honors."

Kari said in a clear, loud voice, "It's a boy." And over the excited talk, "*And* it's a girl too. We're having twins."

"*Oh my god!*" Jade exclaimed over the phone.

"It's a good thing I cleared out the nursery this morning. We need to go back and get a new crib and bassinet," Laurent said.

"I'm taking Friday off and coming early," Perri said.

"I got so caught up in the moment I forgot you were still on the second line. Sorry!" Kari reached for the phone with a grunt and Skye jumped up to hand it to her. "I need to talk to you about something but it can wait until you get here. I need a woman's opinion," she said in a low voice once they were on the line alone.

"Oh god, I can't wait." Perri laughed. "I'm going to die of curiosity before then. Give me a hint."

"I can't. I need to tell you when there aren't ten people around. It's not earth-shattering or anything." She continued to keep her voice down and sound casual. If Skye heard he'd want to know what she was talking about.

"Oh the agony! Fine! Okay, I'll see you Friday morning. Love you," Perri said.

"You too and your dopey husband as well," Kari added before hanging up.

"Well, since we're all celebrating, I think it's time for my news now," Sean announced as he stood up.

"What?"

"Peaches, when you came to us, I realized just how much I'd been missing by not having a Mate all these years. I'd searched but not very hard. Little did I know that she was right under my nose."

"Emma!"

"Exactly." Sean smiled at her. "I realized it just after the wedding. We were standing on the porch and locked eyes and it never felt so right." He shrugged. "I've told her what I am and I've asked her to marry me. We looked into it and she's got some wolf in her gene pool. She's agreed to the change and I'd like to officially request a spot for her in the Pack."

"Oh wow, that's so wonderful. Emma is the coolest. She's good for you, Sean," Kari said. "You have my vote, if that matters at all. I have no idea how this works."

"Well, it does matter. You're Alpha of this Clan, Kari." Andreas walked forward and touched Sean's chest, over his heart. "I'd be honored to have your Mate in Cherchez Clan. Make her, Sean. Bring her over and we'll celebrate at the next full moon."

"There's more. She and I would like to live here and run a clinic in town. Star Lake has no mental health services at all and with only one doctor, we could really use another. Plus, having a doctor here for our own purposes would be ideal."

Kari tried to get up to hug Sean but couldn't get off the couch. Grinning, Skye helped her to her feet. She walked over to Sean and hugged him tightly. "I'm so happy for you both. I'd love to have you both here all of the time. Thank god the next full moon is after my due date. I can barely walk now, I can't imagine running at this size. Someone would have to stay human and drag me in a wagon."

Andreas laughed and Jade was still on the speakerphone and crying. "So much good news in one day!"

"Oof," Kari said after she reached around to hang up the phone.

"What is it?" Laurent asked, alarmed. Taking his hand, she placed it on her belly where the babies kicked her ribs with abandon. His eyes widened. "Oh, that's them."

"Yeah, frick and frack."

Skye came over and held out his hand, asking to touch as well. She guided him to where her daughter was.

"Wow. That must really hurt," he said, awe replacing his usual glib manner.

"Yeah, it's no picnic. All of these months I've been saying that it felt like there were eight arms and legs in here, turns out I was right. But I'm not really complaining, it's pretty wonderful."

The phone rang and she picked it up. *"I hope your bastard baby dies!"* a voice rasped and hung up.

Kari gasped, dropping the phone, hands flying up protectively over her stomach.

Andreas rushed over. "What? Kari, what is it?"

"Star 69! Do it!" she yelled.

"It's a blocked number," Skye said. "What did they say, Kari?"

"They said, *I hope your bastard baby dies*." Tears ran down her face as shock rushed through her that anyone would wish her babies harm.

Andreas roared with anger, slamming a fist down and shattering the oak coffee table. The empty milk glass flew along with the plate. Making a visible effort to rein his anger in, he came to her, still shaking with rage. She went willingly into his arms and breathed him in.

They were all quiet for a few minutes, huddling around Kari and Andreas. "Why, Andreas? Why would someone hate me that much? That they'd wish our babies harm?"

"I don't know, Kari. I don't know. But they won't. I promise you no harm will come to our children."

Sean and Skye leaned forward. "We promise you too."

"And me," Jack added.

"Me too," Ryan said and Laurent growled with barely restrained rage.

After Anna bullied Kari into eating dinner and drinking some decaf tea, Phillip and Ryan took Kari up to bed. Phillip took a post inside the room, stretching out on the chaise lounge, and Ryan on the futon outside the door.

Downstairs, Andreas paced in his study while Laurent, Jack and Sean looked on. "This must stop."

"Three months ago you offered to change me. I'd like to take you up on that now," Jack said. "I can protect her better from inside the Pack. I'll be stronger and faster. The threat is from one of your own, Andreas."

"I know. Are you sure? Do you want to talk with Kari first? Changing isn't very pleasant. The bites have to be deep and cause severe trauma. That means at least a few days in the hospital."

"I'm sure. Let me talk to Kari tomorrow. I want to do it before the babies come."

"Okay. I'd be pleased to welcome you into the Pack," Andreas said and the others agreed.

"First of all, there will be two guards on Kari at all times. Phillip and Ryan can be one team and then trade off every twelve with Skye and Laurent."

"No, Andreas. We have to assume that you're in danger too. You need a guard as well, that's my job. Call in Jon or Craig. We can trust them both, I'd stake my life on it," Laurent said.

Sean nodded. "He's right. But let me do it. I'll go ahead and leave my practice now. I'll move in here and change Emma when we change Jack. They can be in the clinic at the same time. We'll avoid the hospital if we can to keep suspicion down. I'll work with Skye. That'll give us Phillip, Ryan, Skye, Laurent and me here full-time for at least the next month. Jack and Carey will be around when they aren't working."

"What am I? An old woman?" Gregory asked, stalking into the room.

"Of course not, Gregory. I consider you as able as any of these males. You already have a job though. Running this place is important. Kari needs to feel that things are normal. The babies are coming. She'll want to be able to enjoy the air and the decks and gardens with them. That's your domain. If you see a threat, I have no doubt you'd take care of it," Andreas said and Gregory nodded, his honor satisfied. Even an eighty-year-old werewolf had his pride and wanted to be useful.

"Laurent has finally convinced me that a security system is necessary. I want the lodge wired up. Motion detectors, cameras, the whole thing. I want it as non-obtrusive as possible. I don't want it to feel like I live in a prison. Kari would hate it and we'd never hear the end of it."

Jack laughed. "True. Look, I've been offered a position here in town. I haven't told Kari yet because I didn't know if I wanted it or not. But with all of this going on, I think I'll accept. I can get a place in town and be nearby."

"You can have one of the cabins if you'd like. The one you're in now or any of the others. I know Kari would want you here but if you'd rather be in town, that's okay too."

"Really? Sometimes your generosity seems too good to be true. You treat my sister like a queen."

"Well, she is a queen," Andreas said with a shrug. "I'm quite serious. Jack, your sister is my world. I'd do anything for her."

"So why does someone want her dead?" Jack asked.

"Why indeed?"

"To weaken the Pack so they can take over maybe?" Skye said.

"If something happened to Kari, Andreas would crumble. Leave a vacuum."

"Well, what about Sean and Devon? They could take over, couldn't they?" Jack asked.

"Well, I could," Sean said matter-of-factly. "Devon couldn't because Perri can't bear children. It's part and parcel of the Alpha deal. You have to have children to succeed you. He could divorce Perri and have another wife who could bear children but she wouldn't be his Mate and something like that might divide the Pack instead of uniting it. But I was in the car with Kari when we took her to the hospital and the pitcher was put in the dishwasher. I could be working with an accomplice, of course." He shrugged his shoulders.

"If Sean wanted Kari dead, he could have killed her thirty times over by now. He's been alone with her and has been trusted with her in situations where he could have easily hurt her," Skye said.

"So let's work outward, then. Let's just assume that everyone here isn't guilty. The Inner Circle has had enough access to Kari that if one of them wanted her dead, it would have happened by now. That means Andreas, Laurent, Sean, Skye, Phillip, Ryan, Anna, Gregory and me. Who else can we positively eliminate? Let's not let *I'm pretty sure* rule here but *I'm positive and here's why*," Jack said, thinking like a cop.

Andreas sighed, running his hands through his hair. "I'm positive that my mother and father are innocent. I thought my mother was going to have a stroke when Kari was poisoned. They love her and me. My father's family has led this Clan for eighteen generations, even before we settled in the United States. There's no way he'd want anyone else running Cherchez. Devon has never wanted to run the Clan. He's got a nice life with Perri in Portland. He's not very involved with Pack governance. I can't see that he'd want to hurt Kari."

"That's assuming the reason is to take over. I don't think that that's a safe assumption. It's an idea. You're saying Devon is an *'I'm pretty sure'* and that's not good enough. I'm not trying to cause trouble or even to say that I think Devon did it. I don't actually. I just want us to be able to *positively* eliminate people and then move from there."

"My brother isn't a killer. He just isn't. He is just one of those guys who likes to cruise through life and not put out a lot of effort. He's got a good heart and he loves Kari. He loves our family. He loves his wife, and when other werewolves from an Alpha family might have gotten rid of a Mate who couldn't bear children, it doesn't appear to have affected his devotion to Perri at all," Sean said. "And Perri is easily Kari's closest friend. They're on the phone together constantly when Perri isn't here. Perri could have killed Kari if she'd wanted to, as well."

"But Perri's slept with Andreas. Jealousy could have been a motive," Laurent said, throwing the idea out there.

Jack raised an eyebrow but stayed quiet.

"Still, we get back to the point that she's been alone with Kari numerous times. If she'd wanted Kari hurt, she could have done it over and over by this point," Sean said.

"Okay, you win. Let's add Perri and Devon, Jade and Tomas to the list. That leaves a lot of people. We can add Elaine and Henry. If either one of them had wanted Kari dead, they could have killed her in the hospital when Michael first attacked her or even later, when she was in the hospital after the poisoning."

Andreas nodded. "Alex has wanted to challenge me for three years but hasn't. He's got motive."

"But not the opportunity. At least not for the poisoning. From what I understand, he wasn't near the shed, or wasn't seen there anyway."

"Wasn't seen being the operative phrase there," Sean said, and Skye nodded.

"Good point. That leaves Michael, Bert, Taryn, Pierre, James, Ellen, Drew, Carey, Alex, Jon, Craig, Luna and Peter. We know it wasn't Johanna."

"Let's think on it. I need to get up to Kari. You all get some rest. Kari's birthday dinner is Saturday and I want it to go smoothly." Andreas rose to go upstairs, Laurent in his wake.

* * * * *

Laurent went into his room and Andreas into his. He went to the chair where Phillip was stretched out and tapped him gently, waking him up and sending him out. He quickly shed his clothing and slid into bed, pulling Kari's small body into the shelter of his own. Helplessness seized his heart. Having something he wanted so much made him feel scared for the first time ever and he didn't like it one bit.

"Hi." Kari stirred drowsily, eyes still closed.

"Hey there, little wolf. How are my kids?" His hands moved to caress her stomach.

"Rambunctious. They haven't stopped moving all night. One will sleep and the other will wake up and play my ribs like the xylophone."

He laughed softly. "I love you, Kari. It's going to be all right."

"I love you too," she answered quietly, snuggling her ass into him.

"Hey, careful what you wake up there," he teased softly.

"I know what I'm doing." She turned in his arms to face him. "Everyone's up anyway." She pressed her stomach into his and he laughed, reaching down to capture her lips.

He broke away, as always slightly breathless after kissing her. "Elaine said we should take it easy now that you're approaching your due date."

"So you planning on being celibate for the next six weeks then? I can't have sex for a few weeks after the babies come." Deliberately, with as much sensuality as she could muster in her current state, she moved up his body to nibble on his ear.

"Are you purposely trying to tempt me?"

"Yes. Are you really that thick?" she laughed and he gasped as she licked down from his ear to take the tendons in the place where neck met shoulder between her teeth, his pulse beating sure against her tongue.

She let go after he'd growled low and sexy and she knew he'd relent and fuck her. She looked at him and smiled. "Anyway, Elaine said to be careful, not that we couldn't have sex."

"Well, not to brag, but I do have an exceptionally large cock so I'm worried that intercourse will hurt you now that the babies have dropped."

She laughed and nipped at a nipple. "Ego much?" Chuckling, she reached down and took the aforementioned large body part in her hands, and he thrust through her grasp slowly.

"God, the way you touch me." He groaned. "You first, you insatiable little wolf. Lie back. Let me show you ego," he said, laughing. He helped her to lie half on her side. He looked down at her body, ripe with sexuality and life, oh how she took his breath away. Gently palming her nipples, he drew his hands up, lightly circling his fingertips over the sensitive nipples. Unable to resist, he dipped his mouth to her, paying homage to breast and nipple with his lips and tongue while his roaming hands brushed over velvet-soft skin.

Her soft sighs and squirms ignited the spark of desire that had been smoldering. Now flames of ravenous want consumed him.

Nudging her thighs open, he moved to lie between them. She chuckled sexily. "Okay, that's good. I'm liking the direction this is moving in."

He laughed in response and opened her with his thumbs and stared. He couldn't get enough of her, of looking at her so intimately. The geography of her sex was different at this stage of pregnancy, everything swollen and extra sensitive. At this stage, her orgasms were much more intense and even the lightest of touches could set her off.

Tracing through the pretty, glistening furls of her pussy, he moved his mouth to her, kissing her passionately. Her breath caught and she arched into him. He loved how she felt under his mouth as he licked long and gentle over her over and over. Orgasm seized her body quickly and he lay, head on her thigh, and watched her face as she recovered.

She reached down caressed his jawline and up into his hair. "Thank you, oh big-cocked one. Now fuck me."

Startled laughter barked from his gut. "You can't ride me, sweetheart, I get too deep. I can't be on top of you. And when you're on all fours it drives me to distraction and it's hard not to pound into you."

A sexy smile curved her lips. "That's a lovely compliment, I must say. Lie on your side, facing me," she said and then backed up, arching her ass into him. He helped her put her thigh up on his and he gently slipped into her. Desire-slicked and superheated, her body welcomed his. His arm encircled her, hand over her breast. Instead of thrusting, they rocked together slowly, languorously until he climaxed. He fell asleep still inside of her.

Chapter Twelve

ꭍꭍ

"No, I can shower alone thank you very much," Kari told Phillip through clenched teeth. Andreas was downstairs on a conference call. Phillip and Skye were in her room and one of them was insisting that he be in the bathroom with her in case she fell.

"Kari, we've seen you naked dozens of times. You said yourself that your balance was off. Let one of us come in and help you."

"For god's sake, this is ridiculous! Other women do this every day and don't need two assistants to help."

"You aren't other women, Kari. I can go and ask Andreas about this, you know what he'll say," Skye said.

"I'll close my eyes," Phillip said.

She rolled hers. "It's not that. I'm not worried about either one of you copping a feel. Frankly, the state my body is in now, I'm even less worried. In any case, a girl just needs to be alone sometimes. And might I remind you that I'm an Alpha of this Pack as well so I don't care what Andreas says about it. And I don't particularly care for you threatening to tell on me like I'm a two-year-old either, Skye!"

"You put us in an uncomfortable position between you and Andreas, Kari. Are you saying you need alone time to get yourself off?" Skye asked matter-of-factly and she sighed.

"No, and I can't even believe I'm discussing this with you! But if I wanted to, I'd need to be alone. I just want to take a shower by myself. I can't handle not having a minute of time alone. For the last two days you guys have double-teamed me twenty-four hours a day. I have to sneak off to go pee for goodness' sake."

Sean came into the room. "What's going on?"

"Kari won't let one of us in the bathroom when she showers. She told me yesterday that she was having balance problems..."

And in the middle of the sentence she ducked into the bathroom, locking the door behind her. "I'll yell if I need anything! You're a superwolf, break the door down if you need to save me," she said, bending over to turn the water on, smiling at her small victory.

When she stepped out of the bathroom, all clean and changed—oh and having taken Skye's suggestion, her pregnant body couldn't seem to get enough sex—there were four sets of eyes frowning at her. Andreas had come up and stood, arms crossed, glaring at her.

She walked past them all and started down the stairs, Phillip coming to take her arm as she went.

"Kari, we discussed this," Andreas started as he followed her downstairs. Phillip pulled out her chair and she sat down heavily, continuing to ignore Andreas.

Andreas sat down and Kari felt the weight of his disapproval and it pissed her off. "Kari."

"Get off my back, Andreas. All of you get the fuck off my back. I know I need guards, I agree with that. But I draw the line at the bathroom door. I need some space! The toilet and the shower are two places I will not negotiate about. I already have two of you in my bedroom at night—severely curtailing my sex life I might add—one of you outside my door and another in a connecting room. We have a state-of-the-art security system, food tasters like some fucking French royalty. This sucks large. I don't like it and I'm doing as much as I can to bend and make it acceptable for everyone. You're the only one I'll accept in the bathroom during a shower. And if you are there you'd better get me off. Sorry to be vulgar but I don't care at this point. Werewolf pregnancy is making me one horny bitch and you guys are totally cutting in on my action. No one will be in the bathroom with me when I pee, period."

She said all of that while buttering and putting syrup on pancakes and eating two slices of bacon and some apple. She looked up to see them all trying not to laugh.

"What now?" she demanded.

"You're one horny bitch?" Skye repeated and they all burst out laughing.

"Laugh while you can, monkey boy," she muttered and kept eating. "I can't wait until you meet your Mate."

"Andreas, clearly you're not satisfying Kari. Do you need help with that? If so, I volunteer for that duty," Ryan said, trying not to laugh.

"She's a machine! I can only do so much. We're down to one position and I'm going to get carpal tunnel. My face is going numb," Andreas said.

"Hello? I'm right here!" She should have been embarrassed but she was so horny it was insane.

"Shall I show you how it's done?" Skye asked Andreas.

"Ha ha. Give me a week. I might just take you up on it."

She got up and walked out of the room. "You boys keep on playing. I'm going to call and see if the bedding is ready for the nursery."

Andreas got up and caught up with her. He tried to put his arm around her but she slapped him away. "Think again. Rest your face. Oh and your hand, you'll be needing it for yourself," she hissed at him.

"Sweetheart, I was only joking," he said in that neutral tone he'd adopted when she'd gotten pregnant and anything could set her off. "Let me show you how much I was just joking."

"Maybe I should let Ryan show me," she said, raising an eyebrow at him.

He growled at her. She could hear them laughing in the dining room and struggled not to snicker at the look on Andreas' face.

She darted around him and called the seamstress to see if the crib bedding was done. In the background she heard the door to the office close and smiled to herself.

Andreas came to her, standing at her back, kissing the back of her neck as his nimble fingers pulled up the hem of her dress.

She hung up and he gently pushed her forward so her hands were braced on the desk. "Relax," he murmured as his fingers found their way inside her panties and up into her wet heat. "Damn, always ready. You drive me crazy with wanting you."

Two fingers alternated sliding from side to side over her clit while he held her hair in his other fist, his teeth at her neck. The cool air on her exposed legs, his fingers in her pussy and that bit of control with his hand and teeth and she shot into climax rather quickly.

Standing there, panting, he righted her panties and smoothed down her dress, pressing a kiss to the nape of her neck. "Better? You forgive me now?"

"You're certainly on your way," she murmured, smiling.

"Again? Jeez, you two," Jack said as he came into the study. Thank goodness Andreas' hands were out from under her dress.

"Hello to you too. Try knocking on closed doors. Have you come to take notes while I pee?" she asked sarcastically.

He put his hands up in defense. "Hey, I'm on your side on the bathroom thing. I start here in Star Lake at the end of the month. It'll give me time to heal from the change." He grabbed a cookie and stuffed it into his mouth. "If it's okay, I'll move into cabin four next week."

"I'm so happy you're moving in!" She kissed her brother and brushed crumbs off the front of his shirt. "I need to go to town to pick up the bedding, who can take me?" she called out as she sashayed into the dining room.

"Let one of us go and get it. You don't need to come too." Skye grabbed her hand and kissed it.

She eyed him and considered unleashing her grumpiness at him. Her swollen feet and her back pain and general misery made her want to rip peoples' heads off. But he was sweet to want to take care of her so she bit her lip and smiled instead. "I'm grumpy, Skyler, my love. Fair warning now. I want to go and pick up my babies' bedding. It's a normal thing and my life is incredibly far from normal these days. *So,* you can take me or Ryan and Sean can take me or Andreas can take me. Hell, I'll go with a fox in a box. I don't care but I'm going and I want to go now so you had better make up your minds." She tapped her foot as she craned her neck to see his face.

He smiled down indulgently. "Andreas really should bring on the farm team to keep you happy in the sack."

"Cheeky!" She laughed.

"Come on, I'll take you. Laurent can come too," Andreas said, laughing along with her.

"I hate this car," she grumped as Andreas had to pick her up and put her in the seat because it was so high off the ground. She was so pregnant she couldn't get in on her own.

Laurent sat behind her and Phillip came along too. Andreas threaded his fingers through hers as they drove into town and helped her out of the car when they got to Marva's house.

"Oh, this is perfect!" Kari said as she looked at the bedding that Marva had created for the babies. One comforter and bumper set was midnight blue with silver threads, and had the moon and stars on it, the other was a deep green with light green and blue waves embroidered all over it. She'd also made bassinet bedding, sweet blue and yellow flannel sheets and blankets.

"I'm glad you like them. I'm so tired of regular old pink or blue so it was a nice change to do something bold. If I do say so myself, it suits you. You are due any day, aren't you?"

"A little over two weeks now."

"Well, congratulations. Bring those babies by after you have them, you hear?" Marva said as she handed the bundles to Laurent and Phillip.

"I will, thanks, Marva," Kari grinned as she bounced out the door, Andreas waiting for her on the sidewalk. "I need pie," Kari said. "Let's stop by the bakery and get one for dinner."

"You know Anna is making a huge cake for dinner tomorrow," Andreas warned.

"That's tomorrow and Perri will be here soon. I'm sure she'll want a slice too."

"Oh, so we're supposed to pretend that you aren't going to eat the whole chocolate cream pie on your own?" Laurent asked.

"Duh. Of course you are! You know, you guys aren't being very nice to me," she groused as she headed toward the market that held the bakery.

Once back home, she put the bedding on the cribs and looked at the mural she'd painted on the wall with non-toxic paint. It was a picture of the lake, with the trees surrounding it and the moon rising. She'd painted grass and wildflowers along the base of the wall all around the room. It took awhile but the effect was worth it. The babies would be in with her and Andreas in the bassinets for a few months. She wanted them to sleep in their beds but Andreas was so huge and such a heavy sleeper that she was worried he'd roll over on them so they got bassinets instead, with sides that pulled down so she'd be able to nurse in the middle of the night more easily. Her boobs were already the size of Mount Rushmore so she was pretty sure she'd have enough milk for them.

She looked at herself in the mirror. She had a backache, she had to pee every twenty minutes, she was leaky and horny and grumpy as all get out. When she wasn't grumpy she was crying. How did women survive nine months of this? Her heart went out to human women.

"It looks perfect," Andreas said, coming up to check on her. "Frick and Frack will love it."

They'd been arguing over names since Monday, when they'd found out they were having twins. He wanted Tomas for a boy and Helene for a girl. She'd wanted Jack for a boy and Maya for a girl. "Let's ask Perri what she thinks. She just pulled up," he said to her.

"Oh good!" She rushed past him. He grabbed her arm and carried her downstairs.

Perri came in while Devon carried the bags to their cabin. "Hey, babe. You look marvelous," She rushed over to hug her and smooch Kari's belly. "How are my fabulous niece and nephew?"

"Fine. Come up and see the nursery. I just got the bedding today."

"So dish. I've been waiting all week," Perri asked and Andreas raised an eyebrow.

"Girl talk. You wouldn't be interested. I don't suppose I could have some time alone with Perri?"

"You know the answer to that. Come on. Skye and I will come up. We love girl talk," Phillip said, leading the way.

Once in the nursery, they sat down on the glider rocker for two and Kari turned to Skye and Phillip. "You two, what I say stays in here. If you blab about this I'll make your lives miserable."

Skye laughed. "We promise, *reine*."

Mollified by his use of her official title, she turned to Perri and dug into a very large slice of chocolate cream pie Anna had brought a few moments before, to fortify herself before explaining what Luna had said at the hospital.

"Oh my god, she didn't!" Perri exclaimed, eyes wide.

"She did, and right in front of Andreas. Of course Andreas thinks it's my hormones."

"He said that and he's not walking with a limp?"

"Not in so many words. Plus, he was driving so I couldn't injure him at the time."

"It was obviously meant as a dig, one of those casual comments that is a total burn."

"See! I told him that and he didn't believe me. He said 'Phillip kisses you on the lips' when I brought up the fact that she always goes for the kisser."

"Oh my god, that is so totally different!"

"I said that exact thing!"

She looked around at Skye and Phillip who watched the exchange, riveted.

"What?"

"I feel like I've been initiated into a secret club," Skye said, smirking. "Who cares what Luna thinks anyway?"

"That's not the issue. I *don't* care. It's the way she did it. Sneaky bitch."

"Like she has a chance," Perri snorted.

"As if!" Kari added.

They all went down to dinner half an hour later and Andreas cornered Skye. "What was that all about?"

"I'm sworn to secrecy but it was just girl stuff," he replied.

"Will this cause me trouble?"

Skye snorted. "Kari is a troublesome female, is she not? But how often does she prove to be worth it?"

Dinner was an informal affair and they all sat and talked until nearly midnight, when Kari begged off and headed upstairs. Her back pain was terrible and Anna sent up a hot water bottle with Ryan, who lay behind her in bed, holding the water bottle to the small of her back, and read to her.

She woke up sometime later and quietly got up to get some water. Triumphant at those few minutes alone, Kari stood and looked out at the lake and the beauty of her home with a smile.

Not wanting to push it and have a freaked-out Andreas come hunting for her, she put her glass in the sink and headed back to bed. On her way back upstairs, her eye caught movement in the television room just behind the stairs and she walked through the darkened hallway to see what was going on.

Ryan and Phillip sat together on the glider sofa, talking.

Guilty, but not so much she stopped trying to overhear, she listened for a moment.

"I know you feel an attraction to her. We all do. She's pregnant and putting out a lot of hormones. All the males are climbing the walls right now," Ryan said softly. One of his legs pushed the glider slowly back and forth.

"I'm so ridiculously horny. I masturbate like five times a day when I manage to get the time alone and it's not enough. I haven't been out on a date in months. I'm almost desperate enough to have sex with Luna."

Ryan laughed at that. "I know. Being on lockdown here makes it hard on my sex life too."

Silence stretched between them for a moment. A bit embarrassed that her horny hormones were affecting them and they couldn't do much about it, she was still happy to see them relaxed and free of having to guard her every moment. She moved to go back upstairs. That is, until Phillip leaned over and kissed Ryan.

A silent gasp caught in her throat and a hot flush burst through her. Frozen, she stood there in the dark and watched them, unable to tear her eyes from these two beautiful men as they kissed and put their hands all over each other.

A low groan came from one of them, bracketed by the soft sound of their clothes rustling as they moved closer in their embrace.

Phillip leaned in and touched his lips to Ryan's. Slow at first, not quite tentative. The kiss deepened, Kari could see mouths opening wider and the first lazy and then more firm and frantic slide of tongue against tongue.

The popping sound of buttons being yanked loose, flying around the room, sounded over the wet sounds of kissing as Ryan ripped the front of Phillip's shirt, shoving it off without breaking the kiss.

Reaching around, Ryan grabbed Phillip's braid and wrapped it around his fist, holding his head where he wanted as the kiss continued to intensify. Phillip's eyes had snapped open at first when Ryan grabbed his hair but they slid shut and his hands slid up Ryan's belly and the wall of his chest.

Rapt, Kari watched as Phillip's hand moved down again, going straight to Ryan's zipper. With frustrated groans, they both stood quickly. Breaking the kiss, they panted as they yanked their jeans open and kicked out of them quickly. Ryan pulled his shirt over his head. They stood there, totally naked and staring at each other, breath heaving, cocks so damned hard they stood flat against their bellies.

Kari's mouth watered. Her hand went to her throat as the heat of their sex made her body throb. She knew she should stop watching but she was enthralled at the sight of these two hard and masculine men wrapped up in this intensely passionate moment.

Breaking the tension, Ryan reached out and grabbed Phillip's cock and Phillip gasped, thrusting his hips. His eyes locked on Ryan's hands and Kari saw him slide his thumb over that glistening slit at the tip of Phillip's cock. Kari choked back her own moan as Ryan brought that thumb to his lips and tasted Phillip's pre-cum. Phillip did not. He moaned, ragged, full of desire as his head dropped back.

All of their earlier hesitation and slow exploration was gone. In its place was a surety of action.

Lazily but with a sure hand, Ryan pumped his fist over Phillip's cock over and over. Kari watched as Phillip's muscles first relaxed and then began to tighten. With his head back like that his body was arched forward, thrusting his cock into Ryan's grip. The tip of his braid reached the back of his calves. He looked like a beautiful statue there. They both did.

Kari was moved by the magnificence of these two adult male werewolves in their prime touching each other in such a raw way. The way Ryan held Phillip's cock was sure and much tighter than she would have held Andreas'. There was so much muscle there, so much strength just beneath the skin that she felt her wolf move within her.

Phillip's head came up as if in slow motion and he moved Ryan's hand. They stepped, body to body, and met in a brief kiss on the lips before Phillip's mouth skimmed down Ryan's throat and across his collarbone, down over his nipples. Kari's own throbbed when she caught sight of Phillip's tongue flicking over Ryan's flat copper-colored ones. Ryan hissed and arched into Phillip's mouth.

Ryan reached around and freed Phillip's hair and it fell like a river of copper around his shoulders and down his back. Their hips rolled, thrust into each other, and Kari saw, in the flickering light of the television, the wetness on each man's belly as cock rubbed against cock.

They tumbled to the carpet and thrust into each other, grinding, pressing cock to cock. Kari's breathing was shallow as she imagined what it must feel like to have the ridge of the crown of one cock slide against the other.

It must have been pretty damned good because the writhing and grinding became more and more frenzied, the moans louder and louder until Ryan broke away. Pushing up to his knees, he faced Phillip, who was on all fours.

And suddenly Phillip moved forward, taking Ryan's cock in his hand and then moving his mouth to him. His tongue slid around the meaty head and then sucked it inside. Kari wished she could see more but Phillip's hair played peek-a-boo with the scene as he moved his mouth on Ryan.

"Fuck. That's so good. God. Yes," Ryan murmured.

Phillip moaned around the cock in his mouth. Ryan's hands slid through Phillip's hair and gripped. Tossing his head back, Ryan began to thrust into Phillip's mouth, fucking into him. There was no finesse, no slow perusal of the other. It was hard and fast as desire took over. A sheen of sweat glistened on Ryan's back. Phillip cupped Ryan's balls in one hand as the other braced his weight on Ryan's thigh.

"You're next, Phillip. Oh yeah, damn it. I'm so close..." Ryan's voice became strangled, his face tightened and a harsh whispered roar broke from his lips.

Kari had to lean back against the wall. She was unbelievably turned on. The taboo of what she was watching along with the fact that she was watching in secret—watching these two incredibly masculine men—made her skin itch with desire and longing.

Moments later, even as Phillip had been sitting there regaining his breath, Ryan pushed him back to the carpet and took over. Sure and quick, Kari saw the muscles in Phillip's stomach tighten and his hips rock as Ryan's mouth sucked his cock deep inside.

Really inside. Ryan took all of Phillip's cock over and over. She watched, entranced as Ryan's mouth pulled up, exposing the wet and hard flesh of Phillip's cock, and then slid back down to the root.

"God damn, you're good at that. Fuck." Phillip reached out and slid his hands through Ryan's hair and held on.

Phillip's hair was spread out around his head on the carpet like a Titian painting, but his body was hard and muscled and straining with pleasure. The juxtaposition of that beautiful and flowing hair with the body easily used as a weapon was part of Phillip's allure. Part of what made him so sexy. And he lay there, back against the carpet, his cock in another man's mouth, and was no less masculine for it. More so in fact because it seemed to Kari that the interlude, while clearly sex—and hot sex at that—was also about connection and camaraderie as Pack.

Kari saw when his moment came, as his hips thrust up and his grip on Ryan's head tightened. His lip caught between his teeth as his back arched. He was beautiful. They were beautiful and Kari slowly backed away and crept back to bed, richer for that secret sharing of those stolen moments.

Settling back in her bed next to Andreas, her hand slid down to her desire-slicked pussy and she made herself come in the predawn darkness, the sounds of their moans and sighs, the sight of them kissing and loving each other burned into her brain.

* * * * *

Kari woke up in her favorite way, wrapped up in Andreas' arms. He had her cuddled up against himself with his hands protectively spread across her stomach.

"Happy birthday, little wolf," he growled into her ear and started off her day with a few rounds of fireworks.

"Where are my presents!" she exclaimed as she sat up afterward. Andreas still lay on his back, slowing down his breathing.

He struggled to speak once he got his breath back. "No presents until tonight. You know the rules. And wow, what's gotten into you?" he said, grinning at her.

"Oh, a little dream I had last night." She decided that she'd keep the interlude between Ryan and Phillip to herself. It was their business, certainly nothing for them to be ashamed of. But she was embarrassed that she'd stood and watched it all. "I'll let you name one of the babies if you give me some now," she replied hopefully.

He laughed. "Nope. And are you really going to tell my father that you're going to name our son after your brother instead of him?"

"Blackmail. And anyway, your father, though wonderful, did not nearly raise me. Jack did. Why not Jack Tomas? Tomas is such an old-fashioned name."

"And Jack isn't?"

"No. It's a strong name! How about Sean Jack? Or Skyler Ryan? I'm partial to Phillip Ryan myself."

"We can't. How will Laurent feel? Or Devon? Or anyone else? If we're going to name our kids after anyone it has to be after my brothers, father or grandfather or your brother. Sean Devon, Sean Tomas, Devon Jack. That sort of thing."

"We could just reject all family names and go out on our own. Something like Liam or Piers."

"Piers? Uh, no." He rolled his eyes at her.

She sighed. "You know, you really just should let me have my way all the time. But especially on my birthday." At his rolled eyes she snorted. "Okay, let's shelve this for now and go down and get breakfast. I know Anna will do something special for me."

"A multiple orgasm isn't special?" he challenged, and she fell back into him.

"You're so right. Thank you. It's the kind of birthday present you can give me every year." She giggled and got up. "Wow. They're low today," she said, looking down at herself.

"You must be getting close." He got up and danced around the room, pulling on a pair of jeans and forgoing the shirt.

"You have to wear a shirt, Andreas. Honestly, you look so sexy it'll drive me insane."

He grabbed a shirt out of the dresser and turned back to her, pulling it on slowly. "I'm a lucky, lucky wolf," he said, winking at her.

Moving back to the bed, she looked at him over her shoulder and let her robe fall away. "Wanna get lucky some more?" Grinning, she raised an eyebrow suggestively and he laughed and started back toward her until Jade pounded on their door.

"You two up?"

"Why does she do that?" Kari moaned and pulled her robe back on. "Just a sec."

Andreas opened the door and Jade rushed in, laden with baby things. "Just a few things for the babies," she said and Kari had to laugh. The woman had bought so many "just a few things" that Kari had had to get another dresser just to hold it all.

Accepting the loss of an opportunity for more sex, she shuffled past her mother-in-law, pressing a kiss against her cheek on her way past. "Hey, *Maman*. See you all in a bit." She padded into the bathroom, shutting and locking the door behind her.

When she came out she threw on a favorite pair of maternity overalls and headed down to breakfast with Phillip and Sean.

"Hi, Emma! It's lovely to see you." She gave her sister-in-law-to-be a hug.

"Happy birthday. I hope you don't mind that I'm here."

"Emma, you're welcome here any time. Both now and after you change. Please, this home is the family home. It's as much Sean's as it is Andreas'."

Sean smiled at her as if to say *I told you so* and Kari warmed at their easy unspoken communication.

Kari allowed herself to be pulled into the dining room and sat down. Of course, as usual, everyone bustled around to serve her and she watched with a smile.

Jack walked in and tsk tsked at her. "You're a spoiled one."

"Says the man who rubs my feet." She snorted.

As breakfast wore on, more and more members of the Pack began to stream into the lodge. Kari had to remember not to refer to the babies as multiples when people asked about her health and the pregnancy. They hadn't told the Clan yet about the twins, just a few people knew. Andreas wanted to announce it at dinner.

Her back beginning to ache, Kari got up to stretch.

"You all right?" Andreas asked.

"My back and the contractions are making an appearance again," she said and Elaine smiled at her.

"It's your body getting ready. I can see that you've dropped."

"Yeah, speaking of that, please excuse me." She walked out of the room to go to the bathroom. Of course, Phillip and Ryan came along to wait outside and she tried not to act any differently. But man, oh man were the two of them sexy.

When she came back out she went to the great room and sat down on the couch. Ryan rubbed her lower back. Andreas was on the phone in his office. She loved the normalcy of the moment. Of her family.

Michael came in, shyly dropping a present in the hall and greeting her sweetly. She gave him a quick hug.

Henry and Luna came in. Henry came over and greeted her while Luna just waved and headed into the dining room. Perri gave her a look. Kari shrugged. It wasn't a formal gathering, she didn't owe any sort of formal greeting to Kari anyway.

Alex came in with several presents. He smiled at her and dropped the boxes off on the table. "Hey, hot stuff. I tell you, if all women looked as good pregnant as you, I'd be for keeping the entire gender pregnant all the time."

She snorted. Despite Andreas' dislike for Alex, Kari found him oddly charming. "Thanks, I think."

It had started to snow on and off and some had gone off for a run while others decided to do a bit of backcountry hiking. The house was quiet, the kids were off making snow people outside and Kari read while Perri, Ryan and Skye played a brutal game of cards.

Andreas was on the phone and in his office pretty much all day. The babies had been pretty quiet but Kari's back hurt and she couldn't shake her lethargy.

"I'm just going to lie down here," she said and Ryan got up to grab an afghan from the other room to tuck around her.

She woke up as the sun was going down and Andreas was laying sweet kisses on her face.

She was one lucky girl, wolf, whatever.

"Hey, *petit loup*, wake up, baby. It's nearly time for dinner."

She sat up and let him help her off the couch. "I'm going to go upstairs and freshen up then."

"I'll come with you," he said.

"Laurent, Devon, can you stand guard please?" Andreas said quietly to them, and they both nodded.

When they got to the room both guards stayed outside, having a drink and playing backgammon. Apparently werewolves were big on board games and cards. Kari hadn't played so many games since she was a very young child.

"Now," Andreas said huskily as he shut the door behind him, "I believe that this morning, we were on the verge of getting lucky yet again when my mother decided to barge in. I've ignored you woefully today, *mon amour*," he said, stalking toward her.

Giggling, she fell back onto the bed and let him make amends for his neglect. Twice.

* * * * *

They appeared downstairs forty-five minutes later. Kari had changed into a gold and eggplant dress that Drew had brought her for her birthday celebration.

"HAPPY BIRTHDAY!"

The love and celebration in their voices made Kari blush. She smiled and clapped when she saw the heap of presents. She loved getting presents. Big or small, expensive or handmade, it didn't matter. It was the surprise and the wrapping and the fun that she loved so much.

Andreas came forward after she'd opened everyone else's gifts. "Kari, I want to say in front of everyone here just how much I love you. You're it, little wolf." He handed her two boxes. Blue boxes. She looked up at him and gave him the "you are going to get so lucky later" look.

The first box held a diamond and sapphire bracelet, to match her ring. It was so breathtaking she'd probably freak out wearing it in public, afraid to lose it. The second box held a pendant with a locket.

"It's empty now. But we'll put pictures of the babies in it when they come."

"Babies?" Drew said.

"Yes, more news. Kari is carrying twins. A boy and a girl."

"Oh my goodness!" Ellen exclaimed. "How wonderful."

Jade sat and preened, the grandmamma to the first set of twins ever in Cherchez and for the first set of werewolf twins to be born in over a hundred years. Tomas grinned like a fool.

"Dinner!" Anna called out and they all made their way into the dining room, chatting excitedly about the news.

As they sat and devoured all of Anna's goodies, Luna leaned forward and asked if they had names for the babies yet.

Kari snorted. "We're currently in negotiations for that. The boy name is hardest. We've narrowed it down to Maya or Helene for a girl."

"Oh that girl will have her daddy wrapped around her finger in about five seconds." Perri laughed.

"Like her mom," Sean said dryly, grinning.

"He'll have a harem, like the old days!" Luna exclaimed and Kari looked at her, confused.

"Harem?" Kari asked, smiling.

"Back when Andreas couldn't get enough of me and Perri and all of the Pack females," Luna laughed.

Kari's smile slid off her face and she turned to look at Andreas, who scowled in Luna's direction.

"What's Luna talking about, Andreas?"

It got very quiet.

"When a Pack Alpha is unmated, he often couples with the females of the Pack. That was all before you, of course," he added. "Now that there's you, there's no one else."

"Are you telling me you slept with Perri? With Luna? With Ellen?"

"Yes, but Kari, that's all in the past. Why be upset?"

Which of course was *sooo* the wrong thing to say. "Hmm, because you lied to me? Because you've told me in detail about lots of other Pack history but completely left out the fact that you've fucked some of the women in our Pack?"

"All of the women in the Pack. Except for Anna. And Jade of course," Luna added and Andreas turned to her, growling.

Horrified, Henry grabbed Luna's arm. "That's enough help," he whispered.

"What? So we had sex with him, big deal. It's not like, even when it happens in the future, that she still won't be his Mate, our Alpha," Luna said lightly.

Kari narrowed her eyes at Andreas. "In the future? You think you'll be fucking other women in the future?" Her voice lowered dangerously.

He put his hands up in surrender. "No, no. Of course not. Kari, even though it can happen that the Pack Alpha Mates might share their sex with others in the Pack at Gatherings, I have no plans to do so. I have no desire for other women. You're all I need, all I want."

"Oh how very grateful I am that you don't plan to dole me out like a platter of chocolates to the rest of the Pack! Thank you so much." She stood up and looked at Perri. "How could you not have told me?"

Perri looked stunned. "I…it wasn't a big deal. It was all over a year ago. You're his Mate, he loves you. I love Devon. It's nothing, I promise you."

Kari walked toward the door and Andreas got up and grabbed her, stopping her. "Kari, please. I'm sorry you're hurt, but all of this happened before I even knew you existed. How can you be mad that I slept with women before I met you?"

"The *point* is that you lied to me. That day in my old apartment when you wanted to know my entire prior sexual history and I told you. You could have told me then but you didn't. You've had a dozen chances to tell me before now but you haven't."

He winced. "Okay, I should have. I didn't know how to bring it up. It was meaningless. But you said you weren't interested in my past sexual life."

She wanted to hit him. "That is *so* not what I meant and you know it. I didn't want to know how many women you'd slept with but I had a right to know that you'd slept with women I know. With people I thought were friends. God, Andreas, how can you stand there and pretend not to understand what this is about?"

She looked down to where his hand was holding her arm. "You need to let go, please. I need to go to… Where can I go that isn't someone else's? This whole place is yours. God." She pulled away roughly.

"Jack, can I come to your cabin for a while?"

Jack jumped up and came to her side. He felt so bad for Kari and for Andreas too. The guy should have told her. "Yeah, come on, baby."

"Phillip, Ryan, you too," Andreas ordered.

Jade stood up, "Andreas, do something! You've hurt the poor girl."

"I need you all to leave me alone," Kari mumbled, letting Jack pull her into his arms.

"Phillip and Ryan will be coming, Kari. I'm not negotiating on that," Andreas said, hands on his hips.

"Fuck off, Andreas. You have no room to negotiate anything," she said and walked out of the house, Phillip and Ryan keeping a discreet distance.

"I *told* you to tell her," Laurent thundered.

"What were you thinking?" Sean turned to Luna. "Why would you bring that up?"

"What? I had no idea it was supposed to be a secret."

"But it was tasteless to bring it up on her birthday. Why would anyone bring up former women in front of a wife or girlfriend?" Elaine asked her.

"You fucked him too!" Luna said.

Elaine sighed. "Yes, I did but that isn't the point, Luna. You were hurtful to Kari, a woman who's been nothing but kind and generous to all of us. I don't think that some decorum is too much to ask."

"Andreas, you have to make this right," Jade said.

"Sean, you and I need to talk," Emma said quietly.

Sean nodded his head and they got up and walked outside. He hadn't told her about the more casual sexuality the

Pack had. He wasn't Alpha so he hadn't coupled with all of the women in the Pack, but he had slept with Perri and Ellen.

And then there was silence as the weight of what had just happened settled on Andreas. He leaned his head into his hands with a heavy sigh. Some mistakes came with a heavy price. He hoped like hell it wasn't a toll he couldn't pay.

* * * * *

"Kari, you know he didn't mean to hurt you," Jack said as he smoothed her hair back. She lay curled in a tight ball on his bed.

"He should have told me. My god, to find out in front of the whole Pack like that." She shook her head and big tears fell down her cheeks. "I'm so mortified. They all knew and no one said anything. That bitch Luna! She did it on purpose."

Phillip sat on the porch with Ryan, listening to Kari weep. "I hate this. She's so upset. She was right about Luna. That one wants to be hurtful."

"What do you mean she was right about her?" Ryan asked.

Phillip told Ryan about Luna's comments at the hospital and Kari's reaction.

Ryan sighed. "Andreas has made his bed. He should have told her of this. She grew up human, she doesn't understand this world."

Andreas approached them and sat down on the steps. "I really messed up."

"Yep," Phillip said.

"Laurent told me months ago that I should have told her. That she was going to find out and that it should come from me. Fuck all, I hate when he's right. I just didn't want to hurt her, to have her think it meant anything. How could she think that anyone I've been with in the past means anything compared to her?"

"Andreas, if you don't mind my saying, I don't think that's what she said. She knows you love her. Tonight she was humiliated in front of the whole Pack. Something she didn't know was used to hurt her. That's the problem. You not telling her something she needed to know created a situation where she was hurt ten times more," Ryan said.

"I agree," Jack said from the doorway.

Andreas turned around. "Is she okay?"

"What do you think?"

"You must think I'm an asshole."

"I think you should have told her. I think that watching my sister cry is something I really hate and it makes me want to kick your ass. But since you're a werewolf king and she loves you, I can't shoot you. So I'll have to stick with knowing you feel like shit."

"Jack!" Kari called from the other room, sounding so alarmed they all ran into the cabin together.

She was kneeling on Jack's bed, looking pale, her eyes red and puffy from crying.

Andreas went to her. "What is it?"

"My water broke." She motioned to the mattress. "Sorry about your bed, Jack."

Jack began to laugh. "You're so strange. You're in labor, doofus. Who cares about my bed?"

"Let's get you to the house. Elaine and Ellen will help with the delivery," Andreas said and Kari just looked at him. "Kari, please. God, I'm so sorry you got hurt. I should've told you. I'll make it up to you after you have these babies, I promise. For now, let's be sure everything is okay. Please."

"Phillip can carry me." Refusing to look back at Andreas, she smiled sheepishly at Phillip. "I'm wet. You might want to wrap me in a blanket."

"What's a little amniotic fluid between friends?" he asked and she laughed as he picked her up.

Ryan reached out and squeezed Andreas' shoulder. "Let's go and get this all moving."

They ran ahead. Jack and Phillip stayed with Kari and carried her up to the house.

"Kari, let's get you in your bed. I've had Ellen go up and lay down padding. It's a regular labor and delivery room in there now. Everything is going to be all right," Elaine said. Kari wouldn't meet her eyes. Elaine looked to Andreas.

Perri and Jade hovered around. "What can we do?"

"You've done enough already," Kari said.

"Listen, Kari, I'm sorry. The last thing in the universe I'd do is hurt you. I love you. You're my best friend. What happened happened ages ago. Andreas should have told you. I had no idea you didn't know. I'm sorry. Please, please let us be in the room with you, to help you," Perri said, tears in her eyes.

Kari sighed. And doubled over with a contraction.

Phillip settled Kari on the bed and Ellen set pillows behind her back. Elaine put on gloves as Perri helped Kari out of her dress.

"Just leave me naked!" Kari screamed out, batting away the gown someone proffered as another contraction hit.

"Kari, this'll be a bit uncomfortable. I need to check your cervix."

Uncomfortable would not have been Kari's word for what it felt like. "Holy poop on a stick! OUCH! *This* is your idea of uncomfortable?"

Elaine smiled and threw away the glove. "You're at seven centimeters, Kari. You're moving quickly. I'm going to have Ryan bring up some warm towels for your back. This part is uncomfortable but pain medication isn't very effective with our metabolism. We tend to burn right through it."

"Oh I'm so lucky tonight. This is early, is everything okay?" Kari gasped out.

"Yes. Twins tend to come early and you're only two weeks from your due date anyway. Everything looked fine on the ultrasound. It's all going to be okay, Kari."

Andreas stood at the door, looking forlorn. Kari looked at him and he looked back, misery on his face. "I'd like to be alone with Andreas for a while, please." Worriedly, those Pack members in the room looked between the two of them and quickly left, closing the door as they did.

He came to kneel next to the bed. "Please, Kari, don't stay mad at me. I hate it. This moment...our babies, you...it's the best thing that's ever happened to me. You shouldn't have found out the way you did. I'm sorry you felt betrayed and humiliated. I love you. Hell, I adore you. You know that."

She reached out and touched his hair. "I do know that. I just don't know how I can face them all, knowing you slept with them."

"None of them meant anything to me. As Alpha—as an unmated Alpha—they were part of the...benefits, I suppose. You've seen our attitude about nudity and sexuality in general. It's more relaxed than human standards. The moment I saw you I ceased wanting anyone else."

"Okay, in the first place, put away the shovel, you're digging yourself a deeper hole. Benefits?" She sneered. "But *they* were all mated, were they not? I mean you say...*OH MY GOD*!" Kari writhed as a contraction hit her.

"Breathe, honey. Remember to relax through the contractions," he urged softly, taking her hand.

"You breathe!" she hissed out, squeezing his hand so tight he thought he'd lose feeling.

It tapered off and he remained holding her hand. When she didn't pull away, he let out a breath of relief.

"Yes, they were all mated. It's hard to explain. Some mated couples do continue to share with others during Gatherings and still remain happy and committed to each other. It's not my choice. I don't want any other women. Believe me!"

"So I could? I could just go and fuck, say, Phillip, at the next Gathering?"

He scowled at her. "Well, it's complicated. No actual fucking of anyone below you in rank except for Sean and Devon because they're my brothers. Everyone else is below you in Pack structure. You could have some kind of sex with any of the others in the Pack, just no intercourse."

"Oh for cripe's sake! You people have *everything* stratified, don't you? A blowjob? Sure, but only the Fifth and above. What's a hand job, Andreas? And wasn't Luna below you? I mean, I know she was literally," Kari fired back.

Andreas sighed. "I only coupled with Luna in wolf form. And as a male and Alpha, who else could I couple with? Everyone is below me."

"Wait, are you telling me you had sex with Perri and the others in *human* form?" She raised her voice at that and screamed into another contraction.

He waited until the contraction had passed. "Just Perri and Johanna. Johanna because I was dating her and Perri, well, it was a family party and we all drank too much. Devon was there of course, he knew. I wouldn't have done anything without his approval or acceptance."

She closed her eyes. Her best friend, her supposed best friend, had slept with her husband. Only he hadn't been her husband then. Kari knew it was irrational to feel jealous about something that happened before she came along but it hurt nonetheless.

"So if I fuck Sean and Devon we can call it even?"

"No! There will be no fucking of anyone but me, Kari." Frustrated, he ran his hands through his hair and it stuck up in all directions. "This has gone on long enough. I've been an ass. I freely admit it. But you would truly do that to me, to us?"

The last was said with a depth of emotion that she'd never seen from him before, it tore at her heart.

"How can I get past this sick feeling in my stomach? This fear that there's something I don't know?"

He put his head down on the bed beside her. "Kari, I have not betrayed you or our marriage."

"Lying is a betrayal, Andreas."

He sighed. "You're right. But it's now you who's deliberately missing the point. What would you have me do to make this all right? Tell me and I'll do it."

"I don't know! Maybe I need to leave. Maybe this is so big I can't get around it. Do you want me to leave and take the children so you can have your life back?" she asked quietly. She felt desperate. She needed to shut up but she couldn't. She wanted to make things right but she couldn't see her way back.

"No one is leaving. Do you want to? My god, Kari! Would you end our relationship over this? A stupid mistake? I hate seeing you like this. You *are* my life. I don't want another life. I love this one. I love your infuriating tendency to get pissed off at nothing in particular—although I admit this is something to be angry over. I love waking up with you every morning. I love the children you're giving birth to right now. I love you, Kari."

"I don't know how to find my way back to you right now. I'm scared that I'll always distrust you. I've never had much in my life, and all of a sudden I got you and this big warm family who loved and adored me. But it was all a lie."

"None of it was a lie! None of it is a lie. We do all love and adore you. I do, my parents do. The Pack does."

"Except for Luna and whoever it is that tried to kill me. Oh, and Johanna." She snorted.

"Let me love you, Kari. Let this be the last thing between us. I promise you on my life I won't hide anything from you again. This can't be the end. I know you love me. I can see it in your eyes. Let's move on from this. You can extract whatever payment you wish from me for it." He smiled hesitantly.

She sighed. She was so afraid of being hurt but she loved this man and her Pack more than her own life. "Okay. Okay but, Andreas, I'm telling you now, don't lie to me again. I'll walk out that door and never look back if you do."

He smiled at her, nodding, tears in his eyes to match hers. "Thank you," he said. "Oh baby, you won't be sorry." He leaned in and gently kissed her lips and used a cool cloth to wipe her forehead. "Now do you want to walk for a while?"

"Yeah, let me grab a robe." She huffed through another contraction and let Andreas help her up and put a loose robe around her.

When he opened the door she came face-to-face with nearly the entire Pack, all looking worried.

"I tried to make them leave but everyone keeps coming back up," Sean said, looking expectantly at Kari.

"Walk with me, Sean. Andreas, please assure everyone that all is well. I don't want to have to jump over thirty people so everyone needs to wait downstairs."

Andreas looked relieved to have a task to do. Each one of the brothers and Phillip took turns walking with her up and down the hall. Kari spoke to Sean and made sure everything was all right between him and Emma.

"Okay, enough whispering over there. It's my turn," Devon said and came to take his place with Kari. "You okay, sweetheart? I'm sorry, you know. It was a dumb way for you to find out."

"It's over. I don't want to talk about it anymore."

"Can you try to forgive Perri? Honey, she loves you so much. You're her best friend. She's torn up over it." He must have seen her confusion over how he could be so nonchalant over his wife fucking his brother. "It didn't mean anything, Kari. Not like you think. It's part of Pack culture. It won't happen again, not least of all because Andreas isn't interested.

But also because that's not where Perri and I are anymore in our relationship. Neither one of us is bothered by it but it's probably not something we'll do again."

"I can't deal with this right now, okay? I'm in labor and my hormones are all over the place and I just don't want to think about it right now."

"I'm sorry, of course."

Brushing a kiss on her forehead, he continued to walk with her in comfortable silence for a while until she finally slumped down the wall and announced she was done.

Andreas quickly helped her back into the room and onto the bed.

Kari looked up at the full room and gritted her teeth through a contraction. "Not that a queen wouldn't give her life for the Pack or anything, but I really don't want to have a pelvic exam with ten people in the room."

The non-approved Pack members left quickly, quietly shutting the door after they'd gone.

Kari cried out as Elaine did the check. "Let's go. It's time to push. Andreas, hold her leg up. Sean, get the other one," Elaine ordered.

Kari looked at Perri and Jade and held her hands out to them.

It was a full team effort as Kari pushed. She put her all into it and bore down, pushed so hard she saw stars, and felt her son or daughter being born. "Oh!" she said as she saw the baby being pulled out and wrapped up in a blanket.

"This is your daughter!" Elaine said, placing the bundle on Kari's stomach.

Weeping tears of joy and relief, Kari pressed a kiss to her daughter's forehead. Andreas looked totally amazed as he leaned over and kissed mother and baby. "This is Helene, don't you think?" he asked and she nodded.

"Okay, your son is coming. Let's get pushing."

And in seven more minutes she had both babies, healthy and strong, cradled on her chest.

"Tomas Jack Phinney and Helene Jade Phinney, meet your family," Kari said and Andreas mouthed *thank you*.

"Tomas Jack?" Tomas said. "You named him after me?"

"And me?" Jack asked, pushing to get closer.

"Yes. It was Andreas' idea," she said, smiling at him and then Jade. Helene was Andreas' grandmother's name. There were no women on Kari's side that she felt close enough to to name her child after. She felt a slice of sadness at that and then it was replaced by a wave of tenderness and relief. Knowing that her children would have the big family she'd always wanted was a great gift. Tomas and Helene would always be loved. They'd never doubt that they were wanted and cherished. That would be her greatest gift to them.

Chapter Thirteen

A month after the babies were born, the time came to change Emma and Jack and bring them into the Pack. Andreas bit Jack first and once he'd stabilized and rested a bit with Anna watching over him, it was Emma's turn.

As the time to change Emma arrived, Sean still hadn't made up his mind as to who would do it. He'd argued with Andreas that he should be the one to bite her but Andreas felt it would be better to have someone else do it.

"Sean, can you honestly sit here and tell me that you'll be able to rip into her flesh and cause enough pain and trauma to facilitate the change?"

"It should be me! She's the one who has to suffer. What kind of man am I if I leave it to someone else because it'll be hard?"

"Honey, Andreas is right. Let someone else do it. You've seen transformations before. Don't do that to yourself. Emma has to suffer regardless of who does it, but you don't have to add any more misery to the situation," Jade said softly.

"I'll do it, Sean. It would be an honor to change Emma. That way Laurent and Andreas can hold you while you hold Emma," Phillip said.

Sean took a deep breath and looked to Emma. "All right. Is that okay with you, hon?"

She nodded. "Just do it already. The longer we wait the more nervous I become."

Elaine and Ellen stood at the ready. "Okay, Emma. We're right here. You know that we have to wait for several minutes to allow your body to go into trauma, but we'll catch you and we won't let you go," Elaine assured her and Emma, pale-faced and trembling, nodded.

"I love you, Em," Sean said as he kissed her softly.

"I love you too."

They removed her shirt and Phillip changed and padded over to where they'd situated Emma on a low gurney. He gave a soft whine, knowing what he'd have to do.

Sean held both of Emma's hands. Andreas held Sean around the waist and gently took his brother's hands back. "Sean, let me hold your hands. You'll want to save her. Your wolf will take over. If you're free you could hurt Phillip. Maybe even Emma too."

Laurent took one of Emma's hands, standing close to Andreas just in case he was needed to help with Sean, and Kari took the other. Phillip lunged suddenly and nausea roiled through Kari when she heard him tear into Emma's flesh, rending her stomach open.

Emma writhed and screamed and Sean put his forehead to hers, struggling against Andreas to get his hands free to stop Phillip. Tears of terror and fury fell from his wild eyes. His wolf was fighting to rise and Kari spoke gently to both of them, trying to keep them calm. Phillip pulled away and changed back, Jade helped him clean up. Elaine stood at the ready and they all watched as Emma lost consciousness and her vitals went crazy.

Anguished, Sean waited as Elaine and Ellen monitored the machines that Emma was attached to. Andreas kept his hold on his brother and spoke softly into his ear. Holding her breath, Kari watched the two of them, moved by the love they had for each other. Finally, a sigh of relief burst from Sean when Elaine and Ellen sprang into action and began to stabilize Emma.

Afterward they cleaned her up and put her next door to Jack's room. Sean lay next to her, careful not to jar her injuries.

"I wish I could have been with you when you were changed," Andreas said quietly, the emotion clear in his voice.

Kari turned to him and looked up into his face. She put her hand to his cheek, reassuring both of them they were real. "Mistakes were made, Andreas. Why dwell on that now?"

"Knowing you were in that hospital room and being unable to hold you, to comfort you..." his voice broke for a moment. "Not being able to see with my own eyes that you were safe, it tore me apart, Kari. I was terrified that you'd hate me forever."

She closed her eyes for a moment, imagining life without Andreas, without the Pack, and touched an emptiness that she hadn't felt since she'd accepted her new life. Because there were no words eloquent enough to convey what he meant to her, she simply put her cheek above his heart and listened to the reassuring beat of his heart. "I love you, Andreas."

Chapter Fourteen

The quarterly Gathering was upon the Pack as they all worked through their new roles and responsibilities. In the months leading up to it, there had been a few more threats by phone and the two-on-two guard situation remained in force.

Sean and Emma had married in a human ceremony and were living in one of the cabins while their house was being built on the other side of the lake. Their practice was new but already doing quite well.

The lodge was bustling. They had a full house, Emma had announced that she was pregnant at lunchtime and Sean looked very happy and content. Jade buzzed around, giddy to be a grandmother again. Anna agreed to stay back with Gregory, Laurent and Ryan to watch the twins while Kari and Andreas went on the run. Kari hadn't wanted to leave them at all but as Alpha it was her duty to be there. Additionally, it was the first run since Emma and Jack's transformation so they were running as a newly expanded Pack.

Later that day Perri and Kari were in the nursery, playing with the twins. "Does this make you feel bad?" Kari asked softly.

"You mean all of the babies all of a sudden?" She shrugged. "I thought I'd be okay with it you know, but it's hard. We could adopt. But a human child raised by werewolves is a complicated thing. Either we'd have to change him or her later, in their teens, or face their death as we lived three times as long. A parent shouldn't live decades longer than a child. That reality alone makes werewolves adopting human children too painful for most of us. Plus a non-werewolf child in this Pack, where all the children are werewolves—it would make a kid feel left out."

"Tell me to shut up if you want, I know that advice is easy for me to give and all, but have you talked to a fertility specialist? They can do so much these days. I know that there's a shifter fertility doctor in San Francisco. Elaine was talking about her the other day."

"I've been thinking about it a lot lately. I want to, but part of me is afraid. I don't want to get my hopes up. Is it worth all of the money and hassle? For something that may or may not work?"

"I don't know, Perri. Only you can answer that one. We'll support you in whatever way we can. If it's something that you really want though, it seems to me that it's worth a try to at least talk to someone."

A knock sounded on the door and Luna popped her head in. She'd apologized for the incident at Kari's birthday, swearing she hadn't meant any harm, but Kari didn't trust her and neither did Phillip, who came into the room and picked up Tom, nuzzling his belly and garnering a sweet giggle in response. Skye pushed past and scooped up Hellie and gave her a cuddle.

"You guys! I swear, I have to duke it out to get time with my own babies," she teased and got up from the floor, folding away the playmats. "Hi, Luna, how are you?" she asked, trying not to sound hostile.

"Oh good. They're growing so fast!" she said, looking at the twins, and Phillip turned away from her slightly, taking Tom out of her reach. "Well, now Andreas has his legacy. He must be relieved."

"Relieved?" Kari said and she could feel the hair on her arms prickle up as Perri's hostility toward Luna rose.

"Oh you know, when an Alpha mates, getting a son is so important. It's your job, you know, to breed a son. You proved your worth now," she said flippantly.

"Luna, watch how you speak," Skye growled and Helene gave a startled cry. She wasn't used to her number two fan sounding hostile in her presence. He murmured endearments to her and she calmed down.

"I didn't mean anything by it. God, can't anyone say anything around here anymore? You know, being offended so easily isn't really a good thing," she said to Kari.

Kari walked forward until she was nearly touching Luna and raised an eyebrow. "You know, Luna, if I didn't know better, I'd think you were trying to bait me. But I know that's not the case because I'd have to take your challenge and we both know how that would end." Voice low, her power rolled over her skin onto Luna.

Henry and Andreas walked down the hallway and stopped, feeling the exchange. Since Kari had given birth, she'd acquired a lot more power. The electricity of it filled the hallway.

"*Reine,* I meant nothing untoward, I swear," Luna stammered.

"Understand this, Luna—you'll be very sorry if I am actually offended, so thank your lucky stars I *don't* offend easily," Kari said, growling, and Luna went to her knees, forehead on the floor in submission. "Get out of my sight," she said and Luna backed up and then got to her feet and went downstairs.

"What was that all about?" Andreas asked Kari.

"Luna oversteps herself, *again,*" Skye answered, only in a little sing-song voice so as not to scare Hellie.

Henry went to his knees and rubbed his face on Kari's legs. "I am sorry, *reine*. I don't know why she does it. She's jealous."

"Henry, you need to see to your Mate. She'll end up challenged if this continues." Andreas dismissed him without comment on what he'd said.

He stalked into the nursery with *that* look in his eye and backed Kari through the connecting door into their room. "Skye, Ryan, Perri, can you watch the twins for a bit? Get Laurent and Devon up here to help if you want," he growled over his shoulder before shutting their door gently but firmly behind himself.

Her pulse fluttered as she felt her pussy bloom and heat at his perusal.

"God, you're so sexy when you do that." He pulled his shirt off over his head. "I need to see you naked right now." In one swift movement he stood there gloriously naked and hard, his pants down and off.

"Why don't you make me?" Kari challenged, raising an eyebrow. She kept her voice down, knowing how many people were in the other room. The need to be quiet was something new and exciting.

He growled again and lunged at her, catching her quite easily, with a wicked chuckle. "Hmm, now that I have you, let's set about the making."

A few quick yanks and tugs and her clothes were gone and she found herself turned and bent over the bed, feet on the floor. His fingers tested her and found her ready. "Hmm, a little making already I see." She grinned into the mattress even as she blushed.

Nudging her ankles wider, he guided the head of his cock to her and pressed himself inside in a breathtaking movement. She moaned, feeling him, being filled by him that way flipped her switch like nothing else. Although he had plenty other things in his bag of tricks, she liked being taken by him.

He sighed, satisfied. "I needed that. I came up the stairs and felt your power like a wall in the hallway, it went straight to my cock. You're so fucking sexy when you're dominant like that."

"Oh yeah?" She pressed herself back onto him, meeting his thrust. "Seems to me you like being dominant even more."

Reaching around, he found a nipple and teased with rolls and tugs of clever fingers while the other hand slid down, finding her clit.

"Well sure, little wolf. Because there's nothing hotter than making an Alpha bitch heel."

She stiffened and he laughed.

"You're tough shit all day. You run this Pack and they all look up to you. But when I close that bedroom door and look at you and you melt? Oh little wolf, it's so fucking hot it makes me feel like exploding right then and there."

Mollified, she relaxed a bit. "Alpha bitch, hmpf! You're lucky…that's it, god that feels good…you're lucky I like you in dominant mode."

"Indeed. Now I have work to do so let's get to it." He thrust deep into her body and her whimper of pleasure shot through his cock.

He did indeed love it when she submitted to him. Loved to enter her from behind and control her movements, holding her just so. Then, looking down at the long, pale line of her spine, at the gentle flare of her hips, he watched his cock disappear into her body and come out again. His cock was covered in her honey. He made her so hot. His words made her cunt weep and that made his wolf want to howl up in triumph.

At the same time a deep gentleness settled into him. As always, amazed by the way she harbored him. Her body took him back over and over. She arched, wanting more. He gave it to her.

His hands stroked over her skin, the hair on his arms rising from the electric power still clinging to her. The power of her Alpha, cloaking her in warm energy. Nearly sticky, the warmth of it clung to him, drew him to her.

Reaching around, he palmed her nipples, loving the soft sound of delight she made. Rolling and tugging on them, his clever fingers drew her higher and higher. He knew she was nearing that peak. Knew she'd be restless and seeking more sensation.

She writhed against him as he continued to stroke into her. One palm slid down her stomach and found the wet, swollen folds of her pussy and slid through them. Pulling her honey up from where they were joined, he began to tease her slippery little clit.

A sound much like a squeal came from her and he chuckled as he continued to torture her.

In retaliation, she squeezed her inner muscles around him several times, making him groan. "Damn, I love when you do that. But I'm not ready to come yet."

Pulling out, he flipped her over and moved her onto the bed.

"Hey! What about that whole making thing?"

He crawled up over her, taking her arms and moving them above her head. "Oh I'm working on it. On *my* schedule." Disappearing over the side of the bed a moment, he returned with a pair of her panties dangling from his fingers. Eyebrow raised, he wrapped the silk and lace around her wrists and hooked the material over one of the decorative pegs in the headboard.

She tried to move but couldn't. "Oh."

A slow, wicked grin slid over his lips and her lips parted without sound as heat pulsed through her. The look on his face as he devoured her with his eyes, his very large presence above her, having her hands bound—she'd never felt so controlled before. The man did it so well. He dripped with dark sexuality.

"Oh indeed, little wolf. I mean to have my wicked way with you. I find I like you all trussed up and bound for my pleasure. Perhaps the next time we're in Seattle we need to stop at Babeland for some toys so we don't ruin all your pretty panties." All of this was said in a low, quiet voice that somehow seemed even sexier for its restraint.

His fingertips traced over the skin of her arms on his way down to her nipples. Ribbons of sensation rode her flesh in the wake of his touch. He sat astride her but she couldn't reach his cock even when she strained to touch him with her lips. The weight of it teased her as it lay heavy on her stomach. The wiry hairs on the inside of his thighs pressed into her sides.

Wiggling and squirming, she continued to try and get more contact with his hands, with his cock. He looked at her with a smirk. "Ah, ah, ah. No. This is my show. I'm doing the making. You tossed out the challenge. You should remember to be careful what you wish for."

Sliding down her body with his own, he dragged his cock, wet at the tip, down her belly and thigh. Those fingertips found her nipples at long last, slowly tracing circles around them.

"Please," she gasped in a harsh whisper.

"I do so love it when you beg me." Bending, he kissed the tip of each nipple and then nipped first one and then the other with his teeth. "But you have such a fine and varied vocabulary. I think I need you to be specific. Because whatever can you mean? Please make you a sandwich? Please get a gallon of milk at the grocery store?"

"Oh! You're diabolical."

Chuckling quietly, one of his brows slid slowly upward as he waited. Sexy, arrogant man!

"Please fuck me. I want you back inside me again."

He knelt between her thighs and put them over his, opening her up. His fingers traced through her pussy and she arched with a gasp as he caught her clit between his fingertips, squeezing gently. Ripples of pleasure spread through her.

"Yes. Andreas, like that."

"Yeah? And how about this at the same time?" Guiding himself into her, he thrust hard and filled her up again. A cry burst from her lips at the overwhelming sensation of it.

Adjusting her, his hands held her hips, fingers digging into the flesh there as he served her body to himself while he fucked into her hard and deep.

She strained against her bonds to no avail. She could have broken the bed if she really used all her strength but she didn't want to. It thrilled her to be bound like that. To be helpless to whatever he decided to do to her. It freed her to simply receive him, to let him make all the choices.

"Your pussy around me so tight… It's the best feeling in the world." Moving his hands, he dragged his nails down her breasts and belly, lightly scoring her skin until he reached her mound. Tickling over it, he found her clit and looked down, watching his cock thrust into her below his fingers drawing big circles, using the flesh of her clitoral hood to stroke over her instead of direct pressure from his fingers.

"My! Yes, that. What is that? Oh, moremoremore please!" She gasped and tightened herself around his cock, delighting in his groan.

"Look at yourself, Kari. Breasts bouncing each time I thrust into your sweet pussy. Back arched. Those pretty legs spread wide for me. God, your pussy is so dark pink and swollen up. So wet and greedy for my cock. Your nipples…" He leaned down and licked them both over and over until she was a quivering, begging mass.

Pulling back, he locked gazes with her and squeezed her clit gently over and over. "Give it to me, Kari. I want your climax and I want it now."

His command, his cock, his fingers—all so sharp and good—built her up until her body couldn't hold back anymore. Orgasm shot through her, bringing a tooth-gnashing climax that brought her back bowing up off the bed, wrists pulling against where she was tied and an "O" of surprised pleasure on her lips.

"Sweet. Fuck, I'm…" Kari felt the spasm of his cock as he began to come, his fingers digging into her hips, holding her to him tightly as he pressed into her so deep it felt like he wanted to crawl into her body.

Looking up at him—watching as his face tightened and then relaxed, watching the flex of his forearms as he held her body to his—Kari was sure she'd never seen a sexier sight in her whole life. His pulse thundered at his neck, sweat seemed to make his skin glow with sensual intensity. This sexy man belonged to her.

At long last he breathed a long sigh of repletion and pulled out. Bending down, he pressed a passionate kiss to her lips as he reached up to untie her wrists. She saw the panties get tossed off to the side as he collapsed on the bed next to her.

They lay there, legs tangled, the air redolent with the musk of sex, for some time afterward. Just enjoying the silence and each other's presence.

Finally she sighed. "We should take a shower and get back downstairs." Her voice was still lazy as she said it. The sex made her muscles warm and loose.

Andreas stretched and she watched him with a greedy smile. He looked so damned good naked.

He caught her perusal and winked. "You're so good for my ego, Kari. I love to catch you looking at me that way."

Rolling off the bed, he held out a hand for her to take and pulled her to her feet.

"So who made who?" Kari teased as he washed her back.

"Undeniably, little wolf, we made each other."

By the time they returned to the nursery everyone had gone. "I suppose we took a bit longer than twenty minutes," Kari said, grinning.

They went downstairs and the twins crawled quickly over to Kari, who picked them up, one in each arm, depositing them on her hips.

"You could do phone sex and make a million dollars," Skye whispered into her ear and laughed wickedly. She batted her eyelashes at him and Andreas scowled, mimicked quickly by Tom.

"He's going to be a formidable little Alpha," Ryan laughed.

"He certainly thinks so," Kari said. "But who knows, maybe Hellie will be the first female to lead the Pack. There's that woman from Eastern Rock who's the first female to get into the Inner Circle without a mate."

The other females in attendance all made noises of approval except for Luna, who stared at her in stony silence.

"Why are you so sullen?" Henry said to Luna.

"Is a bad mood a crime now?" Luna's pretty face held a sour look.

"No, it isn't. Luna doesn't like me and that's okay. It's not Pack law to like your Alpha." Kari shrugged.

"What do you know about what I do or don't like?" Luna snapped.

"Whatever your issue is, this is my home and I don't have to take any shit from you. Not as a queen or plain old Kari Phinney. You don't have to like me but you can keep your bad attitude to yourself."

"It's not Pack law for me to kiss your ass."

Andreas growled and moved forward but Kari put her hand up to stop him.

"I'm dealing with this, Andreas. Skye, Ryan, can you please help Anna take the twins upstairs and get them down for a nap?" Kari handed the children off and sat down across from Luna.

"I'll be truthful with you, I don't like you either. I don't like the way you hover around Andreas. I don't like your catty remarks. But as I said, you don't have to like me and I don't have to like you. But you'll be civil in this house or you can get the hell out."

"Fine," Luna said and crossed her arms over her chest and Kari got up and left the room, Andreas following her.

"You handled that well," he said, nuzzling into her neck, nibbling on her ear.

"Thanks. I just wanted to clear the air. I doubt she'll be okay with being civil though. It'll end with her and Henry moving to another Clan most likely."

"Henry has asked to separate from her," Andreas said quietly in her ear.

"What? What does that mean and why ask you?"

"He and Luna never got married in a human ceremony. His mating with her was done under my leadership as Alpha. I can declare them unmated and he'll be free to seek another, as will she."

"I thought you all mated for life."

"A true Mate is a Mate for life. Sometimes, though, your cock can lead you in the wrong direction." He laughed. "Or your pussy. You know what I mean. I don't think they're true mates. Things have always been rocky. I know she's propositioned Pack members outside of Gatherings. It's not against Pack law exactly, but it's pretty bad form."

"She's propositioned you since we mated, hasn't she?"

He sighed. "I told you I wouldn't lie. Yes, but I've always turned her down. She hasn't propositioned me since your birthday or I would have told you."

"That whore!" she spat out and Andreas smiled.

"Kari, my vicious little wolf, let it go. I'm going to grant Henry's request. Hopefully Luna will fulfill her needs with someone else and Henry can move on as well."

"Gah! That pisses me off." She rolled her eyes in annoyance. "Would you just let it go if one of the Pack members propositioned me?"

"Probably not. But you're a better person than I am. Anyway, she's jealous. You have two beautiful children and a very handsome husband." He grinned at her.

"You are so full of it." She laughed, playfully punching him in the arm. "But since you just told me something, I'll tell you something in return. It's not a big deal and I haven't been hiding it but I hadn't told you either and it's bugged me. A while back I saw Ryan and Phillip together in the television room."

"And you felt the need to confess this why?"

"Well I watched it and then I didn't tell you. And when I say together I mean together, together. As in naked and hot, hot, and I mean really hot, sex."

Andreas raised a brow. "And you were involved?"

She rolled her eyes. "No! But I watched." She blushed. "They didn't know."

Andreas chuckled and shook his head. "Oh Kari. You are so much naughtier than I give you credit for. We have these males up here pretty much on lockdown. The sexual energy of wolves is high. It's only natural they'd seek each other out. Phillip and Ryan are friends. I'm wagering it's not the first time."

"Oh my god! Have you been with one of them? Because if you have, I want to hear all about it. And you know, if you ever wanted to do it again, I'd be cool with it if I could, well, you know…watch."

Andreas threw back his head and laughed. "Outside of group situations where the odd touch or kiss might have happened, I haven't had any sexual experiences with any of the male wolves. But it's a pretty big turn-on that you'd want to watch it." He kissed her quickly.

* * * * *

The sky was clear and the night was warm. The moon hung heavy and silver overhead. A perfect night for a run.

And it was. Wonderful and free. Kari and Andreas ran side by side, his giant form sheltering hers. Occasionally she would lean into him and he would nuzzle her with his muzzle.

There was much roughhousing and playing by the Pack members. Perri and Devon rolled around in the dust amorously, as usual.

Once at the lake, Kari lay down, head resting on Andreas' body, feeling the rise and fall of his stomach. He rolled her over, pinning her with a bite at the neck. Soft growls rumbled from her throat and he flipped her over and mounted her. There was no wolf in the universe sexier than Andreas. His large wheat-colored body covered her own, belly against her back.

There was a heady mix of sex and violence in the air and Kari was disgusted but not surprised to see Luna coupling with several Pack members who wouldn't have under ordinary circumstances.

With a snort, Kari shook her head and looked back at Andreas and they headed back toward the lodge so she could feed the twins.

When she'd finished nursing them and rocking them to sleep, she tucked them in before quietly leaving the room.

"I think they're still up there. Why don't you go out and join them?" Kari suggested to Laurent as they stood in the hallway watching Anna work on a quilt as she sat outside the door to the nursery. A nursery that'd been rigged with a deluxe security system. It monitored breathing rates and motion. If anything walked in the room other than the children once it was set, it would go off. Anna and Gregory usually sat with the twins until Kari and Andreas came to bed.

"Nah, I think I'd rather hang out here with you guys. Where's Jack?" he asked, groaning as she massaged his shoulder. He'd pulled a muscle when playing horsey with the twins the day before.

"He's coupling with Luna," Skye snorted as he came into the house.

"No! He needs a woman. Coupling with Luna is beyond desperate. He doesn't even like her," Drew said.

"Don't say that for my benefit. Luna's a pretty woman. Apparently lots of the Pack males find her sexy."

"She's okay, but that desperation is unattractive. At least to me," Peter said.

"Me too," Laurent said.

"Ditto," said Craig.

"There were skirmishes and lots of rough play, you know how that stirs everyone up," Andreas said, winking at Kari as he spoke to Drew.

Kari laughed at Peter and Craig. "Um, guys, isn't the unattractive thing the fact that she's female?"

"Well, that too. I mean, I'm gay not dead. I can see a woman and find her attractive. If I were straight I'd do you. Or Ellen. Yes, Ellen is really lush," Peter answered and Craig laughed.

"Thanks. I'd do Ellen if I were a guy," Kari said flippantly.

"Please, tell us more," Laurent growled at her.

"Laurent! You pervert," Kari accused. "Men. Bring up anything remotely lesbian in nature and they all pant." She looked at Peter and Craig. "Well, almost all men," she amended.

"Hey, I'm bi," Craig answered. "I like a good girl-on-girl sex scene as much as any other red-blooded American guy."

"Never mind! It was just a casual remark. Moving right along." Kari waved them to move to another topic.

Right then Ellen and James walked in and all of the males burst out laughing and made cat calls.

"What the heck is going on?" James asked, grinning.

"Kari was just about to tell us all, in detail, how she'd *do* Ellen if she were a guy," Peter said.

James looked at Kari, eyebrows raised in interest. Ellen looked puzzled.

"Oh you perverts! We were discussing what is and isn't attractive about the females of the Pack. Peter said that if he were straight he would do Ellen. I said that if I were a guy I'd do Ellen. Of course at the very hint of two women getting it on the room went crazy and here we are."

Ellen laughed and came to sit next to Kari. "They wish!" She reached out and caressed Kari's neck teasingly. Playing back, Kari arched her back with a moan.

The men in the room got silent. Kari swore she could hear them gulping. Grinning, she looked at Ellen and ran her hands down her arms until they both burst out laughing, nearly falling off the couch.

"Wow," Drew breathed out. Laurent was sitting still against Kari and looking at them both, eyes glazed over.

"Have you ever been with a woman?" he asked.

"Well, I don't kiss and tell but you know, I went to a liberal arts college and lived in an all-girls dorm. You know those panty-clad pillow fights just get out of hand and before you know it, it's all soft skin, hard nipples and sighs." She and Ellen burst out laughing again.

She winked and got up to go and check on the twins.

They were sleeping peacefully and Anna had fallen asleep, feet up, resting against Gregory's side. Kari smiled at them both, touched by their relationship. Gregory looked up and returned her smile. He held up his book and waved her off with it. "Go have fun, we're okay here," he whispered.

Thanking him, she walked back downstairs and noticed the light was on in Andreas' study and went inside to turn it off. She walked into the room and stopped, stunned. Drawing a horrified breath, she screamed out long and hard, over and over.

Andreas ran inside, grabbing her and pushing her behind him. "What…" His words trailed off as he saw the room.

Everyone else ran into the room and stopped, taking in the scene.

Blood had been splattered over the walls and over the furniture and the words "die bitch" had been scrawled on the wall near the desk.

"Get her out of here," Andreas ordered Drew but Kari shook her arm free and refused to go.

"You can't shield me from this!" she shouted angrily. "This is my house. My children are upstairs. Someone did this with people a few feet away."

Laurent yelled from upstairs where he'd run to guard the children when she screamed, "What is going on?"

"It's all right, Laurent. Stay with the kids," Andreas yelled back. He looked at Carey. "Go upstairs and tell them what's going on. I don't want the children left alone."

Phillip came in fresh from their run and blinked at the scene before them. "Jesus," he breathed out as the grin he'd been wearing slid off his face. "Who the fuck would do this and why?"

Michael came into the hallway with Luna. "What's going on?"

Kari stormed out of the study and toward the kitchen, Phillip in her wake. Michael turned back to the room and gasped. "What the hell? Is everyone all right?"

Andreas turned and saw Luna and gave her a searching look. She blanched, backed off and walked out.

"Kari, wait," Phillip said.

He caught up with her as she bent into the cleaning closet, pulling out buckets and scrub brushes and cleaning solvent. Resolve on her face, she pulled on a pair of gloves and stomped past him without a word.

Pushing her way back into the room, Kari began to methodically mix the cleaning stuff.

Andreas grabbed her arm gently. "What are you doing?"

"I'm cleaning this abomination up! Either help me or let me go."

"Let Gregory do it, Kari. You don't need to be in here right now," Andreas said softly.

"NO! This is my house and I'm not going to let someone do this to me. Gregory is upstairs with our children."

Carey came back down the hall. "Wait, don't clean it yet." He motioned for people to back up and he closed the door, leaving Andreas, Kari, Phillip and Skye in the room. "Listen, this is blood, let's examine it. If it's the blood of one of the Pack, we can identify it."

Skye changed quickly, sniffing and then licking the blood. He did this in several spots and then changed back. "It's deer blood. I couldn't smell any wolves specifically. This room has had at least twenty Pack members in it over the last two days. There were no other scents than Pack. It's definitely one of us."

A few other wolves did the same test and they all came up with the same results. Kari stood in the doorway, glowering as she watched them all.

Afterward she silently scrubbed the walls and furniture until the muscles in her arms burned. The others came in and helped at her side, they all stayed quiet as they did it.

As the sun rose, Kari surveyed the room, took her gloves off, tossed them into the bucket and walked out of the room without a word.

Andreas looked at Sean. "What can I do?"

"Let her process it her way. She'll fall apart soon enough but let it happen on her terms and be there for her." He patted his brother's shoulder and watched Andreas go upstairs after his wife.

Kari stood in the shower and let the hot water wash away the sweat and gunk. She willed away the tears and stepped out and swallowed her surprise as she took the towel Andreas handed her. She should have known he'd come in to be sure she was all right. At least that was right and whole. Her connection to Andreas was one of the few things holding her together at that moment.

"The babies are awake and hungry," he said. She nodded, pulling on some clothes, and walked through to the nursery.

Pausing in the doorway, she watched Hellie pull herself up in her crib. "Anna said that Hellie was pulling up on the furniture last night again. She'll be walking soon."

"That's my girl." Andreas watched as Kari picked each child up and settled them in to nurse. The morning sun shone in through the window, lighting the scene, and it punched his gut. This was his family and he would do whatever it took to keep them safe.

Fury seethed from him as he thought about how one of their extended family members was responsible for the terror that kept bodyguards on his wife every moment of the day. Not wanting to let anyone spoil those small everyday moments with his wife and children, he looked out the window over the lake until he got his anger under control.

They stayed close together for the rest of the morning doing normal family things. They went for a walk, bathed the kids, played, read books. It felt almost relaxed at moments instead of being under siege.

After getting the babies down for a nap, Kari bumped into Andreas as she left the nursery. Without a word, he pulled her into their room and closed the door quietly to not disturb the babies.

He stopped when they were standing next to the bed and peeled off her clothing and eased her to the mattress. Quickly spreading her thighs, he entered her in one breathtaking thrust. He took her then, hard and fast, watching her breasts sway with each press he made into her body.

The entire exchange was silent. Everything was said through their eyes and the caresses of fingers and lips. Kari raked the sheets with her nails, bunched the comforter in her hands, bit her lip until she drew blood.

Andreas was single-minded in his lust. His hands gripped her hips tightly, the only sounds in the room were skin slapping against skin and panting. He leaned down and flicked his tongue over a distended nipple. Her eyes slid halfway shut as he pulled it into his mouth. He healed her and took her and gave her a place to hide and took all she had to give and more.

His hands began to roam her flesh, squeezing a breast just to the point of pain, flicking the nipple with a thumb. She began to tremble, a monumental climax looming on the horizon. The friction of Andreas' thrusting overloaded her senses. It ebbed and flowed, coming within reach and subsiding, teasing her. Rolling her hips, she moved to meet each plunge he made into her pussy. And finally her climax broke, showering a thousand stars in her vision. Her mouth opened on a silent cry as Andreas leaned down and pressed his lips to her collarbone, to her ear. His heat, the heat from his skin, buffeted her.

She felt his muscles tightening, hands gripping her body so hard she was sure there'd be a bruise or two. With a last, nearly silent roar he came inside of her and fell onto the bed, trapping her body underneath his own.

Knowing that he was smothering her, he rolled off and pulled her to him, heartbeat hammering against her back. Through the whole experience, neither had spoken a word, their intimacy being the thing to bridge the gap, saying all that needed to be said.

She and Andreas left the connecting door open and fell asleep, listening to the rhythmic rise and fall of breath.

Chapter Fifteen

Despite the continuing threats, life for the Pack continued to move forward. Emma's pregnancy progressed, their house was being finished quickly. Perri and Devon made the decision to try *in vitro* fertilization. They knew the odds but wanted to try anyway.

Kari was terribly grateful for the support and friendship of her sisters-in-law. They'd become so close and had so much fun together, their husbands had begun to refer to the three of them as the "trio of terror". She reflected on that good fortune as they all sat out on the deck in the late afternoon sun together, watching the twins play with Andreas and his brothers.

Fear ripped through Kari as she watched her brother approach, pale-faced. "What is it? Jack, are you all right?"

"Alyssa just called. She's here. In Seattle. She wants to see me." Alyssa was his ex from Boston. He hadn't seen or heard from her in nearly eight months.

"What? Wow. Why?" Perri laughed at Kari's questions.

"She says she misses me. She wants to talk things over."

"Do *you* want to talk things over? Do you miss *her*?" Kari asked, annoyed that the woman had broken her brother's heart.

"I wish I didn't. I wish I could have never looked back but yeah, I do miss her. Thing is, nothing's changed for me. I want to be married. If she can't give me that, I don't know what to say to her."

Kari hugged him. "Go and see her. Tell her that. She's nuts if she doesn't want you, Jack."

"Okay. Will you be all right without me?"

Andreas cleared his throat. "I think I can do an okay job of taking care of her now."

Jack laughed and jogged out to the car, driving off.

Kari looked to Perri and Emma. "She'd better not break his heart again or I'll kick her worthless ass."

"I'll get in line right behind you," Emma said. "Shall we go for a walk? My back is aching."

Kari called in to Andreas that they were going for a walk and he waved absently, keeping his eyes on the twins.

Kari, Perri and Emma were out near the lake, Phillip and Skye trailing them, when something whizzed by Kari's head. Before Kari could even figure out what it might have been Skye had knocked her down, his body covering hers protectively. He pulled Emma behind his body and Perri was partially under Kari.

They heard a car engine rev and tires squeal.

Andreas, Devon and Sean came running down the slope from the lodge. "Kari! My god, Kari?" he called out as he ran in a blur to where she was. Plucking Skye off her, he pulled her into his arms.

"What the fuck happened?" she asked, a little out of it from the force of Skye's body knocking her to the ground.

"Someone shot at you. The bullet hit the house." Ryan ran up with a first-aid kit and Emma took it from him with businesslike calm—but not before Sean could run his hands over her making sure she was unharmed. Devon did the same with Perri, carrying her in the house.

"The twins!" Kari said, pushing her hair back out of her face, trying to shove Andreas aside to get up and rush into the house. Andreas gasped and pulled her hand away.

"Blood. Were you shot, Kari?"

"What? Never mind that! My babies, where are my babies?"

"They're all right. I gave them to Anna and Laurent. They've gone into the office and locked themselves in. Now damn it, why are you bloody? Were you shot?" he demanded, looking at the bloody spot on her forehead

"I don't know. I don't think so. What does getting shot feel like?"

Emma pushed his hands out of the way. "Let's take her inside. It looks like she was just grazed but I can't tell for sure in the dark."

Andreas insisted on picking her up and carrying her into the house, laying her down on a couch. Emma checked her over. The blood had come from a graze. The bullet had taken off a few layers of skin from her neck, nicking just above her artery. Now that the initial shock had worn off, it hurt like a mother. The blood on her forehead was a spatter from her neck.

It was then that she noticed Phillip. Pale as a sheet, his face was covered in a sheen of sweat. "Phillip, what's all over your arm?" She sat up and pushed them all away and went to him. "Jesus, Phillip, you're bleeding! Emma, come here, I think he's been shot."

"Why isn't it healing then?" Sean asked, forcing Phillip into a chair, pulling off his shirt to expose the wound. "Oh my god, it's silver shot."

"Silver bullets? No way! Are you telling me that the silver bullet thing is true?"

"Well, regular bullets can kill us too if we get shot enough times and in important enough places. But yes, silver can kill us. There are those who know of our existence, human hunters who use silver bullets and silver traps and chains when they catch us."

Kari held Phillip's hand while Emma dug the bullet from the wound and disinfected it. He gritted his teeth and grunted in pain but within a few minutes, the wound began to heal up.

"If it had stayed in him for longer than about half an hour, the silver could have gotten in his blood and killed him," Andreas said.

"Oh my god, Andreas. Phillip got nearly killed because of me. This is no way to live. I think we should go away for a while. You can stay here if you want but I'd like to go to New York or to the apartment in Portland. They're in high rises. Much easier to secure than here."

"This did not happen because of you. A crazy person shot Phillip." He sighed, raking his hands through his hair. "You're right. Let's go to Portland tonight. I'll call ahead and have Drew and Craig go down and secure everything, be sure it's safe."

He looked to Emma and Sean. "You two are welcome to come or to stay here. This all seems to be focused on Kari but I don't know for sure if that doesn't mean others are safe without us. Skye can stay here as a guard if you like."

"I have patients to see at the clinic," Emma said.

"As do I," Sean replied. "We'll never keep the clinic going if we leave now. I think we'll stick around. You need to take Skye with you, Ryan as well. Have as many guards as you can. Carey's offered to come up and stay when he's not working. Between him and Jack and me and Gregory, we'll be fine." He hugged Andreas and kissed the top of Kari's head. "Go."

Kari gathered a few bags of clothing for herself and the twins and some toys. The condo in Portland already had a nursery and would be fully stocked with food and anything else they might need.

"Don't tell anyone we've gone," Andreas ordered Anna. "If they ask or come by, you don't know where we are."

Anna nodded and hugged Kari, kissing the sleeping twins. "Let me come with you. Who'll cook for you? Who will take care of you?"

Kari laughed softly. "I'm not as good a cook as you, but I think I can manage for a while. We'll be back."

Andreas took the Suburban with Kari and the twins. Ryan and Laurent rode with them. Perri and Devon followed them back in their truck, Skye and Phillip after them in the Outback.

In the little over an hour since he'd been shot, Phillip was already totally healed. Natural werewolves were like that. All but the most egregious of wounds healed quickly. While changed werewolves were extremely resistant to illness and disease and healed very fast, they had nothing on the hyper-resilience of a natural wolf.

"Gee, you think four guards will be enough?" Kari asked sarcastically.

"No, I don't actually. But it'll have to do for now. Drew will be at the condo on the weekends when he's not at the shop. He offered to stay for the week but I declined. I don't want him to have to take that much time off. Craig will stay three nights. Peter is apparently away right now."

Kari had fallen asleep during the long drive to Portland and thankfully the twins slept the whole six hours. Andreas looked down at his sleeping wife and back at Ryan and Laurent, who still looked outraged enough to kill. The large men each had a car seat next to them, one to a row of seats. Laurent had a lock of Hellie's hair around a finger and Ryan had his arm protectively around Tomas' car seat. If they couldn't find who'd done this and soon, he'd send Kari and the twins to Paris for a while.

Drew and Craig were waiting for them at the elevator in the parking garage and helped carry up the bags. Devon and Perri had gone home and would call the following day. It was three in the morning and Kari looked every minute of it.

Of course, the twins were awake and it looked like they'd be that way for a while. The excitement of coming to their other home and all of the toys they didn't get to play with as often, coupled with the different cribs and environment, only served to wind them up until they actually bounced off the furniture with energy.

Kari sat in the large recliner and tucked her feet up under her, watching the twins run around and play with their many uncles. She was damned tired. Tired of living under the threat she'd been shadowed by for nearly the last year. All of this werewolf stuff was overwhelming. She loved it but at the same time she'd lost her freedom in a big way when she married Andreas. She missed the ability to just walk out the door at a moment's notice to go to a movie or grab a bite to eat.

She'd been so adamant about not giving into the constant threat, about trying to live their lives normally, and yet there she was in a high rise fortress. On the run with no other choice because some fucking maniac hated her and wanted her dead and seemed willing to hurt anyone who got in their way.

Sighing, she pushed away the mini pity party she'd been having and sat up. Ryan brought her a cup of tea and sat at her feet, watching the twins roll all over Skye and Laurent, a faint smile on his face.

"What is it, Kari? I mean, other than the obvious?" Ryan asked quietly.

"I'm sick of this. Well, not this." She waved her hands, indicating the children romping with Skye and Laurent. "But everything else. The tension, the worry. The fact that someone in our Pack wants to harm me and I don't know why. I want a normal life."

Ryan leaned back into her, his beautiful hair cascading over her knees. She ran her hands through it idly. "I'm sorry. This isn't how it's supposed to be. There's always been a slight division in the Clan. It was bad for a while when Tomas was Alpha. So bad that it's part of the reason he stepped down and let Andreas take over."

"I'd always gotten the feeling that there had been some big kerfluffle about something but no one ever said anything. What happened?"

Andreas came over then, eyebrow raised. "Are you sniffing around my little wolf?" he asked teasingly.

Ryan laughed, a deep throaty sound. "Your little wolf is more than I can handle, Alpha. I'll leave that to you. She does give good scalp massage though."

It was Kari's turn to laugh then. She stood up, stepped over Ryan and approached the spot where the twins wrestled with Skye and Laurent. "Okay you two, time to go to sleep. Give your uncles kisses and hugs and let's go."

It was hard to tell who was more disappointed, the adults or the kids. But soon, after many hugs and kisses and promises of more playing when they woke up, Kari and Andreas were able to get them both to bed and surprisingly they both passed out within minutes.

The condo was quiet. They had Craig posted at the outer door, Phillip, just inside Kari and Andreas' bedroom door. Skye slept on the large couch in the living room, Drew in the room next to Kari and Andreas', Laurent in with the twins.

Kari looked over at Phillip, who rested on a chaise, and sighed. "Come over here, Phillip. Snuggle in with us. I want to know you're all right."

Phillip looked over at Andreas, who nodded imperceptibly, before sliding into the bed next to Kari.

It wasn't unusual for wolves to snuggle up together at naptime as well as during waking hours. Kari had often napped with Phillip but never at night before. She turned, pressed her back into Andreas and put her arms around Phillip.

"I'm sorry you got shot. I couldn't bear it if something had happened to you," she murmured and kissed his temple.

"It's part of the job. And it wasn't your fault. Andreas is right, this whole thing is about the crazy person trying to kill you."

Kari took Phillip's hair out of his braid and ran her fingers through it. "I love your hair. The color, the texture. I wish you'd wear it down more often." She put her face into his neck and breathed him in. She stroked her hands over his arms and chest, soothing but inflaming as well, as her small body pressed against him.

Phillip looked over her head at Andreas and raised an eyebrow. Andreas ground his cock into Kari, turned on by seeing her minister to one of his wolves. And admittedly, seeing how much her gentle touching affected Phillip tightened things low in Andreas' gut too.

Kari froze, feeling Andreas' reaction and then his fingertips drawing her nightgown up her thighs.

"Andreas?"

He put his lips to her ear. "Do you want to continue, little wolf? I'm not okay with you fucking another man, but I love Phillip and I'm all right with bringing him into our bed tonight. I'm sure we can work something out that leaves us all satisfied."

Phillip's breathing quickened as he heard Andreas' words. It was impossible to not be sexually attracted to Kari. He was with her all the time. She was one of his best friends and someone he loved dearly.

"Phillip? What about you?" Kari looked up at him even as she arched back into Andreas' touch. Sensuality coursed through her, the raw heat in the air between them thrilled her.

"I…uh." He laughed. "What's not to be okay with?"

"Will *you* be with Phillip?" Kari leaned her head back to look at Andreas, who laughed, startled. In the background, Phillip choked.

"Naughty little wolf!" Andreas chided. Putting her arms above her head, he kissed her hard until she yielded with softness, opening up to him. "Let's take this as it comes, shall we?"

She nodded and he grabbed the front of her nightgown and pulled, ripping it from her body. Her mouth made a silent "O" of surprise but her nipples were hard and he could scent how wet she was.

Phillip reached out to touch her stomach gently. Kari turned to him. "Naked. Be naked. Both of you."

Andreas quickly pulled off his boxers, which were all he had on anyway, Phillip sat up and pulled off his pajama bottoms and Kari came to kneel behind him and brought his T-shirt up and over his head, pressing herself to his back.

The cool silk of his hair seduced her skin, the sensitive flesh of her nipples. She brought her hands up his arms and he turned.

His kiss was so different from Andreas'. Andreas devastated with his kisses. He owned her. He possessed her and seduced her. It was always overwhelming to give herself to Andreas' mouth. Phillip's kiss was soft and reverent. He *needed* her. Needed comfort and sex at the same time. To assure himself he was still alive and that someone cared about him deeply.

Andreas kissed down Kari's spine and back up to her neck. Her head fell back as she leaned against him. Phillip's mouth moved down to her breasts and he licked her nipples, teasing them into aching points. His mouth was hot and wet, his hands stayed at her waist.

She reached and grabbed Andreas' cock with one hand and Phillip's with the other—both men arched into her with sounds of desire. She ached, needing to be filled. Her pussy was so wet and desire-swollen she felt her honey on her thighs.

One of Andreas' hands slid down her belly and questing fingertips slid between slicked labia. With a gasp, she ground herself into his touch.

"Just a quick one to get the ball rolling," Andreas said in her ear and he slid his middle finger from side to side over her clit. Pleasure boiled up from her gut as she began to come almost immediately.

Phillip's cock throbbed in her fist, pre-cum moistening her fingers. "I've never seen anything so sexy in my life," he said over her shoulder to Andreas.

"Wait." Andreas' other hand came from behind and two fingers thrust up into her.

With a sharp cry, climax overtook her as he continued to work his hands over her. Phillip's mouth went back to her nipples as she rode the waves of pleasure that buffeted her time and time again.

And suddenly Andreas moved his fingers and replaced them with his cock. "Bend forward over Phillip, little wolf."

Kari looked up at Phillip and pushed him back to the bed. He straightened his legs around them both and she got to all fours as Andreas slowly began to fuck her, his hand holding her hair.

Phillip's skin was pale as moonlight and stretched taut over hard muscle. Unable to resist, she flicked her tongue over one nipple and then the other. He put his hands on her shoulders and she moved down, pushing Andreas back.

His cock was right there and it seemed only natural to take it into her mouth. Both men gasped at the sight. She rode his cock with her mouth, making him wet, sliding tongue and lips and the slight edge of teeth over him as Andreas continued to thrust deep into her pussy.

Phillip watched her take him into her mouth over and over, her hair tickling his groin and thighs. Andreas had eyes for her and only her. It was so clear, even in a moment when his Mate had another man's cock in her mouth, that he adored her. Each touch he made was filled with emotion and Phillip only hoped that one day he'd have that with his woman too.

The sharp edge of climax cut through his senses and he looked up at Andreas, not knowing where the line was and not wanting to cross it unknowingly. "Kari, oh god, I'm so close," he gasped.

Andreas pulled back on the hair in his fist. "Not in your mouth."

Licking her lips and locking her gaze with Phillip, she took him back between her hands and began to stroke. "Oh yeah. That's the way." He arched up into her grasp, still wet from her mouth, and let go of the climax he'd been holding back to have her just a few moments longer.

His seed, hot and silky, spread over them both and she gasped as Andreas' thrusts increased in intensity and he reached around to her clit. Cleaning up quickly, Phillip moved his body so he could reach her clit too. His fingers played against Andreas', feeling the skin of her cunt tighten each time Andreas pistoned into her body.

Andreas pressed forward, hard, as he began to come and Phillip continued to work her clit. Phillip's hand was so close to Andreas' cock he could feel the spasms as he came deep inside Kari.

With a soft exhalation Kari climaxed, writhing back against Andreas. Phillip took her lips softly for a moment, wanting that sweet reminder of a brief moment of comfort.

The three of them went to shower off and came back to bed, sated and exhausted. Kari pressed back into Andreas, her head against his biceps with a soft sigh.

"I love you, Andreas," she whispered, not wanting to wake Phillip.

"I love you too, little wolf."

* * * * *

Despite the exhaustion of the events of the last day and the intensity of their sex with Phillip, Andreas couldn't sleep. Giving in, he got up and went into the kitchen for a cup of tea and soon Skye joined him.

"Can't sleep?"

Andreas turned and took a sip of his tea. "Damn it, Skye, this has to stop! My children are in danger. My wife is in danger. You're all in danger. I can't have them living like this. I'll step aside and let Sean be Alpha if I have to."

Skye tensed at that. "He wouldn't take it. Moreover, I don't know if he could do it. Devon sure can't. Who does that leave? Michael?" He snorted at the idea.

"You think I'd choose this over my family?" Andreas said angrily.

"No, of course not, but you don't have to choose. We'll find out who did this. Kari would never let you step down over this. You must know that," Skye said.

"How? How are we going to find out who did this, Skye? It's been months. Tonight was the second time someone tried to kill her, if you don't count Johanna. We get threat calls once a month. She's unhappy, Skye. I can't deal with that. I didn't bring her over to have her terrorized and miserable."

"We need to draw them out. We know it's Pack. We know who *didn't* do it. Let's use them to set up a trap and then reel the responsible person in."

"Using Kari as bait? Unacceptable!" Andreas tossed his cup into the sink.

"No, realistic," Kari said, stepping into the room. Skye and Andreas turned to face her. "Andreas, this has gone on long enough. I'm telling you that we've got to find this person and deal with them. I can't live like this anymore and I can't bear endangering the twins. It's either this or I go to live with the twins in Paris. I mean it. I love you more than life itself but this is about our children now and I have to put them first."

"You'd leave me?"

"No. I'd move away with our children so you could lead your Clan in peace and so our children wouldn't live in a place where silver bullets fly. I'd still be your Mate. I'd still be your wife. It just can't continue like this. I realized tonight that I hadn't actually done anything *alone* in nearly a year. None of us is living a normal life. The males who guard me have no life! You can't run your businesses properly because your right-hand men are having to babysit me. We're always on guard. That isn't natural."

Walking to him, she slid her arms around his waist and looked up into his eyes. "I'm intensely unhappy. Not with you. Not with our family. But with the situation. I don't want to live this way anymore."

Andreas looked anguished. Skye was being very still and trying not to hear what was being said.

"Let's work on the plan. I won't lose you. I'll step down as Alpha and we'll all go to Paris."

"You won't. But yes, let's work on the trap."

* * * * *

Jade and Tomas came and met Andreas and Kari in Portland to take the twins to the condo in New York City and keep them out of harm's way. Against her judgment, Emma had gone with them. She hadn't wanted to leave her practice, but after Sean had thought about it all night and had seen the bullet hole in the house in the cold light of day, he'd insisted for the sake of the baby she was carrying. Jack tagged along too. He and Alyssa were going to meet up in Boston after the trap was set and the twins were safe. Andreas and Kari wanted to keep all the plans low-key and quiet. The human staff weren't even alerted.

The Inner Circle knew for sure that Ryan, Skye, Phillip, Sean, Laurent, Gregory, Anna, Elaine, Perri and Devon and Sean were safe to involve with the trap. Kari had argued successfully to keep Perri out of it as she'd just gone in for the first IVF treatment the day before and needed to be at home resting.

A Gathering was called and the planners decided to set up a few situations where Kari would be left alone—truly alone, because another wolf could smell if anyone was nearby.

Andreas was most difficult to persuade on this point. But finally, knowing that he'd lose his wife and children or the leadership of his Pack, he agreed. Kari argued that she was a strong wolf so she'd be able to fight until someone heard. For her safety, while she was in human form she'd wear a small microphone and monitored by Ryan at all times.

The decision was made to have Kari and Andreas be extremely physical with each other. It seemed that the culprit was incensed by Kari's connection to Andreas and so they'd do what they could to drive the attacker to act and expose his identity.

The cherry on the sundae was to announce that Kari was pregnant again. Although the exact reasoning behind the attempts wasn't clear, it was pretty obvious that her presence was threatening. Whether it was because of her tie to Andreas and the creation of children to lead or in her continued ability to please the Alpha and keep her place they didn't know.

When they arrived back at the lodge on Thursday, things were calm. Anna and Gregory had made the cabins and extra rooms ready. Sean was missing Emma already but determined to find out who was responsible for terrorizing Kari and Andreas.

They'd created a cover for Emma that she was off at a medical symposium in Chicago, that Jade had to work and Jack went back to Boston to try to work things out with Alyssa. Perri, of course, had a legitimate excuse. Devon had decided to come to the lodge, leaving Perri ensconced at the condo in Portland, surrounded with state-of-the-art security. Kari and Andreas had wanted him to stay with Perri but she wouldn't have it. "You need him there, he'll just bug the hell out of me here. Plus, I can't have you leaving. Who would I gossip with!"

* * * * *

Friday evening they had a full house. Henry pointedly ignored Luna now that Andreas had allowed their separation. Although Carey showed mild interest in her charms, Luna had noticed Perri's absence and hadn't taken her eyes off Devon all evening. This despite the obvious rebuffs he was giving her. Kari was ready to step in and kick her butt if she so much as touched her brother-in-law. Several people had asked about the twins but Kari told them they were with their grandpapa having a fun sleepover while the adults got to play at the Gathering.

Kari and Andreas were all over each other. He really couldn't complain about that. With the twins gone it was nice to have uninterrupted time with her. They had gotten "caught" several times with hands up skirt or down pants. Everyone had acted amused so far, including Andreas' number one suspect Alex.

At dinner, Andreas stood up and asked everyone for their attention. With a grin, he raised his glass. "I'm pleased to announce to you all that Kari is pregnant again!"

Skye lazily looked around the table to see how people were reacting. For the most part they looked like a happy bunch. He saw concern on a few faces and noted them to himself.

"Let's go on a run before I get too big!" Kari laughed and they all went to the edge of the forest to disrobe.

Andreas let her change first and caressed her fur and whispered, "Careful, little wolf," in her ear and then changed as well, his large body against her small one.

They ran for several miles, past the small lake they usually stopped at. Despite the danger Kari hadn't felt this free since her first run. She veered off to the left and Andreas came around to the right, she knew she should lead off alone just to see if anyone would take the bait. Ellen, James, Michael and Henry all went left when she did. She hunted a rabbit and felt her wolf joy at the thrill of being a predator. They rolled in the underbrush and jumped over each other, knocking into one another with utter abandon.

After several hours of hide and seek, Kari headed back to the lodge. Andreas came around a bend in the trail and rammed into her, bowling her over, giving her a wolfish grin. She transformed and ran back toward the lodge naked, the moon gleaming off her skin, and a human Andreas scooped her off her feet and rolled in the grass until he ended up with her on top, straddling him. She laughed as Andreas reached up and caressed her breasts, bringing a moan to her lips. She hesitated. Coupling in wolf form in the presence of the Pack was one thing. Having sex wearing a human skin on the lawn outside of the lodge was another. She leaned down and captured his lips with her own and felt him harden in the vee of her thighs, nudging into her.

"Kari," Andreas whispered hesitantly when she pulled back from the kiss. He moved his hips up tentatively, in question. He wanted to love her under the moon, out in the air, since he first brought her here. For him it answered a primal need to mark her as his own, not just as a wolf but as his human wife. The danger of the situation only added to the sexual tension building between them.

She sat up and lifted slightly, grabbing his cock in her hand and guiding him into her body. She sat there with him just barely inside of her warmth and looked down at him, smiling. She bit her lip and he moaned at the erotic gesture. At his moan she slid down another inch, her thighs tense, holding herself in place.

"More," he gasped and she slid down another inch and then another, her body stretching to accommodate him. His hands grasped her hips to pull her down on him but she shook her head.

"No. Let me. I'm in charge this time," she said softly. The night air cloaked her skin. The bit of dew beginning to collect on the grass scented sticky in the air. The humidity of the night wet against the flesh of her back and arms.

She slowly, incrementally moved on him, taking in more and more of him until he was seated inside of her completely.

He pulled his knees up and she rested her back against them. Their gazes locked. "God, I love you so much. You're my entire world," she said to him.

"Ditto," he groaned as she began to move on him again, her thighs tensing as she pulled her body up, nearly coming all the way off him, and relaxing again as she took him all the way into her pussy again.

Her pace was slow, incrementally dragging him up to climax. He was a hard and fast kind of man but her dreamy rhythm pulled him deep into the maelstrom of her spell. Each time she brought that hot, tight embrace down and around his cock, he took another small step toward the inevitable. It built in his spine.

They stayed there, under the moon, the smell of the herb garden wafting across the breeze, slowly moving with each other, for goodness knows how long. In the distance, the Pack howled and moved through the brush.

"I'm so close," Andreas panted out, sweat beading down his temple. Kari raked her nails down his chest, her breasts swaying as she moved faster and faster against him. "Baby, now, please, come for me," he panted, adding pressure and speed to his fingers moving against her clit.

The words, the movement of his hands, the feel of him so deep inside of her body all pushed at her and the orgasm exploded around her, the erratic pulsing of her inner muscles squeezing him over his own edge. He roared her name with near violence, his head thrashing from side to side.

Kari collapsed onto his chest while he remained inside her.

"Wow, can I join in?" Kari looked around to see Alex standing, watching with a grin on his face.

"How about me too?" Luna stepped forward and caressed Alex's arm and he looked at her with slight distaste and stepped away.

"You really should share him, Kari. Apparently he's quite the fertile man," Luna said, approaching them.

Kari watched her, sitting up. She gave a low growl that echoed with threat. Andreas shuddered at the threat display and slid his hands to her waist.

"If I were to share, it wouldn't be with you." Kari tightened her muscles around Andreas, delighting in his gasp and the renewed life his cock began to show.

"What do you have to say about it, Andreas? You seemed to like it before," Luna said, looking at Andreas, licking her lips.

Alex started laughing and Kari liked him even more for it.

Without even looking at Luna, Andreas kept his eyes on Kari, hands caressing her. "Luna, if you value your life you'll shut up now that your Alpha has made it clear she isn't sharing. In any case, it was two years ago, in wolf form. It was all right, I suppose, but it was what? Twice? You should probably get past that. I love what I have. I have no need to go searching anywhere else," he said and got to his feet, helping Kari up and bringing her into the shelter of his arms.

"Give it a rest, Luna," Alex drawled in his Midwestern accent. "Now if you ever need a stand-in, Andreas, let me know. I find your queen to be quite beautiful." He winked and walked past them toward the house.

Andreas growled at him as he passed and Kari laughed. "Let's go," she said to Andreas, ignoring Luna.

Skye came out then, as did Ryan and Laurent. Skye had a wicked grin on his face that let Kari know he'd seen them too. Werepervert, that's what he was. Kari shrugged, he'd seen her deliver the twins. It wasn't like he hadn't seen it before. And she had to admit she certainly saw the appeal in a little voyeurism after that little scene between Phillip and Ryan, and she couldn't lie and say that it didn't turn her on just a little bit that they were watched too.

Back at the lodge Kari ran upstairs and took a shower. Phillip guarded her door loosely. They had to stick to basic appearances but still give an opportunity to let the culprit get to her. Still in the bathroom, she put on the small transmitter that was in an earring.

Downstairs again, Kari and Ryan sat on the deck, drinking tea. "I'd like to go for a walk, you want to come along?" Ryan stood up, asking. The plan was for them to walk and talk and then get separated. Laurent was monitoring the microphone. She promised not to go too far away. Phillip and Skye remained naked so they could change quickly and come to her rescue if necessary.

As they walked, Ryan talked about his time in the Pack. About his life. They trailed away from the sounds and lights at the lodge and took the more deserted path to the other side of the lake.

"Hey, you know, the other day you started to tell me about what brought about Tomas' stepping aside and somehow we got interrupted," Kari said.

"Ah yes. Well, Tomas has siblings. A sister who lives in Northern California, and a brother who was his Second, as Sean is Andreas'. Balmont and his Mate, Angeline, were Michael's parents by the way."

"Oh! You know, I've always meant to ask about his parents and his connection to Andreas. I knew he was a cousin but not much more than that."

"Yes, well, Michael is an only child. Angeline's pregnancy was exceptionally difficult, especially for a werewolf. He was very early and had to be kept in a special neonatal unit for nearly four months. He's still very small to this day."

Kari laughed. "Well, I suppose compared to all of you giants, sure. But he's still what, five ten or so?"

Ryan shrugged, grinning. "Well okay, compared to the rest of us he's small. You're tiny. However, you more than make up for it with your attitude."

She chuckled at that. "Good save."

"Anyway, Balmont wanted to be more than Second. He and Tomas were not very close. They'd always been very competitive but the fact that Jade bore not just one but three strong males secured Tomas' place as Alpha. After Michael's birth, Angeline had many more health problems and Jade was...well, she's Jade. She exudes strength and good health. She and Tomas were strong Alphas and their sons grew bigger and more competent each year while Michael, who was a good son, was overshadowed by his cousins.

"As Andreas approached his late teens it was clear that he was going to be the next Alpha. At least to most of the Clan. Balmont did have his supporters, about a third of the Pack, but overall, it was easy for everyone to accept the obvious.

"Andreas went to college at Harvard. Then to graduate school at Yale. He came back here and not only competently ran the construction company that Tomas had started but started two more companies by the time he was thirty. Andreas was a bit of a free spirit in his early twenties but as he approached his thirties he began to take his future seriously. He became not only integral in the life and governance of the Pack, he became someone whom the Pack began to look to when they had problems.

"When Andreas turned thirty-two, Tomas went to Balmont and told him that he wanted to make Andreas his Second. Ready him for taking over as Alpha. Incensed, Balmont took it to the Pack for a vote. This is an unusual thing. A Clan isn't a democracy, it's ruled by the Alpha. In very rare situations, the Pack can be polled, and Balmont decided to make an end run around Tomas.

"Tomas, seeing his brother's distress, backed off and made Andreas his Lieutenant instead. Andreas saw his father's actions as necessary for the time being but so began an intense rivalry between Balmont and Andreas that got worse and worse as each year passed.

"During this time, Balmont urged Tomas to make Michael higher in the Pack. As you know, the family of the Alpha is generally the Clan leadership and occupies the top spots in the Pack. However, everyone else has to challenge and fight their way to the top."

"So you fought your way up?" Kari asked Ryan.

"Yes, I did. I challenged the older Pack members to move up from the bottom and by the time I was thirty I was one of the Enforcers. Skye, Laurent and Phillip as well. Balmont's strongest supporter, Andrew, was a Lieutenant just below Andreas, and he challenged Skye. Thought he'd take him out and relegate a strong supporter of Andreas to the bottom of the Pack. What happened instead was a bloody challenge that ended in Andrew's death. It was supposed to just be a blooding but Andrew wouldn't stop. Skye got first blood, it should have ended, but Andrew came back at him time and again. Finally Skye had to kill him. It was the beginning of a slide into a final face-off.

"So Skye became Andreas' right-hand man. Balmont could see that the tide was turning. He demanded again that Michael be made a higher rank but Tomas refused, saying that Michael had to fight his way up like everyone else. Even if Tomas had been inclined to favoritism, Michael simply wasn't strong enough to hold a high position in the Pack. The Inner Circle has to be the strongest or an Alpha can't hold the leadership. We may have human skins, Kari, but we're still predators. Any sign of weakness will be acted on."

Kari nodded. She understood that more and more each day.

"As time passed, Andreas' friends filled the spots of the Inner Circle and by the time Andreas had turned thirty-three we held the entire Inner Circle with the exception of Second, which Balmont still held.

"Andreas had been looking for a Mate. Generally, males don't take on the Alpha position at such a young age unless they're mated or some major event happens like the old Alpha is sick or needs to be challenged for some reason. Anyway, Andreas courted women and wolves alike but no one stayed around for very long. Angeline was threatened by this, she wanted her son as Second when Andreas took over. She pressed Balmont into action and Balmont tried to negotiate with Tomas for Michael to be Second when Andreas took over. He promised to step down without any fuss if Tomas agreed.

"By this time Sean had returned from medical school and had worked his way up as well and Tomas had Second in mind for him. Devon was always content as a lower Lieutenant and so he didn't really pose much of a threat.

"The tension had gotten pretty bad. Several of Balmont's closest friends were now relegated to the bottom of the Pack hierarchy. This is common of course, as we get older, younger wolves take the spots that strength can hold. But they weren't happy. Balmont had convinced them that if he or Michael were Alpha that they could have their old spots back.

"So at the last Gathering of the year, Balmont challenged Andreas. Now this was eight, nearly nine years ago. If you think Andreas is strong now, imagine what he was like then. Balmont was thirty years older than him and had gotten soft. It was unbelievable to everyone but Balmont and his people. Andreas tried to avoid it, he even transformed back to human to try to reason with his uncle but Balmont attacked him. Andreas had no choice then and, obviously, he defeated Balmont. Balmont surrendered as Andreas stood on Balmont's chest, his neck in Andreas' teeth.

"Andreas became Second and Balmont seemed to be resigned to his falling fortunes. But he wasn't in truth. He was plotting and Phillip and Laurent got wind of his plan to try to kill Andreas and Tomas, and we called a Gathering and confronted them."

"Yes, Ryan, and why don't you tell her how they killed my parents then? Your precious Tomas and Andreas murdered my parents to keep their power."

They spun around to face Michael, fury written all over his face. The truth had been there all along and Kari couldn't believe she never even suspected Michael.

"Yes, after Balmont and Angeline confessed and the plot was fully disclosed they had to submit to the justice of the Pack. To plot to assassinate your king and future king is a death penalty offense. Something they knew, Michael."

"Fuck you, Ryan," Michael said, his jaw clenching. He brought a hand up and the gun flashed in the moonlight. "Fuck all of you," Michael snarled and shot him.

Kari's eyes widened as she watched Ryan sink to the ground. "Silver," he said simply and Michael shot him twice more.

"Michael! Stop," Kari cried out, trying to bend over to help Ryan. But Michael moved to her then, grabbing her, putting the gun to her temple.

She tried to struggle but he dug the gun into her skin. "Don't. Walk with me, bitch, or I'll do you right here." He walked her quickly away from the lodge as her mind spun, trying to figure a way out of the mess, hoping Ryan was still alive, counting on the fact that the others had heard her and were on their way. Kari wouldn't give up. Her children needed a mother and she wasn't going to let a coward like Michael take her out without a fight.

"What are you doing, Michael?"

"What I've been trying to do for a year," he answered calmly.

"You're the one who tried to kill me," she said flatly, not a question.

He laughed sarcastically. "What, you believed my sorry little wolf routine? I knew what I was doing in that alley that night. But you had to fight back so hard it brought Phillip around. Even then you were a pain in my ass."

"Why? I never did a thing to harm you. I tried to help you."

"Help me? Please! You and your fucking children have put up yet another roadblock to my taking over this Pack."

Just then two wolves ran up, Phillip and Skye. They changed back into their human skin and stood there, naked, hands open. Michael bit off a savage curse.

"Michael, why are you doing this, man?" Skye asked, stepping forward.

"Don't!" He shoved the muzzle of the gun into Kari's cheek. "I'll shoot her in the head. It's silver shot. She'll die instantly."

Skye took a step back, hands open. "Okay, Michael. Just calm down."

"Don't tell me to calm down! All of this should be mine. I've had to sit at the long end of the table and watch others have it for too long. This bitch thinks she can just stroll her *human* ass in here, pop out a few mongrels and take over? My parents were both natural wolves, why should a mongrel lead this Pack? Tomas and Jade never shared anything with my parents and then they killed them, leaving me alone. Did Andreas even try to make amends for it when Tomas stepped down? No."

Kari could feel Andreas out there somewhere. His fury roiled in the air, crackling with menace.

"Michael, you can't win now. Can't you see that?" Kari asked softly.

"Look, keep your fucking mouth shut or I'll shut it permanently."

"What do you plan to do, Michael?" Phillip asked calmly.

"I plan on killing this whore. Sure, I won't be leading the Clan but she won't either. In fact, neither will Andreas, because who would support an Alpha who allowed so many murder attempts on his own Mate? Her murder on his own land? If I'm going down, you're all coming with me." He laughed derisively.

"Poor little Michael, too weak to hold power. You all looked at me with pity. Andreas thought he was being sooo good to me to allow me to watch over his human whore. Even when I tried to kill her he didn't punish me. Weak, pathetic and weak. I walked right into their bedroom and put that water there, hoping to take them both out, but only got her. And again, her stupendous luck saved her. I fucking tried to shoot her and got you instead, Phillip. How's the shoulder by the way?" he asked, snorting.

"All the time I danced around in your midst and you never suspected me once. Well, it's too bad I couldn't kill those brats of hers but I'll just have to settle for killing her."

"Oh man, do you have a case of the feeling sorry for yourself! I may be half wolf but I'm ten times the Alpha you'll ever be. Why? Because you are weak. So weak you'd target children instead of openly challenging for a seat you *know* you don't have the power to take much less hold. You'd rather bring down an entire Pack instead of just dealing with the reality life has dealt you. You aren't an Alpha, Michael. Suck it up. Life sucks large some days. Be what you can be and stop crying about what you can't change," Kari, despite her fear, snarled.

"What do you know about it?" His voice was petulant and Kari felt nothing but disgust.

"Oh, you think this was handed to me? I worked for everything I ever had in my life, which is more than I can say for you. Weak. You dare to call anyone else weak? You're a coward! Here's a clue, not everyone gets to be Alpha. Only two people do per Pack. The chances of it being you are astronomical."

He yanked on her hair. "Shut up, you whore! You stole my seat with your mongrels. The only thing that's kept me going all this time is the knowledge that I kept you terrified and worried for your sniveling brats."

At that, Kari had had enough. She stomped back, hard, on his instep, elbowing him in the gut. He doubled over, his hands slipping but grabbing a fistful of her hair.

Andreas was a flash of movement. He was on top of Michael and it was only moments before she heard the sickening crack of bones breaking. Skye and Phillip grabbed the gun and stood over Michael but it wasn't necessary. He wouldn't be threatening anyone ever again. Andreas stepped back, "Michael Phinney, you're sentenced to death for treason against a Pack Alpha."

Kari looked around and saw that the rest of the Pack had gathered around. Sean came to her and pulled her into his arms, turning her face away. "Are you all right? Are you hurt?" he murmured into her ear.

"Ryan? Is Ryan all right?" she asked, weeping into his shoulder.

"Elaine and Ellen are with him. He's lost a lot of blood but they got the bullets out. He'll need to rest but he'll live," Alex said as he jogged up to the scene.

Andreas came to her then, sinking to his knees in front of her and putting his forehead to the ground. "Can you forgive me for letting this get so far? I had no idea he felt so much hatred toward me."

She pulled him up then and stepped into his embrace. "There's nothing to forgive, Andreas. You loved him. You didn't want to think the worst of him. I wouldn't want you any other way. I had no idea, none of us did. He was a really good actor. Too bad he couldn't be bothered to put any of that work into making his own life better instead of plotting to take mine."

She turned to the Pack. "Michael was the culprit all along. I hope that we can all move past this awful tragedy and work to build a better, stronger and more connected Pack."

Kari looked into their faces and saw what she needed to garner the strength to lead them at Andreas' side.

Epilogue

Three Years Later

Helene and her brothers Tomas, Sean and Devon played in the meadow with their cousins Marie and Andy—short for little Andreas. The other Pack children ran out to greet them as their parents arrived for the Winter Gathering.

Emma, swollen with her second child, a brother for Jade, stood with Kari and Perri, watching the children play. Kari smiled at the scene and tried not to grimace as her sons crashed into each other and roughhoused in the snow. Helene, Julia, Marie and Mimi snorted and went back to their expansive snow family.

Jack walked in with Alyssa, her son and their daughter. It turned out that Alyssa had been holding back from committing to Jack because she was a werewolf. Small world. She'd joined the Pack three years before and she'd gotten pregnant with Drea soon after. Jack and Alyssa had followed Sean's example and had built a home about a mile from the lodge. Perri and Devon had considered it but they both loved Portland so much that they didn't want to leave it behind. Andreas, their son, conceived after two years and four rounds of IVF, was a frequent visitor at the lodge though, and was adored by his cousins. He looked so much like Perri, little elfin face and red hair, that it was startling to see them together.

Kari had gotten pregnant again two years before—another set of twins. Both boys. Afterward she and Andreas decided that four children were quite enough and decided to stop there.

The Pack had gotten past the tragic night where they lost Michael. They'd built a family based on love and trust. Each of the members had grown and prospered over the three years that'd passed.

But there was still yearning for a Mate from those who hadn't found theirs yet. Skye had been seeing a human woman from town and it seemed serious for a while but he always held a part of himself back, knowing his true other half was out there somewhere. It did give him pause, the idea that his Mate would be as difficult as he was. He hoped Kari's words were just teasing. Even so, a difficult Mate would be better than none at all. And he liked his women with a little fire.

Phillip wanted that too. Wanted to find the person who would make him whole at last. He dated but never seriously, instead pouring his love into his Pack and the kids. At least he didn't have to guard anyone twenty-four hours a day and had time for other work and for a social life.

Laurent had begun to be antsy with the yearning. He'd traveled around the country to other Packs and gatherings, just hoping to find her. The older the children got, the more he wanted a family of his own. He and Andreas would be taking a trip into Seattle the next week and he hoped he could shake his need. Maybe he'd look up an old flame or two while they were in the city—anything to get his mind off the emptiness.

The Gathering had brought them all. They sat at the newly enlarged table in the dining room and toasted to the good fortunes of the Cherchez Clan for another year. New members had come to them over the last years. Luna had found her true Mate and the change in her personality had been striking. Henry had found his true Mate as well, a man named Ben who'd moved to Seattle a year before. There were three new single females, which made it easier for the unmated males but not so much for the other women. The state of werewolf hierarchy and the status of unmated females led to tension and power plays between them all. Still, things were good, the wolves were happy and thriving.

Andreas smiled, looking down the table at the face of his beautiful wife, his brothers and their mates, his friends and Pack. It was good to be King.

Also by Lauren Dane

eBooks:

Ascension

Cascadia Wolves: Reluctant

Cascadia Wolves 1: Enforcer

Cascadia Wolves 2: Tri Mates

Fire and Rain

Sudden Desire

Sword and Crown

Witches Knot: Threat of Darkness

Witches Knot 1: Triad

Witches Knot 2: A Touch of Fae

Witches Knot 3: Vengeance Due

Witches Knot 4: Thrice United

Witches Knot 5: Celebration for the Dead

Print Books:

Cascadia Wolves 1: Enforcer

Cascadia Wolves 2: Tri Mates

Crown and Blade *(anthology)*

Feral Fascination *(anthology)*

Sexy Summer Fun *(anthology)*

Witches Knot 1: Triad

Witches Knot 2: A Touch of Fae

Witches Knot 3: Vengeance Due

Witches Knot 4: Thrice United

About the Author

Lauren Dane has been writing stories since she was able to use a pencil, and before that she used to tell them to people. Of course, she still talks nonstop, and through wonderful fate and good fortune, she's now able to share what she writes with others. It's a wonderful life!

The basics: Lauren is a mom, a partner, a best friend and a daughter. Living in the rainy but beautiful Pacific Northwest, she spends her late evenings writing like a fiend when she finally wrestles all of her kids to bed.

The author welcomes comments from readers. You can find her website and email address on her author bio page at www.ellorascave.com.

Tell Us What You Think

We appreciate hearing reader opinions about our books. You can email us at Comments@EllorasCave.com.

Why an electronic book?

We live in the Information Age—an exciting time in the history of human civilization, in which technology rules supreme and continues to progress in leaps and bounds every minute of every day. For a multitude of reasons, more and more avid literary fans are opting to purchase e-books instead of paper books. The question from those not yet initiated into the world of electronic reading is simply: *Why?*

1. ***Price.*** An electronic title at Ellora's Cave Publishing runs anywhere from 40% to 75% less than the cover price of the exact same title in paperback format. Why? Basic mathematics and cost. It is less expensive to publish an e-book (no paper and printing, no warehousing and shipping) than it is to publish a paperback, so the savings are passed along to the consumer.
2. ***Space.*** Running out of room in your house for your books? That is one worry you will never have with electronic books. For a low one-time cost, you can purchase a handheld device specifically designed for e-reading. Many e-readers have large, convenient screens for viewing. Better yet, hundreds of titles can be stored within your new library—on a single microchip. There are a variety of e-readers from different manufacturers. You can also read e-books on your PC or laptop computer. (Please note that Ellora's Cave does not endorse any specific brands.

You can check our website at www.ellorascave.com for information we make available to new consumers.)

3. ***Mobility.*** Because your new e-library consists of only a microchip within a small, easily transportable e-reader, your entire cache of books can be taken with you wherever you go.
4. ***Personal Viewing Preferences.*** Are the words you are currently reading too small? Too large? Too... ANNOYING? Paperback books cannot be modified according to personal preferences, but e-books can.
5. ***Instant Gratification.*** Is it the middle of the night and all the bookstores near you are closed? Are you tired of waiting days, sometimes weeks, for bookstores to ship the novels you bought? Ellora's Cave Publishing sells instantaneous downloads twenty-four hours a day, seven days a week, every day of the year. Our webstore is never closed. Our e-book delivery system is 100% automated, meaning your order is filled as soon as you pay for it.

Those are a few of the top reasons why electronic books are replacing paperbacks for many avid readers.

As always, Ellora's Cave welcomes your questions and comments. We invite you to email us at Comments@ellorascave.com or write to us directly at Ellora's Cave Publishing Inc., 1056 Home Avenue, Akron, OH 44310-3502.

CPSIA information can be obtained at www.ICGtesting.com
Printed in the USA
241594LV00001B/96/P

9 781419 964237